"A Lori Foster book is like a glass of
good champagne—sexy and sparkling."
—Jayne Ann Krentz

"Lori Foster is a funny, steamy,
guaranteed good read!
Say YES! to Lori Foster."
—Elizabeth Lowell

"Lori Foster writes smart, sexy,
engaging characters. The pages sizzle!"
—Christine Feehan

"Foster outwrites most of her peers and
has a great sense of the ridiculous..."
—*Library Journal*

"You're gorgeous."

"I—"

Jude dipped that teasing finger into her cleavage, and then up and over the swell of one breast. He sounded hoarse when he said, "And hot."

Heat ran up her neck. "I don't think so."

"That's because you're not male. Thank God."

Her eyes nearly crossed. May frowned, stepped out of reach, then cleared her throat. Whatever game he was playing, she had to make him quit before she did something stupid like grabbing him. "Look, Jude—"

"I'm looking," he promised. "And I like what I see."

May turned her back on him. If she couldn't see him, maybe she'd be able to get her thoughts together and form a coherent sentence. "This is ridiculous." Jude said nothing, and her tension grew. "I don't understand why you're doing this."

"Sure you do." His voice sounded closer. "I want you."

BOOK YOUR PLACE ON OUR WEBSITE AND MAKE THE READING CONNECTION!

We've created a customized website just for our very special readers, where you can get the inside scoop on everything that's going on with Zebra, Pinnacle and Kensington books.

When you come online, you'll have the exciting opportunity to:

- View covers of upcoming books
- Read sample chapters
- Learn about our future publishing schedule (listed by publication month *and author*)
- Find out when your favorite authors will be visiting a city near you
- Search for and order backlist books from our online catalog
- Check out author bios and background information
- Send e-mail to your favorite authors
- Meet the Kensington staff online
- Join us in weekly chats with authors, readers and other guests
- Get writing guidelines
- AND MUCH MORE!

**Visit our website at
http://www.kensingtonbooks.com**

LORI
FOSTER

Jude's Law

ZEBRA BOOKS
KENSINGTON PUBLISHING CORP.
www.kensingtonbooks.com

ZEBRA BOOKS are published by

Kensington Publishing Corp.
850 Third Avenue
New York, NY 10022

All Kensington titles, imprints, and distributed lines are available at special quantity discounts for bulk purchases for sales
promotion, premiums, fund-raising, educational, or institu-
tional use.

Special book excerpts or customized printings can also be
created to fit specific needs. For details, write or phone the
office of the Kensington Special Sales Manager: Attn. Special
Sales Department. Kensington Publishing Corp., 850 Third
Avenue, New York, NY 10022. Phone: 1-800-221-2647.

Zebra and the Z logo Reg. U.S. Pat. & TM Off.

ISBN 0-8217-7802-1

First Printing: February 2006
10 9 8 7 6 5 4 3 2 1

Printed in the United States of America

To all the awesome fighters of the UFC,
but especially my favorites:
Randy Couture, Frank Mir, Vitor Belfort,
and Chuck Liddell.
You guys rock, and the UFC is the *best,*
most exciting sport around.

As a side note: while I've learned quite a few of
the holds and rules, I feared insulting a fighter
with what I *don't* know, so for this book, I
renamed the UFC as the SBC.

And a special nod to Oleg Taktarov, the first UFC
fighter that I noticed also becoming an actor.
He inspired me.

Chapter 1

He blamed May Price for his new affinity toward lush curves. Before meeting her damn near a year ago, he'd been more than satisfied with willowy models and leggy starlets.

Now, Jude Jamison couldn't get the voluptuous Miss Price, or her very sexy body, off his mind. He wanted her. He *would* have her.

But so far, she hadn't made it easy for him. Hard? Yeah, he stayed plenty hard. When it came to May, nothing went as he intended. Thanks to his fame and acquired fortune, he usually only needed to make himself visible and women were interested.

He liked it that way—or so he'd thought before May challenged him with her resistance. She didn't care about money or fame. No, May liked his interest in art. Specifically, she liked his interest in the art she sold in her gallery.

Trying to make headway with May brought back memories of his youth, when getting laid made the top of his "to do" list and occupied most of his energy. He'd worked hard on sex back then, and he'd had the time of his life.

He still enjoyed sex, but without the chase, it didn't seem as exciting. Hell, it had almost become mundane.

May made it exciting again.

In fact, she made everything exciting. Talking with her left him energized; laughing with her made him feel good; just looking at her gave him pleasure—and often had him fantasizing about the moment when she'd give in, maybe loosen up a little, say yes instead of shrugging off his interest as mere flirtation.

He'd turned thoughts of that day into a favorite fantasy—May out of her restricting clothes and her concealing glasses, with her hair loose and her expressive eyes anxious, seeing only him.

He adored her dark brown eyes with the thick fringe of lashes, the way she looked at him, the way she seemed to really see him, not just his image.

But before he could make moves toward getting her in his bed, he needed to go the route of casual dating. She was different from the other women he'd known. More old fashioned. In no way cavalier about intimacy. And she had a big heart.

He appreciated those differences a lot, but thinking of his failed come-ons left him chagrined.

She took his best lines as a joke. Added sincerity left her unconvinced. And at times, she didn't even notice his attempts at seduction. Yet subtlety wasn't his strong suit. She left him confounded, and very determined.

May wasn't an insecure woman. She wasn't shy or withdrawn. Open, honest, and straightforward— that described May. But no matter what Jude tried, she found a way to discount his interest.

He decided the local yahoos in Stillbrook, Ohio, were either blind, overly preoccupied, or just plain stupid when it came to women. For May to be so oblivious to her own appeal, they sure as hell hadn't given her the attention she deserved, the attention *he'd* give her—in bed.

It had to happen soon. With his financial status and number of investments, not to mention the propositions from two other factions, a slew of daily business details demanded his attention. But until he had May, he couldn't concentrate worth a damn.

Hands in his pockets, shoulder resting on the ornate door frame of May's small art gallery, Jude watched her with the piercing intensity of a predator.

Time for new tactics. She hadn't reacted to compliments and innuendos, so he'd spell things out for her instead. After tonight, May would have no delusions about what he wanted with her.

As she bustled across the floor, bouncing in all the right places, he visually tracked her, soaking in every jaunty step, each carefree movement. She hadn't yet noticed him, but she would. Soon.

Anticipation curved his mouth.

No matter the location, no matter the occasion, May always became aware of him within seconds of his entrance. She could deny it all she wanted, but the awareness went both ways.

Fighting it would do her no good.

Jude played to win, always had. If May knew anything at all about his history, she knew that much. And for right now, he intended to win her.

It didn't matter that her denial made sense. It didn't matter that, despite the attraction, she probably feared him—with good reason. He wouldn't let it matter.

Hell, he wouldn't even think about it.

Ignoring the curious gawking of everyone else in the main room of the art gallery, Jude wove his way toward May. She had her profile to him and, as usual, her suit jacket showed wrinkles from an uncomplimentary fit, likely caused by her impressive rack. The seat of her knee-length skirt hugged her generous ass. And somehow she'd snagged the back left leg of her nylons.

Like the finest fetish garb, her rumpled wardrobe made her that much more enticing.

He couldn't help but think about the voluptuous body she tried so hard to hide. Because most women flaunted their assets, her modesty amused him. Well used to bold seductions, her attempts to be demure dared him. Everything about her made his imagination go wild.

What type of panties did she wear under that asexual clothing? Cotton, or something slinky and slippery and barely there?

Soon enough he'd discover the answers for himself.

He was still studying her ass when she finally sensed his approach. Her animated conversation fell flat, and she whirled around to face him, almost dislodging her wire-framed glasses. He liked the front view as much as the back. Slowly, he brought his attention away from the notch at the top of her thighs, to her belly, her breasts, and up to her flushed face.

Their gazes locked, and Jude smiled.

Regardless of the crowd around her, he didn't bother to hide his intent. He wanted her, and she could damn well deal with it.

A look of delight flashed over her face before she transformed it into a polite welcome. Without

even realizing it, she'd dismissed the women clus-
tered around her and took a step toward him. He
loved her candid response, the way she always
greeted him with pleasure. But with so many people crowded inside the gallery to view the display
of artwork by local talent, she could barely move
without bumping into someone.

Lacking her manners, but with twice her determination, Jude pushed forward until he stood
near enough to breathe in the combined scents of
lemon shampoo and powdery lotion. "Hello, May."

"Jude." Eyes big and bright, she beamed at him.
"How are you? I was afraid you wouldn't make it
tonight. You're usually waiting when I open the
doors. When you weren't, I just assumed the rain
had kept you away."

Only with him did she chatter. His presence
threw her off balance. But for Jude, the lack of coy
pretension was cute.

Hell, everything about her was cute. And sexy.
And *real.*

"That lightning's so fierce," she said, "I was
afraid the electricity would go out and I'd have to
cancel. You know how Stillbrook is. It doesn't take
much to shut us down. But so far so good." She
held up crossed fingers. "With any luck, the rain
will blow over soon. But I don't think I could have
fit anyone else in here, anyway. This is the biggest
crowd yet."

He resisted the urge to press a shushing finger
to her lips. If he touched her, he wouldn't want to
stop touching her. "Storms don't bother me." He
stared at her mouth. "If anything, they turn me on."

She blinked at him in what looked like in-
comprehension, before putting a hand to her hair.
"I don't really mind them so much either, at least

when I'm not working. But the humidity plays havoc with my hair. I'm a mess."

"Not true." Curling, light brown tendrils had escaped her pins to trail over her shoulders. She had that just-laid look going on, and he liked it. "You look good rumpled."

Her lips twitched. "Right."

Somehow, he'd make her understand just how she affected him. "You ever made love during a storm, May?"

The bold approach surprised her. She drew an audible breath, stared, finally shook her head, and admonished him. "Behave, Jude." Her worried gaze skimmed the room. "There are people everywhere. Someone might overhear and not realize you're teasing."

"Behaving has gotten me nowhere." Unable to resist, Jude smoothed back one curl, tucking it behind her ear. Enchanted by her warmth and softness, he let his fingertips linger along her jaw, her temple, then recalled his new resolution for plain speaking. "Besides, I'm not teasing."

She stilled, then laughed as if he'd tickled her ribs.

Undeterred, he lowered his voice and stared into her eyes. "So, have you?"

"Have I . . . what?"

Damn, she looked confused and uncertain, and very sweet. He curved his fingers under her chin and tipped up her face. "Fucked with the storm all around you?"

Her mouth fell open, then just as quickly snapped shut. The lenses of her glasses amplified her glare. "I don't like that language."

"Do you like the act?"

Her beautiful eyes widened. "Oh, for crying out loud . . ."

Again, he caught her chin, surprised that she'd given him hell when May never had a cross or contrary word for anyone. "It's not a tough question, May."

She stepped out of reach. With one hand to her forehead, the other propped on her hip, she wavered. "Not that I should, but . . ."

"But?" he encouraged.

"No." She let out a breath—and didn't quite look at him. "I haven't. Made love in the rain, that is."

He asked the obvious question: "Would you like to?"

Her startled gaze caught on his. She laughed again; but when he continued to wait, her eyes flared, turned hot . . . and she stepped backward, almost knocking into a tray from a passing waiter. To keep her from falling, Jude caught her arm and drew her forward again.

Even through her suit coat and blouse, he detected her softness and warmth. His fingers contracted, caressing her, enjoying the plump feel of her.

She leveled a get-serious look on him. "Are you here to see artwork, or to fluster me?"

His hand slid down her arm to her wrist, where his fingers encountered bare skin. "Are you flustered, May?"

Seconds ticked by. She licked her lips . . . and slowly retreated out of his reach.

Hands trembling, she adjusted her glasses. "Don't be silly." She attempted to smooth the wrinkles out of her jacket. "I just don't want anyone to get the wrong impression. Most of the people here don't know you the way I do. They don't know how you like to kid around—"

"Who's kidding? We've got the storm." His voice deepened. "All you have to do is say yes."

Suspicion darkened her eyes and she added, more strident now, "They don't know that we're only friends."

That had him grinning. "May," he chided, "don't be naive. Men are never friends with sexy women."

She started to argue that, realized he'd called her sexy, and clammed up.

Jude stepped closer. "If a guy seems to be your friend, trust me, he's just biding his time until he can get you in the sack."

A dozen expressions flashed over her face before she settled on a frown. "I thought you and I were friends."

Gently, he told her, "I know."

Her cheeks hot, she lowered her chin and stared at him over her glasses. "So . . . you didn't . . . I mean, you're not here for the . . ."

Jude looked at her breasts. "I've been looking forward to this all week."

She pulled the lapels of her jacket together. "This, meaning . . ?"

"You." He lifted one shoulder. "The showing. Both."

She tugged on her jacket again, doing her best to conceal herself.

"That's not going to work, you know."

"What?"

He eyed her breasts. "You've got too many curves to conceal in a business suit."

Color rushed into her cheeks, and she flattened

her mouth. Rather than fiddle with her jacket, she crossed her arms tightly together. "Let's talk about the artwork."

The change of subject didn't bother Jude. May needed him in more ways than just the sexual, so he understood her rush to get to business.

If it weren't for him, he doubted her gallery would stay afloat. He'd learned early on that the arts rarely, if ever, gained priority from the good folks in Stillbrook. The town consisted mostly of farmers and blue-collar workers who were more concerned with their schools, their local sports, and the neighborhood bar than with anything else.

Not only was he her biggest buyer, but also her biggest draw. Much of the crowd showed up at her gallery just to see him. Because he usually stayed secluded behind the heavy gates of his property, an art showing offered photo opportunities to the money-hungry and personal introductions to the groupies.

Her business had grown because of him. He knew it, and he suspected May did, too.

"I'd rather talk about us, but if you insist . . ."

"There is no us!" Her raised voice surprised her as much as it did Jude. With a groan, she slapped a hand over her mouth.

Poor May. She really had no idea how to deal with a suitor. Or with sexual frustration.

He'd be happy to clue her in. "Relax," he whispered. He took her wrist, kissed her palm, and lowered her hand to her side. "No one is paying any attention to us."

She choked. "Of course they are. Everyone always stares at you. They—"

"Do you realize that your showings are one of the few highlights of this town?" He'd have to balance his pursuit with business if he didn't want to scare her off. May had grit, but obviously, she didn't know how to deal with his interest.

The compliment relaxed her enough that the rigidity left her shoulders and she visibly gathered herself.

"Thanks. It's nice to be appreciated." She folded her hands together. "So, is there something in particular you want to look at tonight?"

He couldn't resist. "You mean besides you?"

She missed a beat, and before she could start protesting again, he detailed his artistic needs.

"I'm still working on the downstairs." He had plenty of time left to him tonight, and luckily, the house he'd built had more walls than he could count. He could buy ten paintings, and she wouldn't think a thing of it. "I need some artwork for the home theater and the guest room. Something . . . friendly. Bright. Large."

After several deep breaths, she nodded. "I have some ideas."

One eyebrow lifted. Jude looked her over, lingering in select places. "Wonderful."

"My ideas involve your house."

"Of course."

"The downstairs you just mentioned." She sucked in another deep breath that expanded her already lush chest. "Describe it to me."

"Dark leather furniture. Natural hickory floors in the game room and home theater, light slate around the indoor pool—"

"You have a pool inside your house?"

He hesitated. The way she asked that, heavy with disbelief, made him uncomfortable.

"Of course you do." She snorted. "Forget I asked."

Why the hell did she have to sound disapproving? "I swim for exercise."

Mouth twitching, she said, "I understand."

Damn it, she made him feel defensive. "You should come by for a swim. You'd like it."

She looked appalled by that suggestion. "Uh, no."

"Why?"

"Not a good idea."

Impatient, Jude narrowed his eyes. "Again . . . why?"

"I don't . . . that is . . ." She glanced around, and lowered her voice to a whisper. "I haven't worn a bathing suit in ages."

"You're modest." He watched her closely. "I understand. But it would just be the two of us."

That made her blanch even more.

"Water inspires me. We could relax, have a few drinks. Discuss your . . . ideas."

"One of my ideas is that we could discuss ideas right here, at the gallery, in our regular clothes."

She could be such a smartass. "My ideas would be more fun."

With a droll look, she straightened her glasses. "But mine would be safer."

Safer. As the word echoed through his head, Jude stiffened and retreated a step. Maybe it wasn't the thought of skinning down to a bikini that caused May distress. Maybe the risk of being alone with him—a man with a past, a man with suspicion still hanging over his head—motivated her.

Her lack of trust bit into him.

But with his reputation, the accusations that had damn near ruined his life, how else could she feel?

"You're afraid of me."

Insulted, she went rigid, too. "No."

She didn't want to lose his business by alienating him. Jude could respect that. "Have dinner with me tonight."

"You know I'll be here till late."

"Fine. Then let's go for a drink."

She shook her head hard. "I don't drink."

His jaw tightened. "I'm doing my best here, May. How about cutting me a break?"

Her laugh was too loud and forced to be convincing. "I always thought you were a serious actor, and now I find you're a comedian." She patted his shoulder. "As if I'd be naive enough to fall for your polished lines."

Calling himself an ass, Jude shook off the uncomfortable vulnerability. So May had reservations about being alone with him. So what? After seeing him in the news for a year and a half, and his less than convincing acquittal, any sane woman would be wary.

To lighten the mood, and his own temper, Jude shrugged. "If you change your mind about swimming, come by and see me."

"Uh-huh. Okay. Sure."

She didn't lie worth a damn. "You know where I live, right?"

She bobbed her head. "Yes, yes, I do."

Hell, he was practically a tourist attraction. "Stupid question, right? Of course you do." Having a well-known personality move into the area was big news a year ago. Because of the rag mags teeming with accusations, speculation, and outright lies, his location remained big news. Even here, in a town barely on the map, the past followed him.

Jude ran a hand through his hair. "And you accused me of being polished."

She turned businesslike, using one finger to nudge her glasses higher on her nose while her brows came down in a slight frown. "You have forty acres. Your house is . . . well, magnificent. A mansion. No one around here has ever seen stone fencing like that. The trees alone are so beautiful that . . ." The frown smoothed away, her expression eased. "Well, besides all that, you're a celebrity. I bet everyone has driven past your place a time or two."

"Have you?"

She rolled her eyes. "I wish I could say I drive by there anyway, but you'd know I was lying. Other than your place, there's nothing out there but a few struggling farms."

"So you've driven by out of curiosity?"

She stared at him, weighing her words, then came to some conclusion. "I stopped by last week, just looking at things, and your security camera zeroed in on me. I had the odd feeling that . . ."

"What?"

Her chin came up. "That you were watching me."

"You should have buzzed for entry. I'd have let you in." He hadn't seen her, but perhaps Denny had. Without denying or confirming her accusation, he said, "I'd love to show you around."

"Right. You want people dropping in, which is naturally why you have NO TRESPASSING signs everywhere."

"Those are for the damn reporters."

"You keep your gates locked. The security cameras are always on, scanning the area."

He touched her again, this time just running his thumb along her jawline. "None of that applies to you."

"Well, I feel so . . . special."

She was special, more than she realized. Not that he'd belabor the point when she insisted on making a joke of his pursuit. He gestured at the display of artwork. "Hey, you're the only art dealer around. And like I said, I could use some help picking things out."

A dimple appeared in her cheek. "I appreciate your confidence, but you have incredible taste and you know it. You're more sophisticated than I'll ever be."

Because of his celebrity?

Or because he'd survived one of the most renowned murder trials of the decade?

May had the uncanny ability to sense a change in his mood, and she launched back into chatter. "I do have some new paintings from this wonderfully talented girl, Giselle Newton. She's only twenty-three, if you can believe that. I'd love to show them to you. Her collection blew me away. She screams talent. She does these really bold interpretations—"

Jude interrupted her by holding out a hand. "Lead the way."

With the topic back on art and off her personally, May became animated and enthusiastic. She forged through the crowd while Jude dutifully followed. Hell, he loved walking behind May. She had this perky little way of almost bouncing on her low-heeled pumps, as if she couldn't contain her passion for art and her delight with the gallery.

She darted beyond the crowds toward the back where special lighting showcased larger paintings. Few people mingled here, probably because the size and pricing of the pieces put them well out of their range.

Over her shoulder, May said, "I'd love to see Giselle get a little attention. And we both know whenever you buy a piece, the artist's reputation grows overnight."

True, because every half-ass newspaper and gossip magazine recorded his every move. Thinking that, Jude gave a subtle scan of the gallery's interior. Photographers lurked in every corner, trying to fit in, trying to be inconspicuous.

Vultures.

He detested them all, but never would he show it. Back in the fighting days of his youth, he'd gotten used to cameras. Unlike many of the competitors in the much-criticized, no-holds-barred Supreme Battle Challenge, known as the SBC, he'd kept his face intact. No broken noses, disfiguring scars, or cauliflower ears for him.

Celebrities, icons in the business world, and the rich and famous all attended and bet on the fights. After winning both the middleweight and light heavyweight belts, his popularity grew, and the sport named him an SBC representative. Hollywood noticed him. He received invitations to the right places by both men and women alike.

From there, producers came knocking, first with bit parts, then lead roles.

Almost overnight, his life had changed for the better—and then for the worse. His ability to kick ass, to never quit, to ruthlessly submit other fighters, went from being an admired quality to a suspicious trait. After all, any man who could break his opponent's arm or dislocate his shoulder without remorse was surely capable of murdering a young woman. Right?

Fucking idiots.

The photographers' presence didn't deserve his attention, so Jude looked right through them. He nodded at a few locals who went wide-eyed and twittered in return, turned down a drink offered by a passing worker, and pretended not to see the gaggle of young women batting their eyes at him and licking their lips.

He turned away.

May took one look at him and softened. "I'm sorry. This must be difficult for you."

"It doesn't matter." Jude studied one particularly vibrant painting in immense proportions. He found himself drawn into the scene, reacting to the peaceful emotion depicted, the soothing brush-strokes.

"Five feet long, three feet high," May enthused. "She set the canvas herself. It'll be even more impressive once framed. I don't know about your furnishings, but to complement the painting, I envision a three-inch-wide Grenoble style, probably in bronze or silver, maybe half an inch rabbit trimmed in black. . . . But we can decide on that later." Teeming with expectation, May leaned around to see his face. "Don't you just love the colors? And that definition? And—"

"Yes." In a unique, 360-degree angle, the artist had painted an abandoned, weathered barn, off-set by trees of brilliant fall color and endless azure sky. Only a stark black crow perched on a broken fence post showed life near what had probably once been a working farm.

Jude didn't look at the price. "I'll take it."

For two heartbeats, May went speechless. "Really?" Her hands clasped together, and she went to her tiptoes. "That's wonderful! I wasn't certain about it, you know. I mean, it's so large that not many of

the homes in the area could accommodate it,
but—"

"Before I leave, I want you to show me those
framing suggestions." Jude took her elbow. "For
now, I want to see the rest of her work."

Chapter 2

Within half an hour, Jude had purchased three more pieces, and May could barely contain herself. She could tell he really loved the work. He talked about the scenes with her, the techniques used, and they agreed that Giselle was a most talented young lady. Discussing art with Jude had turned into one of her favorite pastimes. Out of all of Stillbrook, he seemed to be the only one who shared her love of art.

Except for the photographers intruding, mentally spinning ridiculous tales about Jude to go with the various photos they took, things were perfect. After his odd mood when he'd first arrived, and all that silly sexual banter, meant to be teasing, she was sure, she had started to doubt the success of the evening.

But now, not only had Jude purchased some remarkable pieces to add to his collection, he wanted her to have them all framed, too.

Still bubbling with success, May led him to a large back room that held her framing supplies, worktables, and numerous shelves. She could hear the crowd in the outer room, probably gossiping about Jude. If only they'd buy something . . . but they never did. They didn't have Jude's appreciation of talent, his eye for quality, or his aesthetic judgment.

Choosing only what she thought would complement the artwork and Jude's home, May arranged frame samples on a worktable. With him on one side of the table and her on the other side, she displayed the pieces between them.

"When can you have them delivered?"

"Once you make your choices, it won't take long to frame them. Maybe a couple of days."

"All right."

She folded her hands together and waited for him to peruse the collection. But when she glanced up, Jude's gaze was on her chest, not the frame samples. Heat uncoiled inside her. Feeling awkward, she tugged at the lapels of her suit, trying to hide herself. But like a Rubenesque model, her generous proportions bulged out everywhere.

She glanced up and got caught in Jude's gaze.

"Well," she prompted, feeling very agitated and confused, "what do you think? Will any of these work with your décor?"

Rather than answer, he said, "I'm wondering about something."

May tried to joke her way around her sudden unease. "Uh-oh. With you, that's usually a bad sign." She tipped her head, smiling brightly.

"Do you ever wear anything besides suits?"

The question had her blinking twice, and emotionally retreating. "I'm a businesswoman." She straightened her glasses and smoothed her hands over the front of the jacket, but the lapels wouldn't lie flat, not with her more than ample bust.

"And businesswomen can't wear anything else?"

No matter what she wore, the fit was off. Not that she'd let Jude know how he disconcerted her. She'd long ago accepted herself, and if he got his jollies by teasing her, well, so what? He made up for it in art purchases. "Like?"

His gaze slipped over her body. "Something slinky."

"Right." Her laugh sounded strained rather than natural. "Slinky is for ultrathin models."

Jude paused, studying her expression as if he sensed her discomfort. "Slinky is for showing your curves."

"Yeah, well . . ." She made a face. "I've got *plenty* of those."

Her sarcasm couldn't be missed, and she groaned. She wanted to bite back the words, but it was too late. Already, Jude scrutinized her.

"I agree." He reached across the table and touched her cheek. "You have sexy, very notice-able curves. You should show them off instead of trying to hide them."

May went still, held in anticipation and un-certainty. Slowly, he trailed one finger down her jaw, her throat, over her collarbone.

Her glasses nearly fogged. "I'm on the round side and I know it."

"You're gorgeous."

"I—"

He dipped that teasing finger into her cleavage, and then up and over the swell of one breast. He sounded hoarse when he said, "And hot."

Heat ran up her neck. "I don't think so."

"That's because you're not male. Thank God."

Her eyes nearly crossed. She frowned, stepped out of reach, then cleared her throat. Whatever game he was playing, she had to make him quit before she did something stupid, like grabbing him. "Look, Jude—"

"I'm looking," he promised. "And I like what I see."

May turned her back on him. If she couldn't see him, maybe she'd be able to get her thoughts together and form a coherent sentence. "This is ridiculous." Jude said nothing, and her tension grew. "I don't understand why you're doing this."

"Sure you do." His voice sounded closer. "I want you."

Wary, she looked over her shoulder and found him right behind her, eyeing her rump. She jumped forward a step. "Stop that."

"I don't think so." He reached for her.

She spun away, half scandalized, but also . . . half excited. "Jude!"

"May."

She stepped back. He couldn't possibly really want her, not with every bombshell in Hollywood hot on his heels. But . . . he wasn't in Hollywood.

He was in Stillbrook.

She cleared her throat. "We're supposed to be picking out framing, not talking about my clothes or my . . ."

He stalked toward her. "Sex appeal?"

She continued to back up. "I don't believe this."

"Why not?"

"Because . . ." But she refused to say the obvious, that she wasn't the type of woman who appealed to a man like him.

Jude didn't have an ounce of reserve. "Because you don't want me to picture you in something more revealing?"

With a half laugh, she flapped her hand at him. "As if."

Appearing dead serious, he kept pace with her until they'd completely circled the table, with May now on the opposite side. She stopped retreating.

"I do. A lot."

She had no idea what he was talking about. "You do . . ?"

"Picture you in slinky, revealing clothes." He smiled. "Or no clothes at all."

She'd had enough. Taking an aggressive stance, May faced off with him. "Stop being so outrageous, Jude. Stop . . . *toying* with me."

"When I toy with you, you'll know it—and enjoy it."

Breath strangled in her throat at that provocative promise. Her thighs trembled, her stomach tingled. But this was all familiar to him; he'd likely said similar things to a hundred women, whereas she'd never had anyone be so bold with her.

But she wasn't a wimp, and she wouldn't let him rattle her. "All right, that's enough. All kidding aside, we both know I don't have the type of figure that'd occupy your thoughts."

His brows shot up. "Is that so?"

"Or maybe you just think I'm dumb. Is that it?"

Appearing perplexed, he dazzled her with another smile. "I think you're smart. And sweet. And—"

"Gullible? Because I've seen you on television." May said it like an accusation. "And in movies."

He crossed his arms over his chest, a man at leisure. "You mean with women."

"Exactly. And none of them were anything like me."

"Now there's an undisputable truth."

More confused by the moment, she crossed her arms, too, and glared at him. "There. You see?"

"Yeah, I see." Moving too fast for her to react, he reached across the table and caught her arm, holding her in place as he moved around to close the distance between them. "They're actresses, May, assigned to the role. I don't pick them."

"But you sure seem to enjoy them."

He laughed. "Maybe you don't know it, or maybe you're just playing coy, I'm not sure which, but you're every bit as sexy as any of those women."

"You were just making fun of my suits!"

Jude ignored that. "You don't starve yourself or spend hours in a gym or in front of your mirror, but you're warm and soft and you've got a great ass."

Oh good Lord. No one had ever discussed her butt so blatantly before. "Most live bodies are warm and soft," she argued, but she'd lost a lot of her conviction.

"Most people don't smell as good as you do." He touched his nose to her temple. "Or act as sweet as you."

She quit straining away from him. "You really think I'm sweet?" Her brother would argue that point. So would her parents. And some of the people she did business with . . .

"Mmmm. You don't look down on others just because of what they have. You don't judge people by their possessions." He leaned back to see her face, holding her captive with the intensity of his blue eyes. "And you would never chase a man for his money."

Something in the way he said that brought May out of the sensual fog of pure fantasy. Jude looked sincere, at least in this. And so incredibly handsome he made clear thoughts nearly impossible.

His inky black hair hung over his brow, bone straight and shiny as silk. His long, dark lashes were at half-mast, his brows slightly drawn. Hollywood had voted him one of the "Most Beautiful People" and she had to agree. Success at the SBC made him revered as a fighter, and success at movies made him a prime catch for any producer. Wise investments had left him ultrarich.

So maybe most people did look more at the package than the real man. Maybe women saw the characters he played, and not Jude Jamison, flesh and blood. Did anyone else realize his love of art? Or his protective streak that ran a mile wide?

Did anyone else see his vulnerability?

They'd never gotten too intimate in conversation, but after the evening's events, she felt justified in prodding. "Is that what other women have done? They chased you for your money?"

Jude drew back as if she'd smacked him—a very telling reaction.

Had he been hurt? The possibility brought out her own protective instincts. He'd been through so much. Outwardly, he'd dealt with it all; but inside, how did he feel? "Jude?"

"Jesus." He suddenly looked disgusted. "Don't start mothering me, okay?"

"But—"

"I need to get laid, May, not coddled."

Taken aback after all his soft speaking, she flinched and would have stepped away, but he cupped her neck, tipping her face up, holding her close. "Tell me you want me."

"No."

"Tell me, May."

His breath brushed her lips. His hands were big and warm on her sensitive skin, destroying her concentration. To brace herself, she gripped his forearms. "I . . . it's a moot point. I can't get involved."

"Fine. No major involvement." His thumb moved over her bottom lip. "That doesn't mean we can't enjoy ourselves."

May closed her eyes, hurt and disappointed, and embarrassed that, for even a moment, she'd held out some silly hopes. To be sure, she asked, "You want to have sex with me?"

He brought her closer. "I guarantee you'll enjoy every second."

Of that, she had no doubt. But she wasn't a woman who indulged in casual sex. Not even for Jude Jamison. "I don't think that's a good idea."

Impatience sharpened his tone. "You know you want to."

"Maybe. But I'm a smart woman. I don't take chances—" She almost added, *with my heart*, but bit the words off in time.

"Chances?" His expression went cold. "What does that mean, exactly?"

She'd angered him when that had never been her intent. Just because she did want him—more than she'd ever wanted anything—she refused to wear her heart on her sleeve, or give him more reason for amusement. She had her pride, and she'd damn well keep it. "I'm sorry."

"Sorry for what?" He used the edge of his fist to tip up her chin, still close, still appealing. "Spell it out, May. Tell me why."

And then he'd go and never come back? The thought left her shaken, already filled with remorse. In all her twenty-nine years, she'd never known a man like him. If she lived to be a hundred, she'd never meet another. For her, it wasn't about his money or fame. When with him, she felt . . . happy. Somehow more complete.

If only he felt the same . . .

She returned his compelling gaze and made a decision. She would kiss him. Just once, but she deserved that much. If she didn't, she'd never forgive herself. After tonight, she'd probably never see him again.

It wasn't easy, but she held herself in check, maintaining the small distance of their bodies, only brushing her mouth over his, lingering for one heartbeat, two. Her breath accelerated. Her heart pounded.

She forced herself to lean away.

Confused, definitely irritated, Jude scowled at her, running his tongue along his lower lip, as if tasting her. "Tell me, was that a weak come-on, or an insulting kiss-off?"

A half laugh took her by surprise. The fact that she couldn't even kiss him right only proved her point. Playing with Jude was like playing with fire; she already felt burned.

With a groan, she admitted the obvious, "I have the spine of a jellyfish."

Jude pinched the bridge of his nose. "Swear to God, May, the shit you say has no meaning."

Fighting her smile, May looked up at him and wished for a different life. "It means I'm weak." She drew a reinforcing breath. "It means I want—"

"Hello!" Her brother barged into the room with indisputable bad timing, obliterating the moment . . . and saving May from her own foolish babble.

In a drunken slur, Tim Price bellowed, "There you two are." He tripped over his own feet, fell into the table holding the framing pieces, and sent several lengths of wood and metal clattering to the floor. The table skidded away under the impact, and a corner clipped May's hip with bruising force.

Startled, she jerked sideways—right into Jude's arms.

For one tantalizing moment, her breasts pressed against him, her soft thighs nudged his. He'd never held her before, never felt the perfect fit of their bodies, and to experience it now, on the heels of that barely-there kiss, left him raw.

Something dark and dangerous tightened inside him.

If he'd had any doubts at all about the force of his desire for this one particular woman, holding her had eradicated them.

Red faced and disheveled, May pushed away from him. "Good grief. Jude, are you okay?"

"I'm fine." *Just horny.* "You?"

She wouldn't quite meet his gaze. "I'll live." Discreetly, she rubbed her hip where the table clipped her.

Slowly, Jude turned to face Tim. Not since his days in the SBC did he want to take apart another man the way he did now. "Watch what you're doing next time."

Tim just laughed. "Next time? Does that mean you plan to make a habit of molesting my sister in the back room?"

May jumped as if goosed. "Tim!"

Too drunk to listen, he waved away the warning.

"A little hanky-panky never hurt anyone. Hell, it'll probably do you some good."

Face hot, May confronted her brother in a hush. "What in the world are you doing here?"

"What's this?" He flung out his arms, splashing the contents of his drink onto the floor, the wall, and his sister. "I'm not welcome?"

"You know that's not what I meant." After a fast, mortified glance at Jude, May brushed at her sleeve and summoned a sickly smile. "I'm just surprised to see you, that's all." Worried that others would hear Tim and become aware of his drunkenness, she looked toward the open door.

Jude took pity on her and quietly closed it without comment.

Alcohol fumes preceded Tim's guffaw. "Relax, sis. I'm just razzing you. Hell, I'm all for you hooking up with Mr. Celebrity here."

Jude had started out the night with the firm conviction that he'd end it in bed with May. Now he felt like an ass over his own cocky ego, and that left him in a sour mood, one he would more than gladly take out on Tim.

He took a step forward—and May whirled on him. Voice shrill, posture stiff, she said, "I can handle this."

Under the circumstances, her insistent demeanor didn't faze him. "I could handle it better."

Her fists landed on her hips, and her brows clamped down. "What's that supposed to mean? Are you calling me dumb again?"

Jude rolled his eyes. "I never called you dumb." He leaned forward and dropped his voice to a whisper. "I called you sexy."

Tim, the idiot, remained unaware of the friction

he had caused. "So, besides the obvious, what are you guys up to?"

Obliging May, Jude held out his hands, offering to let her answer.

Skeptical at his concession, May turned back to her brother. "Jude's choosing some frames."

"Ha!" Tim saluted them both. "S'that's what we're calling it these days?"

"Tim!"

"You might as well quit screeching, honey. He's too drunk to listen to you."

In an aside, May snapped, "Don't call me honey."

Tim looked between them and broke into a loud laugh. "Shit, May, it's clear he's got the hots for you. Anyone can see that."

"Tim . . ."

"Well, you don't really think he likes all that stuff he buys?"

"Actually, I do."

Almost as one, brother and sister turned to stare at Jude.

Smiling, Jude clarified for them, "Have the hots for May, *and* enjoy what I buy."

Mortified, May covered her face. "Oh God."

Staring at May's bent head, Jude said, "I'm a connoisseur of beautiful things."

Tim grinned. "There ya go, sis. You have art in common, he likes the looks of ya, and it's not like you're gonna find a better catch." In a ludicrous stage whisper, he added, "And in case you've forgotten, he's friggin' loaded."

"Oh. God."

"He's right, May, I am."

May glared at Jude. "You're *not* helping."

Jude shrugged. "I don't give a shit about helping Tim. I just want you to understand my position."

Tim turned to him with a calculating eye. "Yeah, given your black past, God knows you'd be lucky to have her."

Jude disliked Tim—not only for how he treated his sister, but for his general disrespect of the world and his selfish preoccupation. He owned a car dealership, and when sober, he worked nonstop to bag a sale. Not only was he a drunk, Tim epitomized the clichéd car salesman persona.

When forced into his company, Jude only tolerated him for May's sake.

"You want to spell that out, Tim?"

Tim tottered toward him. "Most o' the world figures you for a murderer. Laying low with a nice, small-town girl like May would put a stopper in the gossip mills, eh?"

Anger overtook Jude's tolerant nature. He surged away from the wall.

May didn't give him a chance to react.

She stepped in front of Tim, blocking Jude's path. "You'll shut up right now, Tim Price, or so help me you'll regret it."

Jude pulled up short. He'd never heard that particular tone from May, and to hear it now . . . Was she afraid he'd wring her brother's neck? Or was she threatening Tim personally?

She didn't have to worry about him. He wouldn't really hurt Tim. He might bust a few teeth so the bastard wouldn't talk so much, but . . .

Over her shoulder, May said to Jude, "And that's enough out of you."

Jude straightened to his full height. "What the hell did I do?"

"You're provoking him."

"Bullshit."

"He's drunk, but you're not. Tim probably doesn't even know what he's saying."

"Oh, I think he knows."

"Damn right I do." Tim wavered on his feet. "You're bored hangin' out with us common folk, and you're usin' my sister to spice things up."

Jude reached past May, but Tim flailed back, then fell on his ass.

May positioned herself between the two men. "There, you see. You're doing it again."

"I don't believe this shit. He *insulted* you."

"I'll deal with him, don't worry about that. Now, I don't mean to be rude, but you should go."

Jude's brows shot up in disbelief. She was dismissing him? "You're joking, right?" He couldn't remember the last time a woman had sent him packing.

"I need to talk to Tim."

Through set teeth, Jude said, "Fine, go right ahead and talk. I'll wait for you."

"No." She shook her head. "This might take a while and I—"

Light flashed into Jude's peripheral vision. Shit, shit, shit. He didn't have to look to know that a photographer had just captured their entire conflict on film.

"Ed Burton! You're not allowed back here." Indignant, May pointed a stiff finger at the local photographer who always made a pest of himself. "I want you to leave right now."

Ignoring her order, Ed turned his camera this way and that, catching the scene from various angles. He had his long, thinning hair pulled back in a ponytail, an unlit cigarette caught in his teeth, and one faded blue eye pressed to the viewfinder.

"Damn it." May grabbed her brother, hauled him to his feet, and herded him toward the back exit.

Ed made to follow, but Jude stepped into his path. "You heard her. This is a restricted area. No customers allowed."

"Yeah?" Ed straightened to a height that equaled Jude's, but he was so skinny, a strong wind could blow him over. "So what are you doing back here?"

Jude crossed his arms over his chest and eyed Ed with the same attention he'd give a slug. "How is that any of your business?"

"The public wants to know."

He smiled and said, "Fuck the public."

Raising his camera for a shot, Ed said, "I'll be sure to share your sentiments."

"Yeah, you do that." Jude started forward, deliberately forcing the other man to scamper out of his path until he'd cleared the door frame and was once again in the outer room. More flashes blinded Jude, but he just kept striding forward, deliberately leading the paparazzi all the way to his Mercedes Benz SL, affording May the privacy she needed to send her brother packing.

But by tomorrow morning, he knew his image would be on the editorial desks of every celebrity gossip magazine in the country. Unfortunately, shots of May looking startled and flustered with her brother in a drunken sprawl on the floor would be right beside them.

It infuriated Jude that he could do nothing to protect her from one of the uglier aspects of his world.

He was known as a man in control, yet in this instance, helplessness burned inside his gut.

Maybe May had the right idea, after all. If she got involved with him, even for a casual romp, reporters would breech her privacy, slander her name, and scrutinize her every act. She'd be subject to the same rumor and innuendo that colored his life. He might be rich with some dubious fame, but Tim had nailed it: Most of the world considered him a murderer who'd gotten off the hook, not through innocence, but through money spent.

Despite his disappointment, Jude knew the best he could do for May was leave, and so he did . . . trailed by camera hounds, ripe speculation, and the gaping interest of the crowd.

Even in Stillbrook, Ohio, some things never changed.

Chapter 3

Caught in a riptide of emotions, May bullied her brother, none too gently, out the back door and away from her customers. His drunkenness had caused a good deal of embarrassment. And with the way he'd insulted Jude, she wanted to throttle him.

But damn him, he'd also interrupted . . . something. The way Jude had looked at her, the things he'd said. Astounding things. Maybe true, more likely just a come-on. But . . . *for her.*

So just maybe she should thank Tim for the interruption.

Damned if she would.

Maintaining a fast clip, she dragged her brother along until they reached the side of the building shielded by deep shadows. Outside the air conditioning, her suit was entirely too warm and constrictive. The rain had stopped, but humidity hung in the air, curling her hair, leaving her skin damp, causing her blouse to stick to her skin.

Why Tim had to drink so much and so often,

she didn't know. Why he seemed to take great plea-sure in humiliating her, she'd never understand.

Yanking his arm away from her firm hold, he grouched, "Slow down," and ended up sloshing into a puddle.

To keep him from falling on his face, May caught his shabby sleeve. She shook with unbridled fury. And disappointment. Drawing on lost reserves, she asked, "How'd you get here?"

"I drove."

No. Incensed anew, May shoved him up against the rickety fence that divided her modest gallery from the housing plots behind it. At twenty-six, Tim had her on height, weight, and strength. He'd stopped being her little brother a long time ago, but he would always be her younger brother—by three years.

For as long as she could remember, she'd cham-pioned him, loved him, and shielded him the best she could from their parents. That afforded her certain undeniable rights.

The right to protect him from himself.

Stumbling on the gravel lot, Tim laughed and swatted at her hands as she searched his every pocket until she found his keys.

When he realized her intent, he began a loud protest and tried to grab the keys back from her.

"Shhhh." May clutched the keys tight in her hand. "Do you have any idea what'll happen if someone catches you drinking and driving? You're plastered. God, Tim, you're always plastered any-more. I'm sick of it, and I'll be damned if I'll let you hurt some innocent driver."

"I got here okay."

"Thank the good Lord. But I'm not a gambling woman, and you know it."

His shoulders went rigid. "Is that a slur?"

Oh God. It was too much. Way too much. "You've been gambling again, haven't you?"

Sheepish, he shoved his hands into his pockets and looked away. "Only a little."

May curled her arms around herself, trying to think what to do. By her own accord, a path she'd chosen and accepted, she held responsibility for many things. But sometimes it felt like control spiraled away from her. Sometimes she wanted nothing more than to run away, deny them all, shake off the caring that they took for granted and didn't appreciate anyway.

Sounding sullen and spoiled and . . . hurt, Tim straightened his shirt, then ran both hands through his unkempt hair. "All right, fine, if you're going to mope about it, you can drive me home."

If the tightness in her chest didn't make a deep breath impossible, May would have screamed in frustration. Through her teeth, she said, "I'm in the middle of a showing. I can't leave."

"Oh, great. You don't want me here, but you don't want me to leave? What the hell am I supposed to do, then? Sit out here in the rain and twiddle my thumbs? No, thank you." He made another grab for his keys, and May shoved him away.

"Hey!" He fetched up against the fence, grabbed his side, and winced. His expression bitter, his mouth slack, he muttered, "Bitch," with just enough contempt to cut through her.

She needed to collect herself. She needed to be calm and decisive. She had to *take* control.

All she really wanted to do was cry. Like that would help anything.

Rubbing her forehead, May forced herself to

consider her options. For certain, she couldn't let Tim get behind the wheel of a car. He could barely walk, much less drive. Calling her mother or father was out of the question. If Olympia Price knew about any of this . . . well, Tim came by his drunkenness legitimately.

Her mother mixed prescription drugs with the booze, and stayed in enough of a fog that she considered everything in the world to be about her. May would end up taking care of her brother and her mom, and she just couldn't handle it. Not tonight. Not after everything that had happened with Jude.

Her father . . . well, who even knew if Stuart would be home? More likely he was off with a woman. Any woman. He used her mother's illness as an excuse to duck responsibility—which left it all to fall on her shoulders.

Strangely enough, he expected May to understand his actions. They all expected so much of her. For most of her life she'd done her best not to let them down.

Her stomach roiled. *I'm not like them. I'm not like them.*

"May? What are you doin' jus' standin' there? Give me my damn keys."

Decide, May. Now.

She managed a calming breath, then another. The throbbing in her head receded behind numbness. She dredged up the person Tim wanted her to be, and she turned to him with conviction. "No, you can't have your keys, so don't keep asking."

"Then wha—"

"You can walk to the Squirrel. Wait for me there."

His mouth fell open. His bloodshot eyes went wide. "Hell no. That's a mile away!"

May didn't let his panic affect her. "Maybe the fresh air and exercise will sober you up a little." She hated to unload her brother on the very nice, very *local* couple who ran the small eatery. She just didn't know what else to do with him.

From the time they were children, Tim understood when May meant business. He gave up without much fight. "I'll need some money."

Of course he did. Tim went through money like water through a sieve. "What'd you spend your money on tonight?"

"Not what you're thinking. I only had a few drinks."

"Right."

"Hey, I don't have a movie star chasing me, okay? I have to work for my money."

The conversation quickly deteriorated. But then, she knew better than to argue with a drunk. When inebriated, the most logical person in the world had no sense of reason or decorum. The longer Tim hung around, the more likely he'd be to embarrass her.

Her purse was inside, presenting another dilemma. "I'll call ahead and tell them to put it on my tab."

"Fine. Whatever." Tim shoved away from the fence, swayed on his feet, and stumbled. "But you're not much of a sister, just sending me off."

Fresh fury rushed through her veins. "And you're not much of a brother!"

He looked wounded, making her immediately regret her words. She despised the man he'd become, but she couldn't entirely blame him. Where Tim was concerned, their parents had always found saying "yes" easier than saying "no," even when "no" should have been the answer.

Even when "no" would have showed more caring.

He was the all-important male heir, their pride and joy, the one to inherit the car lot—and yet, he was one more child they didn't have time for, because children detracted from their own selfish pursuits and bit into the funds they wanted to spend on themselves. Somehow, they'd raised Tim in their image, with such a sense of entitlement he'd never learned to stand on his own. In too many ways, she pitied him.

She would never want anyone to pity her.

"I'm sorry, Tim. You've caught me at a bad time. Just go to the Squirrel, eat something, hang out. I'll be there as soon as I can."

A charming smile came and went. "I'm sorry, too." He started to give her a hug, but May moved out of reach. She loved her brother, but she loathed having a drunk hang on her. The smell alone turned her stomach. "Be careful now."

"I'm ordering a steak," he warned with a grin. Then he meandered off, his gait unsteady, his safety unsure—and May selfishly wondered if Jude might still be inside.

She glanced at the back door to the gallery, seeing the soft glow of lights, able to hear the quiet buzz of the crowd. Soon, they'd all leave. They only came to see Jude, anyway. Not a single one of them had a real appreciation for art.

Looking back at Tim, she made herself watch until he disappeared out of sight along the wet streets.

He'd be okay, she assured herself. He had to be.

Her heart picking up speed, she rushed back into the gallery. Common sense told her that Jude only bided his time with her. She didn't fall at his feet, and that made her unique. If he truly wanted her, he wouldn't want her for long.

Not that she expected more from him. Or from any man. She'd long ago resigned herself to a life alone. She'd made her choices, and she wouldn't wish them on anyone else. Maybe some day things would change . . . and she felt guilty for even thinking that way.

The never-ending conflict wore on her.

When she got inside, she found the back room quiet and empty. Her silly anticipation sank beneath the weight of responsibility. She'd scheduled the show to last another hour. She owed it to the artists and the patrons to put on a good face, so she straightened her shoulders, smoothed her rain-frizzled hair, and wiped her glasses clean before positioning them on her nose. Wearing a dignified smile, she stepped into the main gallery.

No one noticed her. Few people ever did.

Except for Jude.

She didn't need to search the room to know he'd left. She felt it, down deep inside herself. Just as she felt it when he got near.

When he hadn't walked through the doors at the opening of the event, she'd been desolate. Greeting guests had occupied her time, but not her mind.

Then she'd felt his approach, and her heart had soared. So melodramatic. So fanciful.

So . . . *fun.*

His silly flirting sent an irrepressible joy into her soul. He made her blush and stammer. He made her feel naked. He shared her love of art.

He wanted her to believe in his interest.

But May wasn't a dummy. She prided herself on being smart enough to know what would and wouldn't be good for her.

Jude Jamison, all six feet two inches of him, was at the top of the "not good" list. Any interest he showed had to be out of boredom. Or because she posed a challenge.

As Hollywood's sexiest hunk, Jude starred in one blockbuster movie after another. Before the awful scandal and the drawn out trial, his smile had graced everything from posters and calendars to billboards and commercials. Every week he'd had a different starlet on his arm, each one more beautiful than the other.

Even now, Hollywood wouldn't let him go. According to the magazines and newspapers, the offers kept coming. Directors still wanted him, maybe even more now that his notoriety had grown.

But Jude stayed out of the limelight as much as he could. He isolated himself on his property—except for the rare appearance at her showings.

The man did like his art.

If only he liked her as much.

Sighing, she walked to her desk and put in the call to the Squirrel. With Jude gone, the rest of the night would drag.

Damn it, she missed him already.

There were times when Tim hated his sister. As if a freakin' fairy had sprinkled magic dust on her, things always went her way.

May got a job as an assistant to a realtor—and loved it.

Tim inherited the car lot—and hated it.

She took a financial risk and opened the gallery—

and a rich bastard like Jamison moved to the area
and kept her afloat.

He bet at the boats—and lost every fucking
time.

If May wanted the sun to shine, she could probably make it happen. Life blessed her while it
cursed him, and it made it damn hard to like her
sometimes.

Because she didn't face his problems, she'd never
understand. His mother's constant blathering, wanting him to dote on her, wanting his undivided attention. His father's endless demands, first about
the car lot, and then about being a man in general.
Of course he drank. He had to, or his life wouldn't
be bearable.

May knew what the docs said about him drinking. It was a sickness. A disease. A source of relief.
But did she care?

Hell no.

Making him walk to the Squirrel. Unfeeling
bitch. He should've just taken his keys back. Not
like she could stop him. But . . . shit. Somehow she
always did. May didn't start things she couldn't finish, so if she said no, she meant it.

He huffed, then cursed as a passing car hit a
puddle, soaking his legs.

Muddy water drenched him, his head hurt, and
he needed another drink. Bad. His throat closed
up, and he had to swallow hard when he started
feeling sorry for himself. Or sorrier. Whatever.

More headlights flashed over him, and he
stepped to the side to avoid another splash. Christ,
he hated the Squirrel with their greasy food and
pasted on smiles. He hated—

Squealing tires made him jump, then a rough
hand grabbed at him, and he fell. His knees barely

met the roadway before a fist clenched in his collar and yanked him awkwardly inside a car. His arm scraped along the edge of the door. His heel cracked the curb, knocking his shoe loose. Panic exploded, but he didn't have time to react. He choked on an automatic shout of fear.

Rock-hard knuckles cracked against his jaw. His head snapped back, pain exploded behind his eyes, down his neck and back. *"What the fuck?"*

Frantic, he tried to look around, but another blow landed, then another. Shielding his head the best he could, he cowered into a tight ball. But the strikes kept coming, harder and faster. Caught in the floor of the rear seat between two men, he screamed, struggled, but it did him no good. He couldn't maneuver, couldn't dodge the assault. Never in his life had he felt so helpless.

Time dragged by; his babbling pleas faded to broken groans of agony—and finally, before he could black out, the punishment stopped.

Pain receded beneath an awful numbness, a pervasive fear that refused to allow him the luxury of a faint. He sensed that the car had stopped, which meant there were three men, two in back with him and one driving. Would they kill him now? Dump his body somewhere?

He strained one eye open, trying to see past the blurry fog. Darkness sank in, from outside the car, from inside his head. His lips were fat, his tongue swollen, his throat raw from screaming.

From the right of him, foul breath assaulted his face. "You still with us, Tim?"

This couldn't be happening. Words tried to crawl up his throat, but he couldn't get them out.

"He's not listening." That cold, uncaring voice snapped from his left.

"I'll wake him up."

No . . . He tried to move away, but he didn't get far. His teeth nearly shook loose with the force of the slap to his jaw.

A fist caught his collar, choking him. "Do we have your attention, now?"

"Yeah . . ." He struggled to clear his head.

"Good. Now listen up, because the choice is yours."

The fist hauled him upward, aggravating his injuries, keeping him half suspended over the floor. He couldn't see a thing. Just endless blackness. And maybe, just maybe, the glitter of malicious eyes in the dark interior of the car.

"You owe our boss some money."

Dear God. This was about his debt? Someone would do this to him over *money*? Held in the steely grip of fear, Tim muttered, "No."

"Yeah, you do, Tim. Fifty thousand one hundred dollars, to be exact." The voice gentled. "That's hardly birdfeed."

His ribs protested at every breath. "I . . . I'll pay it back . . ."

"Relax, man. You've already paid back part of it." A soft chuckle. "This beating takes care of the C-note."

A lousy hundred dollars' worth. How bad would they beat him for fifty grand?

"You're wondering about the rest? That's easy." Gleeful eagerness built. "To even the score, we'd have to kill you."

"*Nooo.*"

Knuckles cracked, accompanied by an anxious laugh, and Tim almost threw up.

Survival instincts kicked in. Clawing, he struggled to get away from the ominous voices. Where he'd go, he had no idea. It was dark, he was badly hurt. And he had no idea where they were . . .

A slug on his ear and a fist around his throat stifled his movements. He tried, but he couldn't suck even a thread of air past the constriction around his windpipe.

All humor gone, the voice snarled, "Sit still, you miserable fuck, or we'll take you apart right now."

His heart beat so hard and loud, Tim wasn't sure he could hear over it.

"Now, the choice is yours. You can either repay the money tonight."

He didn't want to die. A sob seeped out around the tight fist. He barely managed to shake his head. He didn't have it. The most he could cough up would be a few grand. Even May wouldn't have that much in her savings. Maybe his parents . . . but he doubted it. They'd spent his inheritance quick as they could, damn them. But maybe if he mentioned them, he could buy some time.

The fist loosened, cupped his nape. "Or you can take one of your other two choices."

Hope emerged; he had choices?

"One, you can either die to prove a point."

"Nooo, *pleassse* . . ."

"Or you can do the boss a favor. Just a small favor, Tim, no big deal. But it'll square up your debt. How does that sound?"

Unable to move, Tim gulped air, silently praying, afraid to hope again, but more afraid of being murdered. He nodded his head.

"I thought that might interest you. Here, now, why are you still crouched in the floor? Have a seat with us so I can give you all the details."

Because he had no other option, Tim forced his aching body up to the seat and gingerly settled between the beefy bulldogs. Fresh blood trickled down the side of his face, sticky and warm. A piercing pain sliced deep into his side, probably from cracked ribs. He tasted his own fear.

And if May hadn't pushed him away, none of this would have happened.

Clasping his hands together to keep them from shaking, he whispered thickly, "Wha' d'I haf to do?"

Furious, exhausted, and damn it, so worried she felt ill, May paced the floor. Hours ago she'd showered, changed into her gown. She'd tried the phone a dozen times, left that many messages. She'd checked with all his friends, their parents, every bar in the area.

She knew Tim had probably just gone off somewhere to continue drinking, but . . . what if he hadn't? He didn't have his car. It was still in the parking lot of her gallery. By his own admission, he'd been without money. Would he go off to drink when he knew she'd be coming for him?

Of course he would, she told herself. He was a drunk. And irresponsible. And he never truly thought of anyone but himself.

But what if he hadn't?

Tears burned her eyes. Damn him! Where—

The loud thump against her door nearly sent her out of her skin. For two seconds, she held a hand to her heart and just stared at the door, afraid to move, afraid to hope. Midnight had come and gone hours ago. No one ever visited her except her friend Ashley, but Ashley would have called first.

In a squeak, she asked, "Who is it?"

"May?"

Hearing her brother's weak, slurred voice unglued her feet from the floor. Every previous second of worry merged into a blinding fury that carried her across the room to jerk the door wide.

To her shock, a body fell inside, hitting the floor in a broken heap. The battered face was almost unrecognizable. Mud and blood caked his hair, smeared over his face, and his clothes were tattered. Oddly enough, she noticed that he'd lost a shoe.

"Tim?" she whispered on a breath of sound.

He just . . . laid there. Not moving. Barely breathing.

"Oh. My. God." She dropped to her knees beside him. *"Tim!"*

"G'me . . . inside," he rasped through grotesquely swollen lips. "Hurry."

"Tim?" From a whisper to high and shrill, she couldn't control her voice. Tim sounded scared to death, which reflected exactly how she felt. "What's happened to you? Were you in a wreck?"

Had he stolen a car? Taken one from the sale lot? Why hadn't she thought of that? Of course, he had access to a car, lots of cars. He sold cars, for crying out loud.

Putting a hand to her mouth, May prayed for the right answer. "Tim, listen to me. Was anyone else hurt?"

"No."

Awful panic ran through her. "Are you sure? If you left the scene of an accident—"

"No." He gasped, then moaned out a sob. "No . . . no asident."

May bit her lip. If he hadn't been in a car wreck, then what? He looked demolished.

Get a grip, May. Don't fall apart. She nodded to herself, took a deep breath. "Just hold still."

Afraid of hurting him more, her hands hovered over his body. Blood stained his shirt, his slacks, left a track along his ear and his jaw . . .

"May." One bloodshot eye opened. "Hel' me. Hurry."

Tears burned her eyes, and she shook her head helplessly. "I'm not a doctor. I'll have to call an ambulance." She started to stand, and his hand clamped onto her ankle.

"They . . ." He swallowed audibly. "They migh' come back."

Her eyes widened. "They *who*? Someone did this to you?"

"Yeah. Gotta get . . . inside. Lock the . . . door."

The cold chill of terror scraped down her spine. She surged to her feet and peered out the doorway. The hall outside her apartment was empty and dim. There were no strangers, no unfamiliar shadows. May listened but could hear nothing over the broken wheezing of her brother's breath.

Driven by new urgency, she crouched beside Tim again. "Can you sit up?"

"Yeah." His eye closed. "If you hel' me."

He reached out a shaking hand and May clasped it, then put it to her shoulder. "Hold on to me." Bracing one arm around his chest, the other across his back, she struggled to get him upright.

He made it to his knees, and with her prodding, finally lumbered to his feet. Sweat poured down his face, and his every drink-soured breath echoed with pain.

"This way." Gently, May guided him into a step.

He more or less fell against her, and they both nearly toppled.

"Tim!" May balanced him until he collapsed on the cushions of her couch. Never in her life had she seen anyone beaten. This was different from what Jude had done in the SBC. That was sport; this was . . . just awful.

It pained her to look at Tim. "I'm calling 911. Hang on."

"No, you can't."

"I have to." The uncontrolled terror in her tone startled May. She wrapped her arms around herself and took a deep breath. "Tim," she said, sounding more reasonable, stronger. "Whatever's happened, you need to go to the hospital, and we need to notify the police."

On a groan, he asked, "D'you want me . . . murdered?"

Her knees turned to noodles. "You can't be serious."

His eye opened again. "Dead s'rious."

Murdered.

Dead.

Until she'd reached her front door, May wasn't aware of her feet moving. She turned the deadbolt, taking little satisfaction in the quiet *snick* it made. If someone truly wanted in, her locks wouldn't be much help.

Next, she raced to the window, checked that lock, and jerked the curtains shut. The only other window was in her bedroom and as she entered the dark room, her skin crawled, but she didn't dare turn on any lights.

Finally, she came in to sit beside Tim.

Taking care, she touched his face, smoothing aside his brown hair. "You're in bad shape, Tim. You need help."

"Yeah. Ev'rythin's fucked up. I thought . . ." He tried to swallow. "Need a drink."

May considered calling the police despite his protests. It was hard to tell under all the blood, but he could need the type of medical care she couldn't give. Still, knowing her brother, she had to hear the whole story first. "All right. I'll get you something."

When she returned with a tray, she found Tim slumped to the side. "Tim?"

He flinched. "Sorry. Nodded off."

May set the tray on the coffee table and lifted a glass of tea to Tim's mouth. "Just sip it. Easy now."

It trickled down his chin and into his ruined shirt, but he swallowed, drinking half a glass before turning his face away.

She needed to see the extent of the damage, so she dipped a dish towel into a bowl of icy water and began a careful mopping of his face. Except for a wince here and there, Tim hardly seemed aware of her efforts. Beneath the blood, bruises mottled his skin and a cut marred his cheekbone. She ran her fingers along the bridge of his nose, his brow, and finally, his jaw.

"Your face is going to be swollen a while, but I don't think anything is broken."

"Un-fuckin' b'lievable."

Meaning he'd expected some breaks? She wasn't surprised. He had to be in a lot of pain. "What about your ribs?"

"They hur' like hell."

"Take a breath."

He did, wincing the whole time. "The only way to know if any are cracked is with an X-ray."

"No."

"So we'll have to assume they aren't." Her hands shook as she rinsed out the rag and went back to cleaning him. She'd be strong for Tim, but inside, her stomach roiled. "Now, tell me who did this to you."

"Shhh . . ." he whispered, "C'mere."

May leaned in, putting her ear near his mouth. "What is it?"

"We have to whisper."

"Why?"

"I could be . . . bugged."

She drew back in surprise. "That's ridiculous." Maybe he'd drunk so much that he now hallucinated.

"It's true, dam'it. An' you could be bugged. Both of us. Everything. They know things . . ."

"All right. Calm down." She and her brother had their differences, but she loved him, and if humoring him would help, she'd humor him. Matching his hushed tone, she asked, "Why would someone attack you?"

Again, he beckoned her closer. "I owe . . . people."

Damn it. "Tim, you said you weren't gambling."

"I lied."

"All right." May clenched her hands together. "How much?"

While averting his face, he raised himself a little higher on the couch cushions. "A lot."

"What does that mean, Tim?" When he didn't answer, she leaned around, her face in his. *"How much do you owe?"*

In a breath of sound, he whispered, "Fif'y thousan'."

A dousing of ice water couldn't have shocked her more. Her brain went numb at the enormity of such a debt. She didn't have that kind of money, couldn't even raise that kind of money if he gave her a month. "You can't." She shook her head. "It's not possible."

"Sorry, but I do."

"How . . . How could you?"

"Dunno." He touched his bottom lip with unsteady fingers. "I was at the boats. Ran outta money. A guy offer'd . . . to fron' me." His abused face puckered in a scowl. "I was set up, 's not my fault!"

He'd taken money from a stranger? A loan shark? *In Ohio?*

May shot to her feet, but that jostled the couch, and Tim groaned, grabbing for her, his words tumbling out fast and slurred.

"Don't lea' me," he begged. Big tears leaked out, and his lips quivered. "May." He choked on a sob. "I'm *scared.*"

Guilt churned inside her. Guilt, and anger, and resentment. But none of that would help. She reseated herself beside him. Because speaking aloud agitated him, she kept her voice low. "Tim, I don't have that kind of money. Not even close."

He nodded acceptance of that fact.

Hoping to convince him so that he wouldn't upset himself more, she took his hands in hers. "We can call the police. They'll help—"

"You do, an' they'll kill me. They said so."

"Who?"

He shook all over. "Dunno. But they mean it, May. It was dark. They hit me. Over an' over an' . . ."

Trying to be reasonable in the face of his fear wasn't easy. "My door's locked. There are other people in the building. If you don't leave here until the police come, how can they get you?"

He swallowed hard, then lowered his head. "They said they'd be watchin' me, that they had me bugged. They said . . . they said someone would tail me 24/7. They said I wouldn't piss without them knowin', that if I go to cops, I'm dead." He gulped hard. "Fuck, m'sorry, May. So sorry. But they . . . they know you, too. If they don't get me, then . . ."

May's heart skipped a beat.

"They'll get you."

Dazed, she came to her feet. "Me?"

"It'll be 'kay. They wan' a favor. You can help me, then I'll be even."

She didn't want to know, she didn't want to know . . . "What kind of favor?"

"Promise you'll help me." His face crumbled on more tears. "Promise me, May."

Too many times she'd seen Tim cry when drunk, wallowing in his own self-pity, always blaming others instead of taking responsibility. It sickened her. But this time, it seemed he had legitimate reasons for his upset. "Calm down, Tim. Of course, I'll help you. So what is it?"

His damaged gaze met her fearful one. "I haf . . . t'kill . . . Jude Jamison."

Chapter 4

Ashley Miles did a little two-step, jiggling along to the music in her CD player as she pushed the vacuum cleaner down the twelfth floor hallway in the enormous, empty building. Thirty minutes more and she could head home for some serious study time.

She might be one of the oldest students, but she got better grades than the teenagers, so what did she care?

She'd just turned off the vacuum when her cell phone vibrated, making her jump. "Jesus!" Falling against the wall, then laughing at herself, she pulled her headphones off her ears and retrieved the phone from her jeans pocket. "Hey-lo."

"It's May."

Immediately, alarm bells went off in her head. May never, ever called her at work. Heck, May was never even awake at this time of the night. Unlike Ashley, who hooted with the nocturnal owls, May liked to soar with the early eagles.

Pushing away from the wall, Ashley demanded, "What's wrong?"

Voice too light and animated, May said, "I thought maybe you'd come over for a visit."

"A visit?" Ashley glanced at her watch. Whoa. "You want me to visit tonight?"

"Yes."

She could practically see May pacing, her hand gripping the phone. They were closer than sisters, and very best friends. "Sure, May, I could do that. Wanna tell me why?"

"We haven't had a chance to talk lately."

"And you want to talk now?"

"That's right. You had that new outfit to show me, remember? The flashy one?"

Ashley snorted. *All* her outfits were flashy. She liked bright clothes and lots of texture, unlike May who wouldn't give up on her awful suits. "One question, okay, hon?"

"Uh . . . maybe."

"Do you think you can have some coffee ready when I get there?"

The audible relief in May's tone told her everything she had to know. May needed her. Why, Ashley didn't know. It didn't matter, anyway. Any opportunity to pay May back thrilled her. If it weren't for May, she would have given up on herself long ago. "I can be there in half an hour."

"The coffee will be waiting. Thanks."

"Lookin' forward to it, toots. Buh-bye." Ashley disconnected the phone, stuffed it back in her pocket, and began winding up the cord to the vacuum. Judging by May's behavior, she had no time to waste. A glance at her funky pink jeans with zippered hems and a button fly, yellow-and-pink-checked slip-on sneakers, and her stretch lace tee of yellow and pink roses assured her that her outfit would fit the bill.

The only time May ever cared what she wore was . . . Oh, wow. *When she wanted to trade identities.*

The elevator suddenly dinged, jolting Ashley out of her stupor. Being on the twelfth floor, she normally had to wait forever for the elevator to reach her. But not tonight.

She broke into a jog so she wouldn't miss the ride, and reached the elevators just as a male form stepped out in her path.

Too late to put on her brakes. "Oh shit."

Quinton Murphy, hunk in a suit, CPO of a lucrative consulting firm in the building, gave her one startled glance out of piercing green eyes, accepted the impact of her body against his, and managed to catch her in his arms.

"Oof!" His papers scattered everywhere, and together, caught by momentum, they tripped over the vacuum she towed along.

They went down in a heap, arms and legs tangled in the vacuum cord and hoses. Ashley pushed up, saw his still, perfectly sculpted face, smelled his delicious scent, and scampered away from him.

Speechless, heart punching into her ribs, she crouched beside him. He looked . . . flattened.

Their gazes locked, and then he smiled. "Good evening."

Sitting back on her heels, Ashley groaned. "I am *so* sorry. Are you okay?"

He lifted his head to look at his body. "Other than a possible concussion, a few broken limbs . . . yeah, I'm fine."

"Please tell me you're joking."

Another smile. "I'm joking." He sat up, smoothed back his dark blond hair, and dusted off his hands.

Rather than stand, he draped his wrists over his knees and gave her all his attention. "So, in a hurry, are you?"

Busted. She hadn't finished the rest of the floor. Her shift should have lasted another half hour. But shoot, if he got mad and ratted her out, she could always find another seven dollar an hour night-shift job, right?

"Actually, yeah. I was going to cut out a little early." She winced. "I didn't expect anyone to know. I mean, usually the floor is empty this time of night, except for Flint."

"Flint?"

"The guard. He hangs down by the front doors, but every hour or so"—she looked left and right, leaned forward, and said in a dramatic, conspiratorial, hush-hush whisper—"he reconnoiters the floors."

"Ah. How conscientious of him." Quinton leaned forward, too, aligning their mouths, looking directly into her eyes. The impact was awesome. "I bet he manages to linger on whatever floor you're on, doesn't he?"

Ashley almost wished she had more time. Not that she intended to get involved with Mr. Big Shot. Oh no. But flirting was fun. "It does seem that way." She pushed to her feet, then held out a hand.

He accepted, although he stood with no real help from her. "Quinton Murphy."

"Yeah, I know. Heard all about you."

One tawny brow lifted. "From . . . ?"

He kept her right hand, so Ashley gestured with her left. "The females who're leaving work when I'm coming in. And the females who are coming in when I'm leaving."

"They work for me?"

"I don't think so. They're more . . . casual. They probably work in other parts of the building."

"They're casual in dress, you mean? Like you?"

She grinned. "I like color—almost as much as I like gossip."

"You don't say?" He rubbed his chin. "I'm not sure I recall any female employees outside my own company."

"That's all right. They certainly know you. Or, that is, they know of you."

Both brows lifted. "Really?"

"You're the head honcho around here."

That made him laugh. "The curiosity is killing me. Have they run me down or sung my praises?"

"Nothing but song, cross my heart. Unless you consider 'workaholic' a slight. But how could you when it's apparently true?"

"You're sure of that, are you?"

She pointed out his presence and the papers scattered all around them. "From all indications, you put in a lot of hours."

"I see." He released her to right the vacuum and pick up his papers. "So I'm here late, and you're leaving early. Seems we both have odd hours."

"Yeah, uh . . ." His voice was so smooth, Ashley couldn't tell if he was threatening to report her, or making a pact. "I'm a good worker. Never sick, never late. Usually I don't leave early, either. It's just that an emergency has come up and I—"

"Your secret is safe with me. Or at least it will be if you'll give me your name."

Shew. He intended to be reasonable. "Ashley Miles."

"So, Ashley, I say we cement this new friendship with dinner tomorrow before your shift. What do you say?"

The invite was so smooth, it took her a second to digest it. Technically, he broke no rules by asking. She didn't work for him. Quinton Murphy leased space, but he had his own employees separate from the building management. She didn't answer to him, and he didn't sign her paychecks.

But that didn't mean she'd take the bait.

Cocking out a hip and narrowing her eyes, Ashley surveyed him. Slick. Slick in an expensive suit. Despite devastating good looks, an awesome build, plenty of height, and sex appeal that radiated off him in hot waves, she had the sense to smile and say, "Sorry, no can do."

"The day after?"

She shrugged. Her life left no room for men. Maybe in a year or two, but for now, she had only one answer. "I'm busy, busy. Crazy schedule and all that." And before he could ask, she said, "Always." And with drama, "It just never ends, ya know?"

"I see." He lounged half in the elevator so that the doors couldn't close—and she couldn't leave. "You work third shift, so that must be, what? Eight to four?"

"Uh, yeah. That's right." Using the vacuum handle like a cane, she relaxed her stance. "I'm here long after you and everyone else has left."

"Except for Flint."

"And Rudy and Aiden."

"Rudy and . . . ?"

"Rudy is a guard, too. But he's older and doesn't prowl around as much. Aiden cleans the floors below mine." Pretending deep thought, she mused, "And I guess there must be others, too. I mean, I only do four floors. And this is a big building."

"Any other women work with you?"

"Nope, not that I've ever noticed. I don't think women like night shift."

"But you do?"

"It suits me."

"And why is that?"

Not that it was any of his business, but she figured, what the heck? She crossed her arms and straightened. "I'm going to school. My hours have to fit around that."

"I see."

She looked every year of twenty-seven, but he didn't so much as blink.

"What's your major?"

"Nursing." And then, seeing no help for it, she flattened a hand to his chest and gently nudged him away. "And really, I am in a hurry, so . . . if you'll forgive me?"

"Right." He stepped back, but as the doors started to close, he said, "I'll be seeing you around, Ms. Miles."

Ashley smiled—until the closed doors blocked the sight of him. Then she collapsed back against the brass rail and whistled. "Not if I see you first, Mr. Murphy."

Once Ashley got over the shock of seeing Tim pulverized, she checked him out. Going by what she'd already learned in nursing school, he'd live. Not that she planned to celebrate. He made May's life hell, and she for one disliked him for it.

"I promise, May, it's not as bad as it looks. So much blood makes you think the injuries are more severe than they are. Most of it's just bluster—you know, superficial stuff." Of course, the way Tim carried on would be enough to make someone think he hovered at death's door.

"What a relief."

"So, we're calling the police like good, sensible citizens, right?"

"Ah, no. I promised him I wouldn't." May fought her way into the pink jeans. "And until I talk to Jude, I just don't think it's a good idea."

Only for Tim would May come up with such a cockeyed plan. For sure, she'd never do anything like it for herself. Remembering May's warnings, Ashley protested in a mere whisper. "You know this is insane? And surreal. Something out of a suspense movie."

But Tim's injuries weren't caused by a trip on the sidewalk.

"It's the only way I can leave here without risking him." Utilizing a lot of effort, May closed the last button on the jeans.

Ashley cast a quick look at the couch where Tim slept, thanks to pain pills. "I don't know, May. What if there are people out there, and they recognize you?"

May caught Ashley's arm and pulled her into the bathroom. After turning on the shower, they both felt safer talking. Tim could be loony about the whole "bugging" concern, but someone had really done a number on him, so better safe than sorry.

"We've done it in the past, Ash, and we've never been caught."

"Yeah, well, you might not have noticed, but we've changed a little since the good old days. Most notably, you got gargantuan boobs and I didn't." It disgusted her to admit it, but Ashley said, "I'm still the great breastless wonder."

"Ash," May automatically
terrific figure."

"If you can call an A cup

May held up a sports b
could."

"I hope that thing is lin
it's going to take a lot of s

"I'll manage." May bit her lip and
feet haven't grown any, because the shoes fit. I just
hope I don't rip your jeans if I bend. Or move. Or
breathe." Her gaze met Ashley's. "They're *really*
tight."

"They're stretch. Don't worry about it. Actually,
they look better on you than they do on me." Her
personal sense of style began and ended with color
and comfort. Tight jeans were more flattering, but
she preferred them loose to the point of being
baggy. Lots of room to move. Not real attractive,
but what did she need with male attention, anyway?

May stared at the stretch lace T-shirt, at her own
chest, and she paced away with a hand to her forehead. Her hair hung loose to her shoulders, fluffed
out and flirty to match Ashley's curlier style.

Though Ashley's hair was several inches longer,
she doubted anyone would notice the difference.
They shared an identical shade and texture.

As teenagers, they'd often played tricks on others,
dressing alike, acting alike. May's boyfriend in high
school drove past the theater just as Ashley walked
inside on a date. He accused May of cheating.

Once, Ashley's father had thought she worked
in the garden as per her punishment, when really
she'd been in a school play. He never walked out
to check on her, just looked through the window.

"Promise me you'll be careful, May. I mean it."

"Cross my
her head,
ing to
much
In
th

heart." May pulled the shirt on over
then pulled some more, up, down, try-
make it cover more of her, but without
success.

wardly, Ashley cringed; outwardly, she en-
used. "Hey, it fits."

"Sort of." Staring down at her exposed cleavage,
May moaned. "It's so stretched, I can see through
it."

"Lucky for you it's been a rainy couple of days."
Ashley picked up the V-neck, hooded poncho of
florescent pink that she'd worn to ward off the
weather. She dropped it over May's head, closed
the fat button at her neck, and grinned. It fell to
May's hips, concealing her. "There you go."

"I can't believe I'm doing this. I can't believe
I've involved *you* in this."

"We'll stay inside. I'll keep an eye on Tim. Don't
worry about us."

"I know you despise him."

"But I love you."

Tears welled in her eyes as May drew a shudder-
ing breath. "Oh God, Ash, this is . . ."

"A big clusterfuck?" She nodded. "Sure is."

Dismay turned into a laugh. "You are so bad."

"It's what I live for." Ashley hugged her close.
"Now, stop worrying. I'll keep the phone close,
and if anything happens, I'll call the cops, damn
the consequences."

"You better." May took Ashley's hands. "I won't
trade your safety for Tim's. This is his mess. I'll do
what I can, but I don't want you in danger."

"Got it." Ashley patted the cell phone in the
pocket of the housecoat she wore. Beneath the
housecoat, she had on a nightshirt and flannel
pants. She preferred anything to May's hideous

suits, and her friend didn't hav~~~~~~~~
ther dressed for work or wore ~~~~~~~~
"And don't forget, you're go~~~~~~~~
after you get there."

May slipped off her glasses~~~~~~~
large, colorful tote bag Ash~~~~~~~~~
gave her hair one last fluff. "I m reau~~~~

They left the bathroom, and Ashley walked with
her to the door. Filled with misgivings, she gave May
one last hug. In a mere whisper, she said, "Get those
glasses back on as soon as you round the corner."

"I will."

"And drive slow until then."

"I will."

"And think positive. Attitude is everything."

Since May was the one who'd taught Ashley
that, she smiled. "See ya soon."

Holding her breath, Ashley stood by the front
door until May had left the building. She relocked
the door, then rushed to the window to peek
through the curtains until May had gotten into her
banana yellow Civic and driven away. No other cars
pulled away from the curb to follow. No lights came
on. No one moved out of the shadows.

Tim was such an ass.

After a quick prayer, Ashley moved back to the
couch and stared down at him. If he didn't look so
pathetic, she'd be tempted to kick his butt.

Poor schmuck.

One of these days, May would walk out on all of
them. And not a soul would blame her—except
her family.

Sweat trickled down his bare chest and abdomen, dampening the waistband of his loose cotton

lungs labored and his muscles burned.
ion dragged at him, but it wasn't enough.
May, nothing would be enough until he had
After an hour . . . or a day . . . or hell, a week
f nonstop, no-holds-barred sex, then he'd have
his fill and could get his life back.

But not until then.

And that burned more than anything else
could.

He'd hoped physical exertion would dilute the
throbbing of regret, the continual need. Many
times in the past he'd used exercise to clear his
mind, to control his anger. Pumping weights, jogging on the treadmill, and hitting the heavy bag
until his arms felt like lead pipes usually left him
wiped out in thought and body.

This time, it only fueled his frustration. Propping
his leather-gloved hands on his hips, Jude dropped
his head forward and sucked in air.

He had to face facts: May didn't want him.
She'd been real clear about that. She'd babied her
drunken sot of a brother while telling him to get
lost. She'd kissed him—sort of—then acted like it
was nothing.

To hell with her. Let her throw herself at her
work. Let her pass on something he *knew* would be
good. Let her . . .

Shit. She'd crowded into his brain again.

With determination, Jude locked his jaw and
pounded his fists against the bag until his arms
trembled with the strain, and finally, he had to
stop, crouching down to catch his breath. Even fatigued, with his energy totally spent, May's image
lingered in his mind. Smiling. Sweet. *What the hell
is so special about her?*

"You have a visitor."

suits, and her friend didn't have much else. May either dressed for work or wore stay-at-home clothes. "And don't forget, you're going to call me, too, after you get there."

May slipped off her glasses, stowed them in the large, colorful tote bag Ashley had carried, and gave her hair one last fluff. "I'm ready."

They left the bathroom, and Ashley walked with her to the door. Filled with misgivings, she gave May one last hug. In a mere whisper, she said, "Get those glasses back on as soon as you round the corner."

"I will."

"And drive slow until then."

"I will."

"And think positive. Attitude is everything."

Since May was the one who'd taught Ashley that, she smiled. "See ya soon."

Holding her breath, Ashley stood by the front door until May had left the building. She relocked the door, then rushed to the window to peek through the curtains until May had gotten into her banana yellow Civic and driven away. No other cars pulled away from the curb to follow. No lights came on. No one moved out of the shadows.

Tim was such an ass.

After a quick prayer, Ashley moved back to the couch and stared down at him. If he didn't look so pathetic, she'd be tempted to kick his butt.

Poor schmuck.

One of these days, May would walk out on all of them. And not a soul would blame her—except her family.

Sweat trickled down his bare chest and abdomen, dampening the waistband of his loose cotton shorts. His lungs labored and his muscles burned. Exhaustion dragged at him, but it wasn't enough. With May, nothing would be enough until he had her. After an hour . . . or a day . . . or hell, a week of nonstop, no-holds-barred sex, then he'd have his fill and could get his life back.

But not until then.

And that burned more than anything else could.

He'd hoped physical exertion would dilute the throbbing of regret, the continual need. Many times in the past he'd used exercise to clear his mind, to control his anger. Pumping weights, jogging on the treadmill, and hitting the heavy bag until his arms felt like lead pipes usually left him wiped out in thought and body.

This time, it only fueled his frustration. Propping his leather-gloved hands on his hips, Jude dropped his head forward and sucked in air.

He had to face facts: May didn't want him. She'd been real clear about that. She'd babied her drunken sot of a brother while telling him to get lost. She'd kissed him—sort of—then acted like it was nothing.

To hell with her. Let her throw herself at her work. Let her pass on something he *knew* would be good. Let her . . .

Shit. She'd crowded into his brain again.

With determination, Jude locked his jaw and pounded his fists against the bag until his arms trembled with the strain, and finally, he had to stop, crouching down to catch his breath. Even fatigued, with his energy totally spent, May's image lingered in his mind. Smiling. Sweet. *What the hell is so special about her?*

"You have a visitor."

Jude didn't need to glance at the clock to know it was late. Or really early. Whatever.

Keeping his back toward Denny while he peeled off the boxing gloves, he said, "I'm busy. Make my excuses."

"You can make your own damn excuses."

Jude slanted him a look, and Denny thrust out his bristly chin.

Not in the least defensive, but plenty insistent, Denny said, "I'm tired. I want to go back to bed."

Denny wore only a rumpled T-shirt and un-zipped trousers, no shoes. His thinning brown hair stood on end, showing thick ears and a faded tat-too on his skull. At forty-seven, he didn't take well to instructions. Jude doubted that anyone had ever been able to boss him around.

Denny did as he pleased and expected others to do as he pleased, too. He believed in early to bed, early to rise, and since the sun would be up soon, no doubt the visitor had gotten him out of bed.

Down in the gym, Jude couldn't hear the gate buzzer. Every room in his house had monitors to show what the security cameras picked up, and he could have turned on the one mounted on the far wall, but why bother? The only visitors he got were paparazzi, and they could rot for all he cared.

"Fine." Jude tossed the gloves aside and picked up a towel to dry his chest. "Just ignore whoever it is and he'll go away."

Voice edging toward anger, Denny barked, "I'm a light sleeper, damn it. You know that. The buzzer's been going off for ten minutes."

Jude swallowed a curse. Why the hell had he hired an ex-military, cantankerous, martial arts son of a bitch for an assistant?

Oh yeah. He could trust Denny.

"You work for me, remember?" Jude took a long swig from his water bottle, poured some over his head, then dried off again.

Denny's massive shoulders bunched. "Getting rid of girlfriends at the crack of dawn wasn't on the list of duties when I signed on."

"Girlfriends?" Jude lowered the towel. "What are you talking about?"

"Kicking ass, that I'll do. I enjoy a good workout, especially if the one I'm kicking has a camera."

Dismissing all that, Jude demanded, "What do you mean, girlfriend?"

"Meals, cleaning, hey, no problem. I gotta eat, anyway, and I can't abide filth. That's what you pay me for."

When Denny got on a tirade, it took a lot to shut him down. Jude slashed a hand through the air. "The caller is a woman?"

"I take care of your mail and vet your phone calls. But this shit—"

"Damn it, Denny. *What* woman?"

As if startled, Denny gave up his diatribe and crossed his arms over his chest. His green eyes narrowed with indignation. "Chunky little thing. Brown hair. In a real tizz. She's insisting you said she should visit. I told her you sure as hell didn't mean at five in the morning—"

May was here to see him?

Suddenly rejuvenated, Jude pushed past Denny and took the stairs two at a time to the main level. Even as he raced, he felt like a fool. A pathetically hopeful fool. *He did not chase after women.*

But May wasn't just any woman. Hell no. An ordinary woman wouldn't have him up all night beating the hell out of a leather bag just to burn off sexual tension. He hadn't been this antsy since Elton Pascal had taken the stand against him, telling lies that everyone believed, damn near getting him crucified.

In several long strides, Jude reached the security screen located in his enormous stainless steel kitchen. Arms braced on the counter, he leaned in to see the monitor, and sure enough, May filled the screen.

Holy shit.

Just outside the closed iron gate, May paced beside an idling car. Jude narrowed his eyes and stared at her.

What the hell had she done with herself?

Given his past problems and current status quo with the paparazzi, he'd bought the very best security system available. The picture on the monitor wasn't grainy, and it didn't waver.

The crystal clear image showed May with tumbling hair, poured into skintight pink jeans, and wearing some kind of sneakers that appeared to be yellow and pink checked. Her full breasts gave a tantalizing shape to an otherwise boxy, neon poncho.

She looked . . . well, not bad, exactly.

But not like herself, either. He knew May, and something had happened, something that would bring her to him at this ungodly hour. Something that would make her dress so differently.

Worry replaced stiff-necked pride—and relief filled the void of his soul.

He had a reason to let her in.

Without taking his gaze off the screen, Jude elbowed Denny. "Ask her what she wants."

Bemused, Denny eyed him from foot to forehead, then harrumphed. "Already did. She said she had to talk to you."

"Yeah, but ask her why. Hurry. Before she leaves."

"Before she .. ?" Denny drew himself up. "You're standing right here. Ask her yourself."

His temper hit a high note. On the verge of exploding, Jude jerked around to face his friend and employee. "*Goddammit*, can't you just once—"

"All right, all right." Put out and not bothering to hide it, Denny said, "Jesus. Don't have a hissy."

Through clenched teeth, Jude growled, "I'm not. I'm . . ." *Feeling desperate.* A definite difference. "I'm tired. Now ask her."

Grumbling, Denny punched the voice relay button. "Hey there, miss?"

Almost tripping over her colorful shoes, May whirled around and rushed back to the intercom. She got so close, Jude could see through the lenses of her glasses to the darkness of her eyes, wide with some wild emotion. "Yes?"

"Jude's busy. He wants to know what you want."

On a groan, she knotted both hands into her fluffy hair and turned a circle. Seconds ticked by. Finally, she came back to the intercom and monitor. "Please, tell him . . . tell him it's important." She sounded breathless. She sounded pleading.

Jude's stomach bottomed out. "Ask her if she's hurt."

Denny punched the button. "You hurt?"

"No, I'm . . ." Arms around herself, she closed her eyes and shook her head. "I don't know. *Please*, tell Jude that I have to see him."

A thousand possibilities crowded through Jude's brain, but none of them made sense. He refused to act on emotion, no matter that May often drove him to extremes of melodrama. He was a man who weighed his options, who considered all the angles.

Her presence here now afforded him the opportunity to salvage a little pride. He could refuse to see her, as she'd refused him. He could tell her to take a hike, as she'd told him . . .

Right. He already knew he wouldn't do that, so delaying the inevitable only tortured them both. "Let her in."

"You sure?"

"Yeah." For whatever reason, she'd come to him. This time he'd keep the upper hand. "Tell her to wait in the library."

"The library? But that's upstairs—"

"Across from my bedroom, I know." The circumstances distracted Jude enough that he didn't even mind Denny's look of censure. "The sooner you do it, the sooner you can get back to bed."

Denny snorted. "As if I'd be able to sleep now." The buzzer sounded, and Jude heard Denny say, "Drive through, miss. I'll meet you at the front door."

Energized, Jude went up the stairs, then down the hall to the master bedroom. Pausing at the entrance to the room, he formulated a plan, one that would go a long way toward restoring his good humor.

God, if Hollywood could see him now. He'd fended off bloodthirsty groupies of the SBC, as well as some of the sexiest marriage-minded starlets in the world. He'd won championship belts in two weight classes, and beaten a murder rap without ever showing the public his rage, or his hurt. He'd taken good movie reviews in stride and bad movie reviews on the chin. No matter what they threw at him, he'd remained imperturbable.

Now one small female had turned him upside down, and he felt like a junkyard dog around a bitch in heat, surly, angry, and hungry. Being with her, *having her,* consumed his thoughts.

One way or another, he'd reclaim the calm composure associated with his name.

He went to the wall monitor positioned near his door, watching as she drove up to the house. May had finally come to him. Before she left, she'd be his in every way.

Chapter 5

Anxiety churned in May's stomach, making her ill. Was she doing the right thing? If she didn't call the police, would Jude end up hurt, too? Her decisions could cause more problems, could endanger others.

But what if she went to the police, and they never found out who wanted Jude dead?

In equal parts, she wanted to throw up, turn the car around, drive away, and disown her brother. But none of those options would get the results she needed. The responsibility for helping her brother fell to her shoulders, because no one else could do it.

Certainly not her mother or father.

Definitely not Tim himself.

And because she believed the horror of it, she doubted that even the cops could unravel such a mystery. Tim didn't know who had beaten him, and they couldn't put him under twenty-four-hour surveillance.

Without a name, the insane threat against her brother—and Jude—would forever be there.

No one had followed her, she was sure of that. It amazed her that she'd made it to Jude's in one piece. Between her shaking hands, her repeated glances in the rearview mirror, and her nervousness at what she needed to say to Jude, she'd probably been the worst driver on the road.

Her tires slipped in the mud and leaves as she accelerated through the ornate gate to the sweeping drive in front of Jude's mansion. Immediately, the gate clanked shut again behind her. The sun had yet to rise, but gray dawn lightened the sky, and as she neared Jude's house, she could see the enormity of the structure, the aura of wealth.

Wide porches, one for the first floor and one for the second, wrapped around the grand structure of brick and stone. A sweeping cobblestone walkway led to double columns at the entrance. At any other time, she probably would have appreciated the details of his home, the meticulous landscaping, the fountains and faceted windows.

Right now, she only concentrated on getting inside. To her nervous observation, Jude's home looked huge, unwelcoming, cold and dark.

A six-car garage sat to the side, but given the hurried nature of her visit, she parked Ashley's brightly colored car right in front of the entry door. Floodlights came on, blinding her but lighting the yard to make it easier for her to navigate.

She dug out the cell phone from the big tote bag and called Ashley first. The second Ashley picked up, she blurted, "I'm here."

"Inside?"

"About to be." Damn, her voice squeaked. "He's letting me in."

"You weren't sure he would?"

"No." With the way their last encounter had gone, she wasn't sure of anything.

"Okay. Enough quaking—and don't deny it, because I hear it in your voice. But you're too strong for that, May. We both know it. So chin up. Shoulders back. Remember, Jude Jamison is just a man like any other. Flash him some cleavage and he'll be putty in your hands. And if you need the cavalry, I'm only a phone call away."

May smiled. "I don't know that you could get in. He has a tall stone and iron fence around his property."

"Hey, I can climb a fence. No problem. But if it comes to that, God help him when I do get inside."

The image of Ashley scaling a fence and wreaking havoc on someone of Jude's height, weight, and capability left her chuckling. "Thanks, Ash."

"Go get 'em."

The line went dead, and May put the phone away.

Despite tripping over her own feet, she reached the front door and raised a fist to knock. Before her knuckles met wood, the double doors opened and the man from the intercom greeted her with a distinct lack of formality.

Hair on end, he looked her over with a comical expression, shook his head, and said, "Come on in. Jude's upstairs. He'll meet ya in the library."

"Thank you. I—"

He turned away, forcing May to swallow her apology and hurry after him.

He had a long stride and a booming voice. "I'll bring you both some coffee, but I gotta get dressed first."

Filled with apprehension, hope, and a lot of uncertainty, May looked around as they passed through the house. She made a quick note of polished marble floors, soaring ceilings, and masculine hues of brown, tan, and cream. Jude had simple tastes and apparently liked clean lines, but everything he owned screamed of high quality.

Especially the multiscreen monitors flanked by intercoms that graced every room. Though some were turned off, most of them showed various angles around the house and grounds. High tech didn't even begin to describe it.

When the man stopped at the entrance to a stainless steel kitchen with granite countertops and floors, May almost ran into him.

He turned, jumped to find her right behind him, and frowned. "I told ya Jude was upstairs."

"Yes."

"You didn't go upstairs."

Oops. "I was supposed to?"

He crossed bulky arms over his chest. "Be easier to see him that way, dontcha think?"

It took some concentration, but May fashioned a smile. "Yes, of course. The, ah, stairwell is back that way?" She pointed over her shoulder. The house was so immense, a body could get lost going from room to room.

Suspicion darkened his green eyes. He had the most imposing visage she'd ever seen, yet somehow he looked familiar to her.

"Want me to take your wrap and bag?"

"No." Clutching the tote in front of her, May shook her head and said again, "No, thank you. I'll . . . keep them with me."

"Fine." He started back the way they'd come, until they got to the sweeping, double-wide wooden stairway leading to the next floor just inside the foyer. "Go on up, then. To the immediate right is the library. Make yourself comfortable."

May stared up and gulped. Knowing Jude waited at the other end made the stairs feel ominous in the extreme, like the flame that lures the moth, a path that, once chosen, would change her life forever.

And she wasn't ready for that much change yet. "Umm . . ."

The older man's face softened. "I've known Jude a long time. Been working for him for a few years now. No reason to be nervous."

Belatedly, May held out her hand. Introductions would help put off the inevitable. "I'm May Price. Jude buys a lot of his artwork from my gallery."

Her hand got swallowed in a giant mitt. "You can call me Denny. I'm Jude's personal assistant, bodyguard, housekeeper, and general go-to guy." With added curiosity, his gaze went over her again. Satisfied, he gave a brisk nod. "And he buys all his artwork from you."

This time the smile came of its own accord. "I'm so sorry to have bothered you at this time of the morning—"

"No bother. The sun will be up shortly, anyway. Now, go on."

"Thank you." May waited until Denny went back to the kitchen and the all-important coffee preparation, then she forced herself, one agonizing step at a time, to climb the stairs. The closer she got to the upper landing, the faster her heart galloped and the tighter her stomach got.

Deciding to call on Jude was far different from actually doing it. She held tight to the handrail, her gaze darting everywhere as she viewed the upper floor. She could see yet another hallway that led to various rooms—probably bedrooms. She gulped.

She peeked into the darkened, *empty* library that looked as if it doubled for an office. Muted light came through the windows and a set of sliding doors that led to the balcony. Long shadows crept across the floor and over a variety of large furniture pieces.

"Jude?"

No one answered her pathetic whisper, and that amplified her unease. She reached inside the door frame and felt along the wall until her fingertips encountered a switch. She flipped it on, then stared in awe.

Floor-to-ceiling cherry shelves circled the room, topped with detailed crown molding and filled with books of every size and color, some paperbacks, some leather bound. Some very formal, some tattered and worn.

May stepped past an imposing cherry desk that faced two padded chairs and a love seat, situated around a matching coffee table. Her sneaker-clad feet sank into ultrarich burgundy carpeting. At one end of the shelves, she found a collection of classics alongside resource books on everything from sailing to decorating to accounting to natural home remedies. Coffee table books, biographies and dramas, action adventure, and finally, shelved eye level at the farthest end, mysteries, thrillers, and even romances took up a considerable amount of space.

When she pictured Jude lounging in one of those overstuffed, enormous chairs, a paperback romance in his hands, she couldn't help but sigh. He was such a capable man. A *guy* kind of guy.

Long before she'd met him, she'd watched him in bouts at the SBC. She'd paid to watch them live on her satellite TV, and then rented every single competition to watch again. Thanks to her fascination with Jude, she now knew more about mixed martial art fighting techniques than she'd ever imagined existed.

With one punch, he could knock a man out. He didn't swing; he drilled straight forward, hard and fast and on the button. Not just one shot. But two, and three, and four . . . however many it took to drive back and conquer his opponent.

Because he had phenomenal submission skills, he could hold his own on the ground, too. One challenger had said that fighting Jude on the ground was like wrestling with a shark in the water. Not only impossible to win, but you were liable to lose a limb while trying.

Jude matched up with the best of the boxers, and the best of the grapplers.

It spoke of his confidence that he displayed all his books, not just the ones most acceptable by society.

Walking to the wall of windows on the farthest end, she looked out at his property. In the distance, a fat red sun broke the horizon, spreading pink ribbons across the sky. The land was so incredibly beautiful, but isolated—deliberately so. He kept himself away from the public, yet still needed the monitors to ensure his safety and privacy. A sad way to live.

May would rather envision a beautiful painting on the wall, instead of the cold, blinking monitor that took up space. To think of him living here alone . . . Well, he did have Denny.

But it wasn't the same.

"May."

At the sound of his voice, her heart shot into her throat; the time of reckoning had come. She pasted on a bright smile and clasped her hands together. Greetings, explanations, pleas, all hovered near her tongue. She turned—and fell mute at the sight of him.

Good Lord. He must have just come from the shower.

Wearing only loose, faded jeans that hung low on his hips, he braced his bare feet apart and slung a damp towel around his neck. A thick black watch circled his right wrist.

Her gaze slid all over him, from his prominent biceps, to his tightly muscled abdomen, to that silky line of black hair leading down into his jeans. Going up again, her attention moved over wide shoulders, and lastly, his naked chest.

Dark, damp hair, disrupted by a few scars, decorated the sleek muscles across his chest.

Jude helped her regain her wits when, with a snort, he walked into the room toward her.

"That's a new look for you, isn't it? I'm not sure I like it."

A nearly hysterical laugh bubbled out of her tight throat. Like it? Of course he didn't like it. Neither did she. Not only were the clothes not her style, they barely fit.

"I borrowed the outfit from Ashley."

"Ashley? Didn't I meet her once?"

"Yes, at the gallery. But Ashley's not very interested in artwork. She just comes by to see me because we're best friends and . . ."

Her thoughts shattered as Jude went past her toward a chair. May took in the sight of his broad back tapering to lean hips, and that supersexy butt hugged by worn denim.

Oh, *wow*. Once he sat down, she realized that he carried shoes, socks, and a green T-shirt in his hands.

As if her visit were nothing out of the ordinary, as if he dressed in front of her every day, he bent to pull on his socks without saying another word.

May shook her head—but couldn't quit ogling his body. "I'm sorry to bother you."

"No bother. I was up. Working out."

"Oh." Why in the world had he been working out so early? She'd always imagined that movie stars caroused into the wee hours of the morning, then slept in till noon.

He glanced up. "You're all right?"

She shook her head, but said, "Yes." And like an addict, she stared some more, at the thickness of his wrists braced on his knees, the way his thighs strained the denim of his jeans, how the fly had faded from stress . . .

"May, look at me."

Oh, she looked. And his body was even more gorgeous in person than on the big screen.

Slowly, he straightened. "My face, May."

Mortified, she jerked her gaze up to his. Jude cocked a brow. Amusement, determination, and sizzling heat reflected in his clear blue eyes.

She gulped and eased back a step. "I'm sorry. I—"

At her retreat, the amusement fled. "Tell me why you're dressed that way."

Oh God. She was a horrible person! One look at Jude and she'd forgotten about the awful threat, about what she had to do and why she'd come to Jude in the first place.

"Right." She pushed her hair away from her face. "I'm sorry. I'm a little nervous coming here like this, and it's making me scattered."

Silent as death, his intensity piercing, he watched her.

Get it together, May. "Yeah, soooo, I dressed like this because I didn't want anyone to follow me when I left my apartment to come here. I even drove Ashley's car."

"You were that worried about the photographers taking your picture?"

"What?" Her legs felt too unsteady to try to explain everything while he sat there, mostly disinterested and somehow calculating. "What photographers?"

"The ones at your gallery. Last night."

"Oh." She flapped a hand. Pesky photographers were the least of her worries. "I forgot about them."

He frowned. "Then why the costume?"

Somehow, she doubted Ashley would appreciate having her wardrobe referred to as a costume. "I really need to talk with you about . . . *everything*. Would that be okay?"

"All right." He didn't so much as blink. "Take a seat."

She took a step back instead, prompting a laugh from Jude.

"I take it you don't want to sit?"

"I can't . . . I'm too nervous."

He shrugged. "Suit yourself."

Damn him, did he have to be so distant? She was used to his warmth and teasing and now, when she needed it the most, he almost seemed disdainful.

To get her thoughts focused, May briefly closed her eyes. When she opened them again, Jude had finished dressing and leaned back in the chair. His hands laced over his abdomen, his legs stretched out in front of him. He watched her, waiting, openly impatient.

"Anytime you're ready, May."

Never in her life had she been this jittery, and she hated it. She'd learned early on to assert herself, to go after what she wanted, because no one else would do it for her. Right now, she wanted to protect Jude.

She couldn't do that if she didn't explain. "I know you left my gallery annoyed."

He made no comment on that.

"And I know you must dislike Tim. I even understand why. There are times when I don't like him, either, and he's my brother."

The attempt at humor didn't faze him.

Giving up, May said, "The thing is, I . . . I need your help."

Very slowly, Jude pushed out of his chair and stalked toward her. "Let me get this straight." He didn't raise his voice, but then he didn't have to. "You refuse to date me, to even have dinner with me, but now you need my help?"

Pride would be a luxury, so May dredged up her courage instead. But it wasn't easy. Thanks to Ashley's flat-soled sneakers, he towered over her. "Yes."

"Unbelievable." Inky black hair, still damp, fell over his brow, drawing her attention to the heat in his blue eyes.

Like a fool, she felt his gaze deep inside herself.

When he propped his hands on his hips, the soft cotton polo shirt stretched over his hard chest, emphasizing the differences in their sizes.

She wanted to touch him.

More than anything, she wished he'd hug her close and joke with her, somehow put her at ease. But he stood silent and still, deliberately intimidating her.

She licked her lips. "I know this is going to sound totally outrageous, and believe me, I'm very, very sorry. But I didn't know what else to do."

Jude didn't seem to be paying attention. He reached out and fingered the big button at the neck of the poncho. "What is this you're wearing?"

"I . . . what?" Confused, May looked down. "It's a poncho. If you remember Ashley, you know that she's, well, smaller than me."

"Less endowed."

"Right. Same difference." Her glasses slid down the bridge of her nose and she pushed them up again. "I needed the poncho because her shirt isn't exactly a perfect fit and—"

"Take it off."

Breath froze in her lungs. Three little innocuous words, but somehow Jude made them sound like a sexual command. "I beg your pardon?"

"Take off the poncho. I want to see the shirt."

She didn't move, and with a sound of impatience, Jude reached out one-handed and popped the button open. The tote bag fell from her numb hands. *"Jude."*

"What?" With practiced ease, he dragged the poncho up and whisked it off over her head.

At the last second, May shook off her stupor and grabbed it to hold in front of her. "What in the world do you think you're *doing?*"

Jude walked a circle around her; she turned, mimicking his steps to keep him in her sights.

"I figured you'd be more comfortable without

it." He stopped, and then gestured to the doorway. "And Denny is here with the coffee."

Startled, May looked up.

Denny, first guilty, then disgruntled, unglued his feet and huffed into the room. "I wasn't snooping." He plopped the tray on the desk and glared at Jude.

"Yes, you were." Jude filled a cup with steaming coffee. He took several drinks before making a sound of appreciation. "Denny has a bad habit of looming around without announcing himself."

"My *looming* has kept your ass safe more than once." And then to May, "If not for me, Elton Pascal would have gotten to him at least a dozen—"

"That's enough, Denny."

Unperturbed, Denny gestured at the tray. "Ignore Jude's bad habits. He's spoiled. Most of the women he knows woulda had his pants off already. I've walked in on more than one uncomfortable moment—"

"Denny."

May didn't know if she should blush, take umbrage, or laugh.

"On top of everything else, now I gotta play host." After another glare at Jude, Denny bestowed a bright smile on her that showed off one silver tooth toward the back. "Would you like me to pour you a cup of coffee? I tried not to make it too strong, you being a woman and all."

"Thank you." Struck by the tension in the air, May looked between them.

Rolling his eyes, Jude clasped Denny's upper arm and started him toward the door. "We wouldn't want to keep you, Denny. I can serve her."

Denny protested. "But I don't mind none."

"I know you don't. I'm willing to bet you'd love to hang out and visit. But I'd rather you didn't." Jude stopped at the door, and when Denny finally slunk out with some audible grumbling, he said, "Keep your ear off the wall."

"Go to hell." Denny's stomping footsteps faded down the stairs.

Jude eased the door shut—and turned the lock. "Now, where were we?"

Close to hyperventilating, May shook her head. Being locked in a room with Jude guaranteed she wouldn't be able to hold a thought.

"Wait, I remember now." Jude's insincere smile put her more on edge. "I was going to get you coffee, and you were going to quit hiding behind that deco disaster you call a poncho." He strode back to the desk. "I assume you take yours with cream and sugar?"

"Yes, thank you." She did not want to expose herself to Jude.

"So." While fixing her a cup of coffee, he glanced her way. "You going to drop that poncho or not?"

"Not." She retreated another step.

"You've done a lot of that this morning. Backing away, clamming up instead of being your normal chatty self."

"I'm sorry."

"Yeah, so you keep saying." He turned his wrist to check the time on his watch. "Plan to tell me why anytime soon?"

"My brother is in some trouble."

"Shit." He put a spoon in her cup and stirred. "I should have known this had something to do with Tim."

Carrying the cup of coffee, he came to stand in front of May. After a long look, he set the cup on the table and held out a hand, palm up. "Let me have it, May."

She had no doubt what he meant, and seeing no hope for it, she gave up her grip on the poncho.

Jude tossed it and her tote on an empty seat, then looked her over, surveying everything from below her chin to above her ankles. Voice low and a little rough, he said, "Interesting shirt."

She wanted to cover her breasts with her hands, but that'd just make her look more ridiculous. She stood stiff, her arms at her sides, back straight, shoulders rigid.

"Those jeans can't be comfortable."

"They're too tight."

"Wanna take them off, too?" He glanced at her eyes and smirked. "From your horrified expression, I guess I can assume you're not here to get cozy with me. Oh, that's right. You want nothing to do with me. You turn down all my invitations. You're only here because your idiot brother needs some kind of help."

"I'm sorry."

"Enough with the apologies." Casual as you please, he went back to his chair and settled in to drink his coffee. "So am I supposed to drag it out of you? Or do I even need to? History's taught me that when people come to me for help, that usually means they want money."

Oh God, of course, they did. People probably hit him up for money all the time—and now he expected the same from her. In a way, she did need money from him, but not for the reasons he'd think.

No, she couldn't do it. She couldn't be just one more person who . . .

His voice gentled, even if his expression didn't. "You came all this way. Might as well see it through."

Adrenaline rushed into her veins. She had to warn him about the threat. Before she could chicken out, she stormed toward him. "Last night, someone grabbed Tim, pulled him into a dark car, and beat him half to death."

Jude took a small sip of his coffee. "Half to death, huh?"

"Don't you dare be callous, Jude. When Tim fell through my doorway—and I do mean fell—he was so bloody I barely recognized him. One of his eyes swelled completely shut, and the other is so blood-shot it hurts to look at him. His lips are cracked. He has bruises everywhere."

"Apparently, he pissed someone off."

"He pisses everyone off! You of all people should know that."

In the blink of an eye, Jude's expression went cold and hard. "I'll be a son of a bitch." His coffee cup clattered as he set it on the desk. Pure rage brought him out of his chair, sending May to scuttle back. "You think I did it."

Her eyes widened at that barely-there whisper. She started to retreat further, but his hands clamped onto her arms, keeping her immobile.

"You came here, all righteous and pathetically brave to face off with me, the evil outsider, because you think I jumped your poor excuse for a brother."

Words lodged in her throat. How had he gotten everything so wrong? "I didn't—"

"Jesus, I'm an idiot." He worked his jaw before thrusting himself away from her in disgust. "Look at you. You're shaking in your sneakers. You think I'm going to hurt you."

That didn't make any sense. "I'm trying to explain—"

His harsh laugh cut her off. "Your brother provoked me, so naturally I'd want to pound on him a little, right? I mean, what the hell, if I'd hurt a woman, why would I draw the line over a weak-ass like Tim?"

He didn't give May a chance to dispute that.

"And you know what? I would've loved to give Tim one good punch in the mouth because the bastard deserved it. But when I fight a man, it's face to face. I'm not a coward who jumps a man from behind."

"I know."

"I fight fair, and a fight with Tim wouldn't be that. It'd be like fighting a kid, for Christ's sake."

Or hurting a woman? May's heart broke for him. He sounded so wounded that she wondered how many times those accusations had been thrown in his face. For an honorable man like Jude, being blamed for something he wouldn't do had to be unbearable.

"Here." He picked up the phone and tossed it toward her. She didn't move, and it landed on the floor in front of her.

"Call the cops, why don't you? Share your damn theories. Tell them whatever the hell you want. I don't care." He started to turn away.

"Yes, you do."

"The hell I do!" In a heartbeat, he was back, nose to nose with her. "Just because I wanted in your pants doesn't mean you can—"

Nervousness fled in the face of raw anger. *"Will you shut the hell up?"*

He did a double take, his tirade suspended.

Shocked at her own loss of temper, May groaned. She'd lost her control more in the last twenty-four hours than she ever had in her life. She had to get it together. Crossing her arms tight, she tried to contain herself.

But she flared anew when Jude's gaze dipped down to her chest. "Oh no you don't! Don't you dare start eyeing my boobs, damn you."

Jude blinked at her. "I—"

"In all the time I've known you, never, not once, have I accused you of anything." She hadn't slept yet, she was tired down to her bones, and now her head wanted to explode off her shoulders. "But from the moment I walked in here, you've done everything you could to make this *more* uncomfortable for me, when let me tell you, bud, it's plenty uncomfortable already."

Jude regained his aplomb with a vengeance. "If you didn't voice the accusation, you've sure as hell thought it."

"You have no idea what I think."

"It's obvious."

"Apparently *not.*"

He took several deep breaths, and in a more moderate tone, asked, "If you don't think I'm dangerous, then why keep denying me?"

Oh, shoot. Her loss of temper had her heaving and left her brain blank. He was dangerous all right—to her peace of mind, her heart, and her blood pressure. "Ummm . . ."

Jude again closed the gap between them. "Why, May? If you're not afraid of me, why refuse to have dinner with me? If you don't believe all the rumors, then why dodge me?"

Somehow, they'd gotten way off course. She

tried to inch away, and he growled with frustration.

"Why shy away from me all the damn time?"

May pressed her hands to her temples. "Stop yelling at me!" They stared at each other. "I can only deal with one thing at a time, and for right now I have a whopper of a problem with my brother." *And with keeping you safe.*

Jude struggled with himself.

"I mean it, Jude. You've bullied me enough. I don't take it well on a good day, and today is not going to be good. So tell me right now, will you be reasonable, or should I just leave and figure things out on my own?"

"Could you?"

Through her teeth, she said, "I've managed so far." Though how she'd manage this one, she had no idea.

For only a moment, he looked admiring. "Fine. You have a reprieve. For now." He put space between them, slouched into his chair, and gestured at her. "You have the mike, Miss Price. But I'm tired of playing twenty questions. If you've got something to say, say it."

"All right." He had her just annoyed enough that she didn't bother to measure her words. "Tim owes fifty thousand dollars, and if he doesn't pay it, there's going to be some nasty consequences."

To her surprise, the bald statement didn't affect Jude at all. "Tim is an ass."

"I had to leave him at my place. Ashley is taking care of him. Tim claims the men who beat him up said they'd be watching him, and if he tried to go to the police, they'd kill him."

"And you believed that?"

Only because the threat implicated Jude—and Tim's beating made it all too real. She'd get it all said now, while they were both being reasonable, calm adults. "The man he owes . . . he told Tim that they'd be even, that he wouldn't have to pay it back, if he . . ."

Jude closed his eyes and sighed. "If he what?"

He looked bored again—but it wouldn't last long. She sank down to sit on the edge of the chair facing him. "If he killed you."

That got his eyes opened. He stared at her, his expression blank before breaking into humor. "You're kidding."

"No." She bit her lip, sick at heart. "Sorry, I'm not."

He started laughing. "Damn, I didn't see that one coming." The amusement quickly waned. "So tell me, how the hell did I get into this?"

"I don't know." May wished she had the nerve to crawl into his lap and put her arms around him. It couldn't be a good feeling, for someone to want you dead. "All I know is that Tim is pulverized, and whoever did it to him said he'd be watched around the clock to make certain he doesn't go to the cops. He's to pay—either with cash or by . . ." She gulped. "Doing you in, or else he'll be killed."

"Who does he owe?"

It bothered May that Jude seemed to take it all so well. "He's not sure. He borrowed at the boats without getting a name. Tim said he thought it was a friendly exchange . . ."

"Tim never thinks. It's one of his biggest problems." Jude tapped his fingertips together, thinking. "By the way, if I *had* jumped him, he sure as hell wouldn't be able to come crying to you."

"I know." The urge to defend her family burned

inside her, but unfortunately, Tim had no defense. "You have to give him the money, Jude."

Incredulous, he shot forward in his seat. "I don't have to do a goddamned thing!"

This time, May did reach out to him, putting her hand on his forearm. Muscles bunched. Their eyes met. "Don't you see? It's the only way. Tim said they want the money soon, but I don't have that much. I'll have to sell . . . things to get it."

His jaw locked. "It's not your debt. It's Tim's."

"At this point, does it matter whose debt it is?"

"He's an adult. A man. Let him grow up."

If only it were that simple. "A life is at stake here."

"Should I break out my violin?"

He didn't believe her, didn't understand that the threat really did exist. "Tim probably should be in a hospital, but he's afraid to go. Whoever did this to him means business. I realize eventually we'll have to notify the police, but in the meantime, if you'd only give him the money, then he won't have to—"

"Kill me?" There was no amusement in Jude's grin. "I have another solution."

"You do?"

"Damn right." He caught her hand and laced his fingers with hers. Eyes bright and direct, he said, "I could kill Tim instead."

"That isn't funny."

"I wasn't joking."

Maybe he could take death threats in stride, but she couldn't. "Of course you were. You could no more kill than Tim could."

Jude's attention stayed glued to her face. "Where have you been? Don't you watch the news? I'm the scourge of the earth. I murdered a woman. In comparison, offing a creep like Tim would be a piece of cake."

She was in no mood for his sarcasm. "We have to get serious here. Paying them off is the only option. But we need to move soon. Who knows what they might do next?"

Jude tugged on her hand, forcing her to lean toward him. "You don't think I'm capable of murder?"

Distracted once again, May stared at his mouth. "For the last time, Jude. No, I'm not afraid of you, and no, I don't believe you're a murderer."

He released her so suddenly that she almost fell back in her seat. "So now your reprieve is over."

"No way." She rushed to her feet and moved behind the chair. "We haven't figured out what to do about Tim's attackers yet."

Smirking, Jude stood, too. "Look at you, cowering behind the damn chair." And in a taunt, "I thought you weren't afraid of me."

"I do *not* cower."

He took a step toward her, and she scrambled to the side. "Looks like cowering to me. You trust me enough to have in your gallery, to keep me as your best—maybe your only—customer."

"I have customers!" Just not enough to keep her in business.

"But you don't trust me enough to date."

Why did he have to turn insistent now? "It's not a matter of trust."

He stalked her. "Bullshit. You want me to choke up fifty grand to save your brother's sorry ass, but God forbid you have dinner with me."

Anger stirred inside her again; her brother's ass wasn't the only one on the line. "You've got it all wrong, Jude."

"You're no better than Tim."

The insult cut deep, making her rigid. "Take that back."

"He uses you, and you want to use me. My money's good enough—as long as you don't have to touch me to get it."

Infuriated, May launched herself across the chair. Jude stumbled back, but not fast enough. She was on him in an instant.

Poking him hard in the chest, May shouted, "I have *always* wanted you. *Always.* I don't accept your offer of dates because I know exactly how we'd end up."

Jude grabbed for her pointed finger but missed. She advanced, and he backed up. "Yeah? And how's that?"

Sounding demonic, she growled, "*In your bed.*"

Disbelief replaced surprise. "Oh, really?"

"Or my bed. Or on the damn street corner." The look on his face gave her pause, but anger ruled. "Around you anything is possible, because the second you're close, I start thinking insane things that can't be. Around you I'm a jellyfish." She punctuated that with another hard poke that made him jump. He butted up against the desk and came to a halt. "And in case you're still confused, that means I have no backbone. You look at me and I *melt.*"

"Melt, huh?"

May had the awful suspicion he might laugh. "Yes, damn you." She thrust her chin up close to his. "You shake my control and I can't stand it."

"Then why not just give in?"

"Argh!" She knotted her hands in her hair, amazed that he could be so dense. "It would never work, that's why."

"I see." Furthering her suspicions that he found her loss of control amusing, he rubbed his mouth. "Funny how you never told me this before, no matter how many times I asked you out. But suddenly you need my money for your brother, and just like that"—he snapped his fingers right in her face—"you confess all."

"What are you talking about?" He couldn't have meant that the way it sounded.

"Planning a little trade-off, honey? I get a fuck, and your brother gets bailed out of trouble?"

If she'd had time to think about it, if the insinuation hadn't been so ugly, and if she hadn't been running on lost reserves, she might not have swung at him. But before she knew it, her fist flew through the air and connected with his chin.

He grunted as his head snapped back. "Son of a . . ."

May's mouth fell open. "Ohmigod." What had she done? "Ohmigod, I'm sorry." She shook her hand, but it continued to sting—so how must his *face* feel? "I'm so sorry!"

Rubbing at his chin, he gave her a cross look. "Just calm down, May."

"Ohmigod." Mortified at her own awful behavior, she rushed away from him, snatched up the poncho, and tried to jerk it on.

He reached for her. "May—"

Frantic, she screeched, "Don't touch me!" Stupid poncho, it was all twisted inside out, fighting her. Dear God, not only had she screamed at him that she wanted him, but she'd struck him, too. While fumbling with the poncho, she turned to look at him. "I am really, really sorry."

With a long sigh, he crossed his arms over his "Where do you think you're going?"

"Out of here. Away. I should never have come here."

"You didn't hurt me, honey."

Her eyes flared. "I *punched* you."

Mouth twitching, he said, "Yeah, I know. But it's just a little swat. I'll live."

She covered her face. "Not if Tim kills you." Her knees almost buckled at the thought.

"He wouldn't. He *couldn't*. Trust me on that."

"But whoever wants you dead could." And just saying it aloud made her want to be ill. How could he accuse her of using him when the main reason she'd come to him wasn't even for her brother.

No, she'd come because she knew Jude could be in real trouble.

"Tim's probably either lying or exaggerating, so just calm down and take a deep breath."

She'd borrow against her gallery. Between that and her savings and whatever Tim had put away . . .

"May, listen to me."

Giving up, she threw the poncho aside. She had no time to waste now that she knew she couldn't take money from Jude. He'd never believe her motives, not after he'd been hurt so badly by the trial and all the negative press that had followed.

Anxious to go, she grabbed up the straps to the tote.

Jude snatched it away from her. "You're not leaving."

"Yes, I am." She reached for the bag, and Jude held it over his head.

"No, you're not."

"Fine, keep it." She'd call a cab from the kitchen. Denny would help her. When she got home, she'd call the cops, and together, they'd make Jude accept the reality of the situation.

But when she tried to rush past Jude, he caught her wrist. May kept going, Jude didn't let go, and the momentum turned her full circle until she ended up wrapped in his arms, her back to his chest.

Shock rippled through her.

He touched her everywhere, his arms circling her upper body, his feet caging hers in, his hard thighs snugged up to her backside.

Heat rushed along her nerve endings, closing her eyes, parting her lips, making her belly tingle. *A damn jellyfish.*

She tried to explode away, but he easily subdued her, saying, "Settle down, honey."

She could hear his smile, and it enraged her all over again. "Don't you dare laugh at me."

"Wouldn't think of it."

"Jude . . ."

He nuzzled her ear and whispered, "We need to talk."

If not for him holding her, her weak knees would have given out. "There's nothing else to talk about."

"I disagree. We need to talk about your idiot brother. And whoever told him to kill me." His mouth touched her ear. "And most of all, the idea that you want me. Because, you know, thinking you didn't is what made me so mean. Now that I know you do . . . Well, I promise to be Prince Charming."

And finally, he gave her the hug she'd been craving.

Chapter 6

On the one hand, someone wanted him dead.

But on the other, he had May in his house, in his arms, and she'd made a most appealing admission.

A close to fair trade-off.

She started squirreling around again, and Jude sighed. "I'm not letting you go, May." Not for a good long while. "You might as well quit fighting me."

With a groan, her shoulders slumped and she went limp.

"That's better." He hugged her closer, appreciating the luxurious weight of her breasts on his forearms and the cushion of her behind against his thighs. "Is your hand okay?"

She flexed her fingers and winced. "I deserve the discomfort for hitting you."

"Such a martyr." He kissed her ear again, asking softly, "Out of curiosity, why'd you attack me if you didn't want me hurt?"

Eyes closed, she dropped her head back against

his shoulder, giving him better access to her. "I don't know. I've never hit anyone before."

"Really?" That shouldn't have surprised him. May was strong, but also one of the gentlest people he knew. "Well, I have. As a sport, it can be fun."

"Fun?" Judging by her tone, she disagreed.

"Yeah. Exciting, exhilarating. Extreme passion and desperate struggle all wrapped up together. Then you take a guy down, prove yourself superior, and adrenaline floods your system. It's a rush."

"If you say so."

"The men who participate in the SBC respect each other. They learn from defeats, and they learn from wins." He clasped his hands on her shoulders and turned her around to face him. "But in anger, it sucks."

"I'm sure you're right." Sounding formal and stiff, she said again, "I really am sorry. It was out of line and unforgivable."

He took great pleasure in saying, "I'll forgive you."

She frowned, then lifted her nose. "Thank you. Now . . . I'm leaving."

"No," he whispered, "you're not."

"Good-bye." She made no move to walk away.

Jude shook his head. "I don't think so, honey. For months now, I've wanted you, and you've turned me down flat. You've played coy, you've even played dumb. And no, don't start flaring up again. You know it's true."

She had the good grace to look away.

"So tell me again why you kept saying no. I'm not sure I understand all that nonsense you spouted."

Staring at her feet, she said, "It's not nonsense." Her hand settled on his chest, just over his heart. "We're from different worlds."

"Earth. Same world, May."

"You know what I mean."

"Sorry, no. You're going to have to go into detail." And while she explained, he'd have time to think about the situation with her brother and how best to deal with it to his advantage.

Her fingers traced an imaginary pattern over his pec muscle, driving him a little nuts. "You're filthy rich."

Why did it always have to come down to money? "So? I wasn't born that way. Most of my life was spent in lower middle class."

"Really?"

He could tell he'd surprised her. "Sure. I'm not the son of a movie producer or a famous leading lady. I grew up in a little three-bedroom ranch in a crowded subdivision. Public school. Packed lunches. Used cars and worn furniture. But we had clean clothes and lots of laughter. It wasn't bad."

"It sounds pretty nice."

Nice. Jude smiled at her in wonder. Other women, snootier women, had labeled his upbringing novel, fascinating, even touching. But May hit the nail on the head. "Yeah. I remember when I was seven, my mom spent most of the spring cleaning houses for other people so she could buy us a jungle gym for the backyard. She'd work while my brother, sister, and I were all in school. Then Dad bought the lumber, and together, we all built the thing. Dad was no handyman, so it was a little crooked, but it was solid, and everyone in the neighborhood hung out in our yard."

"You have a brother and a sister?"

"Incredible, huh?"

"I didn't mean it that way. I've just never heard much about them."

May had stopped straining away from him, so Jude had no problem talking about family. "Both older, both in the business."

"They're actors?"

"No. Neil's a stuntman, Beth does sound design. My folks loved music and drama, and they loved us. If we showed an interest in something, they encouraged it every way they could. I spent as much time in plays and choir as I did in sports."

Her mouth twitched. "Somehow I can't imagine your mother encouraging you to fight in the SBC."

"That's because you haven't met her." But Jude realized that he'd like for her to.

Unlike the other women he'd dated in the past few years, May was someone he could take home. She wouldn't call his dad boorish or his mother provincial. She wouldn't turn up her nose at baby photos or sugar cookies hot from the oven. He could easily picture her at the kitchen table, where his family always congregated, sharing conversation and coffee and laughter. Or better yet, at the stove helping his mother with dinner.

May would like his folks—and they'd like her.

"No matter what I do, my mom gets behind me a hundred percent." Jude felt himself smiling. "As long as I do my best, she's happy."

"It doesn't bother her when you fight?"

"She worries, but she's also my biggest cheerleader. From the time I was a pip-squeak in elementary, I was faster and stronger than most of the other kids. Mom said those were God-given talents that I shouldn't take for granted. Since Dad knew I wanted to be an actor, it was his idea for me to start in the SBC and make a name for myself. But Mom had a few rules."

"Like?"

Grinning, Jude said, "No tattoos. They're popular with fighters, but she hates them. No shaving my head, either, and I have to be polite. She said just because I beat up someone, doesn't mean I have to talk like an idiot."

May laughed. "I think I like your mother already."

"She also made me promise I'd always come back to the States to live. I did some training in Thailand and Tokyo, and I think she worried that I'd move there. She wanted me to call at least once a week, so I did."

After soaking all that in, May shrugged. "I've never been out of the country. I've never been in the limelight, either. And regardless of your upbringing, you're rich now. Like I said, we're from different worlds."

"In the scheme of things, money means little."

She didn't debate the point, which made Jude wonder if she already knew what it had taken him years to learn: Money could make things easier, and it could make things harder. But it couldn't buy happiness.

"You're also drop-dead gorgeous."

The compliment warmed him. "Thanks. You, too."

She pinched the bridge of her nose. "Come on, Jude. I'm not in your league, and we both know it."

Her plain speaking encouraged him to do the same. "If this is about your weight—"

Her head snapped up. She went rigid, then frowned. Her voice lowered to an ominous whisper. "What about my weight?"

Oh shit. He'd stepped in it there. Amazing how time spent in Hollywood could fool you into believing all women wanted to be rails. "You're sexy as hell." And when she still didn't look convinced, he added with complete sincerity, "Great ass, great rack."

For two seconds she looked insulted, then humor got the best of her. "Well, aren't you the smooth one? I'm sure I've never been so flattered."

The facetiousness of the remark damn near made him blush. "I just meant, you know." Determined to make her understand, Jude ran his hands up and down her arms. "You said earlier how you thought skinny movie stars were my style."

"That's all you dated."

"Because leading ladies come in one size."

"Which is probably why they're leading ladies. But I'm a corn-fed Midwestern girl."

God, he loved how she put things. "Corn fed is good."

"I grew up on meat and potatoes."

Sliding his fingers beneath the warm weight of her hair, he cupped her nape. "You're making me hungry." In more ways than one.

"I refuse to pass up dessert."

"Good. *Love* dessert."

Her mouth twitched. "Jude, this is not just about food."

No, it was about getting her to say yes, so he could end his sexual misery. "I'm waiting patiently for more explanations."

"And in the meantime, my brother and best friend are back at my apartment, possibly in trouble, maybe being threatened. I need to go."

He had to admit she had a point. But without the payment, leaving would do her no good. "So, slugger, you planning to duke it out with the villains? Maybe put yourself in the path to bodily protect your brother?" If it came to that, which it wouldn't, he'd put his odds on May. She was much better equipped to handle herself than Tim was.

"My plans are none of your business."

"Get real." He wanted her, but she could be the most infuriating woman. "You came here and got me involved."

"You were already involved."

"Because someone else wants me dead and your brother is supposed to see the deed done. That makes it very much my business."

She squeezed her eyes shut, nodded. "You're right. I—"

"Swear to God, May, if you apologize again, it's going to piss me off."

She jerked away to realign her glasses. "Fine. Then I'm not sorry." She flapped a hand at him. "But I still have to go."

"Where?"

"The bank will open soon." She inched toward the door. "I need to see how long it'll take to get a loan against my gallery and gather up my savings—"

"No."

The way she turned on him, Jude half expected her to pop him in the kisser again. He held up his hands, feigning fear, and she blushed bright red.

"Stop that!"

"All right." Jude felt magnanimous. Generous. Like a white knight. May had come to him, and he'd solve her problems. "Don't worry about anything. I'll take care of it."

Her jaw clenched. "No, you will not."

"Hush, May." And then to make sure she did, he bellowed, "Denny!"

And Denny, who'd been standing just outside the door eavesdropping, poked his head in. "What's the plan?"

May jumped. Her gaze went from Denny to Jude and back again. "That door was locked."

Holding up a long, thin metal tool, Denny grinned. "I'm good at pickin' locks."

Keeping hold of May's hand so she couldn't run off, Jude perched on the edge of the desk. "I take it you've heard every word?"

"Second nature." Denny shrugged that off. "So, you want me to go get her brother?"

"Yeah, I suppose you should. I have serious doubts that his life is in real jeopardy, but until I know for sure, I'm not about to let May near him without protection."

"No." May glared at them both, tried to tug her hand free from Jude's, and finally gave up. "You can't just go get him."

She looked so worried that Jude put his arm around her shoulders and pulled her into his side. "Yeah, he can."

Denny said, "Course I can."

"No, you *can't*. Haven't either of you listened to me? They're watching Tim. If you try to walk out of there with him, you could get hurt."

Denny shared a man-to-man look with Jude. By way of explanation, Jude said, "She's scared."

"Ah." Full of understanding, Denny took her hand and patted it. "Now, don't you worry about a thing. It's under control."

"How can it be under control when neither of you believe me?"

Denny started to answer, but Jude shook his

head. The less May knew, the less she'd fret, and the less she'd argue. "You can trust Denny. He's an ex-marine, among other things."

"That's right. Grabbing one scrawny brother won't be a problem." Then to Jude, "Should I get the other lady, too?"

Jude said, "Yeah."

But May said, "No. She won't come with you."

"She'll come," Denny told her.

Wide-eyed, May looked at Jude. "What is he going to do?"

Jude honestly had no idea. But he could guess. "Listen up, Denny. Ashley is May's friend. Be nice to her."

Pretending a great affront, Denny said, "I'm always nice."

"No, you're not. You're cantankerous and bossy and you scare women to death."

"Haven't scared any away from you." He turned to May, and demanded, "Do I scare you?"

"Uh . . ." She inched closer to Jude and gave a nervous smile. "No."

Knowing May, she probably didn't want to hurt Denny's feelings by admitting the truth. "May can call Ashley before you get there, but just try to temper your edge a little, okay?"

"I'm tempered."

"Tell her that she needs to bring May something to wear, too. She can barely breathe in those pants."

May stepped out of reach and glared at him. "You really don't possess an ounce of tact, do you?"

Jude laughed. "Never mind, Denny. I'll loan her something of mine to wear. Just get her brother and Ashley here as fast as you can."

"Right."

"Ashley's not like me, Jude. You can't push her around."

He barked a laugh, realized she was serious, and growled, "When have I ever pushed you around?"

"You always do."

"I do not." Hell, she was the one always dictating to him. Telling him no, dismissing him . . .

"Oh, really. What about right now?"

She would have to start that with Denny standing there smirking, tickled pink at his predicament. "I'm trying to help you out."

She leaned close to whisper. "You've been mean and insulting."

"I told you why." Celibacy could be hard on a man, but since meeting May, he hadn't wanted any other women. He gave his attention back to Denny. "Take some backup with you. I don't want anyone hurt, not even Tim."

When Denny crossed his arms and puffed up his chest, he made a most impressive sight. "My backup will be loaded and ready."

May clasped a hand to her throat. "A gun? You're talking about taking a loaded gun?"

"Don't worry," Jude told her. "He won't shoot your brother or your friend."

Denny affected his favorite, most intimidating scowl, and said, "You know who's behind this, don't you?"

On alert, May asked, "Who?"

The very last person Jude wanted to talk about was Elton Pascal. "Forget it, Denny. He's in Hollywood."

"Who is?"

Denny snorted. "When was the last time you checked on him?"

"Checked on whom?"

Ignoring May's questions, Jude tried to get Denny to shut up. "Why the hell would I want to?"

"Because the bastard is capable of something like this."

"Who are we talking about?"

Since May looked ready to combust, Jude decided he'd have to give her a bare-bones explanation. "Denny sees ghosts everywhere we go. If it rains on me, he thinks Elton had something to do with it."

"Elton hates him."

"He's part of a crowd," Jude countered, while giving Denny a *shut-the-hell-up* look. "It's no big deal."

"Your life is threatened! I'd call that a big deal."

Of course, Denny egged her on. "Jealousy can make a man do insane things."

Like a dog with a meaty bone, May leapt on Denny's theories. "This person hates Jude because of a woman?"

"The one who died, poor girl. Elton loved her, but she wanted nothing to do with him. She was crazy nuts for Jude."

"That's enough, Denny."

"When the limo blew up, there wasn't much left of her, and Elton's never forgiven Jude. He's the one who kept the case going for so long. He gave the most damning testimony—all of it lies. He makes sure that the tabloids never forget. And whenever he sees Jude, he—"

"That's *enough*." Jude knew his tone had been harsher than he'd intended when both May and Denny frowned at him with concern. But Christ, he thought about that awful day enough on his own without forced reminders. Guilt was a son of a bitch. And guilt riddled him.

"It's old news." Jude cleared his throat. "Even Elton would have accepted the jury's decision by now. He might not like it, and he might still hate me, but he's not stupid enough to come after me himself."

In the simplest gesture of support, May put her hand in his—and it reminded him of Blair Kane. She'd been sweet, too, but way younger than May, and not nearly as independent. More than anything, he'd considered Blair a pain in the ass, an immature twenty-one-year-old whose body had made her an overnight success and easy prey for creeps like Elton.

Along with a handful of other personalities, they'd attended a Southern California fund-raiser to benefit the homeless. At the end of the exhausting evening, in front of a crowd, she'd asked to share his limo ride home. Jude didn't want to embarrass her by saying no. And he felt sorry for her.

And damn it, he'd been a little lonely, too.

But within an hour of the trip, her clinging and come-ons had gotten on his nerves. It was late, dark, quiet . . . and he couldn't stand the confinement. He'd had the driver pull over to an abandoned highway rest stop, then he'd walked away with the excuse of buying a cola from the vending machines.

Seconds later, the limo exploded.

His chest constricted with the memory, and he glared at Denny. "Get going, will you?"

More subdued, Denny nodded at May. "You're keeping her?"

Denny could use some help with his wording, but Jude caught his meaning just fine. "Yeah."

Approval shown in his eyes. "At least you've still got good taste in some things."

May suddenly caught on. "Oh, now wait just a minute. I'm not . . . I can't . . ."

Cell phone to his ear, Denny left the room at a jaunty pace. He loved to kick ass and was probably hoping for a confrontation. Jude would prefer he'd be disappointed. He wanted things settled with May with as little fanfare as possible.

Shell shocked, May stared at him. "This is not what I wanted when I came here."

"Oh?" Jude caught her elbow and led her to a chair. "You thought I'd write you a check and then send you on your merry way to deal with men ruthless enough to beat your brother and order my death?"

She looked pained. "I don't know."

"Well, I do." And no way would he let her out of his sight until he knew for a fact it'd be safe. But he didn't want her to spend the next two hours worrying about Tim, and he didn't want her to stay with him for the wrong reasons.

He leaned over her, caging her in.

"Now, you listen to me, May. You came to me for help because you're a logical woman and I'm your most logical choice."

"I thought so at first, too, but now I know that I can't take your money."

"Why?"

"Because it'd make me like everyone else."

And to May, that'd be intolerable. He shook his head. If only she knew how differently she made him feel. "Impossible. You're too unique."

"Jude." Full of sincerity and that special understanding that turned him on, she stared up at him. "I care about you."

Outwardly, Jude didn't react. But inside . . .

Inside, his heart stuttered and his muscles warmed. Looking somewhat hopeful, May waited, but damn her, after all her denials he refused to be taken in that easy.

Jude fashioned a bland smile. "Great. Then you understand why I can't let you take out a loan on your gallery. You'll end up losing it, and I like buying my artwork from you."

The spark faded from her eyes. She folded her hands in her lap and her shoulders slumped. "There's nothing else I can do."

"Try trusting me." And with trust would come intimacy. Whatever trouble her brother had gotten into, he'd resolve it quickly, and then he'd have May to himself. In his bed. Exactly where he wanted her. "That'd be a good place to start."

"And then you'll say I used you. No thanks."

Determined to get everything out in the open, Jude looked first at her exposed cleavage, then her soft mouth, with blatant suggestion. "You could always find a way to repay me."

She pressed back into the chair, a little vulnerable, a little peeved. "I had planned to."

That surprised him, even as it tantalized him. But how far would she go? How far would he let her go? "Then we're in agreement."

"I doubt that."

The urge to kiss her burned inside him. He leaned in until her breath teased his mouth and he could feel her trembling. "You know I want you."

"You've been obvious."

But she hadn't. She'd made him work for every hint of her feelings, leading him on a damn chase that left him floundering. Now, thanks to her brother's antics and her overactive imagination, he had the means to uncover her true feelings.

Half hating himself, Jude said, "Let's make a deal."

"What kind of deal?"

"One that'll make us both happy." He looked into her wary eyes and prayed she'd give the right answer. "Stay with me. Let me take care of this situation for you, and in the meantime, you'll stop saying no."

A tiny shiver went through her body.

"Do you understand, May?"

"I think so."

"Let's be sure." And he spelled it out. "You say you want me. I admit I want you. So for as long as it takes to uncover this little mystery of who your brother owes, you'll share my bed. After we have everything straightened out, we can call it even."

Her hands curled into tight fists, gripping the arms of the chair. "No."

"What about Tim?" he prompted, more than willing to push her to get the reaction he wanted. "What about the fifty grand you need? I thought you wanted to repay me."

"Not that way."

"Then how?"

"I could offer you artwork minus my commission, combined with monthly payments until the debt is cleared."

Wow, she said that fast, as if she'd already given it plenty of thought. As if . . . that might have been her plan all along. "Your way could take a while."

"Yes. Is that a problem?"

On the contrary, the idea of keeping May indebted to him for an extended period tempted him, because it guaranteed their association wouldn't end anytime soon. Jude didn't want to dwell on how that thought pleased him.

Ever so lightly, he touched his mouth to hers. "You're saying you won't sleep with me—even to save your brother?"

Her eyes sank shut.

Stomach twisting with regret, Jude whispered, "May?"

When her eyes opened, they were bright with fury. "Despite my earlier display, I'm not a violent person, or else I'd hit you again."

Relief washed through him. "So the answer is no?"

"No!"

Jude grinned. Then he laughed. He cupped her face and before she could dodge him, he planted a soft smooch on her mulish mouth. "Good."

Lost in confusion, May hesitated before shoving him away with disgust. "You're playing games with me."

"Maybe a little. But I needed to be sure we understand each other. And for the record, I'm damn glad you said no."

"You are?"

"When we crawl between the sheets—and we will, no doubt about that—it won't be for you to sacrifice yourself. It'll be because you want me as much as I want you." He rubbed his thumbs along her soft cheeks and kept on smiling. "You spend so damn much time worrying about and caring for Tim, I wanted to be sure you wouldn't give in just for his sake."

Still visibly annoyed, she glared at him. "Satisfied?"

"When I haven't had you yet?" He grinned. "Hell no."

"Jude."

He hadn't slept all night, and he'd done one of the most strenuous workouts of his life, but Jude heard the prudish tone in her voice, and damn it, he felt pretty good. With a wink, he told May, "But I'm getting there."

Chapter 7

"Now, the first thing we have to do," Jude told her, "is call the police."

In an about-face, May stopped being angry and instead looked desperate. "No. No police."

"Be reasonable, May. Every villain everywhere always tells the victim not to call. But it's dumb not to."

"Normally, I'd agree, but this time is different."

Understanding her worry, Jude gave her a promise. "I'll pay for Tim's debt, so don't give it another thought. But since it's going to cost me fifty thousand, I insist we go by my rules."

She turned away from him. "No cops."

"I'm not asking, honey." And to soften that a little, he added, "You know it's the right thing to do."

She shook her head. "No."

"I can keep him safe, May."

"*No.*"

Her lack of faith in him rubbed him raw. Why come to him in the first place if she didn't trust him to set things right? "This is ridiculous. I'm not going to let anyone hurt your brother."

"Damn you, it's not Tim I'm worried about!"

Jude stared at her, blank. "Then what the hell are we talking about?"

"Oh God." She shot out of the chair. "And you called me ridiculous."

"No," Jude said, "I did not. I said the situation was ridiculous."

"The situation is that someone wants you dead." Her hands landed against his chest. "*You*, Jude. Tim is just a pawn. I have a feeling that money was loaned to him just to get to this point—of getting to *you*."

So she'd come to him, humbled herself, eaten her pride . . . for him?

"Don't you see?" Her hand knotted in his shirt. "If you call the police, they'll start poking around, probably scare off whoever wants you dead, and we'll never find out who it is."

Jude stiffened. "What do you mean, we? You're not involved in any of this."

"You're kidding, right?" She tried to shake him, but Jude curled his hands around her wrists. "Tim is my brother. He's being used to get to you."

"So I'll figure things out, but you'll keep your nose out of it." The thought of her poking around in dangerous business made his head pound. The only way to know she'd be uninvolved would be to keep an eye on her. "I mean it, May. Promise me you'll stay here until I know it's safe."

She shrugged. "Impossible. I have to work."

"You only open the gallery on the weekends."

"And the rest of the week I work at the realty office."

Damn. He'd forgotten about that. "So take a vacation."

"Without notice?"

"Say you're sick. Flu. I don't know and I don't care. But you're staying here."

More agitated by the second, she pulled her hands free. "I'm not a liar."

"I know. It's an admirable trait." As he considered the situation, he shared his thoughts aloud, "I wish Tim hadn't come to your apartment. If there was anyone following him, then they know where you live."

"According to Tim, they already knew."

Jude's heart almost stopped. "What are you talking about?"

She eyed his rigid stance. "Well, don't overreact, but they told Tim that if they didn't get him, they'd get . . ." She winced. "Me."

In an instant, everything changed. Jude changed. His perspective on the situation changed. This was no longer a mere threat to Tim, or even to himself. An eerie calm settled over him, the type of calm he felt before a fight, the calm that earned him a reputation of always being in control.

His tone and manner were civilized, but his mood bordered on savage. "You didn't think to mention that before now?"

"I was too worried about . . . you. And then once I got here, I realized I couldn't take money from you anyway."

Since she damn well would take his money, Jude strode to the phone and dialed Denny's number. As soon as Denny picked up, he said, "It seems you were right, after all. This suddenly stinks of Elton."

"Told you so."

Jude was so pissed he could barely get the words out. "He threatened May."

"Bastard."

Leave it to Denny to get right to the point. "Get them both out of there, and watch your ass."

"No problem. My ass is a favorite part of my anatomy."

After Denny hung up, Jude stared at May. By threatening her, someone had crossed the line. If it was Elton, God help him. Jude protected what was his—and whether May liked it or not, she fell into that category.

Yet until last night, he hadn't even kissed her.

As if she sensed his mood, she came to him. "It wasn't like that, Jude. He only threatened to hurt me to keep Tim in line."

"That's what Tim told you?" He'd already known Tim was a coward, and this proved it. "And you believe him?"

"I didn't really think about it one way or another."

"You better start thinking about it, because Elton doesn't mind using women to get to me."

"What Denny said is true? He hates you that much?"

Jude ran a hand through his hair, disgusted at himself. He'd let ego get in the way of his instincts. May had left herself exposed to come to him, and all he'd thought about was using the situation to get her into bed.

"Yeah, Elton hates me."

"How do you know him? Is he someone in the movie business? I don't recognize his name."

"He owns a string of nightclubs popular with the Hollywood crowd. He's rich, obnoxious, and foul as it is, I don't doubt your brother would hand you over to him if he thought it'd keep his own hide safe."

"Jude?"

"Hmm?"

"If I go along with any of this, and I'm not yet sure that I will, will you do me one favor?"

Surprised that she wasn't fighting him tooth and nail, Jude paused, raising one eyebrow. "What's that?"

"Quit insulting my brother."

He didn't want to give her a chance to change her mind. "Right. I'll put that top of my list—right behind making sure that neither Elton nor Tim can lay a finger on you."

Shaking her head, May said, "You're looking at this all wrong. You're the one—"

"Now let's get you out of those clothes."

She dug in her heels. "Jude Jamison!"

He pulled her into his arms and kissed her hard. Now that he knew how she felt, he couldn't help himself. Every kiss was sweet, and made him want more. "Will you always turn me upside down and inside out?"

"I don't mean to."

"I know." He kissed her again, this time slicking his tongue along her lips until they parted so he could take a brief taste.

She didn't object, but he had to keep it short or he'd forget himself. A taste of May affected him more than sex with other women.

When he ended the kiss, May's eyes remained closed, her cheeks were flushed, and her glasses were crooked.

Jude smiled. God, he had it bad.

"Come on." Deliberately distracting himself, he slid his arm around her and tugged her out of the library. "You can borrow a few things after I show you what room to use. Hey, know what? I can even show you my pool now. Maybe we can swim together later." He moved his hand down her waist to the flare of her hips. "And since you don't have a swimsuit with you, maybe I can talk you into skinny-dipping."

"Not a chance."

"Come on, May. Live a little."

Disgruntled, she stomped along beside him. "I wish you wouldn't treat this like an adventure."

"I have the elusive May Price in my house." Jude grinned. "Trust me. It's an adventure."

"I haven't agreed to stay."

But she would. He'd see to it. "You need to put in that call to Ashley before Denny shows up. I'd just as soon she didn't start screaming, alerting the entire neighborhood to our plans." He led her down the short hall to the second door on the left.

Sounding less than enthusiastic, May said, "I'll have to call my parents, too." As if trying to ease a headache, she rubbed her forehead. "I don't think Tim will be able to make it into work for the next couple of days, and they're bound to wonder about him. I don't want to alarm them on top of everything else."

Because if they got upset, she was the one they'd call. May had "caregiver" stamped all over her, and he'd be willing to bet everyone in her family unloaded on her with regularity. Would they blame her for Tim's predicament? It seemed likely. Maybe he could talk to Ashley alone, get a little more information on May's background. It'd help in dealing with her brother, and maybe even her mom and dad, too.

It unsettled Jude to realize that he'd just decided to interfere in her entire life. But what else could he do? Much as he'd like to deny it, he cared, too. Probably a lot more than May did.

With a silent curse, he opened the bedroom door. "This is the room you can use."

She peeked in. Her gaze swept the room, paused on the monitor, and frowned.

"You don't like it?"

Full of suspicion, she considered him over her glasses. "It's not your room, is it?"

Surely she knew he could be more subtle than that. "No."

"Those monitors only see out?"

His brows came down. "They're installed in every room, along with the intercom system. The house is big enough that we need the intercom so Denny can let me know when there are deliveries or phone calls. The monitor in here can be set to see anywhere outside the house, or for multiple views. The one in my room, the kitchen and library, and a few downstairs, can also be set for views inside the house."

"Are any set to see in—"

"Damn it, that's an insulting question. I wouldn't spy on you, and I'm not a perverted Peeping Tom."

She thought about it and nodded. "Okay. Sorry."

Jude simmered. Never before had it been so difficult to keep his emotions in check. May pushed his buttons sexually, but she also nudged his temper with every other turn. Around her he couldn't be distant or complacent about anything.

Unconcerned with his inner battles, she went back to examining the room. "It's huge."

If she thought the guest room spacious, what would she think of his decadent sleeping rooms and private bath? Watching her, he said, "I'm right next door."

She glanced across the hall at the double doors. Before she could put too much thought into the proximity of their sleeping quarters, he prodded her into the room. "The bedding is clean. Feel free to use the computer and line three of the phone; it's private for this room. You have your own bath, already stocked with everything you might need."

"Really?" she murmured. "How convenient— for you."

"Jealous?" He hoped so, but said, "Don't be. My family visits sometimes, and I like to accommodate them."

"I am *not* jealous. What you do with other women doesn't—"

"Look around, make yourself at home. I'll be back with a change of clothes in a minute." He touched her cheek, and then forced himself to walk away. Having May so close to a bed, even while hostile, wreaked havoc on his touted control. But no way in hell would he blow it now by coming on too strong.

Head spinning, May sat on the edge of the queen-size bed made up with a lavish cream satin and chenille spread. The room Jude expected her to use was bigger than her whole apartment. The closet was as big as her bedroom.

It intimidated her and reinforced the differences in their lives.

The call to her parents would be less than pleasant, and Denny had already left, so she called Ashley first. She could only guess what Ashley might do if

Denny knocked on the apartment door without warning.

She answered on the first ring, saying, "Hey, toots. How's it going?"

"Hi, Ash. There's been a change of plans."

"An agreeable change?"

"Yes." Sort of. "Jude wants you and Tim to come here until we figure out what to do."

"Gee, that's real nice of him, but I don't think I can drag Tim out the door by myself. He's awake now, and whining worse than an injured pup."

"Jude sent Denny, a friend of his, to pick you both up." She quickly described Denny so that Ashley wouldn't be alarmed when meeting him.

"You make him sound like a real character."

"He is that. Denny seems to think he can take on dragons or bullies or whatever, and still ensure your safety. But be careful, okay? I got you into this, and I'd never forgive myself if you got hurt."

"Hey, careful is my middle name."

A tap sounded on the open door, and May looked up to see Jude in the doorway, clothes in his arms. His warm gaze skimmed over her, then across the bed, and came back to lock on her face with unmistakable intimacy.

Very aware of her positioning, May stood and signaled Jude to come in. "No, Ash, your middle name is insanity, but I love you, anyway."

"Not to be a drag, but should I point out that you're the one who went off to visit a movie star at the crack of dawn wearing my clothes? That makes you way more insane than me any day."

Actually, it made her desperate, but why split hairs? "Yeah, well, he's here now. Um, waiting for me." And looking far too appealing for her frame of mind. "So I should go. I just didn't want Denny to scare you."

"I don't scare easy." Ashley's voice dropped to a hush. "Where are you?"

Feeling more conspicuous by the moment, May turned her back on Jude and matched Ashley's low tone. "At his house."

"Yeah, I know. But in what room?"

"Ash . . ."

"Ha! You don't have to say a thing. I can already tell it's a bedroom just by that scandalized whisper of yours. Good for you, hon. Give him a big ol' sloppy one from me, okay? See you soon!"

Left with a dead phone, May smiled at Jude, put the phone in her purse, tossed the purse on the bed, and then . . . just felt awkward. "She'll be ready when Denny gets there."

"Good." Jude came into the room and set his load on a massive dresser topped by an ornate mirror. "I brought you a T-shirt and drawstring shorts. They should be more comfortable."

Shorts. Great. She cleared her throat. "Thank you. I'm fine for now."

Jude surveyed her a moment, then let out a sigh. "Speaking of shorts . . ."

"Were we?" Because she didn't want to. She hadn't worn shorts since she was ten.

"Yeah. You see, we have a few more stipulations to cover, and it'd be better to get them out of the way now, while we're here alone." He kept glancing at her legs. "In case you want to yell again."

Both insulted and embarrassed, May lifted her chin. "I don't yell that much. In fact, I almost never do."

"Huh. Can't prove it by me."

Jaw clenched, she said, "You have my word that I

won't lose my temper—that is, as long as you're not trying to make another deal with me." It still made her furious that he'd thought she'd sleep with him for Tim's sake.

Jude didn't reassure her. "Then take a breath, honey, because it's another deal, and this one is nonnegotiable."

Holding her head, May said, "Oh God."

Jude gestured toward a chair situated beside the doors to the balcony. "Take a seat."

After a sleepless night, she gratefully accepted any excuse to get off her feet. "This sounds serious."

"Yeah." He stood in front of her, hands clasped behind his back, expression stern. "First of all, I'll find out from your brother where he was supposed to take the fifty thousand. Then I'll deliver it."

Awful scenarios blasted through May's mind, leaving her shaken. Someone wanted Jude dead, and that made him the least appropriate person to meet with the men who'd attacked her brother. "Absolutely not."

"If your brother is as bad off as you say, then he can't go. And I sure as hell won't let you go, so don't even start arguing."

May stiffened. "If I wanted to go, I'd go. You can't allow me or disallow me one way or the other." Jude's expression darkened until she added, "But as it is, you'll get no disagreements from me. I freely admit to being a coward. The idea of facing off with someone like that gives me the willies."

"You're not a coward," he argued. "You're sensible. It's one of the things I love most about you."

That "L" word shocked May silly. Her eyes widened, and she almost slid out of the chair, her bones felt so limp. Jude kept talking, but whatever he said, she missed. Her heart beat too loud for her to hear.

Luckily, Jude paid her reaction no mind. Hands behind his back, he stood at the balcony doors, staring out at nothing in particular.

Sounding pensive, he said, "Someone has to deliver the payoff. I won't ask Denny to go. He's like a live wire waiting to tear someone apart, especially if he thinks that person means to harm me. You might not know it about him, but he was one of the most respected trainers in the SBC. That brings a lot of confidence and—"

The pieces suddenly fell together. "Denny Zip," May repeated. "He goes by DZ when he's training."

"That's right. You've heard of him?"

She leaned forward in her chair. "Do you mean to tell me that the Denny who works for you is also DZ, the one the camps are all named after now?"

Jude lifted his brows. "You're familiar with the DZ camps?"

"I've watched all the SBC fights." And she owned all the fights on DVD that featured Jude. "I know that training from a DZ camp carries a lot of clout. I know anyone who was trained personally by DZ is almost revered."

"True."

"Oh, wow. He trained you, didn't he?"

"Yeah." Wearing a quirky smile, Jude asked, "You're a fan of the SBC?"

She was a fan of Jude Jamison, but he didn't need to know that. "It's sort of grown on me."

"How many competitions have you seen?"

All of them available for rent. "Enough to know the competitors and understand some of the different fighting techniques and the different submissions. I know you're both the middleweight and light heavyweight champion."

"Only because I dropped out after the movie career got wings. There've been a lot of tough contenders since then."

May snorted. "Who? That young guy they call Havoc? He has a glass jaw. Even Frost took him, and anyone can see that Frost is too slow for you. And Miltman, the egomaniac, doesn't have your ground skills."

A look of delight spread over Jude's face. "Miltman might be an egomaniac, but he has the right to challenge me. I just don't feel like accommodating him."

"He hasn't earned the right to challenge you! Let him fight at your level before he thinks he can come in and take a belt."

"Miss Price, you never cease to amaze me." Jude rubbed his chin. "So maybe this fascination of yours with the SBC is where you learned such a mean right jab."

If she lived to be ninety, she would still feel guilty for hitting him. "No. That was pure reaction."

Humor faded beneath understanding. "Because I compared you to your brother."

What could she say? It was the worst of insults.

"It's not easy to hit a target, you know. Lots of people swing without ever making contact."

"I'm not proud of it, Jude."

"You should be. Few trained fighters have ever managed to get me on the chin. And no other woman has slugged me."

"Oh God." She covered her face. "Let's drop it, okay? It won't happen again."

"But I sort of liked all that fire." He leaned down, putting himself eye level with her and grinning like Satan. "I always knew you weren't as reserved as you let on."

Peeking through her fingers, May said, "I plan to be very reserved from now on."

"And here I was," he said, his voice low and sensual, "hoping to grapple a little." He straightened again. "But back to business. Since your brother isn't reliable, I'm not about to let a woman go, and I can't send Denny, that leaves me to deliver the money."

"We could hire someone—"

"Another reason for me to go is that it'll give me a chance to see if Elton is involved. I know most of his cronies. I know how to ask the right questions." His eyes glittered. "And I know how to get answers."

"Meaning you intend to get physical?" She had faith in his abilities, but not if someone shot him in the back.

"That's right. And there might be repercussions, so if it takes a day or a week or longer, I want you here with me until I know the problem is resolved. That's part of the deal."

The idea of Jude putting himself in that type of danger was bad enough, but the added possibility of a long visit in his home left her reeling.

Then the rest of what he said sank in. "*Part* of the deal?"

"Yeah." Jude stared down at her, smiled, and said in apology, "There's more."

Chapter 8

Jude hated to keep pushing May. She not only looked exhausted, but very out of her element. And that made him want to keep her around for more than just the obvious reasons. Never before had he felt so emotionally protective of a woman. The need to make her life easier, combined with the gut-churning desire to have her in his bed, made for a potent mix.

He wanted to tell her to lie down, to sleep, and that he'd take care of everything. Unfortunately, he knew May would never let someone, let alone a man, take over her life. He had to be honest with her and hope for the best.

"First, this is your brother's debt, not yours, and he'll damn well work it off."

"I agree it's his debt. And believe me, I'd love to see him be held accountable. It's just . . ." May removed her glasses to rub her tired eyes. "Knowing what's right and getting Tim to do it are two different things."

Jude could see the lack of sleep catching up to

her. She'd probably run herself ragged in preparation of the gallery art show, so she would have been weary even before her brother got stomped. She needed sleep.

But then, so did he.

The idea of curling up with her appealed in a big way.

"I've never liked the way Tim treats you, but until now, it wasn't my business."

"You don't understand how it was when we grew up." Like a shield, she replaced her glasses before looking him in the eyes. "My parents are . . . different."

"Different how?"

"Not like yours."

"My parents are great, but we've had our bumps in the road, too."

"Bumps?"

He shrugged. "Everyone has problems with their family, May."

Her smile held no humor. "Yeah, that's what people tell me, that mine is no different. Until they meet my folks." After a heavy sigh, she looked out at his yard. "My mom and dad have always babied Tim beyond all reason. As his sister, I've never really understood."

Because they didn't afford her the same pampering? Jude knew that some parents picked a favorite. He didn't approve, but he'd seen it happen.

"For as long as I can remember, anything he wanted," May continued, "they thought he had to have, and they went out of their way to give it to him. If he screws up, they make excuses so he doesn't have to own up to his mistakes. He never has to learn. They . . . feel sorry for him, which is really bizarre. He's a handsome young man, healthy and intelligent. But they've almost crippled him with their attitudes."

"They're enablers."

"Yes."

Gently, Jude said, "But then, so are you."

Rather than deny it, May lowered her head. "I've tried to be different, but I guess I fell into the same rut. My parents expect me to treat Tim the same way they do, and sometimes it's easier to just go along with them."

"It doesn't take a genius to see that you feel responsible for Tim. But you aren't his mother, so there's only so much you can do."

As if admitting a grave sin, she whispered, "Sometimes I really resent him."

"You'd have to be a saint not to."

One side of her mouth lifted in a slight smile. "Thanks. But my parents would disagree with you."

It wouldn't be easy to like her folks. Already, Jude wanted to cut them out of her life. "Obviously, their perspective on the situation is skewed. I'm sure they think they're doing the right thing, but their way hasn't been working. In fact, it's almost gotten Tim killed, right?"

Given the present circumstances, she couldn't deny it. "Yes."

"So now you'll let me give it a try." And God willing, he'd make a difference.

Her hands twisted in her lap. "How can I say yes when you're talking about putting yourself in danger?"

With a smile, Jude crouched down in front of her and took her fretful hands. "Look at it this way—what have you got to lose?"

Warm fingers curled around his with surprising strength. "You."

Her soft voice caused his heart to miss a beat. He hated to admit it, but in so many ways, May had the power to do what a bogus criminal charge hadn't; she could destroy him.

And that scared him.

Dumb, he told himself. He wasn't a kid to fall headfirst into gentle brown eyes, a big heart, and a stacked bod. He'd had women, some that he'd liked a lot, some that he'd lusted after. But never before May had he suffered such an awful excess of sensation. It plagued his mind, heart, and body all at the same time.

Trying to regroup, to shield himself, Jude choked out a laugh. "Don't bury me yet. I'll be fine."

She didn't look convinced, but Jude let that pass for now. He pushed back to his feet and smiled down at her. "There's no reason to worry about your brother, either. I'm not going to abuse him, I promise. But I will hold him responsible. I have some ideas on how he can repay the money, ways that'll keep him out of trouble, but with good men to keep him in line."

"He has to work at the car dealership."

"He'll show up for work, but with supervision." Pleased with his plans so far, Jude explained, "He'll hire a man I trust, someone who'll report to me. If Tim tries to sneak off to gamble or drink, I'll know about it. Until he repays me the fifty grand, I own him."

With a groan, May slumped back in the chair. "My parents aren't going to like this. Tim's supervision of the dealership is the one thing they're adamant about, even though Tim's made it clear that he hates it."

"Why is that, you think?"

"I have no idea. My dad still hangs out there a

lot, and my mom butts in constantly. Yet they want him as a figurehead. They left him little choice in running it, even though they haven't turned it over completely to him."

"You're older," Jude pointed out. "Why didn't you get it?"

"I'm female."

"A noticeable fact. So?"

"Well, for my parents, that excludes me. My mother's famous sentiment is that she's not leaving anything to 'a damned son-in-law.' My dad says if I want a dealership, I should marry a man with one." She slanted a look at Jude. "I told them both that I wanted nothing to do with cars."

Anger burned inside Jude. Sure, all parents favored a kid at various times, depending on the different stages children went through while growing up, their personal interests, and how much trouble they got into. But parents should love their kids equally, and they should at least make a pretense of being fair. "It's a wonder Tim hasn't lost it yet."

"It's been a close thing a few times. But in that, Tim's not much different from my folks. They aren't into saving money, so they pretty much live off what they have. It'd take one small catastrophe, like a major health issue or something, and they'd all be broke."

No, Jude thought, unable to keep his gaze off May for long, *they'd look to her to save them.* "Have you put away for a rainy day?"

"Since it rains a lot around here, yeah."

Jude grinned with her. "It's always amazed me when a celebrity goes bankrupt. Do you know how much money they squander on absurd luxuries? Took me forever to get used to it, and I admit, I spend my fair share now, too. But I also have a magic touch when it comes to investments. I make more than I spend by a long shot."

May peered at him uncertainly. "I wasn't asking . . ."

But for whatever reason, he wanted her to know. "When you boil it all down, I'm the same person I was before the movies. I'd still rather make money than waste it, so with my input, the dealership will gain value. Your parents won't have any reason to complain."

"They're real protective of Tim."

"Their idea of protection has left him weak. Without you, what would he have done with this current mess?"

"Good question." Typical of May, she leveled her shoulders and lifted her chin. "But he does have me, and I can't just turn my back on him."

"You'll be helping him in the long run, but if it'll make you feel better, I promise to tell you ahead of time what I'm doing with Tim and why. So what do you say? Are we in agreement so far?"

"I don't understand you." Knees pressed together and expression fretful, she leaned forward in the chair. "You're being so generous."

"I can afford to be generous." Jude caught her hands and pulled her to her feet. "But I'm not finished. I also want a special arrangement with you."

In exaggerated frustration, she collapsed against him. "I'm afraid to ask."

Jude kissed her forehead. "Never be afraid of me, May. I wouldn't hurt you."

"Jude Jamison," she said, only half teasing, "you would break my small-town, country-girl heart, and you know it."

More likely, she'd break his. So far, she'd proven efficient at fending him off—while he'd run the gamut of emotions trying to get past her defenses. In so many ways, her strength awed him. "I guess I'll have to prove you wrong." He leaned back and put his hands on his hips. "But first, the rest of our agreement."

"I hope you don't expect me to sign anything."

"I want to dress you."

She laughed—but when he didn't, her face went first blank, then hot with color. "You have to be kidding."

"We've already concluded that I've got money to burn, so let me have the fun of buying you clothes."

"No."

Such a weak denial could be easily ignored. "What you wear isn't the least bit flattering. You have a kickin' body, and I know just how to show it off."

She pushed out of his hold. *"No."*

Jude headed for the door. "Denny will be back soon. Go ahead and get changed so you'll be comfortable, then come down to the kitchen. I haven't eaten yet and I'm starved. We can all talk over brunch."

"Jude." May scrambled after him.

He started to pull the door shut, but at the last second, he caved. Damn it, he didn't want to walk away while she looked so flustered. "How about a kiss to tide me over?"

May frowned, but she puckered up and kissed him. It was a virginal kiss, mouths closed, no tongue—and he still loved it.

"Nice." He flicked the end of her nose. "Do you

realize we can buy you an entire new wardrobe over the Internet? We won't even need to leave the house."

"I won't wear it."

"You haven't even seen it yet. I have great taste in women's clothes." He winked. "But if you want to go naked, hey, I promise I won't utter a single complaint."

The door shut in his face. A second later, he heard a thunk that could have been her head hitting the door, followed by a groan. Poor May. He was starting to confuse her as much as she confused him.

All things considered, not a bad sign.

Feeling like an idiot in the man's jacket and backward baseball hat, Ashley leaned on the doorbell—and continued to lean on it while examining a broken nail. Next to her, Denny grumbled—but then, he'd done a lot of that. Like May, he wanted to take care of everyone. He'd alternated between treating her like a lost orphan and a favored niece. He might be old enough to be her dad, not that her dad ever gave her as much attention, but she wasn't a child. She could take care of herself.

The sooner Mr. Zip realized that, the better they'd get along.

The door opened, and there stood Jude Jamison in the flesh. Wow. Ashley had met him before, but familiarity hadn't reduced his impact. A lesser woman might have sighed in pleasure just looking at him, but she held it in. How the hell May kept resisting him, she didn't know. The man was a certified stud.

He smiled his megawatt movie star smile at her. "Hello, Ashley. Thanks for coming."

She pulled the hat off her head and let her hair fall down her back. "What, no butler?"

"I'm the butler," Denny pointed out.

"Now, why didn't I know that?"

Grinning, Jude pulled the front doors open wide, and Ashley stepped inside. She wanted to see May. Her friend had strange ideas about romantic relationships—most specifically that she couldn't have one. Being in the home of a man she secretly adored probably had her out of sorts.

With a low whistle, Ashley took in the interior of the mansion. Everything matched and looked new and . . . *perfect.*

As a lover of clutter and comfort, she knew she could never live that way, but she said, "Nice digs, Jude."

"Thank you."

She didn't spot May, so she called out, "Lucy, I'm home!" The words no sooner left her mouth than the twelve-foot ceilings sent them back to her. "Cool, an echo. Imagine that."

Jude laughed, but Denny didn't share in the amusement. He glared at Ashley. "I had a hell of a time getting her into those clothes."

Ashley cast him an evil glance. "Most guys bitch because they can't get me out of my clothes."

"They must not know you well."

She made a tsking sound. "I told you once, Denny, a little politeness wouldn't have hurt anything. One of these days, you'll learn."

"I was trying to save your skinny ass, not flatter you."

"Oh, trust me, no one would ever accuse you of

flattery." Then, just to shut him up, Ashley gave her attention to Tim. "Hallelujah. For once, Tim's not complaining."

Actually, Tim occupied himself by sizing up Jude's home. He had stars in his one good eye and a look of connivance on his beat-up face. Anyone could see that he wanted what Jude had.

To sneak them out of the apartment without notice, Denny had worn dark glasses and a baseball cap similar to Ashley's, but in a different color. He'd more or less muscled Tim—who whined and carped the entire time—into threadbare jeans and an Aerosmith T-shirt. With mussed hair, more dark glasses, and a lit cigarette hanging from his mouth, he looked less like Tim the Wimp and more like every other twentysomething guy.

Keeping the cigarette between his bruised and swollen lips had proved tricky. The second Denny had them both in the car, Tim had tossed it. He'd lounged in the backseat while Ashley rode up front with Denny.

Tim said, "Whas goin' on? Why'm I here?"

Jude started to answer when May appeared at the top of the stairs, and he became riveted on her instead.

And no wonder. Not since they were kids had Ashley seen May so . . . dressed down. Her hair was even more tumbled now than when she'd left her apartment. Cell phone to her ear, she hesitated at the top of the stairs. "Mom, I really have to go now. No, I can't . . . Yeah, I know. I won't. I promise. Yes, Mom, I'll take care of it. *Yes.*" She waved to Ashley, her bare feet shifting anxiously while trying to end the call to her mother. "*Mom,* I need to go."

Unless Ashley missed her guess, May had removed the too-tight sports bra. Only an enormous, well-worn SBC T-shirt and a pair of loose navy blue shorts covered her.

Judging by the rapt expression on Jude's face, he noticed the loss of a bra, too.

"Look," Ashley said, elbowing Jude in the side, "she's got knees. Who knew?"

"I did." In a near trance, Jude started forward, but May finally disconnected the call and, holding the hem of the shirt as low as possible, rushed down the steps.

"Sorry about that." Bouncing in a dozen places, May came to a halt in the entryway. "I had to call my mom and dad, and naturally, they're . . . concerned."

Ashley snorted.

"Chris', May," Tim complained, "you did'n tell 'em anythin', did you?"

"I told them only as much as I had to without lying."

"Freakin' wunnerful."

"You should have been the one to call them," Ashley pointed out to Tim. "You had plenty of opportunities."

"They know we're here now, at Jude's home." May sent Tim a look of apology. "Mom wants you to call her as soon as you can."

Denny spoke over the top of Tim's moan. "I was planning to put him in the guest rooms downstairs."

Without much interest, Jude said, "Works for me." His focus remained on May.

Fighting off her smile, Ashley looked from Jude to May and back again. A hungry, blatantly sexual glimmer lit Jude's eyes—which was probably why May wouldn't look at him.

"Downstairs?" Tim limped toward May. "Why'r they puttin' me downstairs?"

"It's close to the pool and sauna," Denny explained. "I've seen fighters beat up way worse than you, and water always helps the recuperation process."

That only agitated Tim more. "Will someone tell me wha' the hell's goin' on?"

Seeing Jude struggle between his fascination with May and his self-assigned obligation to Tim thrilled Ashley. She wondered if her friend understood the significance of his involvement. Knowing May, she doubted it. Guys could ogle her all day, and she never paid the least bit of attention.

Before May could address Tim's concerns, Jude put his arm around her and turned to Denny. "What's the verdict?"

"Other than a bad case of wuss-itis, he's fine. Lots of colorful bruising, but nothing's broken."

"What about his ribs?" May asked.

"They're fine."

Just to keep Denny riled, Ashley said, "I agree, but you can't rule out breaks without an X-ray."

Right before her eyes, Denny seemed to swell. "I keep telling you, I've had years of experience in treating injuries."

"Then you should know what I say is true."

Typically, May fretted. "Should I take him to the hospital, do you think?"

Tim said, "No!"

Denny stepped past Tim to confront Ashley. "Even if he went for X-rays, they don't do anything for broken ribs except rest. And, Ms. Smarty Pants, sometimes even an X-ray's inconclusive."

Ashley glanced at Jude. "Is he always such a hard-on?"

May gasped.

Jude grinned and said, "Pretty much, yeah."

And Tim started moaning again.

"Damn young people today think they know everything."

Enjoying herself, Ashley replied, "And cranky old farts think they can boss everyone around."

"Old!"

"Well, sure. Compared to a young person like myself, forty's old."

"I'm forty-seven."

"Really?" Ashley lifted her brows. "You're in great shape."

Denny had his mouth open for more arguments, but when the compliment sank in, he snapped it shut and glared at her in suspicion.

Jude stepped between them. "Let's all go to the kitchen for now. Tim can answer some questions over a meal."

Liking that idea, since she hadn't yet eaten, Ashley asked, "Do you have a cook?"

Through his teeth, Denny said, "That'd be me."

"A jack of all trades, huh? The Amazing Denny Zip. I'm proud to know to you."

"For today," Jude said, "I took care of the meal."

"*You* cook?"

"Course he does," Denny snapped, taking exception to everything she said. "Does he look helpless?"

"No, just filthy rich. But hey, admittedly I don't know squat about the habits of the rich and famous. If you say they all cook, then I believe you."

That took the wind out of Denny. "Jude here is the only nabob I know well, but he's not like the rest."

"Thus my confusion." Ashley walked away to

hook arms with May, saying in a stage whisper, "Some guys can dish it out, but they sure can't take it."

"I heard that, young lady."

More or less dragging May with her, Ashley laughed. "So where's this kitchen? I'm starved."

May stared at her brother in dismay. "What do you mean you don't know how to repay the money?"

Slumped in his seat with an empty plate in front of him, Tim looked like a petulant child. Much of the swelling in his face remained, but he could now open both eyes and speak more clearly. Not that what he said helped much.

"I didn't have the money to pay, so I didn't ask."

Jude smirked. "You just figured you'd kill me and be even-steven?"

Tim was wise enough to avoid Jude's gaze. "They beat the hell outta me, okay? I wasn't thinking straight."

"You never think at all, or you wouldn't be in this situation—a situation that now involves your sister."

Face coloring, Tim glared. "If she hadn't made me walk to the Squirrel—"

May started to object, but Jude beat her to it.

"Enough."

Tim shrank back in his seat.

"I'm going to tell you this one time only, Tim, so I suggest you listen. This is *your* mess. You took the money, you gambled it away, and you'll be the one to repay me—on my terms. May is the only reason I'm willing to help. You won't insult her, you won't blame her, and you won't attempt to involve her further. If you do, I'll cut you loose, and you can fend for yourself. And don't look at your sister, damn it. If she had fifty thousand to give you, neither of you would be here now."

Very quietly, May said, "That's not true."

With a smug smile, Tim straightened, until May said, "I came here because you were threatened, too, Jude. Otherwise, I'd have convinced Tim to go to the police."

"Now, wait a minute," Tim protested.

"Oh, shut up," Ashley told him. "Let your sister talk."

May couldn't help it. With everyone picking on Tim, she did feel sorry for him. A lifetime habit wasn't easy to break. "I still think the police should be notified. But I didn't want to do anything that might jeopardize Jude. He needs to know who wants him dead."

Pointing his fork at Jude, Denny said, "I already know who it is, even if Jude won't admit it."

"*I'm* the one in trouble here," Tim reminded everyone. "They said they'd kill me if I went to the police. That means *no* police."

Under his breath, but not under enough, Denny muttered, "Chickenshit."

Affronted, Tim glared around the table. "Okay. I get it. No one cares about me. Let them kill me. I won't be missed."

Jude rolled his eyes.

"But you should remember, they said if they couldn't get me, they'd get *her.*" He pointed his finger at May.

"I'm not going to let that happen," Jude told him in an icy, controlled tone.

Wound up, Tim lifted out of his chair to address

everyone at once. He braced himself with one hand flat on the tabletop, his other hand at his ribs.

"They said they knew I could get to Jude, because he hung around May. They said I'd be doing May a favor by getting rid of him, before he got rid of her."

Denny slammed down his fork.

"They said if I didn't care enough about her welfare to protect her from him, why should they care? They said—"

"That's enough." May was so furious, she shook all over. "You know what you're saying is nonsense, Tim. You know it's all lies. How dare you—"

"It's all right, May." Calm personified, Jude squeezed her hand while addressing Tim. "You won't raise your voice to your sister. Ever. Do you understand me?"

Heaving, Tim stared at Jude, then at May.

"This is between us, Tim. Quit waiting for your sister to defend you, and tell me you understand."

Finally, he relented. "I understand."

"Tomorrow morning, my banker will deliver papers that spell out the terms of the loan and how you'll pay me back."

Surprise slackened Tim's expression. "Pay you back?"

"Did you think it'd be a gift?"

Obviously, he had, but he pinched his mouth shut and reseated himself without a word.

"Wise decision." All business, Jude leaned forward and crossed his arms on the table. "You'll sign the loan agreement with witnesses present so there won't be any mistakes."

"I'll be no better off with your so-called help. The only difference is the loan shark."

"Fine." If May could have reached her brother, she'd have kicked him. She shot to her feet and flattened her hands on the table to lean toward him. "Then *don't* take the loan. Be an idiot. Get up and leave right now. Take your chances with . . . with whomever."

"Calm down, May."

"Calm down?" She turned on Jude and found him eyeing her rear in the awful shorts. Good God, she'd forgotten she wore them.

To better conceal herself, she plopped back down in her seat and considered screaming.

Tim's behavior both shamed and embarrassed her. And Jude shrugged it off as nothing. To Tim, she snapped, "At least Jude won't kill you over the money!"

Totally deadpan, Jude said, "Don't make promises you can't keep, honey."

"Jude."

He laughed—when it was far from a laughing matter.

"You might want to give your sister's suggestion some thought. No, I won't kill you. But I won't let you weasel out of the loan, either. You might prefer another beating to dealing with me when it comes to money."

"But you're loaded," Tim reasoned.

"And I intend to stay that way."

Scoffing, Tim asked, "Why would you even care? Fifty thousand is nothing to you."

"There's where you're wrong. It's a debt that you *will* pay back. But I'll be generous." Tim looked hopeful, until Jude said, "I'll give you until tomorrow morning to think about it."

Snickering, Denny stood and gathered up the empty dishes. Nodding at Jude and May, he said,

"You two should get some sleep. You both look beat."

That sounded like a wonderful plan to May. She was so tired that it hurt her eyes to blink.

His voice a little too deep, Jude said, "I'll see that she rests." He caught May's hand and pulled her to her feet.

"In the meantime," Denny said, "I'll start working on getting Tim back in shape."

Horrified by that prospect, Tim whispered, "No."

"We'll ice what's bruised, then work out the stiffness with some swimming, and finish up with the sauna to relax everything."

Both hands in his hair, Tim slumped forward and moaned.

"Sounds like you guys have everything all set." Ashley pushed back from the table and stretched, then looked at her watch. "Just in time, too. I need to run to my place to shower and change, and then get to school."

"Ash," May protested, "you have school this morning? Why didn't you say something?"

"I have school every morning during the week."

"But you were up all night, too." To Jude and Denny, May explained, "She works from eight at night to four in the morning, then catches some sleep before school. But last night I called her, so she hasn't even been home."

"It's no big deal, May. I've pulled all-nighters plenty of times."

"But not under these circumstances," May insisted.

"And not," Jude said, "with probable danger. I agree with May. You should stay here. At least for the rest of the afternoon."

Typical of Ashley, she shook her head and laughed off the idea of protection. "No can do. I've got a test today, and if I miss it . . . Well, let's just say my instructor scares me way more than the idea of some idiot who thinks with his fists." Determined on her course, she added, "The professor can fail or pass me. But the idiot who thinks with his fists would have to catch me first. And truthfully? I'm too busy to slow down for him."

Chapter 9

Jude could feel May's tension when she said, "That's not funny, Ash."

"Sure it is." Ashley gathered up her purse and pushed in her chair. "Besides, why would anyone want to hurt me? I'm not a part of this."

"What if someone saw you come here?"

Ashley's mocking gaze went to Denny. "Then that'd mean he's not as good at watching for tails as he claimed. Surely, you don't want to insult Denny like that."

Denny snorted.

"She's right, you know," Jude said. "Denny's good, but there could still be a risk involved."

"Sorry. School comes first." She waggled her brows at Jude. "Even before hunky movie stars."

"What if someone sees you leave here?" May asked. "What if someone comes after you?"

"The mood I'm in, the sorry SOB will wish he'd never met me."

Denny laughed. "You've got *cojones*, child."

"Yeah, I know." And then to May, "Now, stop looking like that. For crying out loud, I'll be fine. I'll catch a nap before work."

"Work?" Denny asked. "You're working tonight, too?"

"Yeah, we middle-class stiffs have to pay the bills."

"*Both* jobs?" May asked, and Ashley just shrugged.

Denny scowled darkly. "What do you mean by *both*? She has more than one job?"

"She waits tables at a restaurant a couple of times a week, too."

"I get great tips. It's all the personality, ya know." Denny scoffed.

The way May looked at him, Jude could tell she wanted him to fix things somehow. But his impression of Ashley Miles was that she made her own decisions, and neither wanted nor needed input from a near stranger.

Still, he tried. "If you'd like to take the night off, I'd be happy to compensate you for your wages."

"Nope, but thanks anyway."

"You've been an enormous help. It's the least I can do."

"It's not necessary."

"Stubborn," Denny groused. "Will it offend your independent nature to log my number and Jude's into your phone, so you can call us quick if you have a problem?"

"Good thinking." She tossed her cell phone to Denny. "Have at it."

In seconds, Denny had both numbers programmed in for her. "You had May as number one, so now I'm number two and Jude is number three. Just push a button and you're bound to get one of us."

"Aye aye, captain." She tucked the phone back into her pocket. "May, you got my car keys?"

Reluctantly, May handed them over. "Please be very, very careful."

Flashing a glance at Jude, Ashley said, "Yeah, you, too."

"Come on, Ashley," Jude said, "I'll walk you to your car." He didn't want her warning May away from him, and he needed a chance to talk with her, anyway.

To his surprise, May didn't try to follow. Instead, she hugged her friend good-bye, thanking her profusely for her help and making her promise to call if she needed anything. Then she turned to Denny and asked if he'd show her where Tim's room would be.

As soon as they left the kitchen, Ashley told him, "She's up to something."

Because he'd been thinking the same thing, Jude raised a brow. "Do tell."

"Normally, she'd dog my heels all the way to the car, then stand in the driveway waving until she couldn't see me anymore."

"Elton Pascal," Jude said, thinking aloud. "She probably plans to drill Denny about him."

"And he is?"

Someone Jude didn't want to talk about, and a person May would never get near. "No one important. Just a nutcase who doesn't like me."

"Ah, yeah. I have some of those people in my life, too. Best to ignore them."

"That's what I always say." They stepped outside into a warm September day, humid from the recent rains and still a little overcast. "So you work and go to school, both?"

"Yeah, ain't I amazing?"

Pretty much, yeah. Compared with someone like Tim who waited for a handout, Ashley's attitude was more than admirable. But Jude didn't say so. He could tell she treated her determination and motivation with sarcastic wit. "What about your parents?"

She unlocked her car door. "Pretend I don't have any."

Oh. That stumped him, and made him respect her that much more. It couldn't be easy for her, facing life completely on her own. Sure, she had May, but every young woman needed familial support and caring parents to back her.

Turning to lean against the side of the car, Ashley shook her head. "Don't feel bad for me, Jude. I was the lucky one."

In so many ways, she looked like May, just leaner and lankier. They were both such pretty women, with intelligent, kind brown eyes, dark feathery lashes, and high arched brows. But this was the very topic he'd meant to discuss, so he put his visual comparisons aside and kept her talking. "Meaning May was unlucky?"

"Are you kidding? I take it you haven't met her folks yet."

"They're that bad?"

Ashley drew in a deep breath and let it out slow while staring off at the immense fountain gurgling in the side yard. "She's got the psycho mom from hell, the father who's a habitual liar about *everything,* and into the mix comes Tim, who in their eyes can do no wrong."

"And that leaves her . . ?"

"To take care of them all."

"I figured as much."

"It's totally weird. May's mom blamed her for anything Tim did wrong. Not Tim. *May*. And when Tim needed something, even if it was something May had worked hard for, her folks expected her to give it to him."

"Why?"

"Who the heck knows? They'd say, 'If he had it, he'd give it to you,' as if that'd ever happen."

Jude knew the type. "Easy enough to claim, because Tim would never have anything May needed, so the theory can't be proved."

"Exactly. It's easy to slap noble intentions on someone who won't ever have to live up to them. Money, introductions, time, attention . . . they expected May to give to Tim. School was the worst. She couldn't get involved in much because Tim was involved—and she had to take him to events, cheer him on, and then take him back home. Her mom forever claims to be sick, and her dad is too busy chasing skirts."

"Damn." It sounded worse than he'd imagined.

"She fought his fights, propped him up and hugged him when he needed it. She even did his homework, if you can believe that crap. Olympia, May's mom, threw on the guilt, telling her that Tim didn't understand the work, but she did. It was easy for her and hard for him. It's a wonder the creep graduated—and he probably wouldn't have without May."

"And her mom and dad?"

"She runs for them, too. Every little thing falls on May. And if it interferes with her life, too bad." Ashley's voice dropped. "The amazing thing is that she's still so damn nice. To all of them."

And the responsibility she felt was deeply ingrained. Anyone who cared for May would have to understand her priorities and accept her unusual duty to her family.

It couldn't be easy, yet she and Ashley remained friends. "You two are close."

"Like sisters. I care more about her than any blood relatives. More than anyone. May thinks it was a big deal for me to do without a little sleep for her today, but she's done so much for me, I'm glad for a chance to repay her whenever I can."

Jude bent his knees, bringing his gaze level with Ashley's averted face. "What'd she do for you, Ash?"

Shaking her head, she said, "A better question would be, what hasn't she done?" She laughed. "So I owe her. And God forbid I be like Tim, forever a taker without ever giving back."

"I don't think anyone would accuse you of that. From what I could tell, you're a damn good friend."

Her eyes, so much like May's, met his. "May deserves the very best. In all things."

"I agree." Jude propped one arm on the top of the open car door. "So, are you going to lecture me about hurting her?"

"Nah. May's an adult. She can take care of herself—she's been doing it since she was born." Ashley turned her head toward him, giving him a hard stare. She looked lethal, but her tone was soft, almost teasing. "Only a real asshole would deliberately use May. And c'mon, Jude, you're not an asshole, are you?"

Jude couldn't help but laugh. "I have no intention of doing anything to hurt her."

"Yeah, well, keep that thought in mind for when you meet her folks." She climbed into the car and put the key in the ignition. "Wherever May is, one of them shows up. And given what you've got . . .

let's just say, I imagine you'll have a visitor before
too much longer."

"What I've got?"

"Money, fame, influence. Yep, they're gonna
love you." She pulled her door shut and spoke to
him through the open window. "If you really mean
to have Tim sign loan papers, get it done as soon
as possible, because her dad will be on you before
you know it."

Jude stepped back as she started the car and
drove away. So Ashley thought May's father would
drop in on him? His biggest problem with that
possibility was that it meant he'd have little time to
get closer to May.

Better get to work on it now—while he could
ensure some privacy.

Jude started toward the house, determined that
May would get the rest she needed . . . after he got
what he needed even more.

Her.

May tuned out Tim's complaints as they went
down to the lower level of Jude's house to the
rooms he'd use. She'd already noticed the elaborate wine rack in the kitchen, and the first thing
she saw downstairs was a long, well-lit, mahogany
wet bar that filled an entire wall. In front of that
and to her right was a game room. To her left,
through an oversized arched doorway, was the
home theater. On the farthest wall behind her was
an elaborate gym area that contained a heavyweight bag, a speed bag, a treadmill, and an assort-
ment of barbells and weights with a bench.

The mahogany bar, though elegant and rich,
might as well have contained blinking neon lights

for the way it held all her attention. Glass shelves sported a variety of glasses, while a tinted glass cabinet protected more wine bottles and hard liquors.

Her stomach churned at the sight of so much alcohol. Did Jude imbibe while watching movies on the sixteen-foot screen? Maybe while he exercised? Did he consider drink an accompaniment to anything he did?

Most women wouldn't care. They'd love Jude's company, no matter how they spent their time. Other women didn't have her loony family to contend with, either.

A glance at Tim told her that he'd noticed the liquor supply, too, and that couldn't be a good thing. Her brother had adopted their mother's unfortunate habit of overindulging. Right now, he looked at all that alcohol with covetous greed.

Trying to sound enthusiastic, May turned a full circle to see everything. "I can't believe the size of this house."

"There's a lot more to see," Denny told her. Then, denying Tim the opportunity to ogle the bar, he said, "This way." Down a short hall, he opened a door to a moderate suite of rooms, including a bedroom, bathroom, and sitting area with a television, DVD player, and the requisite monitor—though this monitor wasn't on.

Tim made a beeline for the bed and cautiously stretched out atop the beautiful quilt with a heavy sigh. "God, I'm sore."

Crossing his arms over his chest, and with a look of distaste, Denny eyed him. "Lying around will only make it worse. The pool and sauna are at the other end of the floor. You've got ten minutes, then I'll be ready for you, so don't fall asleep."

Eyes closed, Tim said, "I don't have a swimsuit."

"Don't need one. There aren't any ladies here except your sister, and she'll be resting." And in a final warning, "Ten minutes."

May touched her brother's foot. "Denny will have you feeling better in no time."

Giving her the cold shoulder, Tim gingerly turned to his side without a reply. It embarrassed May that her brother could be so childish and un-appreciative, especially when she saw Denny's jaw flex in anger. She strode out of the room—but again stopped to stare at that elaborate bar with worry.

"Surly jerk," Denny muttered as he joined her. He patted her shoulder and said, "Even the young and stupid have to grow up, whether they want to or not. Life has a way of seeing to it."

On the pretense of cleaning her glasses, May ducked her head. But Denny, not one to miss much, noted her preoccupation with the bar. Scowling, he took two quick steps back into the room to confront Tim. "By the way, alcohol might dull the pain, but it does more harm than good."

"Oh God, not a lecture on top of everything else."

"I'll lecture you whenever I damn well feel like it, and you'll either listen, or take a hike down the driveway to deal with your problems on your own."

Tim curled a little tighter on the bed but refrained from arguing.

"Now here's a lesson you should take to heart. Booze might appeal to you right now, but it's a downer, and you're lower than a snake's belly already. It directly affects brain cells—in those who have them, that is. I'm still undecided about you."

"Ha-ha. Don't make me laugh."

Unfazed by Tim's sarcasm, Denny continued,

"It increases the workload on the heart, making you more tired than usual, and causes high blood pressure, vomiting, and ulcers. It widens blood vessels, which'd make your headache worse and cause a drop in your temperature. Because it reduces your body's ability to make blood cells, it can leave you more susceptible to infection. And it can stop your kidneys from maintaining a proper balance of body fluids, meaning it'll bloat your not-so-pretty mug."

"All that, huh?"

"And more."

"So why the hell does Jude have a supply if it's such awful stuff?"

Denny smoothed his hand over his hair, and for the flash of a second, May could see a tattoo on his skull. "For parties and guests and a responsible social drink here and there. But drinking is forbidden when you train with me."

"I'm not training with you."

"As of right now you are, so understand this. I know exactly how much alcohol is in every bottle. If you touch so much as a single drop, I'll make sure you regret it."

Tim said something May couldn't hear, but she saw Denny nod before pulling the door shut.

"Thank you." After years of practice, making excuses for her brother came naturally to her. "He's out of sorts, but I'm sure he appreciates all you're doing."

"No, he doesn't. But who cares? Ain't doing it for him, anyway."

May wondered about that but let it go when Denny took her arm. "So what'd you want to talk to me about?"

Surprised, May gave a self-conscious laugh. "How did you know . . ?"

"You're easy to read, missy. A refreshing quality, if you don't mind me saying so."

"No, I don't mind." They walked together through the game room and beyond. Denny was all business, whereas she took in her surroundings with awe. Just as Jude had claimed, he still had plenty of bare walls. The pieces he'd purchased would look wonderful with his décor, but she had a few more in mind that would really fit the overall tone of his home.

She'd discuss it with him, May decided. And whether he liked it or not, she'd gift him with a few pieces out of appreciation for all he'd done and still intended to do. She couldn't personally afford many of the artists that she represented, but excluding her commission would help.

"This is the racquetball court," Denny explained, letting her poke her head through a thick door where tall white walls and a glass viewing area framed light, highly polished wooden floors. "Jude loves the sport. And of course, this is the pool. That room at the end there is the sauna."

"Wow." Seeing the enormous indoor pool that resembled a natural pond almost made her forget the questions she wanted to ask. Lush plants, smooth rock, and boulder walls were everywhere. At one end of the irregularly shaped design, a small waterfall trickled into the water, rippling the surface. A space had been sectioned off for a connecting hot tub. "This is incredible."

Denny laughed. "According to his mamma, Jude's a water baby. He's happiest near the ocean, a lake or pond, or even a mountain creek. There're waterfalls everywhere in the house, and that big fountain in front, and the stocked pond out back."

"I love water, too."

"S'that right?" Crossing his arms over his chest, Denny lounged against what appeared to be a wall of chiseled rock softened by hanging vines. Across from the pool, floor-to-ceiling windows let in sunshine and reflected off his piercing green eyes. "Maybe you and Jude could take a swim later tonight."

That got May back on track. "Oh no, thank you, anyway. But I did want to talk to you. You told Tim he could have a few minutes, so if you're not too busy right now . . ."

"You wanna know about Elton Pascal, don't you?"

Disgruntled, she crossed her arms, too. "It's weird how you do that. What are you, a mind reader?"

He rolled one big shoulder, which was decorated with an elaborate tribal tattoo. Jude had said tattoos were popular among the fighters, and she'd seen for herself how most of the men sported them on limbs, backs, and like Denny, their heads. Some weren't bad, some looked overdone.

Denny's tattoos fascinated her.

He chuckled. "Got this one on my arm when I first started competing. The one on my head was a moment of adrenaline-related weakness, and a dare I should have passed up. But hey, live and learn."

He'd known her thoughts again.

"Like I said, you're easy to read. And since Jude's no idiot, you should make it quick. He probably figures you're down here grilling me now, and let me tell you, Pascal is not one of his favorite topics. If he had his way, the man's name would never be mentioned."

Taking Denny's warning to heart, May shook off

her distraction and started grilling. "You said he's harassed Jude, and that he's been very accusatory."

"He outright lies, and some idiots believe him."

"Isn't there anything Jude can do about it?"

Shaking his head, Denny pushed away from the wall and went to a stone bench with a wood cabinet built beneath it. "You gotta know Jude. He has a chip on his shoulder the size of this house." After pulling out some towels, he glanced at May. "A lot like your little friend."

"Little friend?" May laughed. "You mean Ashley?"

"Yeah. Nice kid—but she works the tough routine to the bone. She needs to relax a little."

"Yeah, well, good luck getting her to do that. I've been trying forever."

"With a helping hand from me, she'd have more free time."

Denny didn't know Ash well if he thought she'd take his help. "For as long as I've known her, she's been on her own."

"You two have that in common, huh?"

"We share a background, but our upbringings were different. Ashley's parents were superstrict to the point of being mean. Mine just . . ." She floundered for the right words.

"Favored your brother?"

That was a nice way of putting it. "Yes. But Ash didn't have any siblings to deflect her parents' attention. Whereas I never went without, they were always dirt poor, at least when it came to Ash. There were times that she wouldn't have lunch money, but her dad had a motorcycle that he took out every weekend, and her mom got her nails done all the time."

"Kids should come first."

"I've always thought so."

Denny smiled at her. "She didn't like me helping her. Pitched a real fit about it."

Coming from Denny, the observation sounded like a compliment. "When Ash was a kid, her family willingly accepted help from anyone and everyone. They were on food stamps, and every holiday the church gave them food and sometimes cash. The school even offered her family some second-hand clothes, so Ashley could dress better. I don't think she ever got over it."

"She shouldn't have been through it in the first place."

May agreed wholeheartedly. "When we were in eighth grade, this one bully started saying mean things to her. He wouldn't stop, and I could tell it was hurting her."

"I bet she chewed him up and spit him out, didn't she?"

It had taken years for Ashley to get the take-no-prisoners attitude she affected now. Lost in the memories, May whispered, "She was different back then."

"How so?"

"A lot more vulnerable. She tried ignoring him, but he wouldn't let up—so I lost it. I jumped on his back and pulled his hair, and we both hit the ground hard. He broke his wrist, and I knocked the wind out of myself."

"Good for you."

May laughed. "I got suspended for two days for fighting in school, but so did he for antagonizing Ashley. And it was worth it, because after that, he left her alone."

"Wish I could have seen it," Denny commented. "Too bad you didn't punch him in his face."

That reminded her of how she'd slugged Jude, and she winced. "These days, Ashley looks at an offer of help like an insult. She takes it to mean she's weak or something."

"If she were my daughter, I wouldn't let anyone hurt her."

Denny really was a very sweet guy beneath the rough, kick-ass exterior. "She and her father haven't spoken in years."

"Stupid bastard."

"Yeah." Ashley could use a father figure like Denny in her life. But if he hoped to befriend her, he'd have to tread carefully. "I think Ashley needs to do things for herself now, or else it doesn't mean as much to her."

Nodding in sage understanding, he said, "Bull-headed, like Jude. He gets an idea in his head, and he won't let it go. Like all those damn accusations Elton flings around."

"You think Elton is still doing it?"

"Damn right, he is. If a reporter gets within ten feet of him, he takes it as an opportunity to trash-talk Jude. I'm not saying the scandal around Jude will ever disappear completely, not with the guilty one still running loose. But Pascal won't even give it a chance to cool down. He can't stand the thought of Jude being happy."

"He blames Jude, doesn't he?"

"For stealing Blair, if for nothing else. Christ, she was better than twenty years younger than Elton. A confused kid, trying to adjust to fame." He shook his head. "And Elton, like an old fool, thought he'd found true love or some such shit."

"I read that Jude's limo blew up with Blair inside."

"Blair and the driver both. Since Jude left the

limo to get a cola out of a vending machine, and there wasn't anyone else around on that stretch of highway, it looked really damning."

"But you know him well enough to know he's not capable of murder."

Sharp-eyed and surly, Denny growled, "Damn right, I do. Jude's about the fairest man I know. Hell, he goes out of his way to give back to others, to help when he can."

May tipped her head and asked very softly, "Are you talking about me?"

He snorted. "About myself, actually. Jude gave me a home, and at my age, putting down roots was important."

Appreciating his protectiveness and honesty, May reached out and squeezed Denny's hand. "I'm so glad he has you in his corner."

"I figured I was there for all his fights, I couldn't skip the biggest fight of his life. And he won. He got acquitted. But it still haunts him—just as Elton wants it to."

May paced a few feet away, thinking about the awful circumstances of that day. "Since he's been found innocent, couldn't Jude sue Elton or something? Wouldn't his accusations fall under slander or libel?"

"Maybe. But Jude says he's done nothing wrong, so he shouldn't have to defend himself over anything Elton says. When Elton shoots off his mouth, Jude just ignores him—like your friend tried to ignore the school bully. He figures that his true friends will see through the bastard."

And in the meantime, most of the nation figured Jude had just bought himself out of a guilty verdict. How awful it would be to live with that.

Opening the storage area beneath another bench, Denny pulled out a bottle of water. Before he could close the discreet contraption again, May saw the tumblers and ice bucket.

Good grief, did Jude drink everywhere and any-where he went? Would he drink while she stayed with him?

She couldn't very well criticize him for doing so. Unlike many of the people in her life, she knew for a fact Jude wasn't a drunk. But she had a unique phobia concerning alcohol, a phobia she couldn't control.

She realized Denny watched her, and that he'd seen her disgust over the hidden stash. Her face heated as she stared back and muttered, "Sorry."

"Discuss it with Jude," he suggested. "He might surprise you."

The words no sooner left Denny's mouth than Jude strode through the door. He looked wary and primed, but the second he spotted May, he stopped, and his expression softened. That sexy little half smile curved his mouth, and his eyes brightened. "There you are."

"Did you think I'd run her off?" After a quick wink at May, Denny started out of the room. "I was showing her the pool, but now I'm ready for Tim."

Jude paid Denny no mind at all. Gaze locked on May, he asked, "So what do you think?"

She couldn't think, not with him staring at her like that. "About?"

"My pool."

The door clicked shut behind Denny, leaving them in isolation with only the sounds of the gur-gling waterfall and May's uneven breathing. But their moment of privacy wouldn't last. Denny would return soon with her brother.

May straightened her glasses and cleared her throat.

"I love it." She didn't mean to, but her gaze skimmed over Jude from head to foot and back up again. In a flash, she took in every inch: the muscles, the strength, the raw sex appeal. Her stomach did a little flip-flop in excitement—a familiar feeling whenever she got near Jude.

"Keep looking at me like that," he warned softly, "and I'm going to have to dive right in."

"What?"

"The water." He looked like a rogue, smiling in a sexy, teasing way. "But I'm not sure it's cold enough to help."

Embarrassed and turned on, May jerked around to face the pool. "The rocks are fabulous. And all the plants. The big windows. It looks so natural, like something you'd find in Tahiti."

"That's the point."

Blast her nervous blathering. "I love it." She faced him—and saw the lust in his expression. Oh, wow. "I assume you have people who come over to keep it so sparkling clean?" *Oh God, May, could you not say something so stupid?*

Jude grinned. "Denny more than earns what I pay him without responsibility for extras like the pool. So, yeah, I have people that come once a week. For the pool. The yard. The house. Mondays I catch up on phone calls while the maintenance people are here, supervised by Denny."

"He really is invaluable to you."

"And he knows it." Jude took a few steps closer to her. "He'll want this room for your brother. And you've done enough worrying about Tim for one day." He held out a hand. "Come on. You look ready to collapse."

He had to be every bit as tired, so she said, "I'm fine."

"No." His voice went hoarse. "Time for bed, May. I insist."

Oh, the way he said that. Her heart skipped a few beats, then galloped wildly. She couldn't delude herself: Both she and Jude were exhausted, but neither of them had sleep on their minds. If she went with him now, it'd be to make love.

And it'd be wonderful, but . . . temporary.

Did that still matter, when she wanted him so much, and when she sensed that he needed her, too?

He stood there, hand extended, patient, expectant.

Slowly, May slipped her hand into his.

Chapter 10

Jude didn't move a single muscle. May's compliance meant so much to him, more than he'd expected. When he'd started linking intimacy with trust, he didn't know. He only knew that she would never get sexually involved with him if she doubted him, if she didn't genuinely like him.

Celebrity, popularity, power . . . those things meant nothing to May. He thought of how the night would end, how he'd make it end, and the heated thoughts expanded his lust. No matter what, he wouldn't let May hide from him any longer. She claimed to want him; now he'd see how much.

He'd been patient far too long.

The intrusion of Tim's whining voice jolted Jude into action. Her brother made him see red, but he kept his voice moderate. "Let's go."

She didn't say a word, but he could feel the trembling in her hand, see the added flush to her cheeks. Driven by urgency, he hurried her along, giving her no chance to console her brother, and Tim no chance to cry on her shoulder.

He and Denny worked well together, because while Jude led May one way, Denny led Tim another. As Tim's complaints escalated, May looked over her shoulder with fretful concern.

Because he wanted her attention on him, and only him, as soon as he got her out of sight of Tim, Jude said, "I'm going to strip you naked, you know."

She faltered to a stop at the bottom of the stairwell. Feathery lashes fluttered, her lips parted, more color rushed into her cheeks.

The subtle, sexy scent of her skin intensified with her blush. Jude breathed it in—and knew he couldn't wait to kiss her.

Out of view, Tim's and Denny's muted voices placed them near the pool. The memory of each earlier kiss came back to Jude with the effect of a tsunami. Lust tightened his muscles and thickened his breath.

"Jude?" she whispered, sounding pretty turned-on herself.

He caught her arms above the elbows and lifted her to her tiptoes. Her eyes widened, her lips parted—and he took her mouth with all the savage intensity that boiled inside him.

On a groan, she went limp, slumping against him, her mouth warm and wet and open to his. His tongue thrust in, withdrew, entered again for a more thorough tasting, lazily twining with her tongue, exploring her mouth. It was a kiss of complete possession, whether May realized it or not.

She pushed closer to him, and he could feel her stiffened nipples on his chest, her belly against his crotch. From one heartbeat to the next, he got an erection that even a virgin wouldn't miss.

With a sound of approval, May rubbed against him, countering his every move. Soon he'd kiss her like this again—with them both naked, her legs around his waist, her nails on his back.

Only when Jude heard the loud splash and Tim's curse did he recall the here and now.

"My room," he whispered against her lips. "Tell me yes, May."

Eyes still closed, she swallowed, nodded, and breathed, "Yes."

"Thank God."

One hand on his chest, her face tilted up to his, May laughed. And that, as much as anything else, caused the coiling tension to snap. His patience was at an end.

In all the many times that he'd imagined making love to May, not once had he thought of racing her up the steps. He'd never considered his loss of finesse, or hearing her giggle at his haste, or the heavy, nearly impossible weight of his heart as it seemed to expand in his chest.

In the carpeted second floor hallway, she stumbled, and Jude scooped her up. Mortified, she flailed around, trying to get loose, but no way in hell would he let that happen.

"Settle down, May."

"You can't carry me!"

"Apparently, I can." He kissed her mouth, hard and fast, and took the last few steps to his room. Her mortified groan fired his blood, and he added, "I like holding you, May. You're a very soft, warm armful."

Knotting one hand in the hair on the back of his head, she growled, "Is that another crack on my weight?"

Jude looked down at where her hefty breasts

smashed up against his chest. "No." He shifted his arm, jostling her behind, and he kissed the frown off her forehead. "You're perfect, every ounce of you."

Shoving his bedroom door open, then kicking it shut again, he strode for the bed.

May looked up, and her mouth dropped open. "Holy crap."

"Like it?" He didn't pause in his trek toward the bed, but when he started to lower her to the oversized mattress, she clung like a vine. "May?"

Reaching out, she ran her fingertips lightly along the bottom left Corinthian column of his iron and walnut bed. "I've never seen furniture so big."

"It's a big room."

Her dark eyes focused on the plush down comforter. "And you're a big man?"

Damn. "You won't have any complaints."

Her smile came and went. She looked at the curving wall of windows and the double doors that led to his bath. Her gaze skimmed over two paintings he'd bought from her, the wall monitor, and then the floor-to-ceiling fountain on the opposite wall that supplied the soothing sounds of running water. "You actually sleep in here?"

"It's a bedroom. What'd you think I'd do in here?"

Perplexed, she stared up at him. "It's so big. Don't you feel . . . lost?"

"No." He pried her loose and followed her down onto the bed, sliding his hands from her shoulders down to her wrists and beyond, until he could twine his fingers with hers. He stretched her arms up high, and then just stared down into her beautiful dark eyes. "This is my favorite room. I love the furniture, the fountain, the view, and especially the incredible artwork that one very talented gallery owner helped me choose."

Tipping her head back, she studied the majestic columns at each corner of his bed, visually tracing the fluted wood up to the broad, masculine finials, and then up to his ceiling.

Her eyes rounded. "Jude?"

Already knowing her thoughts, adoring her more by the minute, he said, "Hmmm?"

"Why is there such a bright light right over your bed?"

Grinning, Jude slid his right hand under the hem of her shirt, up her waist, and over her breast. Her eyes closed, her lips parted on a sharp breath.

Feeling her, the plump flesh, the stiffened nipple, made it difficult for him to speak. But he enjoyed playing with May too much not to take advantage of the silly questions.

Instead of pointing out how much he enjoyed reading, Jude said, "During the day, the windows let in plenty of light, but at night, it can be dark as Hades in here." He gently squeezed her breast. "But I'm a guy who likes to see what I'm getting into."

She started to protest when he stroked his thumb over her velvety nipple, and all that came out of her mouth was a small sound, barely heard, not much more than an aroused whimper.

Knowing exactly what that female sound meant, Jude shoved the T-shirt up, intent on replacing his hand with his mouth. Haste rode him again, but around May, he had no choice.

Before he could put plan to action, her hands tangled in his hair, holding him off.

Behind her glasses, her brown eyes looked

solemn and too serious. "I'm not a skinny starlet, Jude."

"Thank God." Again, he leaned forward. May's fingers tightened to the point of pain. "Ow."

"Listen to me."

"Couldn't we talk later?" He turned his head to kiss the inside of her elbow, then studied her soft, swollen lips, now damp from his kisses, and the pulse that tripped wildly in her throat. "I have the sexiest broad on the earth in my bed. I'm finally about to get her naked—something I've wanted to do from the second I first saw her. She's ready, I'm anxious, and if I don't get inside her soon, I'm going to self-combust."

Her shaky laugh made her breasts shimmer. Such beautiful breasts. Later, he'd take his time with her. For now, he wanted her enough that he hurt.

Using only his fingertips, Jude rolled her nipple and got a heated gasp in return. "Can I please take that as agreement?"

She nodded, removed her glasses, and handed them to him. Jude quickly set them aside, and by the time he turned back to her, she'd already whisked the shirt off over her head.

Sitting up on his haunches astride her thighs, Jude got to look at all of her.

He'd expected May to be shy. Overly modest. But instead, she smiled and stretched, putting her arms above her head and arching her neck, thrusting her breasts toward him. The shorts rode low on her shapely hips, displaying her belly and the tops of her hipbones.

On fire, Jude opened his hand over the sexy rise of her belly. "You are so soft."

"And you're so hard." She made a purring

sound, squirming under him. "After seeing you, other men look like boys. You're so solid in layered muscle, so strong in body and confidence."

"I'm just me, May."

She shook her head. "I'm not talking about you the movie star. Or even you the fighter, though I like the fighter a lot."

He started to question that, until she went on.

"I'm talking about you the man who takes whatever life throws at him and is still so damn successful, and so honorable." Her voice lowered. "And so sexy."

Jude smiled. "But?"

"We've known each other a while now."

"True. And it's made me nuts, wanting you while you kept me a safe distance away."

Appearing reserved, she stared at his throat and whispered, "From what you've said, how you are, you enjoy all things . . . carnal."

"I'm a guy." He kneaded her breast while speaking. "Of course I do."

"It's more than that. When I'm near you, I can feel your masculinity, your iron will." Her legs shifted on the bed. "Your sex appeal. You think women stare at you because of your reputation or your fame or your money. But you're just so macho, so . . . powerful."

Because Jude knew women, he knew that's what most of them saw. For them, his appeal was his wealth and celebrity, and most didn't even bother to deny it.

But May confounded him. From the word jump, he'd had a hard time figuring her out.

"Don't you see, Jude? You could be a poor street cleaner who no one had ever heard of, and you'd still draw female attention everywhere you went."

He didn't want her idolizing him. When he fucked up, as all men did on occasion, he wanted her to understand and forgive. If her expectations were too high, he'd never be able to live up to them.

"As long as I have *your* attention, I don't care about the rest of it." Staring down at her body, at the luscious swells and dips and her soft, pale flesh, he couldn't even remember any other woman. She was his fantasy come to life, an ache in his heart and groin, a need he'd never fully appease. The more time he spent with her, the more time he wanted with her.

"You have it," she promised. "You've had my attention for a very long time."

"Good." From May's breasts to her hips and up again, Jude touched her, teasing them both.

"I hope you like what you see," May whispered, "because I'm not changing."

"Trust me, I like you just as you are." Using both hands, he cupped her substantial breasts. "God, you're stacked."

She laughed—but only until he tugged on her nipples.

When she started to lower her arms to reach for him, Jude rasped, "No, leave them up there. I like seeing you like this, all stretched out across my bed."

"All right." She pressed her head into the mattress and closed her eyes—but she didn't move her arms.

"Do you know I get light-headed just looking at you?"

Her hips lifted in a bid to hurry him along. Needing no more encouragement than that, Jude shifted to sit beside her. "Don't move."

Untying the drawstring at the waistband of the shorts, he eased them down until he could just see the top of her underwear. He'd often wondered about it, curious as to what type of lingerie she'd choose. But what he found shouldn't have surprised him. "Pink cotton?"

"Shut up, Jude."

Even while making him red hot, she amused him. "And little blue flowers?" With one finger, he traced a tiny bud that decorated the waistband of her undies.

"I mean it."

"These are cute."

Eyes still closed, arms raised, she said, "I'm warning you."

He felt his smile in his heart. Hell, he even felt it in his soul. "Yes, ma'am." Skimming the shorts down her thighs, her calves, and finally, her feet, he admired her silly underwear, how whimsical they seemed on a woman usually hidden in a boxy suit.

And then he removed her panties, too.

Amazed, breathless, caught in a whirlwind of desire, May gave herself over to the moment. It helped that without her glasses, she couldn't really read Jude's expression. He'd slept with some of the most beautiful women in the world.

If her very average body didn't satisfy him, she wouldn't see it.

But the way he touched her, the added heat pouring off him, and the intent way he explored her told her that he had no complaints.

"This isn't really fair."

His fingers tickled lazily up the inside of her thigh. "What's that?"

"You seeing me naked when, without my glasses, even after you do finally get rid of your clothes, I won't be able to see you that well."

She felt his pause, then the brief skimming of his fingers through her pubic hair. The bed dipped, he stretched away, and then came down close. "Here you are, ma'am."

Using great care, he slid the armatures of her glasses onto her ears. May opened her eyes—and the burning need in his stole her breath.

"Better?"

She nodded.

His mouth took hers in a claiming kiss that destroyed all doubts. With her limp and overheated, he sat up, and in one quick movement, pulled his shirt off over his head.

The sight of his body always aroused her. But now . . . now she'd get to touch him and taste him, too. She started to lower her arms to do just that, but Jude caught her wrists.

"Not yet, honey. I've thought about this too many times to rush through it, but I swear, I'm not myself."

"You look like Jude Jamison to me."

"No. Normally I'm a decent lover."

Her mouth quirked. "Meaning I should expect substandard treatment?"

He closed his eyes. "Meaning there's always been something about you that just pushes all my buttons. Holding back at all is killing me, but I'll be damned if I'll fuck this up."

Judging by his strained expression, his loss of control really nettled him. He looked pained. And almost angry.

Maybe . . . explosive.

Ignoring his order to stay still, May put both

hands on his chest and stroked his burning skin. "It's all right, Jude."

On a raw laugh of frustration, he sat back on his heels, his knees spread wide. Breathing hard, he let her pet him, until in a sudden burst, he threw his shirt against the far wall. "It's not all right."

"Jude—"

He lowered himself over her again, taking her mouth, his hands everywhere.

Caught up in a whirlwind, May could do little more than cling to him. His tongue thrust into her mouth, exploring, hot and wet. His right hand kneaded her breasts while his left held her head still for ever deeper kisses. The denim of his fly scraped against her belly as he started a slow, methodical rhythm that mimicked lovemaking.

"Jude."

He covered her mouth again, and slowly, tantalizingly, moved his hand down her waist, over her hip, and then inward . . . until his fingers delved between her legs.

Overwhelmed by the bombardment on her senses, May opened her legs more and heard Jude's rumbling growl of approval.

Finally freeing her mouth, he kissed her throat, her shoulder, and then, just as his middle finger gently sank into her, he latched onto her nipple.

The combination of sensual assault melted her modesty. Acutely aware of his finger inside her, his knuckles pressing against her mound, his forearm brushing the tender insides of her thigh, May felt every nerve ending in her body.

She'd never been the type for demonstrative sexual displays. For her, intimacy had been restrained and polite. She'd enjoyed sex, and felt fulfilled, yet no one would ever call her abandoned.

But Jude magnified everything, both sexual and emotional. The raw moan that ripped from her throat made her sound like a wanton—and she didn't care. She couldn't hold back the evocative sounds, not while Jude made love to her. Each moan, each frantic twist of her body, seemed to urge him on.

He sucked at her nipple, nipped and teased, and licked with his rough tongue. He pulled out of her, then pressed deep again, this time with two fingers, stretching her, working her. Using his thumb, he circled her clitoris, all the while sucking at her nipple.

An unfamiliar tightening began inside May. She clenched her muscles, trying to hold on to his fingers. Her hands gripped his shoulders. She lifted into him, groaned, and whimpered. She was *so* close . . .

Jude thrust himself away from her.

Cold, panting, May opened her eyes only to see him shucking off his jeans in furious haste, then fumbling with a condom. He glanced up and caught her stunned gaze. "Sorry, honey."

May held her arms out to him. "Hurry."

He laughed, groaned, and with the condom finally in place, stretched out atop her. Cupping her face, he said, "We'll go slow later. I'll show you how good it can be. I'll—"

Frantic, May wailed, "Stop talking about it and just *do* it."

His nostrils flared. Using his knee, he nudged her legs wider apart and wedged one hand between their bodies. His fingertips slicked over her damp, sensitive flesh, and she felt him opening her, then she felt the broad head of his penis pushing into her.

Her eyes started to drift shut.

"No," Jude said, his voice harsh with lust. "Keep looking at me. I want to see you when you come."

May nodded. "Okay." But it wasn't easy. Her eyelids felt heavy, her emotions exposed. She wanted him with her, every bit as wild as she felt.

Lifting her legs and wrapping them around him, she dug her heels into the small of his back to hurry him. She wanted all of him, right now.

Jude locked his jaw. His shoulders went taut. And then he thrust hard, burying himself inside her.

They both gasped, going still as May adjusted to his size, and Jude tried to find lost control.

But May didn't want him controlled. She wanted him as lost as she felt. Needing to push him, she touched his mouth with her fingers and tightened her legs around him. "Jude? You feel so good."

His expression darkened as he fought it, but he lost the battle. "Shit," he snarled, even as he began riding her hard, driving into her, pulling all the way out, thrusting in again.

"Yes." The feelings were so much more than physical. Seeing Jude, breathing in his scent, seeing his excitement and lust while holding him, all made it more than she'd ever experienced. Sharp sensation came in ebbs and flows, growing stronger each time until the tension snapped, flooding her body with pleasure. "Yes, yes, *yes.*"

Jude held her closer, their gazes still locked, and through the clouded haze of her orgasm, she saw the moment he went taut—and the incredible release that slowly drained him.

Seconds ticked by. Jude let out a long breath, smoothed her hair back from her face, and low-

ered his weight onto her. So in love she felt sick
with it, May turned her face into his throat and just
hugged him.

"Damn," he muttered, kissing her temple. "I'm
sorry."

She sighed. "Why?" For her, it had all been
pretty wonderful.

He shifted his weight, leaving her body and
turning to his side, but taking her with him so that
they stayed in a warm embrace. "I didn't do half of
what I wanted to do."

Sleepily, she asked, "Like?"

"Like feel your hands on my cock, or your inner
thighs on my jaw."

Her eyes popped open, and even though they
were both naked and had just indulged in some incredible sex, she blushed. "Um . . ."

But Jude wasn't finished. "I didn't make you
come with my hands and my mouth, the way I've
dreamed of doing."

"Jude . . ."

His hand smoothed down her back to her behind. "And I didn't tell you how incredibly beautiful you are."

Her heart turned over, making her eyes damp.
"Thank you."

"If you weren't so exhausted, I'd start again,
right now." He raised himself to one elbow, destroying her attempts at hiding. Smiling, sexy, he
made a temptation no woman could resist.

"Well, then . . ."

To shush her, he traced her mouth, his expression intent. "But you are exhausted. So I suppose
I'll just have to bide my time until we've both had
a nap."

May would have protested that decision, but in a

diabolical act sure to distract her, he left the bed and, his back to her, stretched.

Wow. She should commission an artist to paint him just like that. She could have prints done and make a fortune.

Over his shoulder, Jude said, "I'll just go clean up. Get comfortable. I won't be long." And he strode across the room, through the double doors to the bathroom.

Feeling very satisfied, May curled to her side and nestled her head into the pillow. Her body seemed to sink into the sinfully soft mattress. The gentle sounds of the fountain lulled her. Lethargic and sexually replete, smiling from the inside out, she closed her eyes.

Within seconds, she was asleep.

PLACE
STAMP
HERE

||...|..||||....|||.|.|.|.||.|.|.||.|..||.|.||..|.|

Zebra Contemporary Romance Book Club
Zebra Home Subscription Service, Inc.
P.O. Box 5214
Clifton NJ 07015-5214

THE BENEFITS OF BOOK CLUB MEMBERSHIP

• You'll get your books hot off the press, usually before they appear in bookstores.

• You'll ALWAYS save up to 30% off the cover price.

• You'll get our FREE monthly newsletter filled with author interviews, book previews, special offers and MORE!

• There's no obligation – you can cancel at any time and you have no minimum number of books to buy.

• And – if you decide you don't like the books you receive, you can return them. (You always have ten days to decide.)

Zebra Contemporary Romance

Chapter 11

"Wimp. Can't you swim any faster than that?"

Eyes narrowed, Tim glared up at Denny. He knew exactly what Denny was doing. Goading him on purpose. Challenging him. But damn it, he still put a little more effort into each stroke.

He had to admit that the light exercises Denny took him through, combined with the weightlessness of the water, had eased some of his aches and pains. That is, he'd admit it to himself.

He wasn't telling Denny jack shit.

"That's better." Along the edge of the pool, Denny kept pace with him. "You've got good arms, son. Long. Toned. If you were trained right, that extra reach would be one hell of an advantage."

Tim sealed his mouth shut and concentrated on another lap. He would *not* ask.

He wouldn't.

But when he reached the end of the pool, the words just came tumbling out. "How so?"

Taking a fighter's stance, feet planted, one arm

extended, Denny said, "You can hit without being hit." He made two quick jabs. "See what I mean?"

"What do you know about it?"

"Everything there is to know." The cocky grin left a silver tooth showing. "It's what I used to do. I trained the most successful fighters in the SBC, including Jude."

No way. A trainer? "Are you pulling my leg?"

"Nope. Used to fight myself, too, but that shit gets old real quick. Had to have my knee worked on twice, popped my ankle a few times, and got my arm broke in two places."

Denny pulled up his sleeve to show Tim one of the ghastliest scars he'd ever seen. "Jesus."

"Yeah. Damn near fucked up my tattoo." With another grin, he said, "I've got so much metal in my body now, the airport sensors go off when I walk through security."

Tim couldn't believe the way Denny laughed about it. "So am I done or what?"

"Yeah, haul your sorry ass out. Or do you need help?"

Minutes ago, Tim would have said yes. But now, after Denny joked about broken bones, he was determined to damn well get out on his own steam.

Denny handed him a super-soft towel and crouched down next to him. "Better?"

"I guess."

Grabbing Tim's ear, Denny tipped his head to the side. "You ever think about getting a tattoo?"

Wincing in discomfort, Tim eyed him. "A tattoo?"

"Yeah. Right there on your neck. Every fighter has a tattoo. Well, 'cept for Jude. Stubborn bastard, I could never talk him into it."

Rubbing his neck where Denny indicated, Tim said, "Do they tattoo necks?"

"The guys I know got everything but their peckers tatted up—and some of 'em got that done, too."

No way would he let anyone near his neck—or inside his pants—with tattooing in mind. Besides, didn't tattoos hurt? They were like . . . needles, right? Lots of needles. He shuddered at the thought. "I'm not a fighter."

"No shit. One look at that black and blue face, and anyone can see you don't know squat about defending yourself."

"There were two of them."

"Could be a crowd of ten, and you can bet Jude'd come out looking better than the rest. But yeah, he's good. Better'n most."

Jude, Jude, Jude. Tim was about sick of hearing him heralded.

Denny studied him. "Thing is, a really bitchin' tattoo would add some menace to your otherwise yellow skin." Laughing, he swatted Tim on the back, making him gasp in pain, then stretched back to his feet. "If you'd learn to carry yourself a little better, maybe get some confidence, you could pull it off. And then you wouldn't be such an easy mark for a beating, you know?"

Trying to stifle his groans, Tim lumbered to his feet and quickly wrapped the towel around his naked waist. "Are we done?"

"Quit asking me that. I'll tell you when we're done."

He groaned. "So what now?"

"We'll hit the sauna. You'll love it. In fact, I'll join you. I could use a good sweat." Catching the hem of his shirt, Denny pulled it up and over his head. As he walked away, he began unfastening his slacks.

In awe, Tim stared at his back. Atop the thick layers of muscles, Denny had a web of scars from surgeries and wounds alike, including what looked like a bullet hole.

Forgetting his own aches and pains, Tim awkwardly trotted to catch up. "Were you shot?"

"More'n once." Denny paused to kick off his shoes and peel away his socks. And just like that, he shoved down his slacks and underwear. "But that was during my misspent youth, before I started fighting for money instead of pigheadedness."

Intrigued, Tim followed on Denny's heels into the sauna and choked on the thick-as-butter steam. After he caught his breath again, he asked, "Is there much money in fighting?"

"Depends on whether or not you're any good. The purse can be a pittance, meaning you're fighting just for the experience and exposure, and maybe just because it's fun. Or it can be a fortune."

"Fun?"

"Damn right. I love it. And truth is, I did all right. Supported myself and packed away some savings. Now Jude, he raked in the dough. He has a knack for being the best at whatever he does."

Tim did not want to talk about Jude. The bastard had money falling out his ears, and a blind man would know he wanted May. But what did that get Tim? A lousy loan.

Denny threw a couple of towels onto the redwood benches. "Take a load off."

His mood spoiled, Tim wiped the sweat from his face and rolled his knotted shoulders. "It's so damn hot in here, I can barely breathe."

"It's good for you. Relieves stress and loosens up those damaged muscles." Buck naked, Denny sat on his towel and stretched out his legs. The fronts of his thighs had more scars and a really nasty, jagged white line ran from his knee to midway down his calf. "Now sit."

Tim sat. But after a minute, the silence got to him. "So tell me about some of your fights."

Denny's eyes didn't open and his head didn't move, but a smile curved his hard mouth. "My favorite was when I knocked a guy out in fifteen seconds. He'd been shooting off his mouth, saying he'd make me tap out."

"Tap out?"

Green eyes opened the tiniest bit. "Don't tell me you've never watched an SBC fight?"

Did he have to make that sound like a cardinal sin? "No."

"Huh." And then, with more interest, "I know what we'll be doing the rest of the day."

"May?"

The voice came to her from far away, disturbing the cozy, safe peace of her dreams. More relaxed than she could remember being in years, she sighed, then nestled further into the comforter.

"May," the voice said again, this time in a sing-song, teasing way.

She roused enough to open her eyes a little. She saw murky darkness and blurry images, but she breathed in the most delicious scent imaginable. The air on her face felt cool, while a cocoon of warmth held her body. She closed her eyes again.

"Wake up, honey."

She realized that she had her nose buried in

Jude's chest hair, and that her cheek rested on him. Her glasses were gone, so Jude must have removed them for her. "Why?"

Strong fingers tunneled through her hair, massaged her scalp. "Because I'm going to make love to you, and I don't want to be accused of taking advantage of your unconscious state."

Make love? That sounded promising. After a luxurious little stretch that slid flesh along flesh in a most tantalizing way, she asked, "What time is it?"

"Maybe five o'clock."

"Mmmm. It seems dark."

"I closed the drapes." His hand trailed along her spine to her behind and further down, until she froze in surprise. "I wouldn't wake you, except that Denny will have dinner ready soon, and anyway, I don't think I can wait much longer."

She tipped her head up to see him, but without her glasses, his expression remained a mystery. "I'm usually an insomniac."

"Maybe I've found a cure."

A little embarrassed, she said, "I can't believe I passed out like that."

His fingers continued to touch and explore, smoothing along her cheek, her upper thigh. He dipped lower—and touched her vulva from behind. "I thought it was nice," he said in a voice gone deep and smoky. "So don't expect me to complain."

A rush of heat and intensified feeling swelled inside her. Holding a rational thought became a challenge, but she didn't want him to know he could turn her to mush so easily. "Passed out women turn you on, huh?"

"You turn me on." He insinuated the tip of one finger past her lips, barely teasing, rasping slick, sensitized flesh.

Oh God. She needed two deep breaths before she could ask, "Did I snore?"

Ducking his head down, he kissed her softly. "I don't know. I fell asleep, too." His mouth touched hers again. "I don't usually sleep with women. Sleep, I mean."

"I know what you mean."

He turned his head, deepening the kiss and twining his tongue with hers for a long time. "I liked holding you, May," he said against her mouth. "You're warm."

More like red-hot.

Pressing closer to her, he said, "And now you're finally awake." The kiss that followed left her clutching at him, practically crawling on top of him.

A loud rap sounded at the door, startling a yelp out of her.

"Sorry, May," came Denny's booming voice, "but Jude has a call."

Jude lifted his head enough to say, "Take a message," as if he expected her to carry on with Denny looming right outside the room.

She gave him a shove that sent him to his back while she scrambled to get under the covers.

Jude whispered, "Calm down."

Without her glasses she could barely see, but they were both naked. In bed together. And now Denny knew exactly what they were doing. She pulled the comforter over her head.

Jude fell to his back with a curse. "Go away, Denny."

"It's your rep."

"Tell him to fuck off."

Denny laughed.

May groaned.

"He wants to know if you have a statement about

the movie deal you were offered. Everyone's hounding him to find out if you're going to agree to that action flick or not."

Jude muttered, "Shit," and then, a little louder, "tell him I'll call him back in an hour."

"You got calls from your publicist, too. Oh, and Uma Thurman wants to chat about a birthday bash in Santa Monica next month, and someone from *People* magazine is requesting an interview."

Speechless, May stayed under the covers. She was shocked down to the tips of her toes. Her stomach twisted into a knot. Dumb, dumb, dumb. For a little while there, she'd forgotten that Jude was a bona fide celebrity. A movie star. A man recognized by everyone.

He wasn't a mere denizen of Stillbrook.

He wasn't for her.

Jude tried to pull the covers away from her, and May choked out, "Don't."

Sighing, he called out, "Denny, no disrespect intended, but if you don't take a hike, I'm going to kick your ass."

Denny laughed again. "Okay, but dinner'll be done in twenty."

"Thanks. We'll be down soon."

The second Denny moved away from the closed door, Jude whipped the covers off May, leaving her completely bare. Her mind immediately did a comparison of Uma's slender, toned body. Her blond hair. Her poise and sophistication and stunning good looks.

In every way, May came out lacking.

For once, she was glad she couldn't see without her glasses. Jude's telling silence was humiliation enough.

To her surprise, he settled himself close beside

her. One hand covered her belly, and she felt his breath on her cheek when he said, "Now, where were we?"

He *couldn't* be serious. "This is a mistake."

Damp lips trailed up her throat to her ear. His tongue teased, dipping inside, before his lips nibbled on her earlobe.

When she trembled, he began another trek, leaving small, warm kisses along her tingling skin until he reached her mouth.

He touched his nose to hers. "You mean then or now? Because, woman, you're about two seconds away from being laid. Again."

He rolled atop her, easily nudged open her thighs, and somehow, maybe because she didn't do much resisting, slid into her with one long, deep thrust. "See?"

She couldn't think. Much. "What . . . What about protection?"

"Took care of it while you were cowering under the blankets."

Even though she couldn't see him well, she glared into his face. "I do not cower."

He kissed her, a lingering, tender kiss that somehow made her feel less foolish. "Prove it."

"How?" Okay, so he was a celebrity. So the beautiful and talented Uma Thurman had called him. So what?

Right now, for this instant in time, he was hers.

"You can start by telling me what you like."

Sliding her arms around his neck, she gave in to the delicious rhythm he initiated. "All right." When he hooked her knees, lifting her legs high to penetrate deeper, she moaned, *"That."* Oh God. "I like that."

Jude said, "Yeah?"

"Yeah." She gasped. "Oh, and that, too."

With a husky laugh, he teased, "And this?"

Lord have mercy. "Ummm . . . Oh! Sure." Feeling the start of her orgasm, May panted, squeezed tight, and just barely managed to whisper, "Why not?"

"Damn," Jude said, his breathing still harsh, his body damp with sweat. "I had twenty minutes and only used ten. I suck."

Heart pounding a furious beat, May said, "No, you were fabulous."

Jude grunted. "So speaks a woman who doesn't yet know fabulous. But tonight I'll get it right."

On her side, one leg over Jude's lap, her head again tucked against his shoulder, May asked, "Does that mean I'm to sleep with you tonight?"

"Every night." Jude stiffened. "Is that a problem?"

Not for her, but then why had he given her a room of her own? She said only, "I don't want to intrude."

His laugh dwindled into a groan. "I like the way you intrude. Feel free to keep it up."

Since he seemed to be in such a mellow, easy mood, and the dinner hour drew near, May worked up her nerve and said, "Jude?"

"Hmm?"

He'd returned his hand to her backside. The man did have a preoccupation with her posterior, and it wasn't conducive to calm discussion. "Can you stop that just a second?"

"No." He patted, stroked. "It's irresistible. Sorry."

Of all the idiotic . . . she let that go. "You had several stipulations that you expected me to agree to."

"Right." This time he gave her backside an affectionate squeeze. "I can't wait to show off this sexy bod in the right clothes."

His idea of "right clothes" was bound to differ from hers. But she'd have to tackle that hideous idea later. Right now, the thought of him drinking wine with dinner had her on edge. Knowing how dumb it was didn't help her to deal with it.

She girded herself, then blurted, "Well, I have a stipulation, too."

As if she'd goosed him hard, Jude flinched, then turned still as stone. One second later, he raised his head to glare down at her. "You don't get stipulations."

Of all the unfair baloney! "I insist that I do."

"No."

His dark frown and obvious suspicion unnerved her, but May held her ground. "If you expect me to abide by your rules, you'll have to abide by one of mine."

In a sudden rush, Jude shoved himself away from her to sit at the side of the bed. Elbows on his naked knees, head in his hands, he stewed.

His reaction might have bothered her more, but she was too busy appreciating the sight of his long, muscled back and taut flesh, all naked, and for the moment, all hers. Unable to help herself, she reached out and trailed her fingers down his spine.

Jude jerked around to stare at her. "All right, let's hear it."

His tone and attitude hit her the wrong way. "You don't have to be surly about it."

"Surly!" In a quick turnabout, he loomed over her, so close she could see the whiskers in his five o'clock shadow. "You're laying out ground rules?"

"So? You did the same."

Teeth locked, Jude said, "Tell me what you want."

"I want you to give up drinking."

His expression went comically blank. He blinked, studied her face. "Come again?"

In a burst of passionate expression, May came up to her elbows, forcing him to move back so they wouldn't clunk heads. "I'm sorry, but I *hate* it."

"It?"

Just thinking of it made her shudder, and she wrinkled her nose. "The awful smell, the sight, everything about it. Wine, beer, hard liquor, it all makes me ill. Literally. It makes my stomach churn. If you want me to stay here, if you want to continue with our . . ." She gestured at the bed.

Slowly, eyes piercing and direct, Jude closed the scant space between them, forcing her down again until his body squashed hers deliciously.

Her breasts flattened on the hard planes of his chest. One of his muscular thighs wedged between hers. His forearms framed her shoulders, his fists at either side of her head. Jaw tight, he said, "It's called a relationship."

She sniffed. "Is it?"

"Damn right." He looked livid again.

"Well, I wasn't sure. I haven't had that many intimate experiences."

If anything, that fired him up more. His nose touched hers. "The males in this area must be total buffoons for ignoring you."

His insinuation insulted her. "I haven't been ignored. I've been asked plenty of times, but I usually say no. I don't like smoking or drinking, and then, there's my family . . ."

"Everyone has family, May. Don't try to use them to send me packing."

Shock dropped her mouth open. "I wasn't!" Good God, didn't he realize just how imposing and impossible her family could be? He'd met Tim, for crying out loud. That should give him a clue.

"Good. Because you and I have something going on here."

Feeling her own dose of annoyance, May tried to shove him away. But like most stubborn mules, he didn't budge. "I need my glasses, damn it."

"Why?"

"Because I want to see you clearly while you say stupid things."

He hesitated, but then stretched until he could reach her glasses on the nightstand. "You're the only woman I know who seems to enjoy insulting me."

She took the glasses from him and slid them on. Looking into his gorgeous face, she said, "*You're* the one who claimed to just want in my pants."

"Yeah, so?" As defensive as a sinner, he added, "Now I've been in your pants, and I like it there. I want to get in your pants a whole lot more."

"Jude," she growled, warning him to knock it off.

He grinned. "Sorry. I like teasing you. I like being with you." He pressed his hips in, moving against her. "I like touching you and laughing with you. And I love making love to you. I don't want to stop doing any of the above any time soon."

"Oh."

"Can I get an amen?"

He'd sing a different tune once he met her folks, so why force the issue now? It'd be taken out of her hands soon enough. Why not keep the moment as pleasant as possible until then?

Pretending an indifference no sane woman would feel, May rolled her shoulder. "Sure."

Chastising her, he shook his head. "Gee, May, don't get all giddy or anything. I mean, I know you're enthusiastic, but let's don't go overboard."

The sarcasm annoyed her. What did he want—for her to jump up and down? For her to leave her heart exposed so he could trample it? "I wasn't expecting a relationship. I'm sorry. I'm not sure how to react."

With droll wit, Jude said, "I'm really not all that conceited, you know. You don't have to work on breaking down my male ego."

He wasn't conceited at all. Temperamental, sure. He had more mood swings than a premenstrual girl the night of the prom. But he was also protective and often patient, and so incredibly generous.

"In every way that counts," she told him, "you're exceptional."

For an extended time, their gazes held. Then Jude cupped her face, kissed her softly, and said, "So I can't drink. Anything else I can't do?"

"Badger me."

His grin went crooked. "I'll try. What else?"

"You don't smoke, do you?"

"God no."

She'd already known that but asked just for the heck of it. As a fighter, Jude was too into health to drag smoke into his lungs. "Will you mind giving up alcohol?"

"No."

He said it too fast for her peace of mind. "You're sure?"

"I'm not an alcoholic, May. I can take it or leave

it, and if it's that important to you, then it's important to me."

Her heart lodged in her throat making her eyes water. Before Jude, she hadn't known such a remarkable man existed. "Thank you."

Worry roughened his voice. "Is it because of Tim?"

She really didn't want to talk about her family while lying naked beneath him. "Can I just say that I've had experience with drunks, and it's not a pleasant thing?"

"Yeah." He stared at her a long time, making her wonder if he'd really let the subject go. Then he levered himself up, looked down at her sprawled body, and sighed. "I don't suppose you want to skip dinner?"

"No!" Laughing, May pushed him away and scrambled to sit up in the bed. "I already told you I'm not a starving starlet. And besides, it's going to be hard enough to face Denny as it is."

His gaze moved all over her, lingering in select places, reminding her that, while she might not look like Uma, he didn't have any complaints.

"Don't be embarrassed. We haven't done anything wrong."

Maybe he didn't think so, but May feared that, in Denny's mind, she'd be just one more groupie. Yet she respected Denny and didn't want him to think ill of her.

"May." Jude touched her chin and brought her face around to his. "There won't be any unfavorable judgments. Believe me."

Only half listening to him, she slid off the bed and lifted the now very wrinkled SBC shirt and shorts in dismay. "Please tell me dinner isn't formal."

He leaned forward and kissed her shoulder. "Denny doesn't have a formal bone in his body, and I prefer jeans any day."

"I wish I had time for a shower."

"Wonderful idea. We'll take care of that after dinner. Together." He bobbed his eyebrows—and considering he hadn't yet dressed, it was an impressive thing. "You'll love my shower."

"Let me guess—it's huge?"

"Big enough to house a family of gypsies. Now, get yourself dressed, comb your hair, whatever, and I'll meet you downstairs."

After scooping up his clothes, Jude disappeared into what May assumed to be a dressing room of sorts. A glance at the clock showed that they'd exceeded the twenty minutes Denny had allotted them. Groaning, she scrambled into the bathroom to do the quickest repair job in history.

Chapter 12

Jude paused in the kitchen doorway just in time to hear Tim say, "I don't know how I'm supposed to pay it back."

Sitting at the table, arms crossed, Denny shrugged. "So let's figure it out. You kept saying 'they,' as in more than one person. How many were there?"

To Jude's amazement, Tim seemed far less wary of Denny than he had just a few hours ago. He also looked better, with all the blood removed and much of the swelling gone down. Bruises colored his face, but he no longer looked so pained.

On top of that, Denny had mellowed his obvious contempt for Tim. They almost seemed to be . . . relating to each other. Weird.

"Three, I think," Tim answered. "A driver, the guy who pounded on me, and the one who called the shots."

"Only three, huh?"

Tim rolled his eyes at the obvious insult.

Scents of Denny's famous bourbon mustard chicken filled the air, making Jude's stomach rumble. "Sorry I'm late." He strode in, but since dinner remained on the stove, instead of on the table, he chose to lean against the counter.

Denny turned to him. "Well, hallelujah. 'Bout time you joined us. I thought I'd need to send in the National Guard." Frowning, he looked through the doorway and beyond, then threw up his hands. "Where's May?"

"She's on her way." He hoped. Denny could be a real pain in the ass about punctuality, a side effect of his own strict regimen.

Tim curled his lip. "Don't worry. She won't miss dinner."

Jude's temper sparked, until Denny said, "That'll cost you twenty laps."

"*What?*"

Pushing back his chair and heading for the stove, Denny added, "Right after dinner."

"That's bullshit!"

With a spoon in his hand, Denny turned. "Keep it up, and you'll spend all night in the pool."

Like a petulant boy, Tim slunk down in his chair. The frown, added to his bruises, made him look ghastly. But he didn't argue with Denny.

The interlude with May had refreshed Jude, and now he wanted to tackle some of the problems. "Were you supposed to contact the three men after I was dead?"

"I couldn't. I don't have a number or name or anything."

"Then how would you let them know you'd fulfilled your end of the bargain?"

Tim sank lower and kept his gaze on the tabletop. "They said if they didn't read your obit in the daily within a week, they'd be coming after me."

Denny reached for a bottle of wine, and Jude said, "Let's have tea." He made a mental note to have Denny get rid of all the booze in the house. If something upset May, then out it'd go. And that included her drunken sot of a brother.

They shared a look, and Denny nodded. "That's what I was thinking, too. I've got some fresh tea in the fridge." He set out the pitcher and four tall glasses. "Describe the men, Tim."

"I can't. It was dark."

"So?" One by one, food-filled dishes occupied the tabletop in pleasing array. Potatoes, rolls, asparagus, and lastly, the chicken. Denny did have a thing about making the most of the dinner presentation. "You still have to have some sense of whether or not they were big men or runts, if they had deep voices or any type of accent."

"I don't know."

"Think about it, damn it. You've got a brain—least I think you do." Denny glanced at the still empty doorway, then his watch, his impatience palpable.

May came bustling up to the doorway. Smiling, Jude again noted how she jiggled and bounced in such a pleasing way, as if energy and life just sparked off her. She'd pulled her hair back in a high ponytail that added emphasis to her rosy cheeks and kiss-swollen lips.

The dinner no longer smelled as good, and his previously raging appetite took a sharp turn from food to sex. With May so damn cute and beddable, and *available*, how could he think of anything but her?

"Sorry I'm late!"

Jude noticed right off that she'd put the hideous bra back on, but all things considered, he supposed he shouldn't complain. By tomorrow, he'd have new clothes for her to wear—including lingerie.

He could hardly wait.

"You're right on time," Denny told her, and he smacked Tim in the side of the head, forcing him to stand until after Jude had seated her. "Manners, boy. I'll beat them into you if I have to."

May looked ready to protest that, so Jude took out her chair and updated her on their conversation. "We were just discussing the men who jumped your brother."

"What about them?"

Jude pushed in her chair, and then seated himself beside her. "Obviously, it was dark, but I was just about to tell Tim that the way a man speaks can reveal a lot about him. Did the men sound like thugs, or were they smoother than that?"

With shaking hands, Tim lifted his napkin and arranged it in his lap. He cleared his throat, fidgeted in his seat, and kept looking at May with mixed accusation and entreaty.

Disgusted, Jude slapped his hands down on the table. "I asked you a question, Tim. May isn't going to answer it for you."

Busy serving herself potatoes from the bowl Denny passed her, May glanced up as if only then realizing her brother's dilemma. Stewed potatoes held aloft, she blinked. "I wasn't even there, Tim. I didn't hear them speak."

Jude hated the apology in her tone. But he had enough sense not to try to sever her protective streak toward her brother. Her relationship with

her family was something she'd have to deal with
in her own way.

But he did intend to help.

"Come on, Tim. You must remember something."

"They were big, I guess." Tim rubbed his brow.
"I know I felt squashed between them in the backseat. One of the men had a deep voice, but . . . sort
of . . . I don't know. Cultured. Soft. He enjoyed
hurting me, I know that."

Denny glared at Jude. "Sound like anyone we
know?"

"Many people, actually." Sure, Elton had men
working for him who had affected a smooth way of
talking—but that didn't incriminate him in any
way. "It's not much to give the cops."

"Cops?" Going rigid in his seat, Tim turned his
panicked gaze on May. "But we agreed—"

"You're not the only one involved, Tim." She
passed the platter of chicken to Jude. "When Jude
decides the time is right, we'll need the police as
backup. But it's his decision."

"Why his? I'm the one who got smashed."

"He's the one they want dead."

Everyone ignored Tim's heartfelt groans.

"Elton wouldn't show up in person," Denny
speculated aloud. "Not for a beating. But it could
be his boys."

"His boys?" May asked.

"The bastard has a string of lowlifes working for
him. He fancies himself a modern-day mafioso."

"Oh, great. This gets worse by the second," Tim
complained.

"First thing we need to figure out is how the hell
to repay the loan—"

Tim's cell phone rang, startling everyone at once.

May gulped down the bite of potato in her mouth. Jude pushed his plate aside. And Tim, struggling to his feet, fumbled his flip phone from his pocket.

He was about to open it to receive the call when Denny snatched it out of his hand.

"Let's put it on speakerphone, so we can all hear." Smiling with evil intent, Denny added, "And pretend you're alone, Tim. Answer questions the right way. Or by God, regardless of what Jude wants, I'll toss your ass to the curb."

To keep May from interfering, Jude squeezed her shoulder. But truthfully, she looked impressed with Denny's believable bluster. Did she know it was all hot air?

Denny opened the phone, hit a button to put the call on loudspeaker, and handed it back to Tim.

In the spotlight, Tim paled, but he said into the phone, " 'Lo?"

"Tim, Tim, Tim. You still alive, you miserable fuck?"

Squeezing his eyes shut, Tim asked, "Who is this?"

"You owe me some money. Or have you accomplished the payback without me knowing?"

"Uh, no." As if to draw strength, Tim's gaze locked on May's. "No, I haven't."

"I don't want details, but when do you plan to do it?"

"I, ah, I'm going to pay the money back instead."

An awesome silence fell, then anger ripped the air. *"What the fuck are you talking about?"*

Tim nearly dropped the phone. "The . . . the fifty thousand. I'll pay it."

"Where'd you get it? Did you go crying to that know-it-all sister of yours? She planning to sell everything? Well, forget it. You don't have that kind of time."

With Denny prompting him through whispers, Tim asked, "Um . . . how much time *do* I have?"

"Tomorrow. Think you can handle that?"

Jude nodded at Tim, so he said, "Yes, I can handle it."

Another shocked silence, and then in a vicious growl, "You better not be fucking with me."

Tim looked ready to throw up, until Denny gave him a slight shove. "No, no, I'm not. I wouldn't. I swear." He swallowed audibly. "Where should I send the money?"

"Send it? I don't think so, Tim. I want it hand delivered to me, by you, at midnight tomorrow."

Jude and Denny glanced at each other, shrugged, and nodded to Tim.

With palpable dread, Tim whispered, "Where?"

"I'll call you in the morning to give you directions." And the phone went dead.

Breathing hard, shaken down to her bones, May said, "Oh my God. This is awful. What are we going to do?"

To her amazement, Jude picked up his fork and cut into his chicken. "We're going to eat, then I'm going to return some calls and arrange for the loan papers and money to be here first thing in the morning."

Her mouth fell open. "You can't just . . . *eat.*"

"I'm sure as hell not going to let this meal go to waste."

Looking for help, she turned to Denny. But as if the awful phone call hadn't happened, he dug into his food.

When he realized she stared at him in horror, he nodded at her plate. "Go on, taste it. I'm a damn fine cook, and I'm waiting for appropriate praise from you."

With no one else to share her angst, May looked at her brother. He seemed as shell-shocked as she felt. "Tim, are you okay?"

Tim opened his mouth, but Denny snorted. "Course he is. A man doesn't let one stupid phone call destroy his appetite." He glanced at Tim, eyes narrowed, and said, "Ain't that right, Tim?"

To her further stupefaction, Tim muttered, "Yeah," and though his hands trembled, he picked up his fork and started eating.

May threw down her napkin. "You are all certifiable."

While chewing, Jude sent her a sideways look. One eyebrow cocked, he put his fork on her plate, cut off a steaming bite of chicken, and held it to her mouth.

"Try it," he urged. "You'll see that enjoying Denny's cooking is better than fretting over some yahoos too dumb to realize they're about to get their asses kicked."

When she opened her mouth to argue, Jude stuck the chicken in. May had no choice but to eat it. With Denny's anxious gaze on her, she said, "Yes, it's delicious."

"Damn right." Proud as a peacock, he said, "Told you you'd like it."

"But, Jude—"

"It's the dark brown sugar, the Dijon, and just a *little* bourbon," Denny enthused, "that makes it so tender."

Her idiot brother nodded his approval while stuffing his face. "Juicy."

"Thanks, Tim."

May stared until Jude caught her chin and turned her face toward him. "I already told you, I'm not going to let anyone hurt Tim or you."

"And what about you?"

Denny snorted. "Don't go insulting him like that, May. Jude can handle himself."

Reluctantly, Tim said, "You should see him fight."

"I've seen."

"You have?"

Exasperated, she stared at Jude. His cavalier attitude made no sense. "He's good. But that's different from this."

Disregarding the others in the room, Jude leaned forward and kissed her. "Don't fret, May. I'll take care of everything." And with a pinch to her chin, he murmured, "Remember, I'm Jude Jamison."

Meaning what? That he was impervious to pain? That he possessed supernatural powers that made him invincible?

Then logic kicked in, and she relaxed a little. Jude Jamison was a rich man. A man of incredible influence. He could *buy* safety, at least to a degree. If he hired bodyguards, and security men, and maybe a private eye or two to expose the ones making the threats, that'd go a long way toward ensuring the safety of everyone involved.

But why wouldn't Jude just come right out and say so, if that was his intent?

His plate now half empty, Tim leaned forward on his elbows. "Denny and I watched a lot of DVDs. Bloody stuff. But I liked it."

Laughing, Denny gave Tim an affectionate slug in the shoulder. "He says he liked it now, but when King got his leg broke in two places, I thought old Tim here was gonna barf."

Tim made a face. "The man tried to keep fighting with his knee bent the wrong way."

"Of course he did. He knew his corner would throw in the towel, so why should he tap out?"

Despite herself, May got pulled into the conversation. "I remember that one. He tried to deny he was hurt when everyone could see the breaks. He ended up with months of rehab."

"He's back now," Denny said, "and stronger than ever."

"But he'll be up against Rico. He's going to get his butt kicked, if you ask me."

Jude smiled, while Denny lifted both eyebrows in surprise. "We've got a few more fights to watch. Maybe you'd like to join us in the theater while Jude makes his calls?"

Mention of the calls sent jealousy searing through May. After all, he'd be chatting with Uma Thurman, and that was enough to make any average woman green.

With everyone watching her, May didn't dare show her resentment toward the other woman. Instead, she cut into her chicken and said, "I'd love to." And to foster the blasé attitude, she added, "Pass the salt, please."

Given the looks she received, she knew she hadn't fooled anyone. Well, except maybe Tim. But then fooling a fool wasn't much of a challenge.

Not one to give into fatigue, Ashley smiled her way through the remainder of her shift at the restaurant. After her classes and a couple of grueling tests, waiting tables for a few hours felt like a breeze. Already she'd gotten over sixty bucks in tips.

She only worked at the restaurant on a very

part-time basis, picking up hours here and there around her class schedule and her maintenance job at the business complex. What she made at the upscale establishment rounded out her income.

Tonight the place was packed, so the time passed quickly. In less than an hour, she'd head off for her other job—and maybe run into Quinton Murphy again.

Her heart jumped a beat, and she mentally smacked herself.

Pffft. What was she thinking? So she'd bumped into the man one time? That didn't mean it'd happen again. She didn't *want* it to happen again. She really didn't.

But in the back of her mind, she kept thinking about the possibility, what he'd say, what she'd say. How he'd look, and those super-nice green eyes of his.

Stupid.

Shoving Quinton out of her mind—again—she headed back to the floor to a table where the hostess had just seated several men. They were a rowdy-looking lot, flashy in the way of men unused to their money, the kind that still liked to flaunt it in the most obnoxious ways.

She saw all kinds, and enjoyed most, but the phony ones drove her nuts.

In the restaurant's requisite white blouse and trim black slacks, she would have felt blah. But she'd countered the no-hue outfit with a sparkly lipstick and dangling beaded earrings. Soon as her shift ended, she'd exchange the white blouse for her beaded tank top in an animal print embellished with gold flecks. A little fancy—but she loved it.

To her mind, clothes that made her feel good

didn't need a special occasion. Besides, making money was the best occasion of all, worthy of a good shirt. And she liked the flash of the top under the florescent lights at the office building where she worked.

It had nothing to do with Quinton.

As she came up behind the table, she heard one man mutter, "I can't wait to see the cocky son of a bitch finished. He'll never know what hit him. It's perfect."

The man across the table spotted her and nodded to alert the others to her presence. Not that Ashley paid them much mind. Most of the executives who came to eat spent their time complaining about one thing or another, usually a colleague. These men didn't look much like execs, but who knew?

"Good evening, gentlemen." The hostess had already given them drinks and menus. "I'm Ashley, and I'll be your waitress tonight."

The loud, insulting one sized her up. Built like a squat refrigerator, his blond hair a bit too long and styled, his smile too lingering, he stood out from the others as the obvious leader of the pack. "Well, hello, Ashley."

She pretended not to hear the smarmy way he said that. "Our soup tonight is baked French onion. A light beef broth with caramelized onions and—"

"We don't want soup."

"Ooookay." She raised her brows in polite inquiry. "Would you like to order now, or do you need a little more time?"

Displaying a distinct lack of manners, he continued to slide his gaze all over her. He sucked at one tooth, then brought his attention to her face. "The steaks any good here?"

Ash plastered on her most brilliant smile and launched into the rehearsed description of the steaks. "The absolute best. We serve only Kobe beef, which is extraordinarily tender, finely marbled, and full flavored. We have a New York strip, a rib eye, and if you're really hungry, I'd recommend the T-bone."

"I'm hungry all right." His gaze wandered to her nonexistent boobs and back to her face again. "I'll take the T-bone."

"How would you like it prepared?"

"I want it still kicking."

"Rare it is. And to go with it?"

"A good-lookin' woman would do."

What an ass. "Sorry. That's only on the breakfast menu."

He glanced around the posh interior of the restaurant with confusion. "This place serves breakfast?"

"No." They opened for lunch, but not before then.

Unamused, he bared his teeth in a parody of a grin. "How about you? When does your shift end?"

"Any minute now. So I better get these orders turned in."

The men all guffawed, and finally, Blondie chimed in. But he didn't fool Ashley. Her lack of response pissed him off.

Making it a point to move around the table—away from Blondie—she finished taking orders. With the promise of prompt service, she started to make her escape.

She'd gone only a few feet when she heard one of the men change the subject. "Did you call him again?"

"Not yet. I'm letting the aches and pains sink in first. A little form of incentive to make sure he gets the job done right."

Aches and pains? The job? Struck with a terrible foreboding, Ashley stopped dead in her tracks. But she had no reason to linger, and doing so might make her look suspicious. When the men said nothing more, she checked on a diner, smiled at another, and moved away as casually as she could manage.

Apprehensive, she darted around the tables to the kitchen and turned in her order. She didn't want to raise any doubts by delivering the meal late.

Praying no one would notice, she trotted to the break room. She didn't carry her phone while working—management forbade private calls on the floors, and you never knew when it might ring. But she opened her locker in a flash, yanked the phone from her purse, and smiling at Denny's cunning, pushed the number two button.

Denny answered on the first ring. "Problem?"

Obviously, for Denny to know who was calling, her name had popped up with her number. "Maybe."

Brisk and businesslike, he demanded, "Where are you?"

"It's okay, I'm fine."

"Where?"

He needed to work on that surly temper. "I'm at the restaurant where I work." She didn't know how to pose the question without just asking it. "Can you describe that Elton Pascal dude that Jude doesn't like?"

"Why?"

"I overheard a conversation from some men that's got me curious."

Denny asked no more questions. "He's in his early forties. Stocky. Blonde. Slick. A real asshole."

"Huh."

"What the hell does that mean, girl?"

"It means . . ." Ashley drew in a breath, praying she wasn't wrong. "Well, he might be here. In town. In the restaurant. With some other bulky guys, all ordering steak."

"Shit." She could practically hear Denny thinking. "When did he get there?"

"A few minutes ago. I just turned in his order. What should I do?"

"Stay the hell away from him."

"I'm his waitress."

"Fine. Serve him food. But don't flirt, don't argue, and definitely don't be alone with him."

Insulted, she said, "Did I strike you as the type to go off alone with jerks?"

"I mean it, child."

"I'm not a child," she pointed out.

"Do *not* get stubborn with me now."

"All right, all right." Amazing how he could bring her to near laughter no matter what. "Keep your shorts on."

"Does May know where you work? Can she give me directions there?"

"Sure, but you don't need to—"

"Be careful. And call if he starts to leave. I'll go tell Jude right now."

"Wait. I don't want to alarm anyone—" The line went dead. Ashley glared at the hapless phone, then clicked it shut and stowed it away. "Stupid men," she grumbled to herself.

Wouldn't it be just like Jude or Denny to come charging to the restaurant, fists in the air, tempers crackling, when it probably wasn't even the right guy?

But that menacing voice, and the implied threat . . . she shivered.

Striding back to the kitchen, she peeked out at the dining room floor. The men had just finished off their drinks, so she had to go check on them.

It couldn't be this easy. She couldn't have the source of all the trouble lounging at one of her tables. If he did turn out to be the same creep, she'd feel like a hero. Jude would be able to get rid of him and the threat. And then he could toss Tim out of his house, and with any luck at all, Jude and May would be able to form a lasting relationship.

May deserved that—and more.

Calculating her next move, Ash glanced at her watch. In another half hour, she'd have to clock out. It took her about twenty minutes to get to the office complex, and she had almost an hour between the end of one job and the start of the other. Surely she could figure out his identity by then.

If nothing else, he'd probably pay with a credit card. As long as she didn't have to leave before he finished his meal . . . She prodded the chef. "Can you hurry it along a little?"

Temperamental in the extreme, but also a major flirt, he grinned shamelessly and said, "For you, Ashley-my-love, anything." He added the caramelized shallot port wine butter to the last T-bone, arranged a stuffed tomato "just so" beside it, and put the last plate on the tray. "Here you go."

The hefty tray weighed a ton, but practice had taught her to balance it with ease. The folding stand hooked over her arm, the tray in the air, Ashley made her way back to the table. She couldn't deny her nervousness, or her anticipation. She just hoped she hadn't stirred Denny up over nothing.

Chapter 13

As Jude laughed into the phone, saying, "Now, Uma, you know I'm not like that," he clicked on yet another outfit, adding it to his online order of clothes for May. She might not admit it right off, but she'd love his choices.

Everything from comfortable jeans and colorful tees to flirty sundresses and career clothes that would better suit her lush figure would all arrive tomorrow, thanks to special overnight shipping.

To go with the clothes, he'd order strappy sandals, cute flip-flops, and a pair of sneakers. Purses, belts, and a lightweight jacket rounded out the selections. His favorite outfit, a tiered pink cami and cropped jeans, would make her look luscious. Once he got her in the clothes, he'd take her out to dinner and show her off.

"Yeah, I'm here," he said to Uma. "I'm hanging on your every word." He laughed with her, and at that moment, a shadow moved past the open doorway—a shadow that somehow resembled May's shorter, rounder figure.

Deciding to investigate, Jude left his chair to stride across the carpeted library. He reached the hall just in time to see May tiptoeing toward the bedroom across from his.

Over an hour ago, he'd left her with Denny and Tim, watching old SBC tapes and DVDs. For a while, he'd lingered with them, impressed with her knowledge of grappling and ground skills. Almost as soon as the announcer noticed a fighter's intent, May saw it. She recognized the setup for an arm bar or an ankle pick, a reversal or a rear naked choke. She called the takedowns before they happened and celebrated a win seconds before it could be announced. She knew the difference between Aikido martial arts and Capoeira martial arts, between Freestyle and Greco-Roman wrestling. She favored Muay Thai boxing and scoffed at Karate.

She was, in so many ways, an amazing woman. Rather than watch the fights, Jude watched her watching the fights.

Covering the phone so he wouldn't interrupt Uma's story, he said, "May."

She stiffened, then turned to face him with a frown. "What?" she whispered.

"Come here." Uma finished her dialogue, and Jude replied to her while holding his hand out to May.

Reluctantly, May came to him, and he put his arm around her, drawing her into his side and into his library.

To Uma, he said, "I'll have to let you know about the party." He returned to his chair, tugged May into his lap, and added, "I've got my hands full here right now." To prove his point, he filled his hand with her rump.

May punched him in the shoulder, almost making him laugh. The way she perched on his thigh, all prim and proper, had very improper ideas going through his head. In one more minute, he'd be hard, and he hadn't even kissed her yet.

"No, Uma, I swear. I haven't accepted the role. I'm not sure I will. I'm in no hurry to get back into acting." He grinned. "Of course I'd tell you. Yeah, you, too, hon. Bye." He laid the phone on the desk.

Arms crossed, back straight, May stared away from him.

He caught her chin on the edge of his fist and drew her face toward his. "Why were you sneaking around my hallway?"

With the stoniest glare he'd ever gotten from her, May said, "I wasn't sneaking."

"You were on your tiptoes," he pointed out.

"I didn't want to disturb your conversation with *Uma.*"

Jealousy dripped from her tone. He smiled at how she said Uma's name, with such a sneer. "She's a friend, May. When others in Hollywood relished my trial, she stood behind me."

"She did?"

"She's a really terrific lady."

Her mouth flattened, and she said nothing.

"Did you see her in *Kill Bill?*"

Again, she looked away. "Yes."

"Did you like it?"

She checked out a fingernail. "Yes."

"Much?"

"A lot, okay? I saw it twice."

Laughing, Jude hugged her until she squealed, and then he kissed her—and didn't want to stop kissing her.

She went soft and warm on him, relaxing back

in his arms when he trailed kisses from her mouth to her jaw and her ear. "I've finished my phone calls," he said against her throat, loving the scent of her, how she felt on his lap. "Want to go play around?"

"I don't know—" Her breath hitched as he cupped her breast. "Okay, maybe."

He resented the barrier of her bra, but he still found her nipple with his thumb, and she still trembled from the touch. "Do you know what I want to do to you, May?"

Full of heightened anticipation, she shook her head. "What?"

"You like when I suck on you here?" He tugged at her nipple and she moaned. Moving his hand down her waist, and then between her thighs, he cupped her mound. She made a small sound of excitement and opened her knees. Searching with his fingertips, he stroked over her, following the seam of the soft shorts, and then—"Ah. Right here."

"*Jude.*" She breathed his name.

"You'll like when I have my mouth on you here," he promised her. "Sucking on you. Licking you."

"Oh God."

Footsteps pounded up the stairs. "Jude!"

"Jesus." Jude pulled May upright. He barely had time to slide the chair under his desk to hide his boner before Denny appeared in the doorway.

He took one look at the two of them and said, "Shit, I'm sorry. But Ashley called."

"Oh no." May tried to scramble off his lap.

Jude held onto her; he needed her for cover. "What is it?"

Looking from one to the other, Denny pulled at his ear, looked behind himself to make sure Tim hadn't followed, and finally, cleared his throat.

"She's working at some fancy restaurant—the child works too much and that's all there is to it—and she overheard a conversation that she thinks . . . Well, she thinks she might be serving none other than Elton Pascal."

Jude's brain couldn't assimilate such a thing. "Here? In Ohio?"

"She described the guy and yeah, it sounds like him."

"What did she hear?"

Denny put his hands on his hips. "Hell, I don't know. Does it matter? She said it sounded fishy, so I believed her. He'd already ordered his dinner, so I figured we didn't have much time to waste on questions." He glanced at May again, at her position on Jude's lap, and the way his arms were around her. He cleared his throat. "I think maybe I'll just run down there and check it out—"

"The hell you will." Elton Pascal. In Ohio. Jude shook his head. If it proved to be true, it could only mean one thing.

Already in battle mode, primed, hard, more than ready, he lifted May to her feet. "I'm going."

May clutched at him. "Are you both nuts?"

He paid her no mind. "Where's the restaurant?"

Denny shrugged. "She said May knew, that she could give us directions there."

They both looked to May.

She puckered up in indignation. "Oh no, I'm not telling you a thing." She crossed her arms tight around herself. "Forget it."

Not in the mood for games, Jude towered over her. "Give me the name of the restaurant, May."

"*No.* This is insane. You can't just go charging down there—"

She yelped in surprise when he caught her

upper arm and started out the door with her, hustling her along to his room. They had a few things to clear up, and it'd be better done in private.

"Unhand me right now!"

His jaw locked. "Patience, honey."

Calling after him, Denny said, "I'll pull the Porsche around to the front."

"Thanks."

May said, "You have a Porsche? I thought you drove a Mercedes Benz."

"I have both. Six cars, actually. The Porsche is black, so better for tonight."

"*Six?*"

Unwilling to be sidetracked, especially by a discussion on his indulgence with cars, Jude hauled May into his room. He turned and pinned her against the closed door. Her eyes were wide, her glasses a little crooked, her lips trembling. A few days ago, he'd have taken that look for fright, but not anymore. He had the awful feeling that nothing much scared May, most definitely not him.

"No time for games, May."

In a mere whisper, she said, "This isn't a game."

"No time for your mothering or your lack of trust, either."

"It is *not* about trust."

"The hell it isn't."

Looking very put out, she muttered, "Your reputation for a cool head is grossly exaggerated."

Of all the—

His nose almost touched hers, making her eyes go impossibly wide. "If Elton is here, then it's to cause me grief. You told me you wanted me to have a chance to deal with it. Well, now's my chance."

"Not like this."

"Exactly like this." He cupped her face. "Hell, he's probably hoping I'll call out the cops and make a big scene. Then he can trot out his alibis and whatever trumped-up excuse he has for being here, and he'll make me look like a fool. It's what he does."

He had to kiss her, but he kept it quick and shallow, letting the surge of emotion strengthen his hostility toward Pascal. He'd see the bastard face to face. And he'd make himself very clear.

"Then he's probably hoping you'll show up."

"Possibly. But he won't expect me to confront him alone. So far, I've ignored him, and that makes him nuts. He wants me to react. He's continually prodded and insulted me, trying to make it happen. By involving you, he's gone too far. He'll finally get what he wants, but on my terms, not his."

"Your terms?"

"I'll see him *mano a mano*. The chickenshit bastard won't expect that. He's not big on confrontations, not when he can usually skulk around, ordering the dirty work for someone else to do. But when I push him into a corner, he'll be too proud to turn me down. He won't want his hirelings to see him as a coward. The conversation will be ours alone—and it'll be a conversation he won't forget." Tunneling his fingers in close to her skull, he added, "That is, if you'll *give me the fucking directions.*"

Her soft expression pinched into disapproving lines and she shoved him away. "Do *not* use that language with me." Needlessly, she straightened her glasses. "I can show you."

"*Show* me?" He must have heard that wrong.

Her chin lifted. "I'm going, too."

"Jesus, Joseph, and Mary." Jude threw up his

hands. Just the thought of her getting anywhere near Elton sucked the breath from his lungs and sent rage roaring through him. He vibrated with menace, with an explosive need to shield and protect.

He tried to hold himself back but couldn't. Shoving his face down close to hers, he ground out, *"You're staying here."*

"Don't yell at me."

Her calm only amplified his turbulence. "Then don't talk stupid!"

"So now I'm stupid?" Her eyes narrowed while she waited for his response.

God, he hated those double-bladed swords women flung out with great regularity. They both knew that no matter what he said, she'd give him hell. But screw it.

Jude planted his feet. "If you think for one second I'll take you along, then damn right."

"Apparently, I'm smarter than you, because at least I know you need someone there for backup."

"You?" he asked, so incredulous he nearly choked.

"Yes, me. I'll stay out of sight but have my cell phone ready. I could call the cops if need be. Or I could lay on the horn if things go wrong. Or—"

"You," he said, pointing a shaking finger at her, but words failed him. He could see the stubbornness, the worry in her dark eyes, and he didn't know how to convince her, didn't know what else he could say. Time slipped away. Elton wouldn't spend all night dining. The bastard had revenge on his mind, not food.

Hands on top of his head, Jude gave May his back. Sickened by the turn of events, by the possibility of a lost opportunity, he went cold. "I guess you were right, after all."

Uncertainty ebbed into her militant tone. "About?"

"Us being all wrong for each other." The icy cold spread, lending him a false composure. He laughed and dropped his hands. "I thought I could get you to trust me, that you'd be a little different, but . . ." He shook his head and, with a huff of disgust, started out past her.

She grabbed his arm. "Jude, wait. I told you this wasn't about trust."

He looked first at her hand on his arm, far too small to encircle his biceps, a delicate contrast to his iron strength.

Yet she wanted to lead him around by his nose.

He looked next into her eyes, eyes so dark and compelling they could eat a man alive. "I'm not your brother. I don't need you guarding me and coddling me. I don't need you giving me orders and telling me how to run my life."

Shocked, she dropped her hand and took a step back. "I didn't."

"You want to run the show, honey? Fine. Go find yourself some wimp who gets off on that shit." His jaw flexed in frustration. "I don't." And he walked out.

He got halfway down the hall when her running footsteps sounded behind him. "Jude?"

Refusing to look at her, he said, "Call the cops, May. Send them on a wild goose chase. Me, I'm going to go take a swim."

"But . . . if that's Elton . . ."

"There's nothing I can do about it, is there? Not with you making all the decisions." Hand on the top railing to the stairs, he waited.

Jude thought he could hear the rhythmic thumping of her heart, feel her indecision fluttering against him. That he wanted to turn and pull her close and hug and console her only pissed him off more.

He had every right to be annoyed with her. His grievances were legit. So why did he feel like such a bastard?

Light as a breath, May's hand touched his shoulder. "It'll take you twenty minutes at least to get there."

The tension ebbed out of him. One small battle, but an important one if he had any chance of keeping her safe. Unwilling to look at her, to risk being trapped by the caring and hurt in her gaze, he nodded. "Tell me quick."

"There are some side streets. You'll need to write them down." Dejected, she went back to his room. Jude followed, watching as she sat on the edge of the bed, her hands together, her head lowered.

Aware of the minutes slipping away, he didn't dare take the time to pacify her. He scrounged in the nightstand drawer for a pad and pen and handed them to her. "Write it out for me."

While she did that, he changed into black jeans and a black pullover. When she handed him the paper, he'd already finished dressing.

Hesitating only a second, he touched her cheek and smoothed his thumb over her mouth. "I'll be back as quick as I can."

She turned her head away.

The silent treatment? Did that mean he'd have to sleep alone that night? Like hell. He'd fix things with her after he got back. "Try not to worry too much."

"I'll worry if I want to."

Shaking his head, Jude said, "Suit yourself." He went out of the room and down the stairs at a trot. Denny stood at the open front door. "Took you long enough."

"There's a woman in the house."

"Oh yeah." Denny frowned in comprehension, and then nodded his head toward a monitor. "Someone's out there."

What now? Striding to the monitor to take a look for himself, Jude said, "So there is."

"*Who?*"

Jude had expected May to continue sulking in his room. He should have known better than to second-guess anything about her.

Barreling down the stairs, hastened by her continued fretting, she said again, "Who's out there?"

"Recognize him?" Denny asked Jude.

"The photographer. Ed Burton. I had a small run-in with him at May's gallery."

Against his back Jude felt the rounded curves of May's body as she struggled to see the monitor past him. Already on edge, his awareness at an acute level, he absorbed every nuance of her touch.

Hands braced on his shoulders, she breathed near his ear. "What is he doing here?"

Hoping for a reconciliation, Jude reached back and curled his fingers over her hip. She froze before easing herself away.

He pretended not to notice, just as he pretended not to be disappointed. "He hangs around, hoping for the ideal photo. It's not a biggie. In fact . . ." He ran through a few scenarios in his mind and smiled. "He might actually come in handy today."

The sun hadn't yet set, but it hung low in the sky, sending rays of crimson along the horizon and emphasizing the shadows of early evening. Outside, at the end of the entry walkway, his black Porsche purred.

Stepping out the door and onto the porch, he said, "Keep an eye on her, Denny."

"You betcha."

May ran out after him. "Jude?"

She sounded angry again, so he kept his back to her.

"Please . . . be very careful."

Not mad. He didn't want to admit the relief he felt. He gave one nod, strode to the car, and without a backward glance, shifted into gear and headed for Ed Burton. He had a deal to offer, one that the photographer surely wouldn't turn down.

Bolstered by new hope and anticipation, Tim ducked behind the interior wall. No one had seen him or heard him; they didn't know he'd listened in. They'd all been too anxious about someone named Elton Pascal being in town.

Was he the man who'd ordered him to be beaten, the one who wanted Jude dead? They all seemed to think so, May especially. And Jude, the idiot, wanted to play the hero and run off to meet the man alone. Tim couldn't fathom that kind of stupidity. But then, he didn't have Jude's skills.

After watching so many fights where Jude had knocked out, immobilized, or otherwise forced a tap out to defeat all his opponents, Tim couldn't help but be intrigued. What an ego boost it'd be, taking a man down with one blow. *Pow.* Just like that. A jab to the chin and it was over.

Or to control a muscle-bound hulk until he became as helpless as a child, twisting a limb to the breaking point, forcing another man to surrender. It made Tim's blood rush just to imagine being that strong, that in control.

Jude continued to take great pleasure in insulting him, but Denny claimed he had the tools. All he needed was the training. Denny had hinted that he wouldn't mind teaching him. If he ever got as good as Jude, he wouldn't let anyone boss him around. Not his dad, not some bullyboy with an attitude. Definitely not his know-it-all, self-righteous sister.

He wouldn't need May at his back, constantly running his life, treating him like a weak child.

Wouldn't that knock the wind out of her? Tim grinned imagining it. She'd have to respect him. He could show her . . .

But what was he thinking? He couldn't fight worth a damn, and right now, he wasn't even sure he'd live out the rest of the week.

Unless he could turn this whole situation to his advantage. Mentally rubbing his hands together, Tim thought out his plan.

If Pascal hated Jude enough to want him dead, maybe, just maybe, his position in Jude's house would be worth something. He could spy, as he'd done tonight. He could supply Pascal with useful information on Jude, ways to hurt him, maybe financially or socially, that wouldn't involve the awful risk of being murdered.

Some men were worth more alive than they were dead. Tim prayed that might be the case for him. He shouldn't have to suffer just because of Jude.

Next time the man called, maybe he'd be alone. And then he'd put the proposition to him. It was worth a try. And it was no more than Jude deserved.

Chapter 14

As he leaned against his car in the restaurant parking lot, Jude kept his pose casual. No one looking at him would know what he really had on his mind. He'd gone inside only long enough to let Ashley see him and to verify Pascal's identity.

And now he waited.

A few cars down, Ed Burton hid with his camera at the ready and a high-tech microphone hooked to his recorder. The photographer had proved more than agreeable to Jude's suggestion. Now, with the sun already set and the night dark, he had everything in place.

Was May still pissed at him? Probably. She had a stubborn streak that took him by surprise. But he didn't mind. When he finished this business, he'd make it up to her in bed. Before they curled up to sleep, she wouldn't have a single complaint with him.

The door to the restaurant opened, causing Jude to tighten in anticipation, but Ashley came out, not Elton. She searched the area, spotted him, and started in his direction. Shit. What the hell was she thinking?

Before she could reach him, Jude turned and moved deeper into the lot, out of range of the lights. Ashley followed, but she had the good sense not to call out his name. As soon as he found a heavily shadowed, obscure spot between two trucks, Jude trained his gaze back on the front door. He didn't want to miss Elton's departure. Everything hinged on him getting the man alone.

"Jude?" he heard in a low, feminine whisper.

Shit, shit, *shit.*

"Jude?" she said a little louder, and as she stepped into sight, he snatched her into the shadows with him.

Rather than give a startled yelp, she said, "Oh, there you are."

Too much like May. "You shouldn't be talking to me here, Ashley. If Elton sees you, it could put you on his shit list."

She shrugged as if it wouldn't be the first such list she'd joined, and pushed her hair back from her shoulders. "I had to know for sure if it was him. The curiosity was killing me."

Again, Jude made note of the similarity between the two women. It wasn't just their looks, which were enough alike for them to be related. They shared mannerisms, smiles, and the same depth shown in Ashley's eyes that he'd often noted in May's.

In fact, their eyes were almost . . . identical.

"Hello," she teased in a singsong whisper. "Why are you staring at me like that?"

Jude shook his head, not about to tell her the path his thoughts had taken. Insane, that's what it was. "I'm worried that Elton will see you with me, that's all."

She said, "Uh-huh," and again, her eyes mirrored the same challenge he'd often seen in May. Uncomfortable with his observations, though he wasn't sure why, Jude forced his gaze away from Ashley's face. "You should get going."

"Where's May?"

Good God, were they both nuts? "She's safe at my house, of course."

Ashley stared at him a moment, then twisted her expression into "the look." Did all women know how to fashion that perfect mix of pity, scorn, and skepticism?

"Man, are you going to be in trouble," she said.

Jude rubbed his forehead. "Is that so?"

"Oh yeah. I bet she wanted to come along, and you went all macho and Tarzan and stuff, huh?" She grinned as if male idiosyncrasies tickled her. "If I were you—"

"Wait." The door opened again, and two of Elton Pascal's henchmen preceded Elton, while another man followed. "Hold that thought."

Eyes flaring wide, Ashley started to turn, but Jude gripped her shoulder and pushed her down low. "Stay there," he whispered. "Don't come out, no matter what."

"What do you mean, no matter what? What are you going to do?"

"Shhh." Staying low and in the shadows, Jude moved away from Ashley, putting a good distance between them before straightening and drawing all the attention to himself. Driven by burning satisfaction, he stepped into the path of the men.

His sudden appearance forced them to a halt. Like dominoes, they nearly toppled each other.

As soon as he recognized Jude, the man in the lead went florid. *"Jamison."* He bunched his fists and hunched his shoulders, coiling up like a too-tight spring.

Moron. Jude lounged back on the black luxury SUV that he assumed to be Elton's car. The hulks that surrounded Elton were both taller and wider, providing a wall of protection.

The first guy took an aggressive step forward, and Jude, barely sparing him a glance, said, "If you don't want him hurt, Elton, you better call him off."

Managing a strained laugh, Elton stepped to the front of the group. With one lift of his hand, the men stepped down, giving Jude more space.

"Well, well, well," Elton murmured. "If it isn't the murderer of innocents."

"Keep that lie going if you want. I don't give a shit. But I do have a few things to say to you." Jude never looked away from Elton's taunting gaze. "Alone."

Fear flickered in the green depths of Elton's eyes, but he quickly banked it. "We have nothing to say to each other."

"There's where you're wrong. Now, I can either go through your men first, which would be a piece of cake, or we can walk to the other end of the lot and settle this like mature men." Jude grinned. "Unless you're afraid to be alone with me."

Elton seethed.

Doing his own share of taunting, Jude laughed. "Come on, Elton. I won't give you the beating you deserve with witnesses hanging around. Your boys can keep you in sight, ready to jump to your defense if you need it." And then, softer, "Not that it would do them much good, and we both know it."

"Son of a bitch," one man snarled. "That's one insult too many."

Jude didn't move. He didn't have to. Elton called the man off with alacrity. Showing his satisfaction, Jude gestured toward the end of the lot— closer to Ed Burton, so the photos would be clear and the recordings accurate. "This way."

Elton glanced at his men, and snapped, "Wait here."

Following his stocky form, Jude noted that Elton had picked up weight. At forty-two, he was Denny's junior by five years, but he looked older, more worn, and far softer. Other than money and influence, he didn't have what it took to be a hard-ass. The dissolute lifestyle and hateful nature had aged him. Left on his own, without others to fight his battles, he'd be helpless.

When they'd moved far enough away, Jude stopped near a light post. He put his hands in his jean pockets and studied Elton. "I see you've been eating well."

"Fuck you."

"You certainly try often enough. But not this time."

A trickle of sweat worked its way down Elton's temple. His twitching gaze darted left and right. "If you've got something to say, say it, damn it."

"All right." Jude kept his tone mild, almost gentle. "I'm done playing the game. I've stood aside while you slander and malign me, but now you've gone too far. You should have stayed in Hollywood— out of my reach."

Alarm drove Elton back a step. "Are you *threatening* me?"

"Of course not." To be annoying, Jude reached out and straightened the lapels on Elton's jacket. The older man held his breath until Jude had retreated again. "You know I only fight in the ring"—

he narrowed his gaze—"unless I'm forced to fight out of it. At heart, I'm a peaceful man, completely averse to violence."

That prod pushed Elton beyond sensible discretion. He bunched his shoulders, making his stocky frame even boxier and turning his ears hot. *"Except when you're murdering innocent women."*

"Say it again, Elton." Jude stepped closer, quiet in his menace, lethal in his intent. "I dare you."

Red faced and sweating, Elton blustered, but nothing intelligent came out of his mouth.

"You're a pathetic coward, Elton. Less than a man. You make me want to puke. No one with any sense pays you any attention, so I've been content to ignore you."

"The paparazzi listen."

"I don't give a rat's ass what the rag mags say, any more than I care what a few struggling actors think. The judge and jury didn't believe you, so you should have let it go."

Eyes bloodshot and bulging, voice strangled, Elton rasped, "She's dead because of you. Sweet Blair is *dead*, and now I'll never—"

"For the love of God, Elton, quit whining." He didn't bother denying the charge again. Insanity shone in Elton's gaze and in the deep, panicked breaths he took. He'd believe what he wanted to believe. Jude didn't care. "You never would have had Blair, so you might as well quit deluding yourself with that particular fantasy. She despised you."

"That's not true!"

"The hell it isn't. You sickened her as much as you do me."

Blind with rage, Elton lashed out, swinging hard. Jude leaned back a scant few inches so that

Elton's punch missed the mark, sending him off balance. He found himself kissing the pavement.

Footsteps pounded toward them.

Bending down, his knee in the small of Elton's back, Jude knotted his hand in the coarse blond hair. He wrenched Elton's face, now marred with gravel and grit, up and back. "Call them off again, Pascal. Do it now, before I decide you're not worth the effort."

"Stay back," Elton wheezed. "Damn it, stay back." He panted, wincing in pain as Jude's fingers tightened in his hair.

"Jesus, Elton." Jude dredged up a laugh to conceal his disgust. "I'm too fast, and you're too clumsy and slow, for you to pull such a stupid stunt." Every muscle in Jude's body twitched with the need for violence. But he had Ed taking photos and recording everything, so he wouldn't lose his cool. Dredging up his famous calm façade, he said, "Now, pay attention. Blair Kane is dead. You can't bring her back. I can't bring her back. You might as well let it go."

A sob broke from his throat, and he shook his head, inadvertently increasing the hold Jude had on his hair. "I can't."

Stupid fool. Jude shoved his head away and pushed back to his feet. Staring down at Pascal, he almost felt pity. Almost.

"I've had enough, Elton. I suggest you face reality, that you give up your ridiculous vengeance and accept how wrong you are, how wrong you've always been. Then get out of Ohio."

"I have business here." Slowly, Elton lumbered into a sitting position. With one shaky hand, he smoothed back his hair and wiped sweat from his face. Two deep breaths later, his arrogance semi-restored, he glared up at Jude. "There's property for sale in Newport, just over the river. I might open a—"

"Spare me your details. I don't care what you're doing."

Elton's face pinched up. "I'm just saying, you have no right to try to run me off."

Jude fashioned his meanest smile. "Go. Stay. I really don't give a fuck what you do as long as you leave me the hell alone. I mean it, Elton. The phone calls and the threats stop. Now."

Elton flinched at that commanding tone. "I . . . I have no idea what you're talking about."

Jude crouched down in front of him. Legs spread wide, wrists resting across his knees, he stared into Elton's glassy eyes. "I've let you run your mouth. I've let you slander me. But you finally crossed the line—and we both know it. Now it's time for you to be smart and let it go." His tone hardened, leaving no room for doubt. "Because if you push me again, I'll walk right through your men to get you, Elton. That's a promise."

Back on his feet, temper still primed for a fight, Jude walked away from Elton, deliberately striding into the group of men who waited anxiously for direction from their boss. They had to scramble out of Jude's way to keep from being plowed over, and in the deepest, darkest part of himself, Jude wanted one of them to try something, anything.

The need to battle burned in his gut. He wanted to strike out.

He wanted to make Elton bleed.

No one spoke to him; the men hurried to Elton, dusting him off and grumbling in a low drone. Left with no other recourse, Jude got into his car and watched until they'd loaded up and driven out of sight. He realized his hands gripped the steering wheel with crushing force, and he concentrated on relaxing his fingers.

Seconds later, he saw Ashley dash toward her little yellow Civic. Now that the excitement had ended, she looked to be in a hurry.

Had he made her late for work? He hoped not. But it pleased him that she had enough sense not to risk a wave in his direction. No one could know she'd ratted on Elton. No one.

Ashley drove out of the lot and sped down the street. He'd have to check on her later—after he'd dealt with May.

Ed Burton started his car and with one friendly toot, he, too, drove off. Jude would talk with him later, as prearranged. Hopefully, Ed had gotten some good shots. But whatever showed up on his film, by agreement, he wouldn't run them yet.

No, Ed would wait for the exclusive interview Jude had promised to him. If all else failed, that'd be Jude's ace in the hole.

With everyone else gone, he fired up the Porsche and started home. But the edge on his temper remained. He'd have to work it out in the gym before talking with May. He'd angered her enough for one day.

Paranoia wasn't a normal part of Ashley's psyche, but she could almost swear someone followed her. Lights had flashed in her rearview mirror many times, but then, she wasn't the only one on the streets that time of night. She moved in and out of traffic but couldn't be sure if the lights that reappeared behind her were the same.

Foregoing a turn signal, she took a sharp right into the office building's entrance—and watched the other headlights pass by. She breathed a sigh of relief, but still couldn't shake off the sense of invasion.

The parking garage was dark and mostly deserted, and the idea of getting out alone didn't thrill her. But after hanging around to see that most impressive conflict between Jude and the other men, she knew if she lingered any longer, she'd be late for sure.

Pushing her unease aside, she pulled into the closest parking spot she could find and killed the engine. The sense of being watched niggled on her mind, making her clumsy as she dropped her keys into her purse and opened her door. She stepped out, looked around, and saw nothing but a few deserted cars, shadows, and drifting debris.

The closing of her door echoed like canon blast.

She could hear herself breathing, sucking the hot, humid evening air into her lungs too fast, too deep. "Get a grip, Ash," she told herself. Sheesh. What was she, three years old and afraid of bogeymen?

Thrusting up her chin and straightening her shoulders, she started forward—and something moved behind her.

"Do you always talk to yourself—"

Screaming, Ashley turned and lashed out with a closed fist. She connected with a rock-hard shoulder, heard a masculine grunt, and started to swing again.

"Whoa!" Muscled arms locked around her, pulling her in tight.

Just as she'd been taught, she brought her knee

up hard and fast, only to miss the mark and con-
nect with a thick thigh instead.

"Ow. Damn it. Settle down."

Her purse fell from her hand, dumping the contents with a clatter. She twisted and fought and—

"Ashley, calm down."

Oh, crap. At the familiar voice, her racing heart
slowed to a steadier beat.

"I'm sorry. I didn't mean to scare you. Are you
okay?"

She went limp. The hands holding her loosened. Breath, and maybe a light kiss, touched her
ear.

"You . . ." Words seemed beyond her as she tried
to bank the adrenaline rush brought on by sheer
terror.

"Yes?" came Quinton Murphy's teasing, amused
reply.

"Jerk."

Laughing, he leaned away to see her face but
kept his hands locked at the small of her back. His
smile tantalized. His eyes seduced.

"Now, is that any way to talk to a guy," he asked,
"who's waited hours just to see you?"

His voice . . . Man, Quinton had a nice, deep,
rich voice.

Ashley shoved him away. "You scared the hell
out of me. What do you think you're doing, lurk-
ing around like a blasted serial killer?" She took in
the sight of her dumped purse and groaned. "Damn
it. Now I'm going to be late."

They both bent down at the same time and
clunked heads. Ashley fell back onto her butt.
Quinton cursed.

Rubbing at her forehead, she said, "Go away.
Leave me alone."

One brow rose an inch. "And here I'd hoped you would be happy to see me."

God, she acted like a bitch. "Sorry." The surly reply didn't hold much sincerity, but under the circumstances, she couldn't do any better. "I haven't had much sleep and it's been one heck of a day."

"I understand."

She picked up her wallet, a hairbrush, and a lipstick.

He picked up her spare tampon and sunglasses.

Ashley snatched them out of his hand. Jamming things into her purse, she said with a lot of skepticism, "So you waited this late just to see me, huh? You didn't have work to do or anything?"

Taking her elbow, he helped her to her feet and flashed a grin. "Okay, so I had a little work that kept me over. But I was ready to go forty minutes ago. Then I realized you'd be in soon and decided to hang around."

"To scare ten years off my life." With a quick glance at her watch, she turned to head in.

Quinton kept pace beside her. "When do you get your first break?"

"I haven't even clocked in yet. And in about two minutes, I'll be late."

"You like to cut it close, do you?"

"No. Usually I like to be here early." As they crossed the foyer, Flint, the security guard, spotted her. His face lit up, and he started to wave—then he saw Quinton behind her and the smile changed to a frown.

Quinton lifted his hand in a jovial wave.

Elbowing him, Ashley said, "Stop that."

Together, they got onto the elevator to go down to the basement. The doors slid shut, sealing them inside, and a new tension filled Ashley's stomach.

Silence hummed. Her nerves jangled. Quinton stood silently beside her, looking at her, smiling.

Smelling good.

Giving off heat.

Making her oh so aware of him . . .

She couldn't take it. She rounded on him—and the elevator doors opened.

"Thirty seconds," he said. "Hustle."

With a huff, she jogged to the time clock and punched in her card with just a few seconds to spare. She didn't bother to look at Quinton as she went into the employee break room, opened her metal locker, and stored her stuff.

From close behind her—real close—she heard, "Nice shirt."

Yeah, it had seemed like a good idea at the time. Now the glitzy shirt just felt like overkill. "Thanks," she said with false sweetness. She slammed the locker shut, turned—and he was right there, a scant breath away, a colossal temptation.

His gaze on her mouth, he said softly, "I am sorry I frightened you in the garage."

Wow. Ashley had the feeling that he knew exactly how his close proximity affected her. He probably knew everything there was to know about women. He probably knew how to make a woman sing.

She didn't care, damn it.

That is, she didn't care until he cupped her face in warm hands.

"I tried to forget about you," he whispered. "But it's impossible."

Scoffing, albeit in a breathless way, she said, "What a practiced line. I bet you've said it at least a dozen times."

Wearing a look of concern and confusion, as if his reaction to her took him by surprise, he said, "I swear, it's making me nuts, wondering how you taste."

She would not be the typical female. "Uh-huh."

"I lied earlier." His thumbs brushed her cheeks, went under her chin, and lifted her face. Full of seriousness and molten sex appeal, he looked into her eyes. "Work didn't keep me here. I just . . . waited for you."

She would *not* do the expected, damn him. She was a strong, independent woman, in charge of her life. One super-hot guy would not take out her knees. "Is that right?"

A half smile appeared. "I lay awake all last night, thinking about kissing you."

Ashley stared at him. He wanted her to be flattered. He wanted her to be flustered.

He wanted her to want him—and she did. But she'd play by her rules, which'd keep her ahead of the game.

Cocking out her hip, she grinned. "Poor baby. I was too busy last night to think of you at all." His piercing green eyes cooled a bit. "But, you know, I don't want your loss of sleep blamed on me, so . . ."

Deliberately taking him by surprise, she grabbed him around the neck, pulled his head down, and plastered her mouth to his. She heard his startled inhalation and felt the rigidity of his body . . . for about two seconds.

Then he gathered her close and took over, and there wasn't a damn thing she could do about it except succumb.

She'd meant the kiss to be pushy. More overkill to go with the shirt. But as his hands spread out wide over her back, and he aligned his body with hers, letting her feel every inch of his hard frame, and his tongue touched hers, then sank in for a long, leisurely taste, she forgot whatever half-baked plan she'd had.

The break room turned into a sauna.

Her stupid knees *did* go weak.

How long they kissed, Ashley couldn't say. Her awareness existed only of him, his scent, his taste, the ripening sensation of pleasure all through her body.

Then his hands slid up her waist, higher and higher, until his thumbs were beneath her breasts and she knew he'd touch her. Any second now, he'd be feeling up her boobs and she *had* to get herself together.

Turning her face away, Ashley rasped, "That's enough."

His harsh breathing fanned her neck. Heat poured off him. His fingers contracted, then went loose and slid back down to safer ground. "I'm sorry. That got out of hand."

"Yeah." She needed three more breaths before she could converse in complete sentences. "Give me some room, will ya?"

His temple touching hers, he brushed his mouth over her jaw—and stepped back.

Ash looked at him. Or more specifically, she looked at the signs of arousal that were so clear: the glittering eyes, the heightened color in his cheekbones, the taut muscles. She shouldn't have, but she slid her gaze along the length of his body until she saw the impressive boner beneath his slacks. New desire mushroomed inside her.

"This is crazy."

"Can you please not stare? You're making it worse."

She rubbed her face, dropped her head back against the locker, and closed her eyes. "I don't even know you."

"Get to know me."

He sounded almost urgent, maybe even desperate, edging on angry.

Quinton Murphy was a very confusing man. Ashley worked a believable laugh past the emotion clogging her throat. "No way. What I do know about you keeps you on the short list."

"Short list?"

"Of men not to get involved with." She waved her hand at him, indicting his body, his mind, his . . . everything. "You know, rich men who get whatever they want. Spoiled men."

The description displeased him. "As you said, you don't know me."

She shrugged. "Actually, my list is nonexistent, so it's a moot point. I'm not about to get involved with anyone. But even if I wanted to, you wouldn't be the right man."

Hardened resolve changed his expression. He looked her over and half smiled. "Your body disagreed." Without seeming to move, he was closer again, intoxicating her with that delicious scent. "Your nipples were hard, you sucked on my tongue, and you were moaning enough to alert the night guards."

Mortified heat rushed up her neck.

"And all I'd wanted was a simple kiss." He chucked her under the chin. "I'd say that makes me the right man."

"Then you'd be wrong." Not since high school had she let anyone of the opposite sex goad her into a temper. She wanted to lash out. She wanted to storm off.

But she was a fair person, and he spoke only the truth. She had been all over him. If she'd kissed him someplace other than her work, her reaction might have taken them straight to bed.

And by the looks of him, he knew it.

She laughed, at him and at herself. That she'd let a near stranger get to her so much was hilarious. "Let's call this a temporary loss of insanity and move on, okay?"

More confused than ever, he scowled. "I don't want to move on."

"Sorry, but you're going to have to." So that there'd be no more misunderstandings, and no more kissing, Ashley broke one of her rules and explained. "I don't have time for dating, Quinton, and even if I did, it'd take one hell of a man to be better than no man at all."

Considering that a great parting remark, she walked away. But with every step that separated them, she was aware of Quinton just standing there, watching her go. Likely a little insulted. In no way giving up.

Probably feeling challenged.

She glanced over her shoulder and saw him smiling after her. Oh yeah, definitely challenged. A little thrill of excitement ran up her spine.

Why oh why did she have to meet him now?

Chapter 15

By the time Jude parked the Porsche in the six-car garage and cut the engine, he was, if anything, more furious than he'd been while confronting Elton.

He needed an outlet. He needed to burn off the anger. Denny would understand his mood, but he couldn't say the same for May. Going straight to the gym and talking to her afterward would be a wise choice.

Unfortunately, May had watched for him through the property monitors, and she met him in the side hallway that led from the garage to the main living quarters. Before he could even take a breath, she launched into an inquisition.

"Are you okay?" Leaving no time for him to reply, she clutched his sleeve and asked, "Is Ashley all right? Was it Elton?" She shook his arm. "You didn't fight with anyone, did you?"

Hands on his hips, Jude stared down at her. "Have you been stewing this whole damn time?"

At his tone, which even he had to admit was

surly, her back went ramrod straight and she looked at him over the top of her glasses. "What did you think I'd do? Play cards? Do my hair? Go to bed?"

Her sarcasm unraveled his control. "Any of those things would have been preferable to thinking that I'd let something happen to Ashley, or that I'd let Elton get the best of me!"

Disgusted and taking it out on her, just as he'd known he would, Jude watched her mouth fall open, and a split second later, snap shut in indignation. "You are not invincible, damn it!"

"I'm not a wuss like your idiot brother, either."

She gasped. "You promised to stop insulting him!"

Growling, Jude stomped off for the kitchen, leaving May alone in the hallway.

He found Tim sitting at the table while Denny regaled him with stories from the SBC. Denny's scrapbook of articles, stats, and interviews lay open on the tabletop as he lectured. "Always avoid a street fight when you can, but if you can't, if your back's to the wall, then just do it. You don't talk about it. You don't threaten. You don't boast and blabber on and on. And don't go in timid. Aim for the nose and plan on knocking that head a good fifty feet. Think that in your mind. A little tap is likely to just piss off the other guy. You want to take him out. Let him know from jump that you mean business."

"Sounds bloody," Tim said, but he looked fascinated.

"It should be."

When Denny saw Jude, he went to the counter and calmly poured a cup of coffee. "Here you go."

"Thanks." Aware of May coming in behind him, Jude sipped the hot brew before commenting further to Tim. "If you don't see any way out of a fight, then plan on a lot of blood. Let the guy know he won't be walking away unscathed."

"Speaking of unscathed," Denny said with a smile, "I see things didn't turn physical. Elton must not have had his usual army with him."

"Not an army, no."

"So how many were there?"

He felt May seething behind him, her arms crossed, her bare foot tapping the floor. Confounding woman. "Counting Elton, only four."

"*Only* four?" May repeated. "Are you out of your mind?"

Filled with contempt, Tim rolled his eyes. "Right. You took on four men?"

"Didn't need to," Denny said. "Look at his knuckles. Not a single mark, so they obviously backed down."

Tim's bruised face soured even more. "Because they're *afraid* of Jude? Give me a break."

Forced to honesty, Jude shrugged. "I wouldn't stand a chance against four men, at least not those four. Regular guys off the street would be no problem. But Elton's men are trained. Still, they knew if they started it, they'd be limping away. For certain there would've been broken bones." He winked at Tim. "And plenty of blood."

"Does your head count as a bone?" May asked with saccharine sarcasm.

Snubbing May, Jude spoke only to Tim. "The only sure way to end a fight is to disable your opponent. The best way to do that is to break something, preferably a leg or ankle. If you only break an arm, he could continue fighting, but if he can't walk, then he won't—"

May gave Jude a shove in the back that sent him

staggering forward a step. He nearly spilled his coffee. Stunned that she would do such a thing, especially in front of two other men, he locked his jaw and narrowed his eyes.

Going on the offensive, she didn't give him the opportunity to take her to task. "How dare you fill his head with that violent nonsense?"

Slowly, Jude turned to confront her. Enunciating every word, he said, "Your brother is not a baby just because you treat him like one. You don't have to protect him." He thrust the coffee cup toward Denny, who took it with alacrity. "You don't have to protect me, either."

"Oh, but I need protection? Because I'm the little woman? A member of the helpless sex?"

She sneered every other word, and even though the rational side of Jude's brain knew it was because of her worry, he reacted to it. "If you're asking me if I'm bigger, stronger, faster—"

"If you say smarter, Jude Jamison, I will *not* forgive you."

Instead of anger, Jude now felt energized. Blood sang through his veins. Frustration faded beneath anticipation. All his focus landed on May. "I've never, not once, questioned your intelligence."

"Thank God," Denny muttered.

"But," Jude continued, "if we're talking about experience, especially in dangerous situations, then yeah, I'm heads and tails beyond you."

Hands fisted at her side, May went on tiptoe. "So, genius, just how did you handle this dangerous situation that you insisted on walking into all alone?"

Jude slanted a look toward Tim, who watched with calculating curiosity. "I handled it. That's all you need to know."

Deflated by his lack of confidence in her, she fell back flat on her feet. More hurt than angry, she said, "Oh, really?"

"Let's just say he knows how I feel about any further harassment."

Denny laughed with glee. "Did you tell him you'd kick his sorry ass all the way back to Hollywood?"

"More or less."

Denny nodded. "About damn time by my way of thinking. This taking the high road crap is for the birds. At least now he knows you're on to him. By the way, I took care of that other business—"

"Not now, Denny."

Luckily, Denny caught on and let it drop. "Oh. Right." He tried for a quick cover-up. "I'm glad you got things settled with that bastard."

Realizing that he wanted to keep the topic private, May withdrew. She looked wounded, but Jude couldn't explain to her right now, not with Tim hanging on their every word. He trusted Tim about as much as he'd trust a starving bear.

Tim's shifty gaze darted from one person to the other. "So . . . you're sure he was the one behind it?"

"As sure as I can be." Jude never looked away from May. "He's been a thorn in my side for too damn long. Like I told him, if he'd stayed in Hollywood, I would have continued to ignore him. But by following me here, he crossed the line and forced my hand."

"Hallelujah." Denny clapped him on the shoulder. "Maybe now he'll butt out of our lives."

"You saw Ashley?" May asked, her manner more subdued.

Jude nodded. "Watched her drive off to the next job, unscathed."

That ruined Denny's good humor. "That child works too damn much."

"Elton doesn't know she called us?" May pressed. "He's not connecting her to any of this?"

"Not unless he's a mind reader." Jude gave her a reassuring smile. "I wouldn't do anything to endanger her."

"Great." She smiled back at Jude. "Then if it's all settled, there's no reason for me stay here. I can get back to work tomorrow. My boss will be thrilled."

Words failed Jude.

Tim didn't have the same problem. "What? No! We can't leave yet."

Denny jumped in. "Damn right you can't. Just because Jude handled part of this mess doesn't mean it's all resolved." He smacked Jude in the back of the head, taking him out of his stupor. "Speak up, damn it. Tell her she has to stay."

"Save your breath." May spun around and forged militantly from the kitchen. Over her shoulder, she said, "My mind is made up."

"You're not going anywhere tonight, May." Jude's sharp statement cut the air like a thunderclap.

She laughed, unimpressed. "Of course not. It's late, and I'm tired. But first thing in the morning, I'm out of here. Good night."

First thing in the morning. Jude started grinning. He had another night at least. A lot could happen in one night. He'd see to it. "She has plenty of spunk, doesn't she?"

Denny looked at him as if he was nuts. "She's royally pissed."

Watching her bounce away in high dudgeon tickled Jude. Time spent with May would never be boring. "And I do love the way that girl exits a room."

Denny followed his gaze, raised his brows as May cut around the corner, and nodded. "Nice."

Tim sputtered. "What the hell are you talking about? She said she's *leaving*. But we don't know for sure that Elton Pascal was behind this mess, and until we do know, I don't want to leave."

Jude spared him a glance. "Then don't."

"But May said . . ."

Denny jumped in. "She's not your damn mamma, boy. Stand on your own two feet. God knows they're big enough."

"Sure, that's easy enough for you to say. You don't know how May can be once she's made up her mind. She's stubborn as a mule. She digs in and refuses to budge." He beseeched Jude. "You have to talk to her. You have to convince her that we need to—"

Denny rolled his eyes. "Get a grip. Men don't go hysterical. Besides, Jude will talk her around." He turned a furious eye on Jude. "At least, he better."

"Yeah," Jude told them both with laughable confidence, "I'll talk her around." It might not be easy, but one way or another, he'd convince May to stay. Hell, he had no choice. He wasn't ready to let her go.

He wasn't sure he'd ever be ready.

That thought didn't sit well, so Jude faced both men. "Before I do that, though, I think I'll go work out."

Denny looked at his watch. "Now?"

"I need to burn up some energy."

"Oh." Nodding in understanding, Denny said to Tim, "Then now's your chance to see how it's done. Let's go."

Tim gave his best poor puppy dog expression. "Forget it. I'm beat. I was ready for bed. I was—"

Together, Jude and Denny caught his arms and lifted him from the chair. Tim whined and carped and complained all the way to the basement. But after Jude got the gloves on him, he had to concentrate on not getting hit.

And Jude saw what Denny saw.

With a little training, a little guts, and a lot more independence, Tim just might make a damn fine fighter. If that happened, he'd stop being May's problem.

That was incentive enough for Jude to spend extra time with him.

Midnight rolled around, and May felt like crying. With each second that had passed, she'd become more despondent. She'd asked herself a hundred questions but didn't have a single answer.

She was no Uma, so why had she assumed Jude would follow her? Why had she assumed he'd want her to stay?

Tucked under the covers in the guest room Jude had first given her, she tried to sleep—and couldn't. Damn him, why did he have to be such a jerk? First, he'd left her behind, which okay, she sort of understood. After all, she wouldn't want to deliberately lead him into a dangerous situation. When given a choice, she'd always protect him the best she could.

But then he'd blown off her concern, treating it almost like an insult. And he'd been outright rude in the kitchen.

She didn't want to argue, and she didn't want to sleep alone. Not tonight. When morning rolled around, she'd leave, and who knew if she'd ever spend another night with him?

God, why had she declared such a stupid thing, anyway?

Because she knew it was the right thing to do.

She wasn't a woman who shacked up. With the danger past, she had to get on with her life. Both she and Tim had imposed on Jude enough.

He said they had a relationship. But did that extend beyond her time in his home? Would he call her and ask her out on dates? Would he miss her?

Would he return to Hollywood to party with Uma?

May smashed her head farther into the pillow and curled a little tighter, trying to contain her hurt. *Damn you, Jude Jamison.*

She no sooner cursed him than a thin ray of light danced across the floor, over the bed, and up the wall as her bedroom door slowly opened. Even without her glasses, May recognized Jude's tall, shadowed form when it appeared in the door frame. Her heart punched against her ribs.

Without a word, he stepped into the room.

May squeezed her eyes shut, which only made her more aware of Jude's overwhelming presence and the clicking of the door when he closed it again. His silent footsteps approached the bed. May felt him standing over her, felt his intense study. She even felt his determination.

The muted sound of rustling reached her ears, and she knew he'd just removed his clothes. Oh boy.

Say something to him. *Say something—*

The covers lifted, the bed dipped, and Jude's large, warm body settled in front of her. Every fiber of her being started doing cartwheels of joy. He'd come to her! But because he didn't speak, she didn't either.

Keeping perfectly still, her eyes closed, she tried to meter her accelerated breathing into a semblance of sleep. It wasn't easy, especially when a hairy thigh moved over hers and warm breath fanned her face.

Gentle fingers sifted through her hair, smoothing it over her shoulder, trailing along her back. He smelled of soap and shampoo, and she knew he'd showered.

But that would have taken minutes, not hours.

Voice dark and deep and low, he whispered, "May, honey, I'm sorry I yelled at you. I've had such a hell of a time with Elton, seeing him left me in a rage."

She understood. When Jude had gone to see Elton, a man who meant him harm, she'd done a little raging herself.

"I wanted to pound on him," Jude explained. "God, how I wanted that. But it wouldn't have helped to resolve things. So instead, I was grouchy at you when I shouldn't have been."

He continued to stroke her hair, lulling her with his touch and soft words.

"I spent the last couple of hours in the gym sweating and working out. I beat the heavy bag, and I sparred with your brother."

Her brother?

"You're right. I shouldn't insult him to you."

Which meant he'd insult Tim to other people? And did she even really care?

"Just so you know, I didn't want Denny to talk openly in front of Tim. If I seemed secretive, that's why. I don't trust Tim." His body crowded closer. "But you're another matter."

He said that as if it had special meaning.

"So, I'm telling you now. Denny hired some reliable men we know, guys we've used in the past. They'll keep Elton under twenty-four-hour surveillance. They're from out of town, but they'll be here sometime tonight, and they'll get straight to work. As soon as we have something concrete, we'll go to the cops."

What a service like that would cost Jude, May couldn't begin to imagine.

"I promise you, while Elton's in Ohio, he's not going to make a single move without me knowing it." Featherlight, Jude touched his mouth to her forehead; his voice went hoarse. "I'm not going to take any chances with you."

For one of the few times in her life, May felt cherished. Tears clogged her throat, she started trembling, and her heart melted.

"Come on, May," he teased, "stop playing possum and tell me you forgive me."

Sighing, she opened her eyes. His face was very close to hers, but without her glasses, she couldn't discern his expression. "How did you know I was awake?"

His hand curved over and around her breast, kneading, caressing. "Your nipples are hard." She heard the smile in his words, and it made her smile, too.

How could she not react when Jude got near her? Snuggling closer to the heat and warmth and security of his body, she put one hand on his chest and turned her face up to his. "It seems you always have that effect on me."

His mouth touched the corner of her lips, and he murmured, "Good to know."

That made her laugh. "Like every woman you look at doesn't go all mushy and adoring and . . . well . . ."

His grin widened. "What?"

Feeling it herself, she whispered, "Hot."

"Mmm. Is that right? I never realized. So what about you, May? Are you hot?" He brushed her nipple with his thumb. "Maybe I'll just find out for myself."

Releasing her breast, he ran his hand over the T-shirt she wore, down her side and the dip of her waist, over the rise of her hip, and along her thigh. He brought his hand back up again, this time on the inside of her leg to the crotch of her panties. As his fingers pressed snug against her, he gave a gruff hum of satisfaction. "Very hot."

Closing her eyes, May accepted the pleasure of his touch. Now that the majority of the danger could be over, she wanted to show Jude that she hadn't come to him for only money or protection. He'd been hurt so badly with negative publicity and false accusations. He'd proudly put up with so much from so many.

When it came to her feelings and motivations, she wanted no doubts in his mind. She wouldn't start making claims of love, because that'd be unfair, putting him in a position to reciprocate, or send her packing. She knew he wasn't in love with her, and she didn't want to leave. So it'd be better to give to him sexually what she couldn't give verbally.

Hoping for a level of seductiveness, she said, "Turnabout is fair play."

The stroking fingers between her legs went still. "Meaning?"

Smiling, May trailed her hand downward, over the play of muscles in his chest, through his crisp chest hair, and onto his taut abdomen. His body had probably inspired many female fantasies. All over, muscle sculpted his long-boned frame. He was toned and strong, with dark body hair and an innate cockiness that only made him more appealing.

She toyed with the sexy, silky line of hair that bisected his body, leading a path to his erection. "Meaning I want to touch you, too."

When she paused over his navel, he held his breath. "May?"

"I love how you feel." Without warning, she dipped lower and wrapped her fist around him. He was as naked and hard as a Greek statue, warm and vibrant and throbbing with life. He tightened, pushing himself more firmly into her hand, clenching his fingers carefully between her legs.

Insidious warmth spread through her. "I see I have an effect as well?"

"I think of you, and I want to be inside you. I see you and I get hard. You have an effect all right." His forehead touched hers. "Harder, baby. Squeeze me harder."

Tantalized by the idea of instruction, May did as he ordered. "Better?"

His hand remained between her legs, immobile, but there, burning and thrilling and heightening her excitement. "Yeah. Now stroke. Like that, but slower." He groaned, breathing hard, heat pouring off him. "God yeah."

A sense of power filled her. She felt daring and sexy, and she wanted to push him the same way he'd pushed her. Turning her face until her mouth touched his, her voice a mere whisper, she asked, "Would you like my mouth on you even more?"

Time seemed to stand still. The air around them

went static. And then Jude kissed her, grinding his mouth over hers, his tongue stroking deep, eating at her, possessing her.

She couldn't continue to pleasure him; she could only hold on and weather the storm of excitement.

His hand curved over hers, making her squeeze him tighter still, stroke harder and faster. He started to groan, low and raw, and suddenly he pulled her hand away. Rasping with every breath, he put his mouth to her throat and sucked, marking her, then did the same to her shoulder, the tops of her breasts. With blatant hunger and loss of control, he kissed her everywhere, leaving her with the sense of being devoured.

His hand plunged under her shirt, shoving it roughly out of the way. He plumped up her breast, and then his mouth latched onto her nipple and he sucked hard, drawing on her, wringing a high-pitched cry of excitement from her.

His teeth nipped, tugged, and she couldn't stay still. "Jude, now."

"Not yet." He growled out the words and switched to her other breast, making her wild.

"Now, damn it."

Using both hands, he shoved her shirt up and over her face. While May struggled to get it off, he sucked and kissed a path down her belly. "Open your legs."

Oh God, oh God. "I don't know——"

He ripped away her panties, shocking her, ratcheting her sexual thrill up another notch.

Pressing his face against her, he inhaled. "You smell so good."

Never, not in her most vivid dreams, had she imagined anything like this.

Jude lifted one of her legs over his shoulder and

pushed the other out to her side. "I've thought about eating you so many times. For months. Ever since first meeting you. Now you're here, and I'm going to get my fill of you until you come."

A promise, or a threat?

And then his mouth was on her, hot and wet, and she pressed her head back, arching in acute pleasure. His tongue lapped over her, plunged into her, and curled around her clitoris. The feeling of his tongue and lips was indescribable, so soft and gentle, but wild and burning, too. His fingers moved on her, opening her more, and as he began to suckle, he pushed two fingers deep.

Sexual fulfillment had never been an easy thing for her, but now, she knew she'd climax. Already the pressure built, throbbing throughout her, drawing tighter and tighter. She couldn't hold still, couldn't stop her moans or harsh gasps. She squeezed her eyes shut tight, clenched her teeth, and an almost violent pleasure ripped through her. She gave a harsh, tearing groan—and didn't care.

Jude stayed with her, and as the release began to fade, he gentled her, lightening his touch until he merely kissed her, soft and sweet.

"Beautiful," he murmured.

May lay there, sprawled out, utterly limp and spent, a tiny bit embarrassed, but really, who cared?

As Jude climbed up to rest atop her, she breathed, "Wow," and heard his triumphant chuckle.

"Wow, indeed." He kissed her, startling her because of what he'd just done and where his mouth had just been. But then she decided she didn't mind. Even that was sort of exciting. He licked her mouth and said, "You're delicious." Then he rolled to the side.

Her breathing yet ragged, she asked, "Where are you going?"

"Condom. You, lady, are about to get the ride of your life."

"Oh, good," she said, still with her eyes closed and her limbs spread out. Then she rethought that. "No, wait."

"Can't." She heard the crinkling of the foil packet as he tore it open. "I need to get off. Now."

May got one eye open but couldn't see much, not in the dark and without her glasses. "But I wanted to kiss you, too." She licked her lips, rejuvenated just from saying it. "You know. There."

Jude muttered something she couldn't make out. He hesitated, making her wonder what conclusions he drew, then he said, "I won't be able to last."

"So don't. You already saw to me. I'm good. Better than good. And truthfully . . . I'm curious about how you taste, too."

"Ah, fuck." He sucked air like a drowning man.

"What's wrong?"

"Just hearing you say it damn near sends me over the edge."

May reached out and found his thigh. "Should I say pretty please?"

"Tease." He scooted up, propping his back against the headboard, his big body taking up a lot of space. "Okay, then. Have at it." He drew a deep breath, letting it out slowly, as if preparing himself. "But hurry or I'll be a goner before you even get started."

Encouraged, May asked, "Will I need my glasses?"

"No." He gave a short laugh. "Just feel your way around."

"Good idea." She did just that, crawling over one of his thick thighs so that she rested between his legs. On her stomach, her head propped on her left fist, she carefully reached out until she touched him. "Tell me if I do anything wrong."

"Yeah, sure." His legs shifted. "Whatever you say."

Very pleased with his reaction, she wrapped her fingers around him and leaned forward to brush him against her cheek. His scent was strong and masculine, and a new surge of sexual awareness unfurled in her belly. Oral sex would be nothing new for Jude, but that didn't seem to matter. She couldn't imagine a man more excited than he was right now.

Because she couldn't wait, she moved her thumb over the head of his erection, spreading a silky drop of fluid. He jerked hard, his penis flexed in her hand, and May drew her tongue over him, licking that salty droplet away and earning a harsh groan for her efforts.

"You taste good, too," she whispered, then closed her mouth over him. He was large enough that she wasn't quite sure how to proceed, but she took the head all the way in, rolling her tongue over and around him while she stroked with her hand.

His fingers suddenly knotted in her hair, not hurting her, but grounding her, drawing her closer. "Take me in, May," he begged. "As much of me as you can." And his hips lifted so that he slowly penetrated.

She breathed through her nose, fast and hard because of her own flooding arousal, and opened her mouth wider.

"That's it. God." He stiffened, gasped. "May . . ."

She withdrew a little, pulled more of him in. Getting the hang of it, she began sliding her mouth over him, taking him in, out again, in deeper . . .

"That's it." A shudder went through him. His hands held her head, guiding her in the rhythm he preferred, urging her on, and in a gravelly plea, he said, "Suck on me."

She did—and he went right over the edge. Only the fingers of his left hand remained tangled in her hair; his right hand clutched a fistful of the covers with incredible power. Hips rising from the bed, he strained against her and growled out an incredible release.

Jude wondered if he'd survive his association with the elusive and enchanting May Price. Every time he thought he had her figured out, every time he thought he had a handle on his feelings for her, she managed to throw him for another loop.

A blow job.

He grinned. Never had he expected such a thing from her.

But then, he hadn't expected her to give him hell, either. Or to trust him so completely. Or to . . . care.

Did she? Given what he'd always known about her, he would have said yes. But now . . . she changed more than a damn chameleon, so he just wasn't sure.

Curved against his side, warm and soft and very pleased with herself, she drifted off to sleep. Jude stared at the ceiling, wishing he'd carried her back to his bed. It was bigger and more comfortable, better suited to his size. And he liked the sound of his fountain.

But after that awesome release, he'd sort of zoned out, his body buzzing, his thoughts adrift. The next thing he knew, she'd rearranged the displaced covers on the bed, kissed his forehead, and snuggled into his side.

She was so damn sweet. And exciting. And sexy.

He could trust her. He could count on her. He could probably . . . love her.

Disgusted with himself, Jude rolled his eyes and silently called himself an ass.

He already loved her, so now what he had to do was get her to admit how she felt. They then could figure out what to do about their future. Together.

With that thought gnawing away his peace of mind, he closed his eyes and concentrated on the feel of May beside him, right where she belonged. They'd have time to work things out.

One way or another, he'd claim her as his own.

Chapter 16

The house was dark and quiet. Too quiet. The ticking of the clock fractured Tim's nerves, and he tried to meter his breathing to match it. Everyone else had gone to bed hours ago.

He could make the call now. No one would ever know, not his sister, not Denny. Not that pompous, self-righteous do-gooder Jude.

But he couldn't. Not yet. Soon, he told himself. He'd get off the bed and call Elton Pascal soon.

A drink would help. The stocked bar wasn't that far from his room. A few shots of liquid courage— that's what he needed. The bed squeaked as Tim sat up, almost stopping his heart, making his skin go cold with goose bumps.

Jesus, he couldn't go on like this. He wanted to sleep in his own bed without worrying about who might hear him move. He wanted to come and go as he pleased. He wanted to have some fun.

What other choice did he have except to call Pascal? If he didn't do something, tomorrow May would force them to leave, and then he'd be vulnerable again. May didn't understand because she wasn't the one who'd gotten beaten and threatened. She wasn't the one having to tiptoe around.

Denny and Jude didn't understand because they had specialized training. Earlier, they'd shown him some live demonstrations, sparring with each other in easy camaraderie. For either of them, it'd be simple to disable a man. They knew moves that were quick and fluid, and unstoppable.

Tim wanted to learn.

But then he thought of Jude's confidence, how easy the bastard made it look, and disdain burned in his gut. Sure Jude was good. And why not? He'd had everything handed to him. Looks, strength. One of the best trainers in the world now worked as his fucking lapdog, cooking, cleaning, playing doorman.

And Denny seemed to love it.

He bragged about Jude the way a father should— the way Tim's father had never bragged about him.

Tim grunted. All he ever got was criticism. Sometimes sympathy. He got the stupid car dealership that he hated. He got slapped on the back, and he got expectations that were impossible to fulfill.

But pride? No, he had no idea how it'd feel to make someone like Denny proud.

Watching them while they sparred had been . . . exhilarating. They'd gone at it hard. They'd dripped sweat and strained, and watching them, Tim had wanted to join in.

But he didn't dare.

He was afraid to take the chance.

Denny and Jude didn't make excuses. If one of them made a mistake, they shook it off, cursed, and tried again.

If he tried, they'd laugh at him, and he knew it.

Not that Denny had laughed while instructing him, but that was different. Denny had a gruff way of insulting that almost sounded like a compliment. When he smacked Tim in the head, it hurt, but it didn't feel mean. It didn't reek of disappointment. He liked Denny well enough.

But Jude was another matter.

Mr. Perfect was probably off boning his traitorous sister right about now. And even though May knew the situation, she encouraged Jude. She didn't really care about Tim. She just liked giving him hell, telling him all the ways that he fell short.

Fuck them both.

This time when Tim rose off the bed, his anger concealed the squeak of the mattress. He opened his door. Moonlight and the glow of outside security lamps came through every window, lighting the way. Wearing only his underwear, he crept across the floor, looking around every few seconds, just in case anyone showed up.

Sweat dampened his palms and the middle of his back by the time he leaned against the polished mahogany surface of the bar. The need for a drink had him breathing hard. He could already taste it, feel the burn as it slid down his throat and into his belly. He could almost smell it, too. His chest labored, and he licked his lips.

Sliding around behind the bar, he cautiously searched the shelves. And found nothing.

Where the hell was it?

A little sick, he searched some more, opening empty cabinets and drawers. It had to be here somewhere.

A light came on, blinding him, scaring him spitless.

"Not tonight, Tim. Get your ass back to bed."

Shielding his eyes against the glare, Tim straightened, and there stood Denny, face expressionless, body relaxed.

"Why the hell aren't you in bed? Are you *spying* on me?"

Shaking his head, Denny started toward him.

Jesus. Tim backed up and butted into the glass shelves, causing a clatter. He hadn't meant to shout. Not at Denny, for crying out loud. But every nerve in his body now twitched in need. He'd counted on that drink.

Denny stopped in front of him. "Come out from behind there before you break something."

Wary, Tim tried to decide if Denny hid his anger, or if he really was that controlled. He didn't necessarily look mad. Annoyed, sure, but then he'd gone off to bed hours ago, and he couldn't be happy about being awakened.

With an impatient wave of his hand, Denny said, "Come on. Quit cowering back there. I'm not going to kick your ass."

Amazing how that relieved some of the tension.

"But," Denny added, his tone sympathetic, "I'm not going to let you drink, either."

"I was looking for a bottle of water," Tim lied.

"No, son. You have a problem." Denny scratched at his bristly chin, then yawned, as if they discussed nothing more important than the weather. "But I'm a problem solver, so the drinking is over."

The drinking is over. Panic edged in around Tim. "What the hell are you talking about?"

"The booze is all gone. I got rid of it. Not a single drop in the entire house."

Disbelieving, Tim laughed. No one would throw

away good liquor. It had to be around somewhere, probably hidden. But when Denny didn't join in the humor, Tim's jaw dropped. "You're shitting me?"

"Nope."

Goddamnit. "This is May's doing, isn't it?" Too angry to be cautious, Tim pushed past Denny, intent on a tirade. "She put you up to it, didn't she? She's always playing high and mighty, the bitch—*oof.*"

A fist locking in his hair yanked Tim off balance. He fell onto his ass and found Denny leaning over him, keeping his head bent back, his position awkward.

His lips barely moving, Denny growled, "You won't talk about any woman that way, especially not your sister. Do you understand me?"

Did everyone have to abuse him? Tim tried to jerk his head free and probably got a bald patch for his efforts. "Ouch, damn it, let go."

"Tell me you understand, Tim."

"Yeah, whatever."

Denny released him. He stood there, arms crossed, posture imposing. He didn't look disappointed so much as resigned. And determined. "Go on back to bed," he finally said. "We'll talk about this in the morning."

"In the morning, May's making us leave."

"Maybe not. I've got my money on Jude." Denny winked, as if the whole confrontation hadn't happened. "Now get some rest. And don't wake me up again, because next time, I will kick your ass."

He walked off, his departure as silent as his approach. A second later, the lights went out, and Tim sat on the floor in the dark.

Head down, hands fisted, he scrambled to his feet and stomped back into his room, closing and locking the door behind him.

"Bastard," he fumed under his breath. Where did Denny get off lecturing him on his sister? He didn't have to put up with May and her bossiness, or he'd understand. "Fuck them all."

Denny had no right manhandling him. He could be arrested for assault. With his skills, he was practically a lethal weapon.

Pacing the room, Tim continued to smolder. It really burned him that Denny had accused him of having a problem. May told him that shit, he just knew it. Just because she was an uptight prude who didn't have any friends and never . . .

Mind made up, Tim crossed the dim room to the chair where he'd left his pants. He felt around until he found his cell phone in a pocket. After he flipped it open, there was only a single moment of hesitation before he dialed information.

It took some effort, and he called a lot of hotels before finding one that could put him through to Elton Pascal's room. Surely, there couldn't be two men with that same odd name, not in a ritzy hotel. Not in Ohio.

This *had* to work.

It wasn't that he wanted Jude hurt, Tim assured himself. He didn't. Just because it'd give him some satisfaction to see Jude taken down a notch, that didn't matter. Given a choice, he didn't want anyone hurt. But he didn't have choices. It wasn't his fault that Jude had made enemies with a psycho. It wasn't his fault that Jude pissed people off.

"Hello?"

The lurching of his heart into his throat kept

Tim silent for too long, and Elton started to hang up after muttering, "Asshole."

"Wait." Tim cleared his throat. "I'm sorry. I . . ."

"What is it? I don't have all day."

"Is this Elton Pascal?

"Who the hell's asking?"

The voice alone made him want to wet his pants. "This is Tim Price."

"I don't know any Tim Price," he snapped. "You've got the wrong number."

"No." Damn it, spit it out. "I'm . . . um . . . I'm living in Jude Jamison's house."

Chilling expectation sizzled through the phone line. The tone turned silkier, less impatient. "And why the hell should I care about that?"

He wouldn't incriminate himself to the wrong person. "I need to know. Is this Elton Pascal?"

"What if it is?"

"Then I can help you."

A thick laugh of hilarity came through the line. "I seriously doubt that."

He wasn't buying it. Tim clutched the phone tighter. He had to convince Elton to take part in the plan. He had to get himself out of this mess. "I can find out things."

"Yeah?" Elton gave a heavy pause. "What kind of things?"

"I know where Jude goes, what he does." Sensing Elton's interest, Tim sought a detail that would matter. "For instance, I know he confronted you at the restaurant today."

"I see." Another pause, then, "So tell me, Tim. How did Jude know where to find me? Can you tell me that?"

Relief washed through Tim. "As a matter of fact, I can."

Muffled whispering and more than one voice led to a chortle. "All right, Tim. We'll talk. But I don't like phones."

"Then how—"

"Tomorrow. We'll meet tomorrow. Then you can tell me everything you know."

As May stretched awake, she felt a warm hand move over her backside, pulling her closer. Her eyes popped open, and she found herself staring at a slumbering Jude.

Dark hair mussed, morning whiskers and all, he took her breath away. Some time during the night he had wrapped himself around her with his head near her breast, his mouth less than an inch from her nipple. She felt every brush of his deep, even breathing, stirring emotions within her.

Their legs were entwined. His arm snaked around her, keeping her close, and even in sleep, his hand clasped her behind possessively.

Content just to look at him, to be with him, May saw no reason to wake him up. She studied his face, the way his dark lashes left shadows on his high cheekbones, the shape of his masculine nose, the sensual curve of his mouth, and his stubborn jaw and chin. Few fighters escaped without telltale battle scars, but Jude was as beautiful now as the day he'd first started in the SBC. It was a testament to his skill.

Not that a few scars could have detracted from his good looks. His appeal came as much from within him as from what the world could view.

He looked so peaceful, indefinably different from when awake. Did he carry the memories of the past year with him always, only escaping them in sleep? She wanted to put her arms around him and hold him close, and somehow protect him—odd, given his capabilities and strength of will.

A knock at the door brought his eyes open, and he looked first at her breast before tracking his gaze up to her face. "Morning." He smiled.

She smiled, too. "Good morning."

Denny called in, "Hey, you slugs. The day is wastin' away."

Jude looked back at her breast, his expression oddly intent, growing heated. His fingers contracted on her cheek. "Go away, Denny."

"You've got packages arriving. Okay to have the driver bring them to the door?"

"Yeah." His lashes lowered and he burrowed closer. "I expected them. But use care."

"Will do. Plan on breakfast in an hour."

"Right." Jude leaned forward and drew her nipple into his mouth, sucking softly.

Warm and wet, the suction could be felt in her belly and between her legs. May's breath shuddered. *"Jude."*

"Mmmm?" His hand began to wander.

She pushed him away. "I need to . . . you know."

He scrutinized her, then realized she wanted a run to the bathroom. "Oh." He grinned. "Yeah, me, too. But promise you'll come back to bed naked."

That sounded like a perfect idea to her. "All right."

He fell to his back, and May scampered from the bed, making a beeline for the bathroom. She knew Jude watched her every step—and she liked his attention. Within a single minute, time enough to also splash her face and rinse her mouth, she opened the door and found Jude standing there.

"My turn," he said and went in around her.

May hurried to the bed, climbed in under the covers, and propped herself against the headboard. When Jude came back out, scratching his belly and yawning, she took in the show with utter delight.

"I could get used to this," she said, and Jude looked up, understanding that she'd become a spectator.

He grinned. "Does that mean you don't often have naked men strutting around your bedroom?"

"You know I don't. And even if I did, they wouldn't be you."

He came to stand beside the bed, and without warning, whisked away the covers. May screeched and tried to scuttle away, but he caught her around the waist and hauled her back, climbing atop her and pinning her down.

They both laughed as they wrestled, knowing exactly what the outcome would be. Still, May didn't give up easily, and because Jude treated her with care, it took some doing to finally get her stretched out beneath him, her arms raised high, her legs forced open around his hips.

Panting, laughing, thoroughly aroused, May asked, "How can I tap out if you hold my hands?"

"You don't get to give up that easy." He kissed her neck, her throat, down to her breasts. "Besides, I don't want to get slugged."

"Why would I slug you?"

He lifted his head, and the smile melted away, replaced with incredible tenderness. He brushed a kiss over her mouth, then her cheek, before saying, "You know what I considered the best part of acting?"

Sensing his seriousness, May quit fighting him. "What?"

"Having money to buy gifts."

She knew just where this was going, and warned, "I don't need gifts from you, Jude."

"Never said you did. I said I enjoyed buying gifts. There's a big difference between needing and accepting."

"I won't accept gifts, either."

He must have had his own interpretation for that, because he asked, "Have I ever told you how impressed I am with you? Not just your mouth-watering body, and not just your great attitude about life. But your incredible strength."

That boggled May, and she gave an embarrassed laugh. "Compared to a man who has muscles on his muscles, I'm puny."

"Emotional strength is a more difficult commodity than physical strength any day. I learned that while going through the trial."

Thinking of how hurtful it must have been for him made her hurt, too. "I'm so sorry you went through that."

He skimmed over his own emotional strength. "The way you deal with things, how you sort of roll with the punches, has always awed me."

While the blows he'd suffered had been for public consumption, shown on every news station and printed in every paper, no one really knew of the punches she'd received, not really. But still the compliment filled her heart. Jude was a strong man, so it thrilled her to know he saw her as a strong woman. "I'm happy."

"I know, and I'm glad. Now, don't interrupt my story. I want to tell you about the gift I bought my dad."

"Okay." She wanted to hear about his family, so she had no complaint with that plan.

"All my life we'd had used cars. Dad kept them running nice, and they were clean other than the usual junk and mud kids bring in after a sporting event or a night at the movies. Big cars, with enough room to accommodate two parents and three kids and a dog. You know, station wagons and roomy sedans."

"Family cars."

He smiled. "Yeah, family cars. But I can remember when the family car would die, usually of old age. Mom and Dad would sit at the dining table and go over the bills and figure out how to juggle things so they could get transportation again."

"That's not an unpleasant picture."

"No. They sipped coffee and talked quietly. And they worked things out."

Why the tears stung her eyes, May couldn't say. Maybe because she couldn't recall her parents ever having a quiet time like that. Arguments, sure. The cops had been called to her house more than once, always for domestic disputes that caused her endless embarrassment and fortified her determination to be different.

At least once a month talk of divorce erupted. There were nights when she'd pray it would happen, though she knew it never would. As often as he cheated, and strange as it seemed, her father liked being married. And because her mother had never been independent, she chose to blame anyone and everyone, to feel sorry for herself and insist on help, rather than find a way to stand on her own two feet.

May could recall all the unhappiness, but she couldn't recall them ever sitting down together to work out a problem.

"When I got my first big chunk of money, I

bought Dad this big, bright red truck. Fully loaded. It was really sweet, all detailed out, with a rumbling motor and the coolest wheels I could find. Dad argued with me for a week before he finally accepted it. I even had to show him my bank statements to make him understand that it wasn't an extravagance for me and wouldn't leave me broke."

"He didn't need gifts from you." May wiggled, wishing she could touch him, but he still held her stretched out. "He loved you, you loved him, and that was enough."

An odd expression darkened his blue eyes to midnight. He stared at her, somehow struck by the obvious truth of her words. "That's almost exactly what he said." He cleared his throat and forged on with more stories. "For Christmas, I bought my mom a new kitchen."

That disclosure had May laughing. "A whole kitchen, huh?"

"Yeah. Cabinets, countertops, flooring, appliances—the whole shebang. Unlike Dad, she only blustered about it for a day or so, then she welcomed the designer with open arms and spent a couple of months getting everything just right. Whenever she wanted to order something cheap, to try to cut back on the cost, the designer refused."

"Only the best for Mom."

"Exactly."

"And for your siblings?" May had no doubt that he'd bought them gifts as well.

"They make decent money now themselves, but yeah, there've been gifts. A horse for Beth, then later, the land she'd admired but cost too much. She built a nice house there, with outbuildings enough to stable several horses. For my brother it was every audio and video toy imaginable. For a stuntman, Neil's a real gadget geek."

"So being able to afford generous gifts is what you liked best about acting?"

"Yeah."

May didn't want to ruin the mood, but she sensed his need to talk. "Jude?"

"Hmm?"

"What was the worst part?"

He looked away, and May felt not only the physical disconnection, but the emotional, too. It lasted only a moment, but she hated it. Then he released her wrists, caught her waist, and rolled so that she rested atop him. "You wanna know the truth?"

Finally, she could touch him. She cupped his face and kissed his brow, the bridge of his nose, and his mouth. "Yes, please."

"The traitors." As usual, his hands settled on her tush. "The people who believed the bullshit and seemed to enjoy seeing me knocked down a peg."

"It's hard for me to imagine anyone who knew you buying into the charge."

"Yeah, well, invitations quit coming. People steered clear. I'd walk into a room, and there'd be whispers."

Her heart breaking, May laid her head on his chest and squeezed him tight. "People can be such idiots."

"You have no idea . . ." He stopped. In a much quieter, strained voice, he said, "You can't imagine what it's like to have the cops come for you. I was in the middle of dinner. I greeted them and invited them in. I asked if they had any news." He snorted. "The last I'd seen them was to report what had happened. Then suddenly, they were there, reading me my rights, pulling out the handcuffs."

"They cuffed you?" Incensed on his behalf, May stiffened.

"Yeah, they listed off the charges and I was stunned. I knew I hadn't done a damn thing, and still, seeing the looks on everyone's faces, watching the report on the news, I felt guilty. And then there was Pascal, fueling the fire, making false accusations and egging people on."

"I am so, so sorry you went through all that."

"I'm still going through it," he said, and for once, he sounded bitter, which only made sense. "Oh, sure, Hollywood wants me back. Thanks to the trial, I've got this unwarranted bad boy rep going, and God help them, there are women who like that shit. I draw crowds, as much from curiosity—like a friggin' train wreck—as anything else. But other than a few select people—"

"Like Uma?"

"Yeah." He kissed the top of her head. "Most of those people mean nothing to me. In my situation, you learn fast who the real people are, and who's a phony."

May smoothed her hand over his chest, then settled in on his heart. "It's good information to have."

"You know who backed me up?"

"Denny."

He laughed. "No kidding. Jesus, Denny wanted to go on a rampage and take people apart. Starting with Elton, of course. Reining him in wasn't easy." Jude tucked his chin in so he could see her. "But it wasn't just him. All the guys from the SBC got behind me like a big family. Guys I'd beat in the ring. Guys I'd trained, or who had trained with me. Some who had insulted the hell out of me because they didn't like losing, or because they wanted to trump up interest in our fight. But no matter the trash talk, they knew me. *Really* knew me. And because of that, they stood with me through it all."

Trying to be subtle, May wiped away her tears. "I'm glad you had them."

"Yeah." He lifted his head more. "Hey, are you crying?"

"No." Her voice broke.

Jude said, "Aw, honey, don't." He turned, again putting her beneath him. He smoothed back her hair and rubbed away her tears with his thumbs. "You know what you can do to make me feel better?"

May gulped, blinked out more tears, and squeaked, "What?"

"Take the stuff I've bought you."

Affronted, knowing she'd just been had, she gasped and tried to swat him. Jude only laughed and caught her hands.

"I *told* you you'd slug me!"

"I didn't." She continued to struggle.

"Only because you can't." He gave her a long, tickling, laughing smooch on the lips. "Settle down and just say yes."

"No."

"No, you won't say yes, or no, you won't take the clothes I bought you?"

"I can buy my own clothes."

"You can pay for them, sure, but the question is, should you be buying your own clothes? Considering your style preferences—or lack thereof—you might as well be wearing burlap or hammered armor."

"You're insulting me!"

"I'm insulting your lack of fashion sense. Come

on, May. You're a beautiful woman with a beautiful figure, and I want to show it off."

Show it off? Horror ended her struggles. "Oh God. What did you buy?"

His grin turned wicked. "What do you think? Something risqué? Something revealing? Do you expect me to whip out a leather bustier and leopard print tights? Maybe some pasties or fringe-trimmed thongs?"

"I don't know."

"Well, get your mind out of the gutter. Or better yet, open your mind to new things—like accepting gifts—and let me bring in the packages. You can look everything over. Anything you don't like we can send back."

She couldn't believe his gall. "You have stuff here, already? How is that even possible?"

"I spent some time on the computer and did overnight delivery. It's easy."

May dropped her head back and closed her eyes. "Says a man of unlimited means."

He took the opportunity to kiss her throat. "I have excellent taste. And the bank official will be here later. Do you really want to meet him wearing my clothes?"

"I could just make a run to my apartment, you know. I have more than enough clothes there."

He made a face. "Trust me, what I have is better. The least you can do is look at it. Please?"

Every ounce of pride she had insisted she refuse any gift. But he looked so excited by the prospect, hopeful like a little boy almost. And he'd said he loved giving gifts. She'd feel like an ogre to outright refuse him. "Under duress, I'll . . . look."

"And try things on?"

Her size. She hadn't even thought of that, but good grief, he had to have given a size in order to select her clothes. There wasn't anything petite about her. "I don't know—"

"You're going to love my choices." He kissed her again. "Make me happy, May. Say yes."

He made it sound like a proposal. "All right."

"Thank you."

Exasperated, she said, "You can't thank me when you're the one giving the gift."

"I can when the recipient is a very stubborn, thoroughly independent woman who keeps me on my toes." He jumped out of the bed with the admonition, "Stay put, I'll be right back." Buck naked, he stepped into the hall and disappeared from sight.

May didn't know what to think, but she hoped whatever he'd bought her wouldn't accentuate the fullness of her figure. She didn't have a concave belly or protruding hipbones or a disappearing waist. Her boobs were big, her backside bigger, and damn it, if he bought her anything that'd make her look foolish, she *would* slug him.

Approaching voices reached her. It was Denny and Jude talking on their way to the bedroom, and May took a mad dash to the bathroom to hide. But the voices didn't enter together. Denny's faded away, Jude's whistle came inside, and then she heard the ripping of bags and the rustle of boxes.

Jude tapped on the bathroom door. "Here, try this outfit on first. I think it'll look great to wear today."

Apprehensive, May opened the door enough to stick out her arm. Jude pushed it open more, gently forcing her back so he could step in. He laid a pair of cropped jeans with a pink chiffon cami onto the counter. Smiling, he held up a pair of one-inch heeled sandals of the same cotton-candy pink.

"Promise you'll let me see after you get it all on."

May stared at the beautiful wispy top and the designer jeans. They were . . . lovely. Not at all risqué. But it appeared to be an outfit for a much younger, much skinnier woman.

"No way am I promising any such thing." If she looked bloated, she didn't want any witnesses. If the clothes enhanced her weight instead of minimizing it, hell would freeze over before she paraded around in front of him.

Shoring up her defenses, she put a hand to his chest and pushed him out of the room. "If it looks okay, then I'll show you."

"There's more," Jude said as he allowed her to eject him. "I bought you panties, too, and a couple of bras, but you won't need one with that top—"

She shut the door in his face. He'd bought her bras? *And panties?* Her face burned. Then she glanced at the delicate top. She'd never owned anything like it, had never even dared to think of buying such a thing. It was so feminine and delicate and . . . beautiful.

Biting her lip with growing excitement, she fingered the material, smiled, and slipped it on.

Chapter 17

Jude held his breath when the bathroom door finally opened. He said a quick prayer that he'd gotten the sizes right, because he knew damn well May wouldn't give him a second chance. If anything was too tight, she'd probably take his head off.

In a way unfamiliar to him, she was touchy about her weight. Most of the women he knew, skinny women, went on and on about their weight while picking at salads without dressing and sipping diet colas. Not May. She ate with a hearty appetite that matched his own, and rather than make excuses about it, she dared him to say a word. Jude grinned.

In his attempts to be "sensitive" to her more generous proportions, he'd blundered a few times. He wanted her to know that he loved her figure with the added curves and softness. How better to do that than to dress in clothes that showed her off, while still respecting her personal modesty?

Her head down in unaccustomed reserve, her

fingers laced together in front of her, May stepped out.

"Wow." Even better than he'd imagined. The chiffon top molded around her lush breasts before dropping in a soft cascade to her waist. The cropped jeans hugged her sexy ass without being uncomfortably tight. And the heeled sandals added just the right touch to pull it all together, and to show her off as a sexy, confident woman. "You look incredible."

Her cheeks heated, and a nervous smile flitted about her lips. "It fits."

"I'll say." He reached out for her hand, and when she gave it to him, he turned her in a circle. "If I wasn't so elated over this little wardrobe rebuilding," he growled, "I'd just drag you back to bed right now."

Face lighting up in pleasure, she asked, "You really like it?"

"I'm male, I'm alive, and I have eyes. Of course I like it."

She ran her hands over the top, and admitted softly, "Me, too."

His heart expanded. "Good. Now try on this one."

Laughing, she snatched up the clothes and darted back into the bathroom. Jude sat on the foot of the bed, smiling from the inside out, so happy to see her happy. He didn't think May had ever gotten enough compliments, and he intended to remedy that. He loved seeing her giddy. He especially loved seeing her look as good as he'd always known she could.

One by one, she modeled the clothes for him: more camis, skirts, T-shirts and blouses, sundresses, jeans, and casual slacks. He liked the new, shorter pastel jackets on her, and the summer sweaters. An array of shoes cluttered the floor, one pair to go with every outfit.

Naked again, May collapsed on the bed in high spirits. "I can't believe you bought so much."

Levered on one arm, Jude balanced himself over her, gazing over her body that looked even better nude than dolled up in great clothes. "There's more in the hall."

She groaned. "No."

"Just purses and jewelry and stuff to go with the clothes."

"It's too much."

Her protests had weakened to a mere formality. "Don't steal my fun."

Eyes closed, mouth in a sweet half smile, she made him wait while she considered things, but finally whispered, "Okay. Thank you."

Running his hand from her rib cage to her belly, Jude said, "Know what I want to do now?"

Her smile widened. "I could maybe guess."

"I want to take a bath."

May's eyes fluttered open, and she rose up onto her elbows. "A bath?"

"Yeah."

Giggling, she dropped back. "The way your mind works is not to be believed."

He'd never heard her giggle, but he liked it. He loved it. He . . . No, it was too soon for anything like that.

"Easy enough to explain. I enjoy seeing you naked. Bathing together pretty much guarantees you'll stay naked a little longer." He kissed her again. "See, it's simple."

"What about breakfast?"

"It'll wait."

"But will Denny?"

"If he knows what's good for him." Jude pulled her to her feet, wrapped her in a sheet, and dragged her to the door.

"No way!"

He peeked out. "The coast is clear. Besides, it's your fault we're in the wrong room." He tugged her into the hall. "I want you to see my bath. I want you to see the grounds. I want to show you everything."

Holding the sheet with one hand, May went along. "I can think of a lot of paintings that'd look great in this hall."

"There, you see? I told you that you needed to visit. We'll tour everything later, and you can make a list of pieces to show me, okay?"

With new reserve, she said, "You haven't had many friends to share with, have you?"

"Not here, no. Other than family and Denny, no one's been in my house." Walking backward, he led her into his room. "But I put a lot of work into getting everything just as I wanted it. I argued with contractors, oversaw the small details, and now I can't imagine living anywhere else."

Her expression carefully blank, May asked, "What about Hollywood?"

Aware of her caution, Jude kicked the door shut. "What about it?"

"You don't plan to go back?"

Was she worried about losing him, or just making conversation? "I don't know. But whatever I decide, I'll always have to travel." The SBC required as much if not more travel than acting. "Why?" He pulled away her sheet and tossed it across his bed. "You trying to get rid of me?"

"No, of course not. I just . . . I've never really

heard you say if you intend to stay here, or if Ohio is just a getaway for you."

At first, it had served as a place to hole up and heal. A place where he could have moderate anonymity. Leaving Hollywood had been as much about leaving his problems behind as deciding what he wanted to do for his future.

He'd made some decisions on that, but he wasn't ready to share them with May. Not yet. He didn't want to spook her, and he was afraid he might not like her answers.

"I like it here," he said only. Then he took her into his spacious bathroom. By anyone's standards, it surpassed decadence with every luxury imaginable.

Three wide marble steps led up to his enormous tub big enough to count for a pool. While May looked around in wonder, he turned on the multiple brass spigots. By specific design, the water pressure was such that the tub would fill quickly.

After retrieving thick towels from a built-in wall cabinet, Jude watched as May ran a hand along the ornate, double-bowled sink and the Italian marble top. Lips parted, she moved to the separate steam cabinet, the fifteen-foot-long shower, and the etched glass window that allowed in a stream of sunshine.

"Heated towel bars?" she asked.

"Naturally."

She stopped in front of a niche where water cascaded over a granite wall. "And another fountain?"

"Like it?"

Steam rose around her, already curling her hair and making her skin dewy. "I've never seen anything like this."

"But do you like it?"

"A sultan could live here. Two sultans. It's . . . incredible." She turned flirtatious eyes on him. "And with you standing there in the nude, how could any woman *not* like it?"

Jude fought a chuckle. By the hour, she became more daring and more openly sexual. "Are you telling me I could have saved all the money I spent in here?"

She shrugged. "You've worked hard for what you have—you deserve it all." She sashayed toward him. "But you could stand in a mud puddle and make it look appealing."

The past few hours had been so enjoyable, like a special moment in time. Jude had to kiss her, and once he went down that path, he didn't want to stop. She wrapped her arms around his neck and gave herself over to him, kissing him back, leaving no space between their bodies.

Jude held the back of her head with one hand, and lifting her thigh with the other, fit himself tight against her. The urge to move inside her, to make love to her here and now, tested his control. But he didn't have a condom in the room with him, and he really did have to get a handle on his excesses.

He turned and pinned her to the wall, in the same move sliding his hand between her legs. Fingers moving over her, he found her soft and hot, slippery wet, and he groaned. "You're making me insane, May."

"I don't see how," she breathed, already shimmering in excitement. "I'm so agreeable."

Because she was by far the least agreeable woman he'd met since gaining fame, her words struck him as funny. The shot of amusement cooled his ardor enough to lead her into the tub. "Come on, Agreeable May. You can wash my back."

But rather than soap up a cloth, Jude turned her so she sat with her back to him and settled her between his legs. He shut off the water, turned on the jets, and took pleasure in kissing her temple, in idly touching her breasts, her belly. He lined his feet up next to hers, comparing her smaller, narrower feet to his size twelves.

"Jude?"

Contentment filled him. "Yeah?"

"While I was waiting for you last night, I got on the computer, too."

Only part of her statement registered. "So you were waiting for me? You weren't so angry with me that you wanted to be left alone?"

"If I'd wanted to be alone, I'd have kicked you out of bed."

In two days with her, he'd smiled more than he had over the entire past year. "I figured as much."

"I looked up bombs."

The hair on the back of his neck stood on end. Whatever her reasoning for doing such a search, he didn't like it. "Want to tell me why?"

She twisted free of his arms, turned, and positioned her legs as if preparing for meditation. The pose, which left her fully exposed despite the churning of the water, distracted him in a big way.

Until she said, "I think I know how you were set up."

Jude's gaze shot up to hers. Just that easily, he began breathing too fast, and tension crept into his muscles. "Set up?" he asked with laudable skepticism, almost afraid to hear her out. Only he and Denny had ever made the assumption that he'd been deliberately sabotaged.

She practically bounced with enthusiasm. "It *had* to be a setup. I read through all the articles and news transcripts I could find. The only thing that made you look guilty was—"

"The lack of any other suspect." His guts churned. "I know."

"But the bomb could have been a contact bomb. That's where the bomb doesn't go off by the use of a fuse or a timer. It literally has to hit something, and then it explodes."

"I know what a contact bomb is, May. The experts nailed that little detail right off. You throw the thing, and when it hits, ka-*fucking*-boom. Detonation." Why he felt so angry, he couldn't say. Maybe because he hadn't expected her to go beyond believing him. He hadn't expected her to care enough to want to prove his innocence. More likely because her involvement meant danger for her—and he'd rather die than have her harmed.

"Exactly. So it makes sense that—"

"None of it makes sense. In order for that type of bomb to work, someone had to toss the thing into the limo. It . . ." His jaw clenched. His fingers flexed. "From what they could tell, it practically landed on Blair. Someone made her a damn target—but as the world sees it, I was the only one around."

"No, you weren't."

Knowing it to be a futile discussion, one he'd gone through over and over again, Jude sat up, too. He put his hands on May's thighs while looking at her body, desperate for a diversion. It amazed him, but around her he stayed hard all the damn time—even now, while talking about a subject that left him hollow and cold. "It's a dead issue, May. Let it go."

She disregarded that order. "Did you ever hire your own investigators to find the real culprit?"

Beneath the water, he moved his fingertips closer to the apex of her legs. "The cops did that. I was too busy trying to keep my damn neck out of the noose."

"But the cops didn't!" She pushed his hands away, frustrating him. "They spent all their energy on trying to figure out how *you* did it. I don't think it ever occurred to them that someone else could be guilty. I realize the explosion left little evidence to work with, but—"

"What was there was singed and misshapen and . . . grotesque." He did *not* want to talk about this.

"I'm so sorry, Jude." She reached out to him, her small hands cradling his face. "But I have a theory."

Memories of how the bodies looked when he'd raced back to the scene pounded through his head. He could still hear the broken glass crunching beneath his feet. Still see the smoldering, twisted pieces of metal that had blown yards away from the limo.

His heart thumped too hard and fast, and he felt a prickle on his nape. "I wasn't that far away you know—just fifty yards or so."

"Thank God you weren't hurt, too."

He barely heard her as he relived that awful moment in time. "I had just bent down to get the Coke that dropped out of the machine." He didn't look at her. He couldn't. "I felt the impact in the air. The noise was deafening, the scent acrid. But there weren't any screams. I don't think anyone had time to scream. At first, I didn't know what had happened. I thought . . . I don't know. That a bad wreck had happened nearby or something, even though that didn't make sense."

In a low and soothing voice, May gave him the precious gift of her understanding. "Things rush through our minds when we're startled. Naturally, you didn't realize it was a bomb. The idea that someone could do that would be ludicrous, the last thing to occur to most people."

Yet someone had done it. Someone—some nameless person—had murdered Blair in his limo. No matter how he looked at it, he felt guilty. If he hadn't given her a ride. If he hadn't allowed her inane chatter and immature seduction to get on his nerves. If he hadn't gotten out of the car. So many "ifs" to live with.

And no way to turn back time.

"Even after I saw the limo, it didn't sink in what had happened. I ran back, but it was too late. Body parts were . . . detached. I couldn't tell . . ." He shook his head, unwilling to say it aloud again. Repeating it all helped nothing. "I've been through this a hundred times, May."

"I'm sorry to dredge up such awful memories. I know this has to be hard for you."

Hard didn't begin to describe it. Nightmarish. Horrific. Bloodcurdling. "You can't imagine what it's like to know you're indirectly responsible for such a thing. Blair was so young."

"Twenty-one, isn't that right?"

He nodded. "Despite being discovered by Hollywood, she was still naive about so many things."

"She had a crush on you."

That information had been in all the news, too. It sickened Jude to remember how much he'd hated Blair's infatuation, the silly way she'd tried to cling to him.

God, he'd been such an unfeeling jerk.

"She was a little scared. Unsure of herself. But she had such a promising future. She was adjusting to the popularity. Given a chance she'd have worked it out."

May ran her fingers through his hair, petting him, making him feel like a sappy, sad kid.

But he didn't ask her to stop.

"The reports claimed that the bomb had to come through a window, because the explosion happened from the inside. Isn't that right?"

Grim memories of his interrogation clashed with May's gentler questioning now. "No windows were open."

"But your door was?"

He nodded. "I didn't close it behind me when I got out. I don't know why. I just . . . I felt bad for escaping Blair to begin with. But she kept . . ." He locked his jaw. Blair was dead, and yet her death had forced him to answer questions that portrayed her in a less than favorable light. He didn't want to tarnish her memory, and had caught hell from her fans, friends, and family for doing so. If there'd been any way to keep most of it private, he would have.

But he'd been fighting for his life, unjustly accused. And he didn't lie.

May gave a slight, understanding smile. "She adored you, Jude. What woman wouldn't? I bet you were kind to her."

"She took it for more than it was. I felt sorry for her. I wanted to be her friend, but she wanted more."

"It speaks of your honor that you didn't take advantage of her."

Jude snorted. Honor? During the murder investigation and the trial, he'd felt stripped of any redeeming qualities, especially his elusive honor. He'd blackened Blair's name in order to protect himself. Nothing honorable in that.

"Jude, stop it."

He glanced up, startled. "Stop what?"

"Blaming yourself. You're not responsible for how someone else feels. You had no way of knowing what would happen. You couldn't have done anything to prevent it. While Blair was alive, you were her friend. I'm sure that meant a lot to her."

"Being her friend got her killed."

"No, some whacko running loose killed her."

"Then that whacko is still running loose, because despite a lack of evidence to convict me, the world isn't looking for anyone else to blame."

"Well, I'm looking. And you'll hire some PIs to look. And—"

"You'll stay out of it, May."

She blinked at him, startled by his ferocity, but not deterred. "You didn't do it, so we need to find out who did."

The greatest unease imaginable coursed through him. "There's no *we,* damn it. Not in this, not in some half-baked manhunt. I mean it, May. If anyone realizes you're poking your nose around, it could stir up new trouble."

"I might not have to poke around."

Icy terror gripped him. May seemed oblivious to any danger involved, just as she seemed oblivious to his insistence that she butt out.

"Let's go over what we know."

His hands fisted. "Let's don't."

"The murder happened in the short amount of time it took for you to walk to the cola machines. That means someone had to be close by to throw the bomb. But it was late at night, the roads all but deserted, and you didn't see anyone there at the rest stop." She looked directly at him. "So maybe . . . Maybe it was someone in the car."

Chapter 18

Water splashed when Jude jerked in disbelief. What the hell was she suggesting? Voicing pure reaction, he said, "Don't be idiotic. Blair was unhappy, but she wouldn't blow herself up. She wouldn't kill an innocent driver."

Rather than take offense at his insult, May persisted. "Did you know the driver?"

So that was her train of thought: not Blair, but Sid. He scoffed at her. "Yeah, I knew him. Not the brightest bulb around. Dumb as a rock, in fact. But a nice enough kid. He wanted in the SBC, only he sucked as a fighter. He had a glass jaw, a wide swinging punch, and no control. Didn't matter how many times he heard the rules, Sid couldn't remember them when he got excited."

"Like in a fight?"

"Exactly."

"You never fought him?"

"Hell, no. It would've been a massacre. In the SBC, you have to earn certain fights, and he hadn't even come close to beating a contender in my league."

"So he wasn't happy."

"He wasn't so depressed that he'd blow himself up. Hell, he was getting his life turned around. I told him I couldn't use my influence to get him in the SBC, but I did give him a job as my driver."

Like a dog on a meaty bone, May jumped on that. "He asked you to influence the right people to get him fights, and instead you hired him?"

"Yeah. Sid liked the deal. He made good pay and he didn't have to get his brains bashed in. He accepted the fact that he wasn't cut out as a fighter."

May mentally chewed that over before asking, "Did he know Elton?"

"How the hell should I know? Before the trial, I barely knew Elton. Some of us hung out in his clubs, and he'd sponsored a few of the guys in the SBC."

"Sponsored them how?"

"Paid for some of their training and stuff in exchange for them wearing T-shirts and shorts that advertised his nightclubs. But after all his accusations, they cut him off. They boycotted anything that Elton touched. They stopped going to his places, and during the matches"—Jude smiled, remembering—"a few of the fighters made a point of ripping up the shirts or shorts with his logo on them. With the cameras and reporters around, that made one hell of a statement."

May scooted closer and again cupped his face. "Jude, what if the driver didn't know the bomb would explode on impact? What if he thought he could toss it in the backseat, and then leave the car and get away before it blew?"

"That's an awful lot of 'What-ifs?' isn't it? You'd have to assume Sid was a murderer, and that he had some grudge against Blair."

"Not Blair, *you*." She sank her teeth into that theory. "Think about it. You just said he was desperate and not too bright. He wanted to fight, and instead you made him your lackey."

"I made him a driver," Jude clarified. "He liked cars, and he made a hell of a lot more than he ever had as a half-ass fighter."

"I understand the generosity behind what you did—but maybe he didn't. Maybe someone else was able to twist things around and impress his thoughts in a negative way."

"You mean Elton?"

She shrugged. "It's possible. You said Sid wasn't smart. You said the fighters hung out in Elton's clubs. You're certain Blair wouldn't do such a thing, and we both know you're innocent. That only leaves the driver."

"Jesus."

"It's worth looking into."

Jude hated to admit it, but she had a point. "I know for certain that Elton never sponsored Sid. He only picked the most visible fighters, the sure bets."

"The crowd pleasers."

"Yeah." Jude's mind churned. "I can have Denny check into it. He'd know how to ask around without alerting anyone to our suspicions."

May grinned. "So now it is we?"

"No." He grabbed her shoulders. "It's me. It's Denny. It's professionals. You will keep your sexy little ass out of it."

Her nose went into the air. "My ass isn't little."

"Your ass is perfect, and I'm not about to put it

on the line. So you either give me your word that you'll leave it to me, or it ends right here."

Her expression went flat. "What ends?"

"This whole theory, damn it."

"Oh."

"What the hell did you think I meant?"

Lifting one shoulder and avoiding his gaze, she muttered, "I don't know. Our association?"

Jude shook her—not hard, but enough to get her attention and to let his disgruntlement be known. "Our *relationship*, damn it."

Her smile came and went. "Okay. You have my word—if I can have yours that you won't give up on this, that you'll follow every lead, that even the tiniest hint will get your undivided attention."

"Deal." He looked down at her breasts. "Why don't we seal this with a—"

A voice crackled over the intercom, saying, "The bank official is here."

"Shit."

May giggled again, and that lightened Jude's mood enough that he didn't mind the interruption.

Stretching out an arm to press the intercom button, he said, "Give him coffee, Denny. We'll be down in five."

"Will do."

"Hey, Denny, you alone?"

"Just me and the intercom."

May blinked, then whispered, "He can't hear in here, can he?"

Jude chuckled. "Not unless I push the button." He did just that to say, "Do me a favor. Check around, discreetly, and find out if Sid knew Elton in any way."

For several seconds, Denny didn't reply. "Sid, the driver who—"

"Yeah."

"What are you thinking?"

"May has a theory, and I promised to check it out."

"A theory, huh?" With warm sincerity, Denny said, "Damn, I knew I liked that girl. Consider it done. And Jude? Tell her I said thanks." The intercom went dead.

Jude looked at May, naked in his tub, her skin and hair wet, her dark eyes consuming. Her smile made him feel powerful. Along with gnawing sexual awareness, he detected the warmth of her concern, her trust, and her caring.

He whispered, "Thank you," before giving her a lingering kiss that promised things to come. "Now, wash up and get dressed so we can get this business settled. The sooner it's done, the sooner I can show you around, then drag you back off to bed."

May laughed. "A wonderful plan."

The best laid plans, Jude thought later, as May stared into the monitor with dismay. "It's my parents."

Not another photographer or deliveryman, not the idle spectator? Jude's interest quadrupled. "Really?" He joined May at the monitor. "Well, Denny, buzz them through."

Not minutes ago, Tim had stormed off, full of blustering annoyance over being "forced," as he saw it, to sign the loan papers. Jude didn't give a damn how Tim felt about it, but he knew Tim's behavior had shamed May, and he hated that.

Both he and Denny had seen enough cocky young men to take it in stride. In fact, Denny had half grinned while watching Tim put his signature on the paper and seeing it all notarized. Denny saw it as a step forward, a way to force Tim into being the man he could become, instead of the boy his relatives had allowed him to be.

Now, May's father was here, and as she stared in horror at the monitor, Jude slipped his arm around her.

"Tim must've called them."

Her tension was a live thing, practically putting her hair on end. Jude tugged on one soft, light brown lock resting against her shoulder. "Why do you say that?"

"They're here because of the loan."

"Maybe they're here because their only daughter is living with a man they don't know."

Turning on him in amazement, May said, "I'm not living with you."

Jude cocked a brow. She sounded aghast. "That offends you? Should I say visiting for an extended period?"

Hands to her cheeks, May whispered, "This is getting worse and worse."

"What is?"

"Don't say anything. Let me deal with my folks. In fact, maybe you and Denny could just go downstairs—" She tried to shoo them on their way.

Jude planted his feet. "Not on your life."

When she looked to Denny for help, he scowled. "I ain't budging."

Looking like she wanted to kick them both, May grouched, "Fine. Suit yourself. Stay and suffer it all. But don't say I didn't offer." Grumbling, she started around them to open the front door.

Jude shared a look with Denny. Just how bad could two parents be? Okay, so he knew they weren't the type to win mother or father of the year. Ashley had given him enough clues for him to suspect they'd be difficult to deal with.

But he wasn't without some expertise in that area. He'd trained with fighters who carried chips on their shoulders the size of a wrecking ball. He'd placated sponsors, and pleased announcers. He'd worked with temperamental producers and directors.

He'd gone through a grizzly trial that would have destroyed most men.

Without a doubt, he could handle two overbearing, disapproving parents.

A silver Jaguar screeched to a jarring halt at the end of the drive. Car doors slammed. *Not* a good sign.

Two people stepped out, a short, garish-looking woman and an overly polished man in reflective sunglasses. As if in physical pain, May groaned.

Wishing he could spare her, Jude propped his chin on the top of her head. "Relax," he told her, "I'm good with parents."

"Ha!"

Denny patted her shoulder. "Stop your fretting. Things'll be just fine."

"Go ahead," she said. "Keep telling yourself that while you still can."

Palpable hostility preceded her parents' approach. Jude looked first at May's mother and wanted to wince. Short, bloated, and with hair an unnatural shade of blond that needed touching up two months ago, she looked nothing like May. Her clothes, the total opposite of what May usually wore, looked comfortable to the point of being sloppy, as if she'd worn them for two days, even to bed. A lit cigarette hung from her lips, and she carried a traveler's mug of something in her left hand. She squinted eyes of an indistinguishable color, as if she hadn't seen daylight in some time. Her gaze roved over May with screaming disapproval.

Her father, on the other hand, wore well-tailored casual slacks and a designer polo shirt. Tall, lean and toned, with an air that shouted "on the make," he couldn't have been more opposite of his wife.

They got as far as the bottom of the porch steps—and stopped.

A strange disquiet rolled over Jude.

"Hi, Mom, Dad." In a preposterous show of enthusiasm, May stepped farther out to greet them. The second she started to chatter, Jude realized how truly nervous the visit made her. "You just missed Tim. I think he's coming back here, though. He said he only planned to go by the lot to check on things and to—"

"Good God," her mother interrupted in a rusty smoker's voice. "Where did you get that ridiculous outfit?"

Her mother's cutting criticism obliterated any good will Jude had affected. May looked incredible, and anyone who couldn't see that had to be blind.

"I bought it for her." Wearing a false smile and keeping his anger in close check, he stepped in front of May. "Hello. I'm Jude Jamison." He held out his hand.

Her father pulled off reflective sunglasses. "You're the one trying to do some fast moves on our Tim."

Obviously, there'd be no handshakes, so Jude switched his attention to May's father—and went mute. Good God, he looked exactly like . . . Well, like May. Sort of. But more like . . .

Only that didn't make any sense.

"No, sir," Jude explained politely, while wild suppositions came together in an awful possibility. "Actually, I'm helping Tim."

Flipping ashes onto Jude's porch, her mother said, "Help him by bankrupting him?"

"No." May tried a smile. "You've got it wrong. Jude only—"

Her mother lashed out. "I don't want to hear from you. Do you think I wanted to come here today? Do you think I enjoy this crap? You dragged your brother into this god-awful mess and now I have to fix it."

Denny sidled up next to Jude, saying in a low voice, "Un-fucking-believable."

"Mother, you know that's not true. If Tim hadn't lost the money gambling—"

"He has an illness. The doctors told you so. When he drinks, he loses good judgment."

Crossing his arms over his chest, Denny interjected, "Then he shouldn't drink."

May's father redirected his disdain. "Who the hell are you?"

Before Jude could try to get a handle on things, May again thrust herself into the spotlight.

"Let's start over with introductions."

"It says a lot," her father pointed out, "that we've never met either of these men, and yet you're living with both of them."

The suggestive slur staggered Jude.

"Visiting," May corrected, taking the awful insult in stride.

Her mother snorted. "Whatever you call it, you've aligned yourself with them against your brother."

Jesus, Jude thought. May's parents were beyond horrible. They bordered on insane.

Smile slipping, May said, "Mom, Dad, this is Jude Jamison. He's lived in Stillbrook for about a year or so now. He buys his artwork from me."

"Makes one wonder *why*," her mother sneered.

"I enjoy art," Jude told her.

"You're enjoying something, all right."

Jude opened his mouth, but May quickly said, "And this is Denny Zip, a close friend of Jude's."

Denny nodded. "Not quite a pleasure, but—"

Jude elbowed him.

"Jude, Denny, this is my father, Stuart, and my mother, Olympia." Trying to play the good hostess, May stepped aside and indicated the door. "Why don't we all go in and get comfortable? We can discuss everything over coffee, and maybe clear up some—"

"Tim isn't signing your goddamn papers," her father said, "so you can just forget that."

Jude took evil delight in saying, "He already did." Wearing the impersonal, blank mask he'd perfected for necessary confrontations, Jude expounded on that, to make sure there'd be no misunderstandings. "The terms of repayment are spelled out. My banker notarized everything. It's official."

"You bastard," her mother hissed, and she threw down the burning butt of her cigarette without regard to where it landed, or the damage it might do.

Jude stared at it, watching it burn, knowing it'd leave a mark. Gasping, May started to bend to get it, but Jude caught her upper arm and held her still. He'd let the whole damn house burn down before he'd let May retrieve that butt.

"Don't you have enough money?" Olympia continued, and with every accusatory word, she further revealed herself as a crude, uncouth, and fanatical person. That she had birthed and raised May sickened Jude. "How dare you take advantage of poor Tim that way? How greedy and conniving do you have to be?"

May had been trembling beside him, but she suddenly went rigid.

Only for her did Jude keep from lashing out. "Understand, Olympia, I don't want your son's money, and I don't want to take advantage of him. He put himself in this fix. My only involvement is to assist him with buying himself out of the immediate trouble."

Stuart laughed. "By stealing the car lot from those of us who worked damned hard to build it?"

"I neither want nor need your car lot." Jude transferred his attention to the male half of the dreadful duo, and again, the dark eyes and similarity of features struck him. "As long as Tim repays the loan as stipulated in the contract, there won't be a problem. I can promise you that the terms for repayment aren't unreasonable and shouldn't cause Tim any hardship."

"Fancy words to mask your greed."

"I made the loan official in the hope that paying the money back will teach Tim responsibility. If he learns from mistakes, he won't keep making the same ones."

"Don't preach to me about responsibility! Just because you bought yourself a not-guilty verdict doesn't change who and what you are." May's father uttered that dig with a curled lip and an expression of loathing that detracted from his GQ image. "I don't want Tim anywhere near the likes of you."

That gibe infuriated Jude, leaving him at a loss as to how to deal with the situation. If these people weren't May's parents, he'd dismiss them from his thoughts and have them thrown off his property. But he cared for May. From the beginning he'd wanted to protect her.

Now he realized she needed protection most from those who should have loved her.

"How dare you."

Everyone started at the quiet ferocity of the words, no more than a whisper, but infused with so much anger that they cracked like a whip.

Jude looked down at May, appalled to realize the words had come from her. All color had leeched from her face. Her lips were pale and trembling, her eyes glassy behind her glasses. Deep breaths had her chest heaving.

Oh God. Intent on shielding her, Jude tried to block her with his body. "May—"

Lips barely moving, eyes glued to her father, she held him aside. "It's all right, Jude." To her parents, she said, "Both of you should be thanking him, not insulting him."

"Thank him for trying to steal the car lot?"

"You can't really be that stupid."

Her mother choked. "How dare you—"

"Jude could buy ten car lots more lucrative than ours."

"Not *ours,* missy. You have no part of the lot." Her mother delivered that reminder with grotesque glee.

"You think I should care?"

May didn't raise her voice. She spoke so calmly that it scared Jude, and he took her hand, only to find her fingers cold.

"I haven't lost much, not with the way Tim's run it into the ground. Instead of coming here with laughable accusations, you should be checking on him, supervising what he does."

Her father shouted, "At least he tries!"

"If you actually cared about him at all, you'd help him to grow up. Denny and Jude have shown more genuine, constructive concern for him in two days than either of you have in his lifetime."

Her mother's face, ravaged by alcohol and nicotine abuse, turned florid. "You little bitch. This is how you treat your family?"

Jude's fragile tether on his temper snapped. "Now, wait just a minute."

May jerked her head around to look him in the eyes. "Stay. Out. Of. This."

Taken aback by her desperate vehemence, unsure if she reacted to a sense of family loyalty or to a need to deal with the situation on her own, he clamped his mouth shut.

May nodded, then again faced her parents. She separated herself from Jude by taking a small step forward.

"Someone attacked Tim because of money he accepted while gambling. Not a little money. Fifty thousand dollars."

"That's absurd," her father blustered.

"Yes, it is. Tim didn't borrow from a reputable bank. He borrowed from someone willing to kill to get the money back. Jude not only covered his debt, but took him into his home to protect him until the mess could be sorted out."

"And conveniently ended up with signed loan papers."

"So? He owes Tim nothing. He certainly doesn't

owe you. Would you give away fifty thousand dollars? If it wasn't for Jude's generosity, Tim might've been murdered for his stupidity."

"We'd have handled it somehow," her father claimed.

"I'm glad to hear that." May still stood like a soldier, her arms rigid at her sides, her feet together, her shoulders back. "Then handle it now. Dredge up fifty grand, pay Jude back, and he can tear up the loan papers."

Her mother's eyes narrowed. "Just like that, huh? You tell him to tear them up and he does? Just what the hell are you doing with him to have so much influence?"

Jude couldn't believe Olympia's inference. She wasn't a natural woman, definitely not a natural mother. Sensing his rage, May reached back, took his hand, and gave him a squeeze.

"Jude would tear up the papers because the debt would be paid and he's an honorable man."

"He's a murderer!"

May squeezed his fingers so tight, Jude winced.

"Get off his property."

Again, Jude murmured, "May . . ."

"Right now. Leave. If you don't, I'll call the cops."

"Call them," her mother taunted. "They probably know *him* by name." She pointed at Jude. "They'll know who's causing the problems."

"Of course they know his name. He's a movie star. He's the most respected fighter in the SBC." She glanced at Denny. "Call the cops."

Denny said, "Uh . . ."

Jude said, "Not yet, Denny."

"I'll tell them about Tim," May offered. "I'll tell them that he was gambling and lost money to someone who beat him black and blue. The same people who said he'd be dead if he went to the cops."

Her mother wanted to strike her; Jude could tell.

Had she struck May in the past? It didn't seem implausible. The woman's certifiable demeanor made Tim's behavior, and May's protectiveness toward Tim, more understandable. It also justified his desire to shield her from such ugliness.

If Olympia made so much as a single move toward May, he'd stop her and deal with the consequences later.

"Let's go, Olympia." Stuart took his wife's elbow. "If he robs us blind and leaves us poor, maybe then May will be happy."

"I'd be happy," May whispered, a break in her voice, "if you'd even once asked how Tim is faring."

Jude's heart completely broke in two. He looked at the tears in May's eyes, the difficulty she had swallowing, and hoped he'd never go through such an awful thing again for the rest of his life.

Yet these were her parents. No wonder she didn't date. She probably figured no man would tolerate her relatives long enough to fall in love with her.

"You've only shown concern for the car lot," May pointed out. "And you know what? I'm glad Jude is going to hold Tim accountable. For Tim's sake, because I love him. Maybe with some good influence in his life, he'll finally grow up a little. Maybe he'll learn enough to keep himself alive. Maybe, just maybe, he'll become a man half as wonderful as Jude."

"You're dead to me," her mother said, wringing a tiny sob from May.

Jude wanted to hold her, but she walked off the porch and stepped onto the entryway to watch as her father revved the Jaguar and peeled away, leaving ugly black tire marks on the otherwise pristine drive.

"Dear God," Denny whispered.

"Yeah." Wanting so many things, all of them centered on May, Jude walked up behind her. He wrapped his arms tight around her, holding her close and rocking her side to side. "I'm so sorry, honey."

"Don't be." The gates opened, and the Jaguar disappeared from sight. "I've always been dead to them. This is nothing new."

Jude hesitated, wishing he had the right words, a solution to offer. "Want me to tear up the loan papers?"

Shock rippled through May. She twisted to stare at him.

"I would, you know." He framed her face in his hands, devastated to see her ravaged expression, the hurt that clouded her eyes. "Whatever you want, May, tell me. It's yours."

The tears spilled over, ripping him apart, and then she gave a shaky laugh. She flung herself into his arms and squeezed him. Against his chest, she said, "Keep the loan. Make Tim pay. And most of all—please, *please* don't ever change."

Damn it. Much more of that and he'd be weeping like a woman, too. He returned her hug, tight enough to make her gasp. Emotion overwhelmed him, distorting his sense of caution. He thrust her an arm's length away, ready to make promises of profound portions. "May, I—"

His cell phone rang, giving him a moment of

sanity. He narrowed his eyes, debated with himself, then cursed. "Shit. I have to take this."

May wiped her eyes and smiled. "It's okay. *I'm* okay. Don't worry."

Very deflated, but also a little relieved by the interruption, Jude dug the phone from his pocket and connected the call. "Hello?"

"We've got some trouble."

Hearing from Lyle Elliott, the private detective he'd hired to keep an eye on Tim, was something Jude didn't need. "What's going on?"

As Lyle explained the situation, May watched Jude and reacted to his darkening scowl. "Jude?"

Jude asked, "Where's he at?" and "How long?" and then, "Son of a bitch. Hang on." With no time to waste, he turned and started for the house in a trot. "Denny!"

Denny, who'd been lounging against the column, smiling toward them, straightened. "What's wrong?"

"Bring a car around." Taking the front steps two at a time, Jude bounded up and onto the porch. "Tim's under the old trestle bridge on that stretch of road that heads north."

"Jesus," Denny said, and as usual, he caught on without further detail. "Is anyone else there yet?"

May didn't understand. "What are you two talking about? Why is Tim under the bridge? There's nothing out there except some abandoned trailers and a dry creek."

"He's alone right now." Deciding he'd have to trust in May's strength, regardless of all she'd just been through, Jude spelled it out. "Tim's out there waiting—probably for Elton and his men to meet him there."

"*What?*" She shook her head. "No, even Tim couldn't be that stupid."

"Of course he's that stupid. That's why I've had Lyle Elliott discreetly watching the house with instructions to stay with Tim if he tried to leave. Otherwise, I wouldn't have let him storm off today after signing the loan papers. It's still too risky."

"But Tim didn't seem to think so." She covered her mouth with a hand. "Oh God. He's . . . He's probably trying to make a deal with Elton."

"He's not alone, May. Lyle's keeping an eye on things." Jude cupped the back of her head and pressed a kiss to her brow. "Tim will be okay," he promised her. And as he put the phone back to his ear, he prayed he was right.

Chapter 19

May collapsed back against a wall, shaken to the core of her being. She was already off balance after the blowup with her parents, and now every awful, deadly scenario imaginable crashed through her brain.

In less than thirty seconds, Denny pulled the Porsche up front.

"Come on." Jude grabbed her hand and pulled her out the door with him.

"I'm going?" May asked, flabbergasted by the possibility when he'd been so adamant in leaving her behind last night.

"Yeah. But you damn well better do exactly as I tell you." He opened the back door for her, practically stuffing her inside in his haste. "Denny, you drive."

"I can have us there in ten minutes."

May clicked on her seat belt, relieved that she wouldn't be left alone, waiting and wondering about what happened. At least this way she didn't feel quite so helpless.

Secured in the seat next to her, Jude put the phone to his ear again. "You still there, Lyle? Great. What do you see?" He listened, nodded, and relayed the details to May. "Lyle's out of sight but able to see Tim and the surrounding area. Right now Tim's just pacing around the tracks."

"The fool," Denny said.

"I can't believe this."

Jude put his hand on her thigh and gave her a reassuring squeeze. "Keep him in sight, Lyle, but don't intervene unless you have to. I'm going to set the phone down for a minute." Jude lifted one hip to retrieve his wallet. He dug out a business card and handed it over the seat to Denny. "Call Burton. He should be there for this."

Trying to grasp the turn of events, May asked, "Who's Burton?"

"Ed Burton," Jude explained, "the photographer."

"Oh." Of course she knew that. She blamed her faulty memory on the recent and distressing chaos.

While Denny called Ed, Jude took May's hand. "This might be our best chance to nail the bastard. We don't want to blow it."

May's brain finally kicked into gear. "You want to get there in time to get some incriminating evidence on Elton Pascal."

"Damn right. Tim thought he'd be going behind our backs with this, making some shady deal with Elton. But it's going to work to our advantage. With Burton covertly snapping pictures and recording what's said, we might be able to end this once and for all."

Denny clicked his phone shut. "Burton had a shoot in the area, so he was already halfway here. He's going to blow that off to join us. He says fifteen minutes, tops. Less if he doesn't hit any lights."

May couldn't help but worry. Tim might have unwittingly orchestrated his own peril.

Jude took one look at her face and rested the phone against his thigh, shielding his words. "You've had one hell of a day. I'm sorry."

"Don't be. Tim's the one who made the decision, not you." She told herself what she'd told Jude earlier. "You've done everything you could to help him. More than enough. We're not responsible for what he does. If he hadn't rushed off after signing the papers..." Another lightbulb went off, and she groaned. "He didn't care about the legalities because he plans to blow that off the same way he does everything else. Plus, he probably figured any deal with Elton cancelled a deal with you. If Elton lets him off the hook, then he doesn't owe money, and the loan is null and void."

"I knew he was up to something," Jude told her. "But I thought he wanted to slip off for a drink or to gamble."

"Do you think Elton or one of his men called again when we weren't around and that's when Tim set up a meeting?"

"Probably. I wish I'd taken his phone away from him. If I had, none of this would've happened."

"At least now you have a chance to catch Elton in the act. That's worth something, isn't it?"

"It's worth a lot." Jude lifted the phone back to his ear. "We're almost there, Lyle. Where are you exactly?" Following instructions through the phone, they turned down a narrow dirt road that circled up behind the old bridge. Denny drove slowly, careful not to stir up dust or make too much noise. All the while, he watched for other cars or people.

Jude spotted the PI's car. "There. The gray Jeep." He closed his phone, and they pulled up close.

An aging man with a kind face pushed himself away from his perch on the front bumper. Dressed in baggy brown pants and an open-collared shirt, his head bald, his eyebrows grizzled, he appeared rickety and ineffectual—until May looked into his eyes. They were keen with intelligence, alert and shrewd.

Jude, Denny, and May all got out. One eye squinted against the sun, Lyle sized them up, then shook hands with each of them.

"He's right over here." He led them to where an open patch in a thick line of trees allowed for clear viewing of the field beyond. "Keeps checking his watch."

"He's impatient," Denny noted. "Damn him for being a fool."

Because Denny sounded more worried and disappointed than anything else, May didn't take exception to his continued insults against her brother.

"Over there," Jude said, indicating a car that approached from the side, driving over the forgotten, fallow field now overrun with weeds. He didn't seem to recognize the vehicle, but that meant little. Elton surely had the means to utilize any number of cars.

"Who is it?" Adrenaline, shock, and fear mixed like acid in May's stomach. The car stopped, and four men got out. "Is it Elton?"

Jude shook his head. "No, it's not even the same men who were with him at the restaurant. But I'm willing to bet they work for him. Elton has a small army of goons to do his dirty work. I should have realized he'd be too cowardly to show up himself."

He turned to Denny. "What do you want to do, stay here with May and Lyle, or—"

Denny huffed. "Just try and stop me from coming along."

"That's what I thought." Jude turned and lifted May's chin. "I know you're going to worry, but stay put. No matter what, don't shout out, or think to help, or—"

"I'm not an idiot." She turned her head and kissed his palm. "I trust you, Jude, I really do. But please, *please* be careful."

"I'm not an idiot either." He turned to the PI. "Lyle?"

Lyle grinned and held up a nine-millimeter pistol. "I always come prepared. Don't worry. I'll see that things work out."

A gun! May stared from Jude to Lyle and back again. They seemed to take it in stride.

Jude even winked at her. "Now, we're going to sneak down and see if we can hear anything. If Ed gets here, tell him to catch as much as he can."

Full of misgivings, May nodded, then watched as Jude and Denny crept closer to where Tim waited. They inched up behind a stand of trees at about the same time that Tim noticed the other men.

Calling out, Tim said, "There you are! I was getting nervous."

"Is that right?" The fellow in the lead grinned from ear to ear, stopping Tim in his tracks.

Even from a distance, that grin made May's skin crawl. She wished Lyle had two guns. She wished he had an Uzi.

She wished her stupid brother hadn't embroiled Jude in this awful mess. If anything happened to either of them, she wouldn't be able to bear it.

* * *

Tim took a step back. "Elton Pascal?"

"Not likely."

"But . . ." Everything felt wrong, and fear began worming around in Tim's guts. The man addressing him seemed somehow familiar. Not by look, but by . . . attitude. "Who are you?"

"You can call me Vic."

That voice. Something about it dredged up a bone-deep panic. Looking from one behemoth to the other, Tim said, "I don't understand. I thought—"

"You and I have a lot to discuss, Tim. But first, did you tell anyone you were coming here?"

Maybe Elton just wanted to be cautious. Maybe he needed to know it was safe before he'd present himself to discuss their business. "No."

"You're sure about that? Because if I find out otherwise, you won't like the consequences."

Surely that was it. A man in Elton Pascal's position would have to be very cautious. But if he played his cards right, this could still work out. Tim tamped down on the rising fear. "I'm sure. I even watched to see if I was followed. But no one else left the house behind me."

"Excellent. Now, Tim, I want you to answer some questions for me." He stepped closer.

Even the smell of him wrought a memory. Tim started breathing too fast. "Questions?"

"You can start by telling me how to get into Jamison's place."

These men looked . . . more than malicious. If Tim had to describe bloodlust, he'd point out the eyes boring into him right now. "Why do you want in?"

An iron fist sank into his midsection, forcing all

the air out of his lungs and making him almost hurl. He doubled over in god-awful pain. He hadn't had a chance to entirely heal from the last beating . . .

The last beating. That's why Vic seemed so familiar. He was the one from the car, the one who'd—

A tight hand knotted in Tim's shirtfront, bringing him upright again, and hands gently dusted him off. "Now, Tim, let's try this again." Vic's tone was absurdly kind, which only escalated Tim's fear. "How do we get in?"

Panic tried to steal his thoughts, but then Tim remembered the clothes May wore and . . . "Delivery men," he wheezed.

"What's that? Speak up, man. There's no reason to whisper. After all"—he patted Tim's cheek— "we're all alone here."

Cold sweat popped out on Tim's forehead as he fought to keep from puking. "He . . . Jude bought my sister new clothes." Oh God, he was such a coward. "There've been . . . delivery guys . . . coming and going."

"Ah." Vic nodded. "So all I need is a delivery van, or something that looks like a delivery van, and I can coast on in. Good to know."

Why would they need in unless they intended to kill Jude? Tim squeezed his eyes shut. He hated Jude, but he didn't want a murder on his conscience. And his sister . . . poor May. She meant well. He couldn't just sell her out. He had to at least try.

Brain cramping, Tim forced himself to look directly at the man—and lie. "I heard Jude say something . . . I don't know. Something about more clothes coming tomorrow. In the morning." If he could just buy himself some time, he could warn the others. He'd think of some way to do it without incriminating himself.

"Nice try, Tim. But you're a shitty liar. I see it in your eyes, you know." Vic smiled. "And in the way you're shaking."

Tim's stomach dropped to his knees. "No, I wouldn't—"

"Jamison's been a thorn in my side for too long. Now, thanks to you, I can get him." Still smiling like a preacher, Vic reached into his pocket and withdrew something gold. It had a low luster and looked to weigh about half a pound—

Brass knuckles.

Tim heaved, already feeling that cold metal slamming into his face.

Vic worked them onto his left hand, flexing his fingers and taunting Tim. "Of course, now that I've told you my intent, you have to go."

Tim shook his head and squeezed a faint protest from the constriction in his throat. "You can't."

"Of course I can."

"But . . . like you said, I lied. My sister knows I came here, she'll know what happened—"

"I don't think so, Tim. She's so infatuated with that bastard Jamison, she'd have stopped you. But either way, it doesn't matter. I have plans for that bitch as well."

Oh God, oh God, oh God. What had he done? Why had he been so stupid? They'd all die because of him.

Vic intended to beat him to death. He'd use that awful contraption now decorating his meaty fist, and he'd turn his flesh into hamburger. Would anyone even be able to recognize him when Vic finished? Against a man like that, Tim was helpless.

Vic tsked. "Look at you, Tim. You're turning green." He reached into his other pocket and withdrew more knuckles for his right hand. He held them up like a mirror, admiring his distorted image in the shine. "I'm going to enjoy this, Tim. I take great pride in my work."

A fuzzy blackness closed in around Tim, and he knew any second now he'd faint. He almost welcomed it as a way to escape the punishment that would come.

Then something Denny and Jude told him suddenly popped into his head.

When you're going to fight, you fight. You don't talk about it.

Vic continued taunting Tim about the difficulty he often had getting blood off the knuckles. He told Tim he could devastate his internal organs with some well-placed shots.

Breath choppy and heart hammering, Tim slowly looked up. Just because he'd die today, he didn't have to make it easy for them.

He locked his gaze on Vic, and when Vic paused, surprised at his boldness, Tim growled, "Fuck off, you psycopath."

And with that, he kicked as fast and hard as he could—and got lucky enough to land his foot in Vic's crotch.

A high-pitched, girlish scream of agony split the air, thrilling Tim, bolstering his confidence and seldom felt courage.

When Vic doubled over, Tim launched himself at the fellow who stood right behind him. But his triumphant counterattack proved short lived.

They hit the ground hard, jarring every bone in Tim's body, and with embarrassing ease, the man turned and pinned Tim to the ground. A fist, thankfully bare of metal, smashed his jaw, once, twice.

Stars circled and danced; black oblivion beckoned.

And then the man somehow flew away from Tim.

Automatically rolling to his side in the fetal position, Tim choked on his own blood while sucking in much-needed oxygen. Noise exploded around him, dull thuds, hollow grunts, but he couldn't comprehend it, not with his nose bleeding again and his head pounding.

A body tripped over him, causing him more pain, and Tim looked up to see Denny in action.

He forgot about breathing.

Like a grim, avenging angel, Denny fought with methodical deliberation. Every strike seemed pre-planned but also instantaneous.

Unwilling to miss it, Tim half sat up and scrambled like a crab out of the way. In no time at all, two men were down, unmoving, still as death.

Jude hit a guy in the temple, then kicked out his knee; the man crumpled. Denny kicked another in the face, causing him to sink to the ground in an awkward heap. Neither Jude nor Denny breathed hard. Incredible.

When a light flashed in Tim's eyes, he glanced around and found some bozo taking photographs.

Another old geezer stood off to the side, gun drawn, casual competence displayed in his stance and expression.

And next to them stood Tim's sister, pale as a ghost, hugging herself tight while dancing in place. Tim saw tears in her eyes, and emotional pain.

All in all, she acted like a woman, except Tim suspected she held herself back so that she wouldn't jump into the fray.

For some reason, maybe a touch of hysteria, Tim found that hilarious. He could almost picture May leaping in, fists drawn. If it happened, he'd put his bucks on May.

If his mouth hadn't already swollen too much to let his lips curve, Tim would have laughed.

Man, he'd messed up big time. Not only had he offered Jude as a sacrifice, but he could have gotten his sister murdered, and he wouldn't have lived to tell about it. He didn't blame any of them for hating him. How could they not? They wouldn't understand his predicament. They wouldn't realize that he was afraid and only trying to stay alive.

Maybe he should sneak off while they were all preoccupied. They'd be glad to see the last of him. They wouldn't miss him. They wouldn't care that he was gone.

But . . . Denny hadn't let him die. Sure, he and Jude had taken their time, letting him lose a year off his life out of sheer terror. And thanks to getting punched in the face, he'd be hurting for another week.

But they hadn't abandoned him.

They hadn't even let him get beaten real bad. When Tim imagined those solid, cold brass knuckles tearing his flesh and cracking his bones, his stomach heaved again. If Jude and Denny hadn't intervened when they did, he would have had some serious injuries.

He felt like an asshole. Worse, he felt contemptible.

He'd spare them all and leave now. Maybe hide

away somewhere so they'd never find him. That'd surely make them happy. May despised helping him. Jude made his disgust well known . . .

Sirens blasted the air, startling Tim, and then he lost his chance to escape.

Knuckles bloody, Denny came to stand over him. Tim was too ashamed and too intimidated to look at him, until Denny held out a hand and said, "Men don't cower, you fool. Now, stand up before the cops see what a baby girl you're being."

Thunderstruck, Tim glanced up and saw only the thrill of the fight in Denny's eyes. No revulsion. No hostility.

Denny didn't hate him?

An insult had never felt so good.

Gingerly, Tim took the proffered hand; Denny hauled him to his feet and dusted him off in a way that hurt worse than the blows had. But Tim didn't complain.

"Dumb shit," Denny muttered.

Tim ran a hand over his head, sheepish and scared and relieved enough to feel like collapsing. "I'm sorry, all right?"

"Sorry it didn't work out as you planned. But I swear to God, boy, if I have to, I'm going to beat some common sense and honor into you. And don't think I can't. I've worked with worse hardons than you. Guys come to the SBC because they're angry, or lost. Some of them have criminal records. I teach them control, how to channel that energy. In comparison," he said, giving Tim a slap on the side of the head, "you're no more than a cupcake."

Tim rubbed at his stinging ear and thought of the moment he'd defended himself. That little bit of control had been . . . empowering.

Now that he knew he wouldn't die, remembering it made him feel good. "Okay."

Denny continued to scowl. With hair mussed, displaying the tattoo on his skull, and that particular look on his face, he resembled a lunatic. A crazed lunatic.

Until he grinned.

"At least I know you listened to some of what I said." A rough, gravelly laugh slipped out. "Swear to God, boy, the way you nutted that bastard really made my day. He'll be singing like a soprano for a week."

A tiny flare of hope burst to life inside Tim. Could he salvage this mess, after all? Maybe Denny would be in his corner. "You said not to talk about it, to just do it." Enthusiasm ripened. "I knew he'd kick my ass."

Denny snorted. "He was going to kill you."

Knowing it to be true, Tim gulped. "Right. So I figured, what the hell. No reason to make it easy for him."

"You're learning." And Denny slung his arm around him.

Behind Denny, Jude slapped Vic's face until he came around. The second Vic blinked, Jude demanded, "Where's Elton?"

Vic grimaced. "Elton who?"

"Funny. Real funny."

"Fuck off, Jamison."

Jude laughed, impressing the hell out of Tim. He looked to be in a very controlled, icy rage, but still he laughed.

"You're too stupid to realize that it's all over, huh, Vic? Yeah, I know your name. I heard everything you said to Tim. I know damn good and well Elton sent you."

"I don't know what you're talking about."

"You want to be that way, fine. I'm happy to let the cops deal with you. They're swarming down the hill right now." Jude's eyes glittered with malevolence. "Just imagine what Elton's reaction will be once he knows they've got you."

Vic groaned, locked his teeth, and turned his face away.

"You're in a lose-lose situation, bud. Either the cops lock you up, or they let you go and Elton has you taken off at the knees. One way or another, you stop being a problem to me."

Ed Burton stepped forward. "I've got it all on tape, Jude. Every single word. It'll be in the morning edition of every paper I can reach."

"You haven't got shit," Vic yelled, and he started to struggle. "I haven't said a damn thing."

Jude put a knee to his chest, keeping him still. "Maybe not." His smile turned lethal. "But will Elton believe that after Ed runs his story?"

Ah, Tim thought, watching as Jude easily subdued Vic. Clever of him to get a reporter involved. But then, Jude always seemed to be two steps ahead of everyone else—one of the reasons Tim despised him. Or somewhat despised him.

Most of all, he envied him.

Suddenly, police swarmed the area, guns drawn, and Tim watched it all in fascination. Jude identified himself, let the cops take custody of Vic, then answered questions with practiced ease. As soon as the police finished grilling him, he went to May. He hugged her close, kissed her in front of God and everyone, and then led her to a fallen log to sit down. He pampered her, as if she'd been the one in the fight. But she didn't have blood on her face. She didn't have aching ribs.

Gallant bastard. Okay, so he more than envied Jude. He admired him. He wished he could be more like him.

Maybe, just maybe, Denny could make it happen.

Chapter 20

May fretted. Jude was so quiet on the ride home. He seemed very aware of Tim following along behind them, and she just knew he wanted to take Tim apart.

Not that she blamed him. Tim had endangered them all. As the police had pointed out during their lengthy interrogation, they could have all ended up dead.

But not once did Jude or Denny act rattled. Tim, on the other hand, stammered and stuttered and had a terrible time keeping his story straight. At one point, he'd even gotten tears in his eyes. Denny had snapped at him. Jude had just looked repulsed.

She'd known all along that her family was impossible to take. She hadn't known that Tim would keep endangering Jude's life.

May touched his thigh. "Jude?"

The black scowl disappeared, and he smiled at her. "Yeah?"

"Are you okay?"

He gave her a quick kiss. "Not a scratch."

"But that's not what I mean."

"I know. Yeah, I'm fine. I just . . . I feel like this isn't quite finished."

"The cops believed you. They're going to talk to Elton. They're going to watch him."

Jude nodded—but he looked far from satisfied.

With a sigh, May guessed, "You want to confront Elton yourself."

He didn't reply, but she knew that was it. Did she have the right to protect him from something that meant so much? No. She pulled out her cell phone and dialed her brother. When Tim answered, she said, "Where's Elton's hotel?"

Jude stared at her, amazed.

Tim stammered in confusion.

Denny chuckled.

"Come on, Tim," May told him, while keeping her gaze on Jude. "We know you contacted him somehow. Vic might not have admitted it, but Elton sent him to meet you. So, where's he staying?"

A strange expression passed over Jude's face as she nodded, agreed to let Tim stay on their tail, and disconnected the call. "Unless Elton has moved, he's at the Royal Plaza. That's all the way downtown. It'll take a while to get there."

New tension vibrated off Jude. "You don't mind if I go?"

The mere suggestion almost made May laugh. Had their relationship progressed to where Jude now took her feelings into consideration before putting himself at risk?

Magnanimous, she said, "I know it's something you need to do." She fashioned a smile. "I'll be good and wait in the car."

His face went blank. "No." His brows snapped down. "Hell no. I'll take you home first."

Of course he would. "Your home?" she inquired with false politeness. "I don't think so."

"Yes, my home." His scowl turned blacker than ever. "Where the hell else would I take you?"

"My home?"

Outraged by the idea, he opened his mouth—and his cell phone rang. "Damn it," he snapped, "it's like Grand Central Station anymore with these stupid phones." He dug the cell out of his pocket and barked, "Yeah?" His brows shot up. "Ashley. Sorry. I didn't . . . he is?"

"What?" May asked. "What's going on?"

Jude settled back in his seat. "Yeah, we're not that far from you. I'll be there soon as I can. If he takes off, let me know. And, Ashley? Be careful. Stay the hell away from him, okay? Yeah, thanks." Jude disconnected the phone, then hesitated.

The way he glanced at May, she knew the conversation had to be about Elton. "Is he back at the restaurant then?"

Denny laughed. "You see? Once you know someone, it's easy to read him."

She remembered being surprised at how easily Denny knew her thoughts. "I suppose."

Urgency replaced Jude's tension. "Ashley's shift just started. She said Elton was there when she arrived. He'd finished his lunch but ordered coffee and dessert."

"We should tell the police. They said they want to talk to him."

"Yeah, we will," Denny told her. "In a few minutes."

Jude's hands curled into fists. "The son of a bitch probably figured he'd make a public appearance. That way he'd have witnesses to swear he wasn't anywhere near Tim when . . ." He faltered, allowing that thought to fester.

May closed her eyes. "When Tim got murdered?"

Strong hands cupped May's face. "I can end this, May. But I don't want you anywhere near him."

She pressed her cheek into his palm. "If I'm with you, I'll be safe."

Her conviction left him speechless.

"She's right," Denny said. "Let's call Ed and get him over there. Right before we go in, we'll let the cops know. That should buy us a few minutes."

Jude fought the idea, but in the end he knew they were right. He spent the rest of the ride making May swear she'd stay glued to his side, that she'd cut and run if things went sideways—which she would never do—and that she'd follow his lead in all things.

Fifteen minutes later, they pulled into the restaurant lot with Tim and Ed parking alongside them. He didn't even glance at Tim, but he spoke quietly with Ed, then with Denny. Finally, he dialed the police to alert them to Elton's presence.

Overall, they made a solemn group, entering the restaurant together with Jude and Denny in the lead.

May spotted Ashley right off. She stood with her arms crossed, waiting near the kitchen entrance. And there at a corner table, circled by a small army of suited men, was Elton Pascal.

The second her gaze landed on him, May felt apprehensive. Elton fit her perception of him to a tee—right down to the sense of evil that clung to him like a dirty film.

Jude smiled on his path to Elton, his gait steady and sure.

One of the men noticed them first, and he shoved back his chair to stand—until he saw Denny, and behind him, Tim. Then he wavered, confusion and concern replacing the antagonism. Obviously, he'd expected Tim to be long gone.

Jude reached Elton's table, planted his hands on the tabletop, and leaned in.

Elton pressed back.

"The police have Vic," Jude told him.

Elton's eyes darted this way and that, as if seeking an avenue of escape. "Vic who?"

Slowly shaking his head, Jude smiled. "I see you sweating, Elton. I see the color leeching out of your face. You know your time is up."

Blustering, Elton coughed up a laugh. "Drop dead."

"Sorry, but I'm not that accommodating. You're stuck with me being around, and that means I'm going to keep digging. From now on, I'll be watching your ass day and night. There'll be no more goons like Vic to take the fall for you. No more secretive meetings with drivers."

Elton swayed in his seat, and May knew Jude had hit a nerve. So she'd been right. Sid had known Elton, and he'd turned traitor on Jude.

How must that make Jude feel?

The man sitting closest to Elton ground his teeth together in frustration. He looked at Elton to reply, and when Elton remained mute, he knotted his fists on the table. "Fuck off, Jamison. You don't have shit and you know it."

Jude didn't appear to notice the other man. "I can't prove you're the one who murdered Blair, but I can damn sure set the groundwork to keep you from ever doing anything like it again."

In a rasp, Elton said, "You're delusional."

"You blew her up, you bastard."

Elton made a small sound of distress. "I loved her."

"And she hated you."

"You stole her from me."

"So you had Sid toss a bomb into the limo, and the poor bastard didn't know he'd blow up, too." Jude shook his head. "The irony is that I didn't want her. I felt sorry for Blair, but beyond that I didn't even like her company."

Elton launched himself out of his chair. It clattered back and fell. "Bastard!" Everyone in the restaurant looked up. Silence filled the air.

The men on either side of him grabbed at his arms, restraining him so that he didn't do anything irreparable in front of witnesses.

A flash left Elton blinking hard, and when he finally registered Ed with a recorder and camera, he panicked. "What are you doing? You can't come in and invade my privacy. Where's the manager? I'll call the cops."

"They're on the way. I called them before I came in. Good luck convincing them of your innocence."

Elton and his men went mute, identical expressions of alarm on their faces.

Satisfied, Jude stepped back. "Ed's a reporter. I'm giving him an exclusive, dating back to the day Blair and Sid were killed in the explosion. Once I'm finished, even if Vic doesn't spill his guts, the whole world will be watching you. If anything happens to me, or May, or her family, you'll be the first person they come to. You better hope we all have long, happy lives."

"Check!" Elton looked around, frantic to find his waitress.

Knowing he wouldn't make it out of the restaurant in time to avoid the police, Jude laughed, turned, put his arm around May, and headed for the door. "Now," he said, "I feel better."

She heard the continued clicking of Ed's camera as he backed out, staying close to Jude. She felt her brother's awe and his nervousness.

Inside, she shook so badly she thought her heart might rattle loose. But on the outside, she maintained a look of calm. She was so proud of Jude.

And so very much in love with him.

Once they reached the parking lot, Jude clapped Ed on the shoulder, triumphant and exhilarated. "Thank you."

"Are you kidding?" Ed let the camera dangle from one hand while he tugged at his own ponytail with the other. "I feel like a kid in a candy store. This is going to be my breakout story."

"Just watch yourself. Don't take Elton lightly. If he manages to wiggle out of this one, he might be out for revenge, and I don't want you hurt."

Ed grinned hugely. "I'm a coward at heart. I've already arranged for protection, at least until the story breaks. After that, thanks to your maneuvering, I should be safe enough. Like you said, anything happens to me, they'll know where to look for a suspect."

"If you keep causing me to miss meals," May teased, "I'm not going to be plump anymore."

"Who says you're plump? You're perfect."

She laughed and tried to collapse down over Jude's chest, but he kept her upright with his hands on her breasts. He raised his knees and urged her to lean back on them. He already had a condom on, but he wasn't yet inside her.

He wanted to make it last.

"I don't go on about it, and I don't really care, but you know I'm on the heavy side."

While toying with her nipples, Jude said, "I adore your curves."

She sighed and gave him a very sultry look. "Then quit teasing me. We might still make it downstairs in time for dinner."

"I want to see you come first," he whispered.

"Jude . . ." Her protest broke into a gasp when he slipped one hand between her legs.

It didn't take long before May reached her breaking point. And Jude watched every nuance on her face, the rise and fall of her breasts, the way her belly contracted and she bit her lip while groaning long and low.

"Damn." A little rough and a lot impatient, he gripped her hips and lifted her limp body so that he could slide in. "Now you're nice and wet," he remarked, and even saying it turned him on more. He knew he wouldn't last beyond a few strokes, but when May opened her eyes and smiled at him, a smile of contentment and sensuality and completion, he gave up the struggle.

Flipping her beneath him, he rode her hard and relished the way she stroked his back and kissed his shoulder as he came.

A long time passed before Jude could dredge up coherent words. May had her arms and legs around him, and she didn't seem inclined to let him go when he leaned up to see her face. Despite her hold, she looked utterly relaxed.

"You aren't falling asleep, are you?" Tenderly, he stroked the wild tumble of her hair away from her face. She didn't move. "You want to go downstairs to get something to eat?"

She hugged him tighter, and if Jude didn't miss his bet, a little desperately. "No, not yet."

So attuned to her moods, Jude understood right off that something was wrong. "May? What are you thinking about?"

"My life."

Not *our* life. Together. Some of the peace he'd felt began to fade. Keeping his voice calm, his hold gentle, he said, "That sounds serious."

"Maybe." She rubbed her cheek against his chest. "I can't keep staying here, Jude. I don't want to give you up, but I need to return to my apartment. I need to get back to my own routine."

Jude ran his hands up and down her back and decided, no matter what, he wouldn't let her go. "You said you're going back to work on Monday."

"Which means I need to be in my apartment tonight. I have to start sleeping regular hours again. I have to catch up on what's happened in the office while I was away. I have to . . . to get used to reality instead of this fairy tale you've created."

Her words disturbed him, so Jude decided to tease a little while formulating a response. "You saying I wake you up too much during the night?" Last night, he'd awakened her twice, once to make love to her and once just to hold her close.

He hadn't actually had a nightmare, but he'd thought of losing her, and his blood ran cold.

Nothing and no one had ever scared him as much as the idea of losing May. Touching her was the only thing that made him feel better.

"It wasn't a complaint." She crossed her arms and propped her head up on his chest. "I'm going to miss having you wake me up."

Jude pushed her hair away from her face. He'd seen her with makeup and without. He'd seen her eyes swollen with tears and sparking with anger. He'd seen the hurt he'd caused and the worse hurt caused by her parents. He'd seen her soft from pleasure and determined to be protective.

"We don't know if it's over, May. Until the cops tell me that Vic has confessed all, or that Elton is behind bars, I need to know you're safe."

She leaned forward and kissed him. "But that's something that could happen tomorrow, next week, or a month from now. I can't continue to use it as an excuse. Besides, after what you told him today, I doubt Elton will try anything around here."

Footsteps pounded down the hallway and seconds later, a fist rapped on the door. "Jude!"

Sensing Denny's urgency, Jude levered May to the side of him and pushed out of bed. "What is it?" He padded across the floor to the door.

"I just got a call. You aren't going to believe this."

Jude glanced back to see May modestly covered by blankets while fumbling on the nightstand for her glasses. He opened the door and stepped out into the hall. "Something to do with Elton?"

"I was checking around like you asked, and there are two guys who claim Sid was with Elton the night before your limo blew."

For one of the few times in his life, Jude's knees felt weak. "Son of a bitch."

"That's exactly what I said! But there's more. I called the detective who arrested Vic. He said Vic is spilling his guts. Seems he's more afraid of Elton than he is of going to jail. They convinced him that since he never actually killed anyone, the courts would go easier on him if he cooperated." Denny lifted his shoulders. "And so he is."

"Did . . ." Jude had to clear his throat before he could continue. They were coming at him so fast, he could barely take in all the changes. Would he finally get his life back? "Did Vic say Elton planned the bombing? That he deliberately murdered Blair?"

Denny nodded. "I'm sorry, Jude. But according to Vic, the sick fuck figured that if he couldn't have Blair, no one could."

"But he always blamed me," Jude reasoned aloud, still trying to get it to sink in. "And when he says he hates me, it's not a lie. He really does. I can see it in his eyes."

Denny put a comforting hand on Jude's shoulder. "Vic said Elton hated you for turning down what he wanted so much."

"Jesus."

The bed squeaked, and a second later May joined them. Wrapped in a blanket toga-style, her hair tumbling down her back and her big eyes serious behind the lenses of her glasses, she sidled up close to Jude. "It makes sense, Jude. I imagine many men look at you with jealousy, my brother included. No one sees the hard work and dedication."

Jude stared down at her. From the beginning

May had seen all of him. Damn, he couldn't lose her.

Crediting his silence to the news, May leaned her head on his shoulder and hugged his arm. "Most people only see your accomplishments and how easy you make it all seem. You're a very tough act to follow."

"We could finally wrap up this ugly business," Denny said. "They're going to arrest Elton now. By tomorrow, it should be over." He smiled at May. "We'll be able to live in peace."

Denny walked off whistling, and Jude knew that Denny had accepted May in the house as much as he had.

Once they were back in the bedroom, May asked, "You look a little shell shocked. Are you okay?"

"I'd be better if you didn't insist on leaving." Jude scrambled to find reasons to make her stay. "What if Elton gets away? If anything, this might make him more desperate. I want you here, where I can keep you safe."

She shook her head. "I can't."

"*Why?*"

Her chin lifted, and she peered stubbornly through her glasses. "I need to get hold of my parents."

Jude went blank for several seconds. "Whatever for? They wrote you off. They're done with you."

May used one hand to hold the sheet in place and the other to wave away his statements. "It's not the first time, and it won't be the last. They don't even mean it. They get mad and they say awful things. My mother was drinking, and that always makes her more hateful."

Jude remembered Olympia's red eyes and the traveler's cup she'd carried. Horrid woman. May's mother. Good God.

"Dad doesn't know how to deal with her, and anyway, he doesn't want to expend the energy trying. Tim can't deal with either of them."

"So it all falls to you? That's bullshit."

Her mouth firmed over his language. "I don't expect you to understand, but they depend on me. They need me."

"Incredible." So this was it? May's grandstand and her reason for walking away from him was because she thought he couldn't understand. He'd make her rethink that bit of nonsense. He understood all too well.

She wanted their love. She needed their respect.

But he doubted she'd ever get it.

May stood stiff and proud before him. "They're my parents. That's something that won't ever change. Sure, there are things about them I don't like, but we don't get to choose our parents. We love what we get, and we try to make it work."

"You shouldn't be the only one trying, though."

"I'm not going to completely cut them out of my life just because they can be offensive." Her bottom lip trembled but was quickly stilled. "That's just not something I can do."

"I despise the way they treat you, May."

Sadness filled her eyes. "I know."

Jude stepped closer. "But I'm not about to let you off that easy."

Her mouth fell open. "What?"

"You want to associate with them, then we will. *We*. Not just you. I suppose holidays are a given.

And there's always sickness or financial snafus and shit like that." He paced, thinking it all through. "Of course, we might not always be around."

"What are you talking about?" Her voice was high and breathless.

"I'm not going back to Hollywood. I told my agent to pass on the action flick. It was a great offer, not just money but exposure, but I'm just not interested."

She trotted to keep up with his agitated pacing. "You're not?"

Head down, hands on his hips, he kept moving but glanced at her. "Did you ever see that movie *Get Shorty*?" Before she could answer, he remarked, "Great flick. Travolta's a class act."

"Jude?"

"In the movie, Travolta's character, Chili Palmer, says to someone that most actors don't know their own zip code or telephone number."

May stopped and stared at him.

"That's not a huge exaggeration, you know." Jude laughed. "Actors are notoriously self-absorbed. Sometimes really shallow. I dated a woman once who got collagen injections in the balls of her feet so that she could wear really high heels while walking the red carpet. Do you believe that shit?" He shuddered just thinking about it.

"I have no idea what you're talking about."

"I'm talking about keeping it real. Hollywood's not for me. It was a nice gig, and I appreciate the breaks, but I've been thinking." He planted his feet and faced her. "Actually, your brother inspired me."

"My brother?" May crossed her arms and cocked out one hip. In the blankets, she looked adorable. "Do tell."

"Lots of troubled guys come to the SBC to find new opportunities. Some have been victims of child abuse, some were orphans, and some have done jail time. Once you have a record, it's hard to find work. These guys are looking for constructive ways to channel their anger, and they're looking for a family. Backup. People who care."

May nodded but kept silent.

On a deep breath, Jude said, "That's the SBC. A big family. People you can count on. You watch their backs, and they watch yours. As a trainer, Denny's turned around more than one young man. I have faith he'll work wonders with Tim."

Her mouth fell open again. "You're serious?"

"Tim didn't tell you?"

Mute, she shook her head.

Damn her brother for being a chickenshit. "I think he's going to do a circuit with Denny. I imagine your mom and dad will pitch a real bitch fit, but trust me, it'll be good for Tim. Toughen him up and teach him humility and responsibility and maybe some independence."

May just stared at him.

This wasn't going quite as he'd planned it. "Anyway, I thought about things and how I trust the foundation of the SBC a hell of a lot more than I do any Hollywood gimmick."

When he hesitated, she prompted him. "And?"

"I've decided I want to invest in some programs within the SBC. You know, sponsor some young men who maybe wouldn't be able to get involved otherwise. I'll get some other sponsors to step up, too. I don't have it all worked out yet, but I know I want to do a series of commercials and paper ads and . . ." He smiled, held out his arms. "I bought half the company."

"You . . ." May inhaled. "You *bought* half the SBC?"

"Yeah. I love it. You love it . . . You do, right?"

"I do."

"Great. I was going to tell you about it, but damn woman, I get around you and I have sex on the brain. I'd like to steal your blankets right now and lay you on the floor and—"

"*Jude.*"

"You see? Anyway, it's going to involve some travel. But I figured, what the hell, you could look for artwork while we're in Germany and Japan and Brazil. Right?"

She blinked rapidly. "You expect me to go with you?"

"Well, I'm sure as hell not going if you don't."

She did some more blinking. "But . . ."

"When we're in the States, we'll visit my parents—and yours, of course. I can take it, I swear. I'm tougher than you think. We'll work out something."

As if to contain her heart, she flattened a hand to her chest. "Jude, my parents are not your responsibility. They're not even my responsibility, except that I've chosen to make them such. There's no reason why you'd have to—"

"It's what any husband would do."

Those words fell hard, splitting the air, echoing again and again. May staggered back a step. Her lips formed the word *husband,* but she didn't make a sound.

Jude wanted to kick his own ass. "Jesus, for an actor and all, I didn't do that very well, did I?"

She covered her mouth, looking more horrified than pleased.

Biting the bullet, and still buck naked, Jude

crossed the few steps that separated them. He went down on one knee, but rather than take her hand, he put his cheek to her belly and hugged his arms around her behind. Desperation tried to rise, but he beat it back.

And hugged her tighter.

"Will you marry me, May?" She felt warm and soft, and he wished she was naked, too. "I love you, you know. Without you it doesn't matter what I do because I won't be happy. So please, tell me you love me, too, and that you'll be my wife."

She sank her hands into his hair and pressed him closer. "My . . . my parents will look at you as an opportunity."

"Then an opportunity I'll be."

"No." Her fingers in his hair stung. "I won't let that happen."

"Whatever you want, May." And he meant that.

"They sometimes call in the middle of the night. When they have fights and stuff. Mom might be drunk. Dad might have been . . . carousing. They expect me to settle the disputes."

"Then we'll play dispute settlers."

She sniffled, choked on a breath. "Tim isn't going to turn into a sterling example of manhood overnight."

"Trust me, honey, I have no illusions about your brother." He looked up at her and smiled to see the shock on her face. "I have no illusions about anyone in your family. But you're not them."

"I had Ashley," she whispered. "Together, she and I made a pact to be different. She was the sister I never had."

Jude considered telling her about his suspicions on that score but decided to save it for later. He had his hands full just getting her to admit she loved him. "Ashley's a wonderful person. You're a wonderful person. And I love you. You, May, not your brother or your mother or your dad. As long as I have you, everything else is tolerable."

A shaky smile danced on her lips. She sniffed, then scooted her glasses back up the bridge of her nose. "Yes, I'll go to Germany and Brazil with you. I'll even go to Timbuktu if you want."

"I won't rule out Timbuktu, but as of right now, it's not on the circuit."

She laughed, and he squeezed her butt.

"Hey, give me a year behind the scenes, organizing things, and we'll see."

The smile settled into a big, happy grin. "Yes, I'll meet your parents. I can't wait, actually."

"I'll call Mom in, oh . . ." He pulled the blanket away, then stared at her body. "An hour or so."

"Yes—" May sank down to her knees in front of him. "I love you and I'll marry you."

His heart expanded. The desperation melted away. "Let's start the honeymoon right now."

Chapter 21

Ashley couldn't believe they expected her to be the maid of honor and wear some cheesy chiffon dress and matching shoes. Probably in a disgusting pastel shade of green or lavender or something. And because the wedding would take place in less than a week, she didn't even have time to get used to the idea.

They rushed it because neither Jude nor May wanted a fancy affair that might alert the paparazzi. Other than Ed Burton, no one but family and their closest friends knew of the impending nuptials. Jude's money and influence made it possible to organize in such a short time.

Ashley couldn't wait to see Denny in a tux. As the best man, he'd look smashing, even with the silver tooth and the tattoo on his head. What May's parents would think . . . now that made her laugh.

Until she remembered Denny bitching at her, insisting that she needed to get a date. *Lighten up, have some fun*, he'd said. According to Denny, he was sure she could have her pick of men. *They're probably lining up for a cute kid like you.*

Cute? Ha. No one had called her that . . . ever.

If he only had any real idea how limited her choices would be.

And speaking of choices . . . Ashley forced herself to get off the elevator when the doors opened. It wasn't quite time for her to work yet, but she thought she'd ease Quinton into the idea of escorting her to a wedding by taking him to eat first. Surely, he wouldn't mind that? He'd asked her out, more than once, and been fairly insistent. He'd even made her world spin with that bone-melting kiss.

So what that she'd blown him off? She could change her mind, right? Something about a woman's prerogative and all that. Especially when the woman couldn't get a man off her mind.

Stride long and lanky, Ashley went down the dark hallway to the office Quinton used. Just as she'd suspected, he was still there. From beneath his closed door she could see a faint stream of light.

Picturing him at his desk, his laptop opened, Ashley smiled. And Denny thought she worked too much.

Before she lost her nerve, Ashley raised her hand to rap on the wood. But her fist was still in the air when the door opened and Quinton almost stepped into her.

He was laughing, relaxed—and he wasn't alone.

A blond woman hung on his arm.

It was a toss-up who was more surprised, Ashley or Quinton. The laughter in his gaze faded to something else entirely.

Wanting, quite simply, to disappear, Ashley said, "Oops."

Piercing green eyes zeroed in on her. "Ashley."

"Yeah, uh, hey. Sorry for interrupting." Damn you, Denny. She'd kill him for putting her up to this. "My bad."

Quinton's brows came down in a frown.

Ashley started to ease the door shut. "Carry on."

Flattening a big hand on the wood panel, Quinton held the door open. "Wait one damn minute."

Not on his life. "No can do."

Somehow, in the two seconds it took her to say that, he disengaged from the blonde and stepped into the hall in front of her. "Not another step."

That got her back up. Glaring at him, she took a deliberate step to the side. Then another.

"Ashley," he warned.

She grinned with provocation. "Really, seriously, I don't want to . . . stop whatever you had going on. I mean, I shouldn't have dropped in like that. Blame the bad manners on the finishing school I didn't attend."

"Will you just be quiet a moment and let me explain?"

She glanced at the blonde, who smiled back at her, then returned her gaze to Quinton. "Okay, sure." Ashley lifted her brows. "Go right ahead."

He put his hands on his hips, opened his mouth, and closed it again. "Damn, this is awkward."

The blonde stepped out. "Should this be my cue to leave?"

Both Ashley and Quinton said, *"No."*

Putting a good face on it, Ashley said, "There you have it. You stay, and I'll skedaddle." And again, she started to ease away.

Quinton caught her arm. "At least tell me why you came to see me."

She'd eat raw eggs first. "I forget. It was nothing. If I think of it later, I'll let ya know."

"Damn it to hell, Ashley. You sought me out for a reason."

"Temporary insanity?"

The blonde laughed. "Why do I have the feeling that my timing really sucks?"

Since Ashley had no idea what she meant by that, and it was her timing that was off, she just shrugged. "Look, I've gotta get to work."

"You're early," Quinton accused. "You came to see me."

Never in a million years would she admit that. "Wrong. I was just making up for being late last time, that's all."

"As I recall," he murmured, "you made it with a few seconds to spare."

Why the hell wouldn't he shut up and let her go? To her profound relief, Quinton's cell phone rang, providing all the escape she needed. With a salute, Ashley said, "Later."

She was halfway down the hall when the blonde said, "What a lovely young lady. And I adored her jeans. I wonder where she got them."

Ashley glanced down at her vertically striped turquoise, purple, and black jeans. The bimbo had good taste—but that didn't make Ashley like the other woman much.

Then again, maybe *she* was the other woman. Or at least she might have been if she'd asked Quinton for a date, since an obvious association existed between him and the blonde.

Thank God, she'd missed that trap.

So if it was such a good thing, why did she feel like someone had just ripped her lungs out of her nose holes?

Stupid, stupid, stupid.

All but stomping, Ashley went to the elevator, stepped inside, and punched the button for the floor where the cleaning supplies were kept. Denny Zip could harp all he wanted, but hell would freeze over before she considered asking out another man.

For the wedding, she'd go solo—just as she'd always done. If that wasn't good enough for everyone, then too bad. As of this moment, Quinton Murphy was off her mind. One way or another, she'd make it true.

The ostentatious restaurant chosen for the rehearsal dinner pleased May's parents. Or rather, the cost of the meal pleased them. They'd been gleeful as they ordered the most expensive items, refusing to wait for Tim to join them. Olympia was a chain-smoker, so the hostess had tucked them away in a smoking area, away from the majority of guests.

As May had guessed, Stuart and Olympia saw Jude as an open door for advancement in their own lives. Even for them, they'd sunk below a gross lack of manners by grilling Jude on his finances, making privileged requests, and outright snooping about his business affairs under the guise of parental concern. She'd tried to shush them but without much success.

To Jude's credit, he dodged the inquisition with finesse while bouncing his gaze back and forth from May to Ashley, her father, and back to May. Whenever he chanced to meet her eyes, he took her hand, kissed her knuckles, and smiled very much like a man in love. Everything was almost perfect. Except . . .

May glanced at her parents once again.

Missing the ashtray by a good two inches, Olympia flicked away her ashes while finishing off her fourth glass of wine. Stuart was too busy eyeing every waitress who went by to pay attention to his wife's gaffes. Tim was now over twenty minutes late, and May was the only one worried.

Leaning close to her ear, Jude said, "Grin. It'll confuse them."

And she did, more than able to dismiss her family's current transgressions in light of everything else blossoming in her life.

Seeing that grin, Stuart complained for the umpteenth time, "I'm telling you, May, your brother should be your best man."

"My brother hasn't even shown up for the rehearsal dinner."

"Besides," Jude said, "I don't like Tim all that much."

Somehow, he made the comment sound teasing enough that Olympia snorted a laugh. Or maybe she'd just reached her limit in wine where everything amused her. A few more glasses and she'd hate the world and everyone in it.

Denny rubbed his hand over his head. "How can I show off my tat with a tux if I'm not the best man?" His silver tooth flashed in the muted light. "I can't let anyone deprive me of such a grand opportunity."

The men began a conversation on tattoos and fighting. May watched Ashley and wished she knew what ailed her. Ashley made as many snide jokes as ever, but a light had gone out of her eyes. Now that May was so happy, she wanted Ashley happy, too.

May started to question her, when suddenly Ashley stiffened. Like a deer caught in the headlights, she stared at a beautiful woman who had just walked in.

Denny, so attuned to everyone and everything, stopped talking long enough to follow Ashley's gaze. His brows shot up. "Speaking of dates—"

"We weren't," Ashley snapped.

"—here comes mine."

"What?"

Ignoring Ashley's disbelief, he pushed back his chair and stepped around the table. Everyone stared, most especially Ashley.

Jude wondered if he was the only one not surprised by Denny's involvement with a very sexy, voluptuous female. She looked to be a few years younger than Denny, maybe in her early forties, rich and feminine from her perfectly styled hair to her painted toenails.

She smiled from ear to ear and came to Denny with open arms. "Denny! I'm so sorry I'm late."

While May and Ashley gaped, Denny embraced her, lifting her an inch off her high heels and planting a smooch on her painted mouth.

May giggled.

Ashley looked hostile and uncomfortable.

Jude wondered at them both. Just because Denny was more protective than most dads didn't make him a eunuch. Jude had known him a long time, and just as Denny liked a well-organized routine, he liked female company. A lot.

Smiling broad enough to flash his silver tooth, Denny turned to the table. "Everyone, this is Zara Trilby. She and I met a month or so ago at the grocery store." His big hand opened on the side of her tiny waist in male possession. "Can you believe that?"

"Everyone has to eat," Zara teased. She looked directly at Ashley. "Hello, Ashley."

Jude thought Ashley might slide beneath the table. Instead, she bucked up and produced a megawatt smile. "Hey. Nice to see you again."

"You two know each other?" Jude asked, saving May the trouble.

Zara gave a robust laugh that had plenty of heads turning in the restaurant, including Stuart's. "Ashley caught me schmoozing a prospective client in his office. It looked very indiscreet, but only because I can be so . . . determined when I want something." She said the last while touching Denny's chest.

Denny grinned. "Your brand of determination is one of the things I admire most about you." He pulled out a chair at the table. "Join us."

As if Zara's presence hadn't started enough buzz, Tim came barreling in the doors next, flustered, eyes wide, breathing hard.

What the hell? Jude thought. He squeezed May's hand as he stood again.

Tim wore a suit, sort of. His white dress shirt remained untucked and only half buttoned with his tie loose around his neck. His hair hadn't seen the touch of a comb, and he had a five o'clock shadow.

"He got away," Tim shouted from halfway across the room.

Jude cursed softly, stepped away from the table, and greeted Tim. "Keep your voice down." He led him toward the others. "Who got away?"

Even before he spoke, Jude knew what he'd say, and his muscles clenched.

"Elton," Tim wailed.

Denny grabbed Tim's shoulders. "Take a deep breath and calm down. You're causing a scene."

"But he's out there somewhere."

More than ever, Jude wanted to rattle some

sense into Tim. "I thought they picked him up right away."

With Denny's insistent eye on him, Tim gulped two deep breaths. "That detective . . . the one you spoke with, the one who had Vic. He came by the house."

"My house? You let him in?" For the most part, Tim had remained with him. Which Jude didn't mind since Denny had taken him under his wing.

"No. I was at home. My home. I needed my damn suit."

Denny patted Tim's shoulder. "Keep breathing, son."

Jude noticed that neither of Tim's parents had bothered to raise their sorry butts from their seats. Olympia stared toward her son bleary eyed, and Stuart looked mildly annoyed.

Tim swallowed more air, ready to hyperventilate. "They haven't been able to find Elton anywhere. The detective said that at first they figured they were just missing him. They had other cops watching for him. Something like an APB or something."

"All points bulletin," Denny supplied.

"Whatever. When they couldn't find him, they figured he skipped town, so they checked with the authorities back in Hollywood. He hasn't been to any of his establishments, or his house. No one's seen him. No one's heard from him."

"Shit." Jude glanced at May, but like a trooper, she held it together. She even managed a smile for him.

Denny pushed Tim into a chair. "Sit down. Try to relax." To Jude he said, "I'll call the detective now and find out what the hell's going on."

"Thanks." Jude watched Denny touch Zara's

Lori Foster

cheek in apology, then dig out his cell phone while stepping toward the entrance.

"So much for our rehearsal dinner."

He came back to May's side. "I'm sorry, honey."

"It doesn't matter." She turned her face up to his. "I'm not going to let anything ruin my happiness."

Such an incredible woman, Jude thought. And she was all his.

May's mother waved her glass for the waitress to see. Stuart leaned close to smile at Zara, who had her gaze trained politely on Ashley. Tim heaved and trembled in his seat, more rattled than a grade school girl who's just found a snake in her lunch box.

Paying no mind to Stuart's sleazy attention, Zara said, "I seem to have walked into the middle of something here."

Jude muttered, "Old business. I'm sorry. Could I order you something to drink?"

"You can get me another glass of wine," Olympia insisted.

"No, thank you."

Zara still watched Ashley. "I'm afraid I gave you the wrong impression the other day."

Ashley shook her head. "No."

"You came to talk with Quinton, but then saw me and left. But, dear, we weren't together the way you think."

May perked up. "Quinton?" She looked at Ashley, who shook her head, denying anything and everything May might conjure in her mind.

"Quinton Murphy," Zara explained. "A very nice man who considered throwing me out a window after Ashley went off in a huff."

"No one would dare throw you out a window," Stuart crooned.

Jude felt like throwing Stuart out a window—except that the restaurant was only street level.

"I don't *huff*," Ashley huffed, shocking May and making Jude smile despite the disturbing news of Elton's disappearance. So Ashley had a love interest? Nice.

"Oh, dear, you do," Zara told her. "You huff quite well, actually. I was very impressed."

"Don't be," Ashley said through her teeth.

"But it really put Quinton in a tailspin. Very well done. You should give him another chance."

Ashley pushed back her chair to stand. Jude still couldn't get over seeing her in a dress. This one was glittery in shades of tangerine, lavender, and teal. She looked lovely, and with her hair up and back, she resembled May more than ever.

In two days, when the wedding took place, she'd looked even more like May in her maid of honor gown.

"Oh no." May reached for her friend's hand. "Where are you going?"

"To contact Quinton?" Zara asked hopefully.

Ashley's fists landed on her slim hips. "No. I have no interest in contacting him."

"You had interest before you saw me." Zara preened, as if the idea of making someone jealous pleased her.

Ashley rolled her eyes, ready to spit. Or curse. She controlled herself with visible effort. "Wrong. I was temporarily misguided, that's all."

"Quinton was so upset."

"Oh good grief." Ashley's face colored. "I was going to ask him to be my date for the wedding.

That's all. And that's only because Denny was being a pain in the ass about me coming alone. Trust me, Quinton will be glad he missed it."

"Gee, thanks," May said, her tone dry.

"You know what I mean, May. Only for you would I wear a pale pink dress with lace." She shuddered.

Tim perked up. He cleared his throat. "Hey, Ash. If you're still dateless, I could—"

Jude said, *"No,"* horrified at the thought, given he suspected Tim and Ashley could be related.

At the same time, Ashley snorted a laugh. "Not in this lifetime, Timothy."

Denny returned to the table. "They assured me they should have Elton soon. With more than one division alerted, he won't be able to access his funds, visit anyone he knows, or go any place where he's recognized. A marshmallow like him won't last long on the street."

"Great." Ashley scooped up her purse and slung the strap over her shoulder. "Glad that's settled." She bent to hug May, grabbed Jude next, and then headed for Denny.

May jumped out of her seat to follow her, protests coming fast and furious.

Stuart caught Ashley as she started to pass. "May listens to you. Tell her that Tim should be the best man, not this other fellow." He gestured as if Denny didn't stand right there, listening. Idiot.

Ashley paused on one side of Stuart, with May on the other. They debated the issue, and to Jude's amusement, the two women looked like bookends. Granted, one bookend was a little taller and slimmer, and one had enough cleavage for two females, but other than that . . .

"Oh, shit," Denny whispered, drawing Jude's at-

tention away from his soon-to-be wife. Denny
looked between May, Ashley, and Stuart.

Jude knew the moment he put it together.
Leaning close, he whispered, "Not a word."

"But they're . . ."

"Yeah, I know."

More rattled than Jude had ever seen him,
Denny asked, "Do *they* know?"

"I don't think so." May understood that her father had a lot of shortcomings. She accepted them,
just as she accepted so much in her life.

But what would she think if she found out that
Ashley was her half-sister, not just a best friend?
Given Ashley's upbringing, would May be able to
forgive her father? It amazed Jude that May hadn't
noticed the similarity on her own. Sure, she and
Ashley shared a close resemblance.

But most of all, they each looked like Stuart.

Jude couldn't prove it, so it seemed wise to let it
go for now.

"That son of a bitch," Denny growled low.

May glanced up. "Don't you worry, Denny.
You're the best man, and that's that."

Denny smiled. "Thanks, hon."

"We were talking about Elton," Jude lied. "I
doubt he's any real threat right now, but until he's
found, I intend to keep a very close eye on you."

"Is that a joke?" Olympia lit another cigarette,
then eyed Jude through the smoke. "As if you
aren't already. You look so lovesick it's enough to
turn my stomach."

May went bright red, but her father jumped on
the topic with calculating eagerness. "Tim should
stay at your place, too. God knows you can afford
the security. Now that he'll be your brother-in-law,
you owe him some protection. After all, if it wasn't

for you, none of us would be on the shit list with this Elton person."

Denny took an aggressive step toward Ashley. "You need a little watching too, missy."

She frowned. "From what?"

"Elton," Denny said, exasperated. "Maybe he knows you're the one who first identified him in the restaurant. Maybe he knows you're May's . . . best friend."

Maybe, Jude thought, he even knew they were sisters. Anyone with eyes could see it, and Elton wasn't above using it.

"Good God. Why don't we all just move in with Jude?" Olympia snatched up May's half-empty glass. "You know, it could be this Elton bozo is totally innocent in all this."

"He's not," Jude said.

"I recall that lots of people considered you guilty of stuff, too. I should think you'd want solid proof before persecuting some other poor guy."

Jude kept his calm with an effort. "We can't get solid proof until Elton is apprehended, and the fact that he ran says a lot. But thanks to Vic's confessions, we know he was responsible."

Ashley acted the smart-ass as usual. "Hey, as G.I. Joe would say, knowing is half the battle." And with a wink, she took off, balls to the walls as usual.

Jude strode over to put his arm around May and spoke close to her ear so only she could hear. "Don't worry. I'll call in some men to keep an eye on her."

"Ashley won't like it if she finds out she's being watched."

"I know." He bent and kissed her, unmindful of the way her mother complained, oblivious to anyone else in their vicinity. "But will my fiancée like it?"

The worry disappeared as May bloomed beneath a smile. "Your fiancée will love you all the more for it. Ashley is very important to me."

Jude nodded. "Like a sister."

"Closer than a sister."

"Then I won't let anything happen to her." He kissed her again. "Keeping you happy is the most important thing to me."

May laughed. "Then your life should be easy. Because as long as I'm with you, I'll be happy."

Contemporary Romance By
Kasey Michaels

__Can't Take My Eyes Off of You
  0-8217-6522-1   **$6.50**US/**$8.50**CAN

__Too Good to Be True
  0-8217-6774-7   **$6.50**US/**$8.50**CAN

__Love to Love You Baby
  0-8217-6844-1   **$6.99**US/**$8.99**CAN

__Be My Baby Tonight
  0-8217-7117-5   **$6.99**US/**$9.99**CAN

__This Must Be Love
  0-8217-7118-3   **$6.99**US/**$9.99**CAN

__This Can't Be Love
  0-8217-7119-1   **$6.99**US/**$9.99**CAN

Available Wherever Books Are Sold!

Visit our website at **www.kensingtonbooks.com**.